CARRIE STONE

Originally from the UK, I've spent the last decade living and working internationally. Aside from writing women's fiction, my main work is as a Psychic Medium & Spiritual Coach - www.carriebattley.com.

When not working, my passion is travelling - exploring new places, cultures & nature. I also adore anything to do with clothing, handbags, sunglasses and shoes… Yes, I'm a typical woman and love to look fabulous!

I currently live between Australia & Spain.

www.carriestone.co.uk

@CarrieStoneUK

Kate & Alf

CARRIE STONE

Harper*Impulse* an imprint of
HarperCollins*Publishers* Ltd
1 London Bridge Street
London SE1 9GF

www.harpercollins.co.uk

A Paperback Original 2015

First published in Great Britain in ebook format by Harper*Impulse* 2015

Copyright © Carrie Stone 2015

Cover images © Shutterstock.com

Carrie Stone asserts the moral right
to be identified as the author of this work

A catalogue record for this book is
available from the British Library

ISBN: 978-0-00-812309-3

This novel is entirely a work of fiction.
The names, characters and incidents portrayed in it are
the work of the author's imagination. Any resemblance to
actual persons, living or dead, events or localities is
entirely coincidental.

Automatically produced by Atomik ePublisher from Easypress

*In memory of Johnny Battley & Terry Stone
Both of whom are now making the angels laugh.*

Prologue

Summer 2010

'I don't know what to do to make it better for you.' Alf's voice was uncertain as he gently stroked Kate's hair whilst he held her in his arms – silently pained by the tremble of her body against his; her weeping as unnerving as the situation they'd found themselves in.

Sniffing back tears, she held up her leaden head and met his eyes. 'There's nothing you can do. It's one of those things – I just need some time to heal, that's all.' Or so they'd told her. And it wasn't as if it was the first time she'd dealt with loss. She should have been used to it by now – should have embraced it like the old friend it was steadily becoming.

She saw the love in his gaze, but it was reflected back at her behind a wall of despair and something else. Feeling her breath catch in her throat, she at once felt guilty. Grief. It was grief in his eyes. She'd been so wrapped up in her own emotions that she hadn't stopped to really consider how he'd been feeling.

Alf propped himself up on one elbow, his arm sinking into the duck-feather pillow. He stared at the wall, considering options for a moment. He'd never been good at talking about feelings; he was better at taking the lead in other ways. Yet, how was he supposed to act?

He felt thrown off kilter – the panic and underlying turmoil

"

that he'd been feeling at the news only a couple of weeks previously had now been replaced with anguish and guilt. The only way forward was to support Kate in the way he knew best.

'We could have a day out somewhere if you'd like? You know – take your mind off things. What about taking a drive somewhere?' He drew a figure of eight across her lips and felt relieved as she formed a wobbly smile. 'Come on – it'll be fun!'

They both knew it wouldn't be, but he couldn't stay home and watch her fall apart any more than he'd had to endure already. He'd had enough of feeling helpless; it was hurting him to see her like this.

Wiping a crumbling piece of tissue across her reddened eyes, Kate nodded – knowing that she had to make an effort in some way – as much for Alf as for herself. 'Okay. Sure.' Slowly disentangling herself from his embrace, she sat up, brushing a piece of wet hair from her cheek and forcing a brighter smile. 'I won't take too long to get ready. Why don't you make us some tea?'

He leaned forward, kissing her shoulder before getting out of bed and stretching. 'Okay, babe. Go get ready and I'll prepare us some breakfast.'

Like a reticent child, she eyed the bathroom door along the hallway, relieved as Alf pulled on his jogging bottoms and padded down the stairs.

It wasn't like we'd planned for a baby anyway, she told herself. She'd been telling herself that a lot in the last two days. Besides, neither of them had been particularly sure if it was the right time to bring a child into the world. Yet, on an unexpected level, she'd been so excited – full of amazement and wonder at the little life growing inside her. Even if was only for six weeks. They'd barely had time to bond before nature had decided to intervene....

She felt her eyes brimming with tears once again and mentally willed herself to be strong. Wrapping her dressing gown around her, she couldn't help but feel lightened as she heard the crashing of plates from the downstairs kitchen followed by loud cursing.

In that moment she knew she'd get through it because she had Alf to help her; the Alf that couldn't even boil an egg and was now attempting to tackle a Full English. Just for her. He was always there – her rock and port of call.

She trusted that together they'd weather anything.

It was just a matter of healing. And time.

Chapter 1

Spring 2014

Kate smoothed the delicate layers of cream chiffon over her hips and carefully adjusted her jewelled, scooped neckline, allowing a subtle hint of her ample cleavage. She stood back, admiring herself in the mirror. She hardly recognised the woman staring back at her. Her usually nondescript mid-length hair had been expertly coloured a dark auburn and styled into gentle waves, framing her oval face. Her large eyes, although still their matt dark-blue colour, were sparkling with anticipation. The shimmer of the smoky eye-shadow that she'd been rallied into purchasing really did give her a mysteriously exotic edge. Long, slightly undefined but tanned legs stretched from beneath her knee-length hemline. She'd taken Megan's advice to try a tinted moisturiser and the results were hard to miss; her usually pale skin had a soft, warm glow. She'd forgotten that she, Kate Wilson, could look quite so glamorous.

She felt a harsh realisation wash through her. Where had this Kate been hiding? Where had the carefree, independent and fashion-conscious Kate disappeared to? The girl she'd been before had slowly and unwittingly morphed into sensible, average Kate over the past couple of years. Kate the care-home worker and Kate the home-maker. In a moment of fleeting clarity she realised she'd shamefully got too comfortable, too safe, too conditioned.

She had slipped into a stagnant routine and somewhere along the line, playfulness and fun had flown out of the window.

Quickly shaking off the melancholy, she selected a pair of sparkling drop earrings from the trinket box lying open on her bedside cabinet. Tonight was *her* night: an evening to shine and be lavished with attention from those closest to her. She'd been daydreaming of this party for three weeks – since finding out that Alf had planned something. It seemed like an age since she'd truly been the focus of any sort of celebration and she couldn't remember the last time she'd been this excited about an evening out. It wasn't for lack of offers, but simply put partying, heavy drinking and impromptu fun seemed to have disappeared somewhere amongst the long working hours and many nights in together. Even the odd nights out with friends at their local pub seemed to lack the sparkle they'd once had. Three glasses of wine and a bag of salt- and-vinegar crisps in a wooden booth at The Red Lion could hardly be considered as living it up…

With a pang of regret, Kate realised she missed this – the chance to get really dressed up and the rush of adrenalin at the prospect of letting her hair down and dancing the night away in unfamiliar surroundings. Tonight she was determined that aside from looking both womanly and – dare she think it – rather sexy, she was going to enjoy herself immensely. It was her thirty-second birthday after all.

Alf burst into the bedroom wearing nothing but navy socks and red boxer shorts that had seen better days. His protruding belly, complete with a dark, wiry hair trail wobbled gently as he scratched his neck and took in the scene before him. He stood transfixed, one eyebrow raised.

'Wow! You look amazing.' His eyes swept up and down her body, lingering on her legs and Kate suddenly felt a little self-conscious. It was such a far cry from her regular jeans, top and pumps combination and she knew Alf must be thinking the same as her – why didn't she look like this more often? And why on earth didn't she?

Feeling guilty, she giggled. 'Thanks! I thought I'd make a bit of an effort. I'm pleased you like it... I might have to start wearing dresses and heavier make-up on a daily basis from now on if that's the reaction I'm going to get from you.'

He shook his head dismissively. 'No babe, you always look nice. No need to go changing yourself. You're lovely as you are.'

There was a hint of weariness in his tone and she couldn't help pondering on why he was being so temperamental of late. Feeling a slight wave of the familiar hysteria that had been creeping up on her in the past months, she grabbed a small pot of bronze nail varnish from her top drawer, trying to block the niggling relationship concerns that were sweeping through her.

Alf was already turning away and opening the wardrobe, seeming not to notice the sudden anxiety surrounding her.

'We need to get going soon, though.' Pulling a dark-blue shirt from its hanger, he held it up briefly, before pushing his arm through the sleeve. 'The others are expecting us at eight o'clock.' Grabbing a pair of jeans and slinging them over his shoulder, he walked out of the room – failing to see Kate's questioning glance.

She turned back towards the mirror. The woman staring back at her had lost some of the excited air of moments before. 'Okay, snap out of it,' she told herself sternly, noticing that her curls were beginning to drop a little. 'You're a team. He's just stressed with work. He loves you. You love him. You're creating problems that aren't there.' She gazed into her reflection with determination. 'Besides, tonight is *the night*.'

Remembering the freshly chipped nail polish on her index finger, she sat down on the bed and unscrewed the lid of the bottle. Dipping the small brush into the liquid, she carefully touched up her nail, the distraction helping her to feel slightly calmer.

Minutes later, Alf strode back into the room with a grin, smelling heavily of the expensive aftershave she'd bought him for special occasions. Her stomach danced as she inhaled the woody scent and all at once her mood was lifted back to a blissful place. It was definitely *the* night.

Replacing the brush into the small pot, Kate stood up from the bed and reached for her perfume bottle, spritzing herself lavishly and feeling even more optimistic as Alf selected his favourite sports jacket from the wardrobe, placing it on a chair.

He looked her up and down again as he looped a black belt through his trousers and fastened it a notch too tightly. 'Are you almost ready, babe?' he asked, bending over to retrieve his polished black shoes from the stand.

'Yes, but I just need a couple of minutes to let this varnish dry.' She waved her finger in the air, watching as he tied his shoelaces – noticing with alarm that his head of thick chestnut-brown hair had thinned drastically at the front. She could see the light reflecting off his scalp in places where the coverage was so sparse. When had that happened? Could it be linked to stress?

She sat back down on the bed, failing to notice as the loosely capped bottle of nail polish was jerked onto its side with the vibration of the movement. He still looks dashing, she thought to herself with conviction. Sure, he was greying quite heavily at the temples, and yes, he'd developed a slight paunch – but not only was he thirty-seven years old, he was also *her* Alf, the one that had stood by her side through thick and thin for the last seven years. And, hopefully, depending on tonight's outcome – he would be making an even longer-lasting commitment. Her stomach flipped with nervous energy and she felt herself growing hot.

Finishing tying his laces, Alf stood upright and picked up his jacket. He glanced at Kate's uncharacteristically made-up face and noticed a blush spreading underneath the heavy foundation on her cheeks. 'Are you okay? You look flushed?'

Caught off-guard, Kate jumped up, smoothing down her dress and reaching for her clutch bag with her right hand. 'Fine,' she said hurriedly, looking at her right hand as a sticky substance filmed a layer across the skin. 'What on earth…?' she stared down in alarm at the bronze paint covering her palm and fingers, her eyes immediately darting to the bed and her dress.

'Oh, God! It's all over your dress.' Stating the obvious, Alf's stare was fixed upon the unmissable bronze smear on the delicate cream chiffon.

He looked on helplessly as Kate's expression changed to horror; a wave of both panic and exasperation taking hold of her. 'No, no, no, no!' She hastily grabbed a used make-up wipe and tried to erase the seeping bronze stain. It was a futile attempt. The sticky mess had already formed an inch-wide stain on the material, obvious for all to see. 'Oh goodness, it's ruined, it'll never come out.' Unable to control her deflation, she felt the buildup behind her eyes and tried desperately to hold her head upwards, fluttering her eyelids in an attempt to stop the threatening tears from streaming into her eye make-up. 'What am I going to do?'

Realising the gravity of the situation and knowing that it couldn't have happened at a worse moment, Alf stepped forward and placed his arms around her. 'Come on, it's not the end of the world. You look gorgeous in whatever you wear.' He gently wiped a small tear from under her eye. 'Get changed into something else – we'll get you another dress to replace this one next week.'

She wanted to argue that next week was too late – her special moment was *tonight* – but she refrained. Aware of the ticking clock, she slipped off the beautiful dress that had made her feel so glamorous and exceptional and walked across to her wardrobe. Not having indulged in luxurious or unnecessary purchases over the past year, she knew her alternative options were limited. It was either her faithful black shift dress – worn countless times and a little faded, one of the many dresses she no longer fitted since going up a dress size, or the asymmetrical green party dress she'd bought last Christmas that made her resemble a billowing tree. She deliberated for a few seconds before plucking the black dress from its hanger. It would have to do.

Stepping into it and pulling it up, she struggled to fasten the awkwardly angled rear zip. 'Can you zip me up, please?'

With one swift motion, Alf fastened the rear zipper and Kate's body was snugly embraced in the black material. She walked across to the free-standing mirror. It didn't look bad. Just, well… a bit plain.

Standing next to her, Alf nodded in gratification, a beaming smile lighting up his face. 'Now *that* is the Kate that I know and love. You look lovely. Much better than that fussy cream thing.' He kissed her cheek. 'This is much more you. Simple, classy and understated.'

Looking at him quizzically, Kate didn't say anything. She couldn't help but notice that his sparkling eyes and happy demeanour at her appearance were genuine. She felt herself rile ever so slightly. His words were not those of dishonest encouragement to make her feel better – they were words spoken from the heart. Unsure how to feel about it, she tried to quickly dismiss the thought. *Simple?* What was that supposed to mean?

'Okay, well this looks fine – so I guess we can get going. There's no point me crying over a dress on my birthday, is there?'

'Exactly, babe. It's a special night anyway – you won't even be thinking about the dress once we're out and celebrating.' A hint of a smile played on his lips and intuitively Kate knew what he was referring to. Her pulse quickened.

Alf picked up his wallet and slipped it into his pocket. 'Right, let's make a move, then.'

Re-touching her eyeliner in a final attempt to look as good as she possibly could, she picked up her clutch bag and switched off the bedroom light.

Two years she'd waited. It was just as they'd agreed. Two years in order to allow enough time for travel, the house renovations and, of course, Alf's career advances. It had passed so quickly – much quicker than she'd expected. It seemed almost yesterday that they'd had the conversation – she could still recall the moment she'd blurted out her feelings. It had been minutes before they'd left the house for her monumental thirtieth birthday dinner. He'd been surprised; she remembered the shock on his face. But then he'd hugged her and explained his reasons for not asking sooner. They'd talked about it for what seemed like hours, but it was, in fact, probably only minutes. Two years is what he'd said and she'd remained silent on the matter ever since, not wanting to push him.

And now, tonight – two years later, on her thirty-second birthday – if Alf was true to his word, Kate was about to fulfil her deepest wish – accepting his engagement proposal. Her heart fluttered at the thought.

She was more than ready to become Mrs Alf Stafford.

Alf drove eagerly out of their suburban housing estate as Kate gazed quietly out of the passenger window, scanning the rows of identical red-brick terraced houses. She'd never given much thought to their mid-terrace property until lately. It wasn't that she didn't enjoy living in Ramsley Way – they'd bought the rendered white two-bed home six years previously and had been more than happy living there. Yet, looking at the mass of similar houses, she realised she was yearning to become more individual. They'd never planned to live there long term. It was supposed to be a starter home, but that idea had seemed to have fallen by the wayside…

She noticed that the detached pointed-roof house that sat on the corner of Worthington Road had recently been renovated. Its fresh coat of white exterior paint, potted shrubs either side of the green door and new sweeping brick driveway made her spirits lift even further. She'd been fixated on that particular property for some time now. It seemed so grandiose in comparison to their own home. It was idyllic – the type of marital home that she hoped to one day share with Alf and their children.

'What are you smiling at?' Alf asked, glancing sideways.

Kate grinned excitedly. 'I'm just happy – it's not often a girl gets to celebrate turning thirty-two with a handsome man by her side.' She rubbed her hand on his leg and returned to looking out of the window.

Alf smiled at the comment and stared ahead. His spirits were high, but he hoped Megan hadn't taken it upon herself to interfere and let Kate know the finer details of the surprise he'd planned. Their close friendship puzzled him. Kate's ways were so different from those of the showy and attention-seeking Megan. She wasn't anything but troublesome in his opinion – always filling Kate's head with silly ideas and notions of riches and glamour. Kate was gentle, grounded; it bothered him that Megan couldn't appreciate that.

'So, am I allowed to know where we are going?' Kate asked with a sparkle of anticipation in her eyes.

Alf grinned, feeling himself swelling with pride. Arranging surprises wasn't his forte, but even he had surpassed his own expectations with what he'd organised. He was certain Kate was going to be impressed with the thought behind his idea.

Tapping his nose cheekily, he narrowly missed the left turn needed for the venue and just managed to pull the car onto a verge before hitting the A road ahead. Kate reached out for the dashboard to brace herself as the car came to a sharp, abrupt stop.

'Sorry – I should have taken a left back there.' Putting the car into reverse gear, he cursed under his breath as he waited for the traffic to ease to make his U-turn.

Trying to hide her mild confusion, she remained silent. She had been so certain that they'd been going to the small country pub venue she'd discreetly found bookmarked on his laptop. It hadn't helped that Megan had remained uncharacteristically tight-lipped on the subject. Yet it made sense; the country pub was the typical type of event venue that Alf would go for. It looked cosy, quaint and welcoming. She'd already envisioned herself walking into the pretty beamed entrance to the cheers of her nearest and dearest. Perhaps a DJ playing in the corner…

Why then, was Alf heading in the direction of a nearby town? She tried to think rationally – could the venue have been changed at the last moment? She felt her stomach flutter with nerves and was relieved she'd opted for her trusty black dress – thankful that she wouldn't be dealing with unsightly sweat marks.

She was so looking forward to seeing who'd be there. Familiar faces danced through her mind and she mentally made a note of who she wanted to spend time catching up with. She didn't often get to see those closest to her, what with her long working hours at Oak Park Care Home, especially over the past nine months since she'd taken on more responsibility. She wanted to make the most of it. Thinking of work made her mind drift to Vivian, one of the residents. She hadn't been looking her perky self of late and Kate was a little worried that there was more to it than was meeting the eye.

'I hope you're ready for some fun tonight' Alf said, suddenly animated and fiddling with his top shirt button. He stole a side-ward glance at Kate and was happy to see her radiant expression. These days it was rare these days to see her being spirited about life. It hadn't gone unnoticed, either, that she'd seemed distracted over the past month and he wasn't sure what to do about it. He was hoping the evening would be the key to bringing her back out of her shell.

They'd been driving through country lanes for a while when Kate observed that the car was slowing just as Alf hit the right-side indicator. Her stomach somersaulted. She recognised the road that they were heading into. Pearmont Manor Road. Pearmont Manor was one of the area's most exclusive wedding venues. She'd only seen the stately home in various magazine articles, but its breathtaking exterior surrounded by exquisite landscaped greenery had provided a backdrop for stunning photographic memories. Remembering the various interior event rooms, her heart skipped a beat.

Surely not? Hardly able to contain her nerves and excitement she swallowed back a squeak.

'Everything okay?' Alf asked, eyeing her in amusement as the car smoothly made its approach into the wide tree-lined road.

Pearmont Manor growing bigger on the left side of them as they travelled parallel to it.

Kate suppressed a grin and tried to calm her racing heart. Never in her wildest dreams would she have thought Alf would arrange something so special. She wanted to fling her arms around him and kiss him passionately – but it would have to wait. Soon she could do as she wished – hopefully in front of their guests whilst Alf was down on one knee. Just the thought made her giddy and lightheaded.

The car slowed as the Pearmont entrance came into view. 'Here we are,' Alf said, clicking his left indicator. As the last of the tall hedging bushes and conifers cleared, the full magnificence of the stately home made it presence known, causing both of them to inhale sharply – for completely different reasons. The car shuddered and stalled as Alf fumbled with the ignition.

'Oh, sorry, wrong entrance. This isn't the one.' With a panicked stance, he flicked off his indicator and quickly restarted the engine. Feeling Kate's confused stare burning into him, he tried not to let his tension show. He was well aware that the mishap could well have set him on a fast track to failure.

'It's not?' Kate asked, trying to keep her voice steady as the car gradually picked up pace and the Manor slowly faded behind them. Was there another entrance around the back? It was, after all, a very big venue. There was undoubtedly more than one entrance, she told herself. Trees and conifers clouded her view as the road narrowed in front of them. Minutes seemed to pass before the car slowed for a second time and Alf once again flicked on the left indicator.

Kate clenched her fists in anxiety as the hedging cleared once again and a sign came into view. She could see the word 'Pearmont' and relief washed over her. Thank goodness, another entrance.

'We're here' Alf said, slightly dubious and wondering if he'd chosen correctly after all. What if she hated it?

The car approached a paved entrance and turned slowly left

onto a gravel driveway. Kate looked up at the large sign that had given her fresh hope only moments earlier and tried not to gasp as Alf's hand squeezed hers encouragingly.

Pulling the car to a stop he switched off the engine and gently kissed her hand, pushing aside his doubts and beginning to feel more zealous.

'Welcome to Pearmont Greyhound Stadium, babe.'

He broke into an excited grin; one that made Kate's heart plummet to even further depths, for she could see it was no humorous joke on his part – only genuine enthusiasm.

'You're probably wondering why I chose here?' He looked at her intently and squeezed her knee. 'I thought it'd be special to recapture our first date seven years ago – except this time I'm going to make it an unforgettable night.'

Kate, lost for words, struggled to contain tears, the disappointment and dismay hitting her with full force. This was not what she'd been expecting. Not at all.

'Say something?' Alf said quietly, growing more and more concerned. He knew Kate well enough to know when she was shocked. But her face was telling him that it wasn't a happy shock. 'Look, I know it's not the Manor next door. I made a wrong turn back there. This stadium is really nice, though. I know you'll love it – even though it's not the one where we first met…' He tailed off, suddenly edgy.

Looking into his squinting eyes in the dimming evening light, Kate caught his worried expression. She took a deep breath, forcing a light, reassuring tone to her voice. 'I'm just a little taken aback – it's not what I expected, that's all.' She bit down on her lip, wondering what to say. 'It's a lovely idea, though, so thoughtful.' She was lying, but what more could she do? She felt a lump in her throat and tried to swallow it down.

'You understand the relevance, right? I thought it'd be special. And fun. I thought you'd be excited about it.' Alf sounded a little dejected and defensive. He fiddled with his seatbelt awkwardly.

Leaning forward, Kate gently kissed him on the lips, silencing him. She pulled back slowly, noticing that his air of excitement had evaporated. He looked forlorn. She grabbed his arm and linked hers through hers, trying to be upbeat.

'Of course it'll be fun. We're together and it's my birthday. I know tonight is going to be special, so let's just go inside and enjoy it.'

Pushing aside the mental images of Pearmont Manor and her dashed hopes, she allowed Alf to lead her towards the entrance of the stadium, with a heavy heart and only one remaining thought. He was the man that she dearly loved, spent every available moment with and had been by her side for over seven years…

So how could he have got it so very *very* wrong?

Chapter 2

'You could have at least warned me,' Kate whispered, retouching her eye make-up in the bright lighting of the ladies' toilet. She watched as Megan – who was standing against the hand dryer – shrugged her shoulders uncomfortably and lowered her gaze.

'I'm so sorry, Kate – if Alf hadn't made me promise then I would have. But he was so taken with the idea and I knew how disappointed you'd probably be, but truthfully, Kate – it wasn't my place to warn you.'

'But didn't you try to change his mind?' Kate asked, exasperated. Megan knew her better than anyone – surely she should have intervened in some way?

Tossing her chocolate-brown, wavy hair to one side, Megan sighed. She had known from the moment Alf had sent her the email of his proposed venue that Kate would be less than enthused. Annoyed at his suggestion, for a fleeting moment she had wondered whether to call him on the internal switchboard and suggest meeting in the staff canteen of the large corporate insurance brokers they both worked for; but she'd decided against it. Alf had made it painfully clear over the years that he didn't value her input or appreciate her outgoing personality. She was certain he wouldn't want to listen to her concerns. Besides, she'd already caught wind of a potentially bigger revelation that was sure to rock Kate's world if it transpired. The venue was the least of her worries.

'You know as well as I do that if I'd tried to change his mind, he'd have dismissed me without giving it a second thought.' She gave Kate a wry smile. 'Anyway, part of me hoped that you'd be so bowled over with the romance behind the idea that you'd forgive him for the awful choice.'

Kate sighed. She knew Megan was right. Alf wasn't one to be swayed once he'd set his heart on something – least of all by a woman he didn't favour. Megan did have a point – the gesture behind his idea was romantic.

She could hardly believe that seven years had passed – it seemed like a lifetime ago that Megan had persuaded her to attend her summer works' do. It certainly wasn't the place she'd wanted to spend her evening, yet events beyond her control had led to her finding herself at a dog stadium in an unfamiliar town.

It just so happened that she'd been parted from Megan and the other colleagues in a flurry of visitors placing their bets, and a kind, dark-haired man with a slightly crooked smile had asked if she was okay. From the moment she locked eyes with Alf, she'd had a sixth-sense feeling he was going to be in her life forever. And here she was, tearing apart his romantic gesture because she'd expected something more to her taste.

Glancing into the mirror Megan quickly applied a fresh coat of the clear liquid gloss to her full lips. She'd never been a big fan of too much make-up, but then she'd never really needed it. Satisfied with her appearance, she picked up her purse and tried steering the conversation in a new direction.

'I still can't believe you spilt nail varnish over your dress. Honestly Kate, you are the clumsiest woman on earth. You have got to get that dress dry-cleaned or something. It's too stunning to waste.'

Kate nodded grimly. 'Yes, I was gutted, but then Alf did make a comment that he preferred me in this dress, which was a bit strange. He said I looked more understated and simple.'

Spinning around with her forehead furrowed questioningly, Megan tried not to let her disdain be too obvious. 'Understated? Simple? Are you serious? You looked absolutely gorgeous in that dress.' She shook her head in disgust. 'What is wrong with him? Dearie me, Kate, it seems he'd like to keep you as dull as dishwater.'

Staring at Megan incredulously, Kate angrily picked up her clutch bag. 'Wow, thanks for that – that's really cheered me up! Nice to know I'm as dull as dishwater.'

Despite the tension, Megan laughed lightly. 'Don't over-react – you know what I'm referring to. I've told you countless times you need to get more of a life and when I saw you in that cream dress, it just reminded me of well, *you*, the real you...' She squeezed Kate's arm gently, noticing a shadow pass across her friend's face. 'I just want to see you happy again, you know that.'

Kate's expression softened. 'I know that. But I am happy – Alf makes me happy. Plus it's my birthday and he has another surprise up his sleeve... I can feel it.' Her eyes sparkled in excitement.

Megan wanted to believe Kate's convincing words, but she knew her friend too well. She'd noticed a vast change in her over the last year and couldn't help but refer back to the passing comments Kate had made about Alf on various occasions. Whether she realised it or not, she'd been disclosing a side of her partner that Megan saw in its true colour – insecurity. As well as Kate's growing introversion, Alf seemed to be projecting all of his own issues onto Kate. It wasn't a healthy situation.

Wisely ignoring the reference to Alf having another surprise for the evening, Megan smoothed down her tight blue bodycon dress and turned towards the door. She knew full well that Kate had quietly set her hopes on Alf proposing, given their two-year deadline. But her intuition was telling her otherwise. Anyway, if the office gossip that had filtered down from management was true, Alf would have other life decisions to concentrate on. She only hoped that Kate wasn't going to be too devastated if she didn't get the proposal she was expecting.

'Right then, enough talking – let's get out there and get you enjoying your party.'

Kate followed, feeling more enthusiastic. She could already hear the beat of a song she favoured in the background and she'd noticed so many familiar faces she couldn't wait to catch up with.

'Oh, just one last thing. Did you decide on the colour theme? Or was that Alf too?'

Megan looked around and pulled a face in distaste. 'Do you really need to ask that? I tried to suggest pink, white and silver, but he was having none of it.'

Kate smiled; she'd thought as much. Pink, white and silver would have been so much better. She stepped into the hallway, allowing the heavy bathroom door to swing shut behind her. They both giggled at the green 'Happy 32nd Birthday' banner that had been stuck wonkily on the overhead beam and walked towards the venue room.

Alf watched from across the room as Kate's face lit up at something one of her friends had said. She threw her hands up in a mock shock and broke into a wide grin. She looked so animated. Luminous. He was pleased the venue had paid off. For a moment when they arrived, from the expression on her face, he thought he'd screwed things up, but she'd soon cheered up. The red and green balloons had been a good idea, too. Not pink, white and silver, as Megan had suggested. He knew Kate better than anyone and she wasn't one of these fluffy women who needed pink things in their life. She'd seemed pleased with the decorations, commenting on them as they walked towards the private-event room he'd arranged. He could have easily gone for the country pub venue but this idea was better – he hoped it had reminded her of his unique and creative side. He wasn't a dull person and yet that's exactly how he'd felt lately – grey. He was sure he wasn't the only one feeling it – it was good to see Kate looking happy again.

'Alright, mate.' Josh, Alf's colleague, interrupted his observation. 'Great party.' He took a swig of his bottled cider. 'I've just been chatting with Walshy over there about how hot Megan looks tonight.'

'Wouldn't know about that, mate. Loud-mouthed, arrogant women don't do it for me. She's got a great face and figure – I'll give her that much. Shame about the personality.' Alf glanced at the willowy Megan standing next to Kate and tucking her thick, wavy hair to one side. There was no denying that she was stunning. Yet he couldn't help but dislike her influence over Kate.

Josh grinned mischievously. He was known in Alf's department as the 'wind-up merchant' and was all too aware of the stand-off between Alf and Megan. He'd already been over to Megan and tried his luck tonight, but to no avail. She was also being uncharacteristically tight-lipped.

'Who's the woman in the polka-dot dress by the window?' Josh asked, nodding his head towards a short, slim blonde in sky-scraping heels.

'Jo – Kate's friend, and she's married. Got three kids. It's a no-go mate.' Alf drained his pint of beer and excused himself, drawn to the laughter and shrieking from where Kate stood surrounded by their mutual friends.

Kate took another gulp of her rosé wine and wiped a tear of laughter from beneath her eye. She saw Alf approaching with a grin on his face. He'd loosened his shirt buttons and she noticed he looked relaxed and happy. 'We were just laughing about the old days. Do you remember that time we got lost on our weekend break in Wales and they had to send the rescue team out. Then Ian ended up breaking his little toe after the ram chased him?'

Alf laughed. 'He's always said his toe has never been the same since. The funny thing is, he already had a sixth toe to start with.' Giggles erupted around him as he looked down at his empty glass. 'I'm just going to get a top-up.'

'I'll come with you.' Linking her arm through his, Kate turned to Alf. 'I'm having the best night. Thank you so much for arranging this.' It was true. The music, the people, the wine. It might not have been what she'd expected but the past couple of hours had been a blast.

'There's more to come yet.' Alf whispered, leaning in to kiss her gently on the lips.

Kate felt her stomach somersault. She couldn't imagine a happier ending to the evening than Alf proposing. It was certainly going to be a memory for the future. She tried to contain her excitement as another thought popped into her head.

'Oh, before I forget. All that reminiscing about our weekend break to Wales made me remember the artistic retreat I was going to do. I think I'm going to look into it again.'

Alf stopped in his tracks. 'Artistic retreat? But I thought you'd given up with your art?'

Kate noticed the edge of tension in his voice and felt her enthusiasm falter. She walked slowly ahead of him. 'Well, I know it's been a long time, but painting used to make me so happy. Remembering it made me feel excited again.'

'It's up to you – you do as you please, but I very much doubt considering you haven't held a brush in eight years that you'll pick up where you left off.' They'd reached the bar and Alf turned to catch the attention of the waiter.

'I wasn't expecting to pick up where I left off.' Kate retorted, wounded. She noticed that Alf's body language had changed; he was standing stiffly against the bar, agitatedly drumming his knuckles. 'Just forget I said anything, okay?'

He swiftly placed his order with the barman and turned to look at her with a confused look in his eyes. 'I didn't mean it like that, darling. I just meant – don't expect to have the big opportunities that you once had with it. Things change. Your life is different now.'

Kate felt herself shrinking inside. She was well aware that in the past she'd thrown away a good opportunity to make a name for herself in the art world, but she'd never regretted it. She thought Alf had understood that – hadn't he?

'I know, and I didn't mean about doing it professionally. I just meant I might look into the retreat again and take it up as a hobby. A creative outlet. That's all.'

She felt her hair being tugged gently and instantly span around to see a tipsy Megan behind her. 'Hey doll, are you okay?'

Megan smiled and held up her wine glass, not noticing as the liquid spilled over the edges onto the carpet. 'I was coming to get you for a boogie. I've asked the DJ to play our song.'

Kate caught Alf's cold stare in Megan's direction and felt it wise to keep the pair as far apart as possible. Following the exchange she'd just had with Alf, his happier mood had clearly vanished. The waiter finished pouring a fresh glass of wine and handed it to her.

She smiled at her friend encouragingly. 'I'd love to. Go and get us a good spot by the DJ stand and I'll be right over.'

Megan followed Kate's orders, but not before singing the song loudly as she brushed purposefully – if not a little drunkenly, past Alf.

'And you call that sorry excuse of a drunken woman a sensible friend?' Alf smirked as Megan was barely out of earshot.

'She's just a little tipsy, that's all. Why don't you come and have a dance after, too? Let's bust out some moves together on the dance floor,' Kate replied lightly, doing her best impression of a dancing robot. The wine she'd drunk was squashing any inhibitions.

Alf's face lightened and he laughed, grabbing her waist. 'I'll hold you to that. It's been a while since the world has seen my running man.' Smiling, Kate led him towards the makeshift dance floor just as Rihanna came over the speakers.

'It's your song,' Alf said, visibly relieved at having an excuse to return to the boys. 'You'd better get over to Miss Tipsy and do your dance together. Just don't be there all night.' He watched as Kate sashayed her way over to where Megan was already doing her best Rihanna impersonation and shook his head in disbelief.

It was almost eleven o'clock and Alf knew his time had come. He stepped up onto the small stage just as the DJ cut the music. The heavy tap on the microphone sent a high-pitched shrill sound through the room, causing everyone to wince and still their chatter and dancing. His eyes immediately found Kate amongst the crowd, looking at him flushed and bewildered. She was a little drunk but still as luminous as she had been all evening. He only hoped his final surprise would be one to make her smile with even more happiness. He'd thought about it for a while – uncertain if it was the right thing to do…but his mind had been made up. He was confident it would bring her happiness in a way that he knew she craved.

'Ladies and gents,' he began. 'Firstly, I'd like to thank you for sharing this special evening with us and I'd especially like to ask you all to raise your glasses to my Kate. Thirty-two years old. Happy birthday, babe.' He raised his pint of beer and the guests followed suit.

Kate found herself surrounded by loud cheers and applause, momentarily forgetting the fluttering of nervous energy that was coursing through her in shock waves. This was it. The very moment she'd been waiting for.

Alf's amplified voice cut through the crowd. 'Furthermore, some of you may be wondering why I'm on this stage and why I'm about to ask my darling Kate to join me.' With a shy smile he beckoned her with his hand and Kate watched as the crowd parted before her. Various hands nudged her forward and she was propelled towards him.

Taking a wobbly step onto the low-level stage, her legs were shaking with nerves. The guests were once again applauding and cheering. Looking out at the room of smiling faces before her, her stomach did a flip as Alf took her hand in his and squeezed it. She gazed into his smiling eyes and saw the Alf she'd always known and loved. The Alf she'd spent the biggest part of her life with.

'Kate, you know how much I love you. I wanted tonight to be a special evening and one to remember. I hope in some way I've achieved that. However, there is a reason I've asked you up here and that reason is – there's something special I want to give you.' Taking a small, blue-leather box from his pocket, Alf nervously held it in his outstretched hand.

'For you, Kate. Open it.'

Heart pounding so fast it felt like it would burst from her chest, Kate carefully reached out and accepted the box – not daring to breathe as the intense headiness of excitement and nerves swept her up in a whirlwind. It was every bit as magical as she'd hoped for. Silence surrounded her as everyone waited with baited breath.

Gingerly preparing to open it, she bit down on her lip to stop herself from screaming with elation. Vaguely aware of the entrance door opening and closing beside her, her fingers trembled as she slowly flipped back the leather-bound lid.

She let out a gasp. Nestled softly in a layer of cream silk was a perfectly round, shiny and shimmering disk. A single word was etched clearly onto its surface. Before she had a chance to utter the muffled gasp that was forming in the back of her throat, a box was thrust onto the stage by her feet.

Alf bent down and quickly removed the lid, at the same time swiftly collecting the box's contents in his arms and thrusting it towards Kate. A gasp of surprise swept around the room.

'In keeping with the theme.' He winked at the guests. 'I wanted to get you something that I know you would love and would also be an incentive for us both to take up walking more often.' The crowd tittered at his joke in surprised amusement.

The tiny Cavalier King Charles spaniel puppy gave a timid squeak as Alf placed him gently onto Kate's chest. Kate stood shell-shocked, looking at the puppy in a daze of misunderstanding.

'Kate, meet Sam – our new puppy.'

As a warm, acidic liquid poured out of little Sam and spread across Kate's chest and down her dress, she swallowed back the ball of disappointment lodging itself in her throat. She managed a quick, trembling smile before being unable to hold back any longer. Meeting Megan's sympathetic eyes in the crowd, she burst into tears.

This was most definitely not the ending to her night that she had been anticipating.

Chapter 3

Easing her small hatchback car into the only spot remaining in the Oak Park Care Home parking, Kate wondered how long it would be until the heavens opened. The Monday morning grey sky conveniently reflected her mood – she'd barely been able to sleep through Alf's snoring and the puppy's continual whimpering. Her body felt limp and she could hardly keep her eyes open.

Noting the time on her dashboard, she grabbed her well-worn shoulder bag and the Tupperware tub of birthday cake she'd brought for the residents and dashed towards the entrance – aware that she was already ten minutes late.

Oak Park director, Walter Steinbach, was discussing a matter with the reception staff as Kate tried to inconspicuously hurry past him. Not an easy task, given that all care staff were expected to wear the unflattering fuchsia-pink top and pants uniform that did little to enhance her mood or figure.

'You're late,' Steinbach barked, in the voice usually reserved for non-compliant and unruly kindergarten visitors.

And you're still alive? Kate felt like snapping back at him. With his hollowing facial features and the sparse few hairs that remained on his head, it was often said he was more ancient than the care home itself. It was just as well he rarely made an appearance.

'Sorry, Mr Steinbach' she found herself saying, ignoring his eagle-eyed stare of disapproval as it followed her towards the staff room. Only fellow care-worker Tina was in the staff room as she strode over to her locker to place her belongings and swap her trainers for comfy pumps. Kate exhaled, relieved that it wasn't anyone else from the team. The last thing she felt like undergoing was in-depth questioning.

'Morning, good weekend?' Tina asked, pouring herself a coffee.

'Yes, fine thanks.' She closed her locker and readjusted her name plate on the front of her top. 'Best get a move on. I've already had Steinbach on my case.' Sighing, she opened the door and hurriedly made her way up to the East Wing.

'Morning, Hilda.' She tapped gently against the door, awaiting her usual instruction from the other side. Nothing came.

'Hilda – can you hear me? Is it okay for me to come in?' Kate asked for a second time, impatient. A faint, desperate rasping could be heard in response and she felt her pulse quickening anxiously as she quickly pushed open the door. 'Hilda?'

What if this time it was genuine?

Hilda was propped up in bed, wide-eyed and pointing rapidly to her throat whilst continuing with the awful grating sound from her windpipe. Acting immediately, Kate grabbed a nearby glass of water and tilted back Hilda's small head, instructing her to drink. After just a couple of sips, Hilda's breathing returned to normal and she cleared her throat.

'Thank you so much, dear Kate. I was afraid for a moment there that I was about to take my last breath.' Hilda said in her usual crisp, clear voice. 'It was a bluebottle, you see.'

Relieved, Kate thought to herself that she really must be out of sorts to fall for Hypochondriac Hilda's latest stunt. 'A bluebottle?' She glanced at the little lady now lying angelically in her blue nightgown, her straight, grey, pixie-cut hair sticking up awkwardly in places.

Clearly recovered and bright as a daisy, Hilda threw back her floral duvet and shuffled her weight to the edge of the bed, gripping Kate's hand as she struggled to stand.

'Yes, it's been in here the whole night buzzing away, keeping me awake. It was only as I heard you on the stairs and was about to call out that it flew into my mouth!'

Helping Hilda walk the short distance to the en suite, Kate returned to the dresser, selecting Hilda's 'Monday' outfit.

'Goodness, that's terrible, Hilda. Especially as it's the third time this has happened. What with the bumble bee and the spider last month...'

A small sigh came from above the washbasin, where Hilda was gently soaping her face with a flannel. 'I know, dear. I am beginning to wonder if the Lord has other plans for me. Don't forget the cockroach, either. It's only a matter of time before those eggs it laid in my ear canal begin to hatch.'

Kate smiled broadly for the first time that day.

Hilda was patting her frail frame dry with a small towel as the first of the questions came unexpectedly. 'So, dear Kate, you're ever so quiet and we all know that it was your surprise party this weekend. Don't keep me in suspense. Anything special happen, dear?' she asked with a twinkle in her eye.

Kate blushed and inwardly grimaced.

By the time she had helped Hilda to dress and guide her walking frame to the breakfast room to join the already nearly full tables, she had divulged the highlights of her weekend. She wasn't one for lying – it wasn't in her nature – but instead of focusing on the main disappointment, she instead concentrated on the few special markers. Namely, her new puppy, Sam, who she'd already grown to adore.

Just as she was about to continue her round, she smiled weakly as she saw a squat, rounded woman with flame-red hair approaching. Her heart sank a little. Fellow care- worker Tasha lived up to her Scottish reputation and fiery hair. She also had such a loose mouth Kate was in no doubt that the details of her party would be wormed out of her and circulated around the entire home before the first spoonful of porridge was even served.

'Morning, luv, you look tired. I heard you were late – and Steinbach's on the prowl today.'

Kate averted her glance from the care rota on the wall. She still had three residents to attend to for the breakfast shift. 'Morning! I know, it was just my luck that he caught me on the way in.'

Tasha angled her body and discreetly took her electronic cigarette from her pocket and faced the wall, inhaling deeply. 'So how'd it go? Did he propose? Where's the ring – come on let's have a look!' Using her free hand, she reached out for Kate's.

Feebly holding her own ringless hand out, Kate waved it in front of Tasha, trying to hide her embarrassment. 'No proposal, unfortunately, but it was such a lovely party. I had a great time – Alf really did go to town on the thought behind it. Plus he got me a puppy.'

Tasha spluttered on her electronic cigarette vapour. 'He got you a puppy? What the blooming hell did you want a puppy for?' She looked at Kate with an incredulous expression.

Kate felt her face flush with heat and hoped her cheeks weren't burning a bright- crimson colour. 'Oh, he's very cute. We've called him Sam. I happen to feel it was a lovely gesture. Alf's already commented how much more of a family home it feels now we've got Sam – and I have to say I agree.'

Tasha replaced her cigarette in her pocket and raised an eyebrow mockingly. 'Well, I suppose it's good practice for you – all those pisses and shits you'll be cleaning up will be great preparation for when you decide to have your own wee 'un.'

Flinching at her choice of words, Kate raised a warning eyebrow as Steinbach appeared on the far side of the room. 'Best get back to work. I don't want to be caught out a second time today.'

Grateful to Steinbach for the reprieve, Kate felt her heart aching as Tasha's words echoed in her mind. She mounted the stairs towards Alan's room and tried not to allow the recurring agony she'd desperately spent the past twenty-four hours squashing. It had been four years since the miscarriage; four years without either of them really acknowledging the elephant in the room that lurked silently between them – the prospect of future children and the loss of the child they had created. Sure, Alf had made the odd reference to the future with a family of their own. But gifting her a puppy? Was this his way of trying to pacify her quiet need for something more? She couldn't help but torment herself with the underlying reasons of his gift choice.

She'd tried to share her concern with Megan – although rather cryptically and indirectly, for it seemed no one, even Alf, was truly aware of how the miscarriage still affected her. Yet Megan hadn't questioned his motives in the same way that she had… her friend's theory was set upon the puppy being a tactical distraction to delay the proposal further.

Internally, she couldn't find much peace around the answer. Alf had never been of a manipulative nature... Surely he hadn't assumed that a puppy could replace her deeper yearning for a child?

Taking a deep breath, she reached the top of the staircase and turned right into the corridor, determined to stop the negative thoughts and concentrate on the notion that his heart had been in the right place when he'd considered the puppy as something she would love. It was of little consequence that he hadn't given a second thought to the fact that both of them worked and a puppy needed constant attention…

'Ah, there she is, the very woman I was hoping to see on this fine Monday morning.' Alan stood tall and wide in the doorframe wearing a cream tweed woollen suit and brandishing a shiny silver pocket watch in her direction.

'Morning, Alan.' Kate smiled, always happy to see the man who transported her to a flamboyant and well-mannered bygone time. Despite nearing eighty-eight, he was as able-bodied and fit as any man half his age.

Picking up his copy of *The Times* from his sideboard, he gently closed the door behind him.

'There isn't anything much I need assistance with this morning, Kate, yet I would be honoured if you'd accompany me on the short journey to the breakfast lounge.'

'Of course.'

Walking carefully beside Kate, Alan felt compelled to ask. 'I couldn't help observing the frown on that beautiful face of yours as you approached. Is something rather the matter?'

Never being one to pry and more likely to discuss quantum physics than one's personal life, Alan's question caught Kate off-guard. Was she really emitting such a distracted energy that even Alan had needed to comment on it?

Trying to lighten her mood, she shyly brushed a stray hair from her face and gave a nervous giggle. 'I had a bit of an unexpected turn of events this weekend, if I'm honest. Not exactly panning out the way I had thought it would. The result was that my partner gifted me with a puppy. It's the cutest little thing, but I guess I'm a bit worried about how I'll cope. What with working all day and it being left to its own devices…'

Alan nodded silently, considering Kate's predicament. He wasn't a man of many words when it came to relationships, especially since living out the last seventeen years of his life as a widow at Oak Park. Yet he'd heard a thing or two along the grapevine about Kate's partnership. Her admission didn't sit well with him. He'd been expecting to hear news of a marriage proposal. At least, that's what the women had been discussing at dinner last night.

'Why don't you allow me to have a word with Mr Steinbach. We're at a loss for animal companionship here and I'm sure I'd not only be speaking for myself when I say we'd welcome a puppy amongst our ranks. Your daily shift ends at four – I'm more than certain we can find a way to keep the little chappie entertained and out of trouble whilst you work.'

Kate felt an overwhelming surge of relief and gratitude as she looked up into Alan's smoky grey eyes in surprise. 'Oh Alan, would you really do that for me?'

'Well, I can't make any promises – you know how stiff Steinbach can be at times. But I'm certain if anyone can, it's me that can convince the old fellow.' He winked at Kate.

Reaching the breakfast room, Alan promised to inform Kate as soon as he'd had a chance to speak with Steinbach.

Vivian took another generous sip from her can of Guinness and looked at the clock on the wall of her sitting room. Kate was running late. Not that she minded; she rarely bothered with the breakfast round – she'd never been able to stomach a morsel of food before eleven anyway. But today was special – their Kate was likely to be full of beans about her proposal. They couldn't wait to hear the full details. They only hoped things had gone as she'd expected and Alf hadn't let her down.

'I bet you it's Hypo Hilda's fault – probably got a case of incurable warts to moan about.'

Lillian chuckled at her friend's comment, fidgeting nervously with the buttons on her cardigan and ignoring the gentle grumbling sounds from her stomach.

'Oh, I do wish she'd hurry up, Viv – I ain't half hungry.'

A knock at the door caused them both to smile in excitement. 'Come in, love, we're all ready for you.'

Kate opened the door in a flurry and swept into the room briskly, clutching the Tupperware box of birthday cake to her chest. 'Morning, ladies. Sorry I'm late. Alan asked me to walk him down to the breakfast lounge and then I got caught up with Hilda – she had a fit and choked on her boiled egg.'

'Good riddance, I say' Vivian piped up, eyes immediately scanning Kate's ring finger and noticing its lack of sparkle.

'Viv, you mustn't talk like that!' Lillian scolded. 'It could be you next.'

'Over my dead body' Vivian retorted, taking another generous gulp of Guinness.

Turning her attention to Kate, Lillian quickly took in her harassed appearance and tell-tale lack of engagement ring. She stole a glance at Vivian, who pursed her lips ever so slightly in disappointment. It was just as they'd feared.

'So how was the party? Did you have a nice time? We'd like to hear all about it. Come and sit down,' Vivian said tactfully, patting the spare seat they'd purposely prepared for Kate's arrival.

Looking into the kindly eyes of her two best friends and charges at the care home, Kate felt her façade crumble even before she'd sat herself in the comfortable chair they'd set out especially for her. 'Oh, Viv, Lil – I feel so stupid.'

Hiccupping through tears, for the first time in twenty-four hours Kate could finally open up about her feelings on the matter.

Vivian and Lillian sat quietly as they listened in silent compassion to young Kate's dilemma. Neither commented or tutted in the usual way they would behave towards the other residents, because for both of them Kate was like the daughter they'd never had. And both of them could feel the disappointment and pain in each word.

Only when Kate finished spluttering through her tears about her confusion on the whole matter did Lillian finally pipe up.

'Let me tell you a story, darling, about my second husband Bobbi...'

It was then that Kate grinned. She'd heard the story countless times. Bobbi was the second of five husbands that Lillian had worked her way through. She happened to also know that Bobbi was the only one who had failed to propose to Lillian for a whole year before Lillian took matters into her own hands.

She had a feeling it was time to pay more attention...

Chapter 4

Sinking back against the cream leather sofa cushions, Kate's eyes swept around the small living room of the house she shared with Alf. Its soft pastel-green walls had once seemed so welcoming and relaxing, yet now the paint was marked and scuffed in places. The ash wood furniture no longer looked fitting – it appeared bulky and dated. Even the imitation flowers that when new had often been mistaken for being real, had faded with age. She sat up straighter, noticing that the laminated flooring was uneven and bubbled in places – most likely through water damage at some point. She looked down at Sam as he whimpered loudly, readjusting himself in the nook of Kate's arm.

'It's okay, sweetie, I'm not going anywhere.'

Sam gently closed his eyes again and Kate relaxed back into place. The house was in silence, save for the ticking of the wall clock. It was a rarity that she could just sit in complete stillness; her day had been long and demanding, not to mention emotionally exhausting. For once she was grateful that Alf was working late. She'd even decided that she didn't have the energy to prepare dinner and would be suggesting a takeaway as soon as he arrived home.

Yet the room decoration unsettled her. How long had they been living in ignorance? It seemed astonishing to her that she hadn't noticed the grubbiness and lack of warmth in the room previously. Granted, they hadn't decorated properly in four years, but it was still a shock to her to realise that things had become so neglected.

Is that what had happened to their relationship too? She couldn't get away from the overbearing thoughts that had been playing on her mind since the party. It had helped a little to chat with Vivian and Lil, but on reflection, they'd not really provided any answers; they'd only listened to her. She knew that she should have opened up to Alf yesterday; he'd been concerned by her lack of talkativeness and expressed it on more than one occasion, but they'd both been enthralled with the puppy and she'd feigned a hangover every time he looked at her questioningly.

She didn't have the energy for the discussion that they needed to have. There were so many things floating around in her head, but she needed first to access her true feelings. She'd been so fixated on the proposal that she'd failed to pay attention to the niggling doubts that had been creeping into her emotions of late. She knew deep inside that all these months of focusing on an engagement was simply a way of getting some sort of commitment from Alf. A commitment that he hadn't given her in another respect; that of discussing trying for another baby together at some point. She'd been convincing herself that if he was ready to marry her, then a baby was sure to follow…

She hadn't been ready to acknowledge her subconscious need for a family before now, but things had come to a head inside of her since the party. She'd been deluding herself for so long; she desperately wanted a child. Yet, what if by the time they began trying, she couldn't have any more children? She was thirty-two… the clock was already beginning to tick fast….

There was no doubt that she loved Alf more than anything, but everything about their situation was an indicator of them not being as on top of things as they could have been. Their relationship was dulled and in desperate need of repair. Why hadn't either of them noticed it sooner? Addressed it sooner?

Sam's eyes flew open and his small head lifted instantaneously as Alf's footsteps could be heard on the gravel outside the street door. His body tensed and he whimpered softly, looking at Kate for reassurance.

With a start, she glanced at the clock, wondering why Alf was home earlier than he'd said – then realised with dismay that she'd spent almost an hour lost in her thoughts.

The street door closed gently and Kate heard a thud as something heavy hit the wooden laminate flooring in the hallway.

'Hi babe, I'm in here.' Remaining on the sofa, she made no move to get up.

Alf pushed the half-glass door open and smiled at Kate as he took off his black suit jacket. 'Hey, darling. You look relaxed.' He walked over to kiss her, loosening his pink tie as he bent down and placed a peck on her forehead. 'Why's the place in silence?' He ruffled Sam's fur. 'Hello, mate. Hope you're behaving for your mum.'

'Yes, he's been good,' Kate replied with a yawn as Alf flopped down in the armchair opposite, kicking off his shoes as he did so. She watched as he picked up the TV remote and pressed the standby button. The room was flooded with sound, making her wince.

'It's weird coming home and seeing you sat in here. Usually you're off doing a thousand things,' he joked, lowering the volume of the TV a little. 'Did you have a good day? Hangover wore off?'

Kate nodded and stood up, placing Sam on the floor. 'I just had a demanding day with Hilda.' She noticed Alf's attention had been caught by something on the TV. 'I was thinking we could get a Chinese takeaway? I don't fancy cooking.'

Alf shrugged. 'Sure, whatever you fancy. I'm easily pleased.' He didn't look away from the screen.

'Okay, I'll go and ring them. I'll just order the usual.' She walked into the hallway to pick up the handset, immediately noticing the large sports holdall at the foot of the stairs.

'Er, Alf, what's this bag?'

Alf's head appeared around the doorway and she noticed by the dark circles under his eyes that he looked as tired as she felt. 'Oh – I forgot about that. It's Marcus'. He suddenly looked sheepish. 'I had a call from him out of the blue this morning. He's split up with his missus and moved back down from Leeds.'

Kate rubbed her face in confusion and sighed. 'Marcus? Is he the one that you grew up with?' What was Alf doing with his bag?

'Yes, he's stuck for a place to stay, you see. So I told him he could crash here for a few days.'

'Are you serious? You're only just telling me this now?' Kate replied, her voice rising and suddenly irate. She shook her head in disbelief.

'Calm down. He's not a bad fella – you'll really like him. I didn't know what else to do. He's in a right state. It wasn't until after I spoke to you that he dropped off his stuff at my office. I didn't expect him to actually take me up on the offer.'

'Fine, whatever.' Kate shrugged, defeated. She really didn't have the energy for an argument. Ignoring Alf's glare, she sighed and walked over to the hallway dresser, scrabbling around in the messy drawer to find the Chinese take-away menu.

'Don't be like that – it's only for a few days. Besides, I told him it's best to come first thing tomorrow. He's made arrangements to stay with his sister tonight. What with her four kids and the brother-in-law that doesn't like him – he won't be welcome there any longer.'

'Look, it's fine,' Kate snapped, picking up the phone handset and punching in the take-away number. 'I'll get the spare room sorted.' She heard the line starting to ring and was grateful for the distraction.

She turned her back toward Alf, silently seething. Did they not have enough of their own unsaid issues without those of a childhood friend?

Alf watched as Kate picked at her food, barely lifting the fork to her lips. He'd tried endlessly to make light conversation, but she'd shot him down with one-word answers. He was tired of the tension. Even Sam seemed to have picked up that something wasn't right and was wisely tucked away in the corner of his box.

He reached for another prawn ball and dipped it into the sweet and sour sauce, taking a bite. 'Can I have your water chestnuts?' he asked, pointing his fork to Kate's plate. 'I know you don't like them.'

Kate looked up with a troubled expression. 'Sure.' She stabbed her fork into the visible chestnuts and using her knife, scraped them off onto the side of Alf's plate. 'I do like them, but I'm not very hungry tonight.'

'I can see that. You've barely touched your food. Is everything okay?' Concerned, he set down his cutlery and looked straight at her. 'This isn't about Marcus staying is it? Because if so I can always tell him that plans have changed.'

She was quick to answer. 'No, don't do that. It's fine for Marcus to stay – besides I've already put clean bedding in the spare room now.' She met his eyes. 'I just feel tired, that's all.'

'Okay, as long as you're sure.' He reached across to squeeze her hand. 'You look shattered, though – and you must be if you're imagining that you do actually like water chestnuts.' His smile ceased as Kate snatched away her hand.

'Why do you always think you know everything about me?' She narrowed her eyes. 'Yes, I do like water chestnuts and I have done so for a long time.' She stood up from the table, taking her plate with her and walked to the dustbin. 'Clearly you haven't been paying attention.'

'There's no need to snap at me, Kate. And, for the record, I do know a great deal about you. In case you haven't noticed we've spent the last seven years living together.'

Scraping her food off the china plate angrily into the dustbin, Kate didn't rise to his remark. It was on the tip of her tongue to point out that she had very much noticed they'd spent nearly the last decade living together. And that was the problem. Was it ever going to be anything more than just two people living together, like two flatmates? Was there ever going to be any real mention of a family or proper future together?

'Like I said, I'm tired. I think I'll have an early night.' She rinsed her plate under the tap, before plunging it into the bowl of soapy dishwater. 'Just leave everything in the sink. I'll do it in the morning.'

Alf took a sip of water to stop himself from saying something he'd regret. Replacing his glass on the table, he picked up a napkin and dabbed at his mouth. Kate was already walking out of the kitchen. 'Okay. Good night.'

He heard her walk slowly up the stairs and found that his own appetite was suddenly waning. She was behaving oddly out of character and had been ever since the party. It was true that they rarely had big nights out any more, but surely her surliness couldn't still be attributed to the aftereffects of alcohol? Alf felt there was something more to it.

Picking up the remainder of food on the table, he began to clear away. Had the puppy been a mistake? Was that why she was being odd? He couldn't imagine his sweet, lovable Kate being angry at him for giving her something she'd always hinted at. She loved animals, she was always the first one to reach out and show attention to anything with a fluffy tail. Why would she be constantly fussing over Sam if he was unwanted? It couldn't be the puppy?

Josh's comment also came to the forefront of Alf's mind. Walking into the office that morning, he hadn't been surprised to hear about the party amongst the weekend gossip, but he had been surprised when Josh had said they'd all thought for a moment there that he was going to propose. He'd scoffed at the idea, momentarily stunned that his gesture had come across that way. Josh had said it was the small box that did it and his words preceding the puppy.

Part of him now wished he hadn't taken the advice of the

kindly dog breeder, Evon. She'd been so overawed with his idea of presenting the puppy as a birthday gift that she'd insisted on contributing the name-tag. In hindsight, perhaps he should have just put the tag on the puppy and instead presented the puppy first. Yet Evon had told him she'd made the tag look presentable in a nice box and it would be more of a surprise for Kate to see the tag first. He couldn't argue with that. Kate's face had been a picture. Not to mention the tears of joy she'd shed when he'd placed the puppy in her arms. For a moment he'd been distracted and horrified when he'd noticed the pee all over her party dress, but she'd quickly reassured him with a kiss and a smile.

No, he was pretty certain that Kate hadn't misconstrued the box as a proposal. She knew him too well. If and when he did propose, it would never be done in front of an audience. She'd know that. He'd want it to be special and private. Besides, they'd agreed to give it a few years yet. They'd had a long chat on her 30th birthday – both of them feeling it would be better to wait a while until their work and financial situations were more stable. She hadn't even mentioned the idea of engagement or marriage since.

He knew from experience that when a woman was getting itchy feet about an idea, there would be unmissable hints. Kate hadn't done any of that. She'd seemed happy enough with the way things were and she surely would have mentioned it if there were any problems he wasn't aware of... So what else could it be?

He was stumped.

Kate pulled the heavy, patterned duvet up further until it covered her ears. The disruptive sounds from the television could still be heard wafting their way up the staircase and through the landing into the bedroom. She could just about make out Alf's loud snores from the sofa, amongst the din.

Sniffling into her pillow, she closed her eyes and exhaled – trying to concentrate on nothingness and let her wandering mind rest. Her body was exhausted and she could barely move. Yet her head was a whirlwind of activity.

Suddenly remembering her morning alarm, she reached toward her bedside table and begrudgingly set the timer to 5.30am. Her early-morning starts at Oak Park had never been a problem for her before. She'd always loved her job – the residents, especially Vivian and Lil, were like family to her. However, for the past couple of weeks she'd been contemplating her future an awful lot. Even before the party, when she'd been so sure that Alf would propose, she'd wondered how married life would change their routines and life together. Now, with a strong and urgent feeling that all wasn't right with their relationship, she was beginning to wonder if she truly was happy with other parts of her life.

Snuggling back under the cover, she thought about Lillian's story and drastic measures to prompt her second husband into marrying her. If only she had it within herself to be as proactive and bold. But she knew that wasn't the answer. It wasn't even about engagement or marriage… It was about their lack of communication and the unsaid things that lay between them. The crossed wires and dashed hopes.

The simple truth of the matter was that she wanted Alf to want her and only her, to think of her as the future mother of his children and his *forever* life partner. She didn't want to have to influence his decision in asking her to marry him. Wasn't his love for her true self, flaws and all, enough to warrant that?

As she drifted into a fitful sleep, a small voice in her head wondered whether his reluctance to move forward together was because his love for her wasn't *great* enough. Ignoring it, she concentrated on happy memories until the voice became so faint it could no longer be heard.

'Turn the alarm off, babe.'

Alf's sleepy voice caused Kate's eyes to fly open of their own accord – her mind taking a few moments longer to process the situation. She felt his heavy arm draped across her body and, turning her head ever so slightly to the left, his face so close to her she could feel his heaving, rhythmic breathing against her neck.

She disentangled herself from the duvet, only half covering her body, and pressed the silence button on the clock. The beeping tune immediately ceased and Alf's heavy breathing became more insistent. Not wanting to wake him again, Kate tiptoed toward the bedroom door, reaching for her dressing gown on the hook as she passed. Wrapping it tightly around her, she carefully closed the door behind her and made her way downstairs.

Despite being early spring, dawn had yet to break and darkness loomed in at her from the kitchen windows. She turned on the under-cabinet lights and filled the kettle.

Placing herself at the dining table, she heard the excited whimper of a sleepy Sam as he padded out of his dog bed with a vigorous wagging of his tail. Picking him up, she noted that he'd managed to wee on the special absorbent pad that Alf must have left out for him the previous evening. She smiled, pleased that the effort had paid off.

'Good morning, sweetie. What a good boy you are for peeing on the pad.' She allowed him to lick her chin with his over-enthusiastic tongue. The kettle began to boil and Kate yawned, wishing that she could forgo her usual morning routine and instead, with a click of her fingers, be ready for work.

'Wishful thinking, huh, Sam?'

The puppy tilted his head from left to right, as if pondering her question. She smiled tiredly, placing him gently on the floor.

A soft tapping sound, coming from the hallway, made her jump. Unsure if she'd imagined it, she stood rooted to the spot, senses on high alert. A second tap, this time slightly louder, emanated once again into the kitchen. Sam's tiny body tensed, his attention fixed beyond the kitchen door, into the darkened hallway. Kate noticed him quivering with fear. 'Shhh, it's okay. It's just a noise.' She bent down, picked the puppy up and walked into the hallway.

Through the slim, coloured, leaded-glass panels in their heavy, dark-wood street door, Kate could just about make out the silhouette of a person. She watched as the silhouette leaned in closer and tapped once again at the glass. Sam began to yap wildly; a piercing, high-pitched sound.

'Hello?' she called out, stepping closer to the door and putting the safety catch on.

A strong, husky voice came back at her. 'Alf? It's Marcus, mate.'

'Hang on.'

Trying to calm a noisy, wriggling Sam, Kate one-handedly removed the safety catch and unlocked the top bolt, opening the door.

As the door flew open with the force of the wind, she flicked on the hallway light, squinting as her eyes adjusted to the stark brightness.

She stared at the man on her doorstep, all at once feeling self-conscious of her flannelette ensemble and tired appearance. His messy, dark hair, with its hint of a curl crawling down onto his forehead, framed an olive-toned face with the most perfectly symmetrical features she'd ever seen.

He stuck out his hand toward her – long, thin fingers and tanned, soft skin. 'You must be Kate. I'm so sorry for arriving at this ungodly hour. I was going to wait in the car, but I saw the kitchen light come on and assumed Alf was up.'

Unable to remove her eyes from his startling face, she limply shook his hand, aware of a sudden rush of heat travelling up her neck and towards her face. She struggled to find the right words as a cloud fogged her mind.

A loud creak on the stairs broke her gaze and she automatically spun her head to the right, seeing Alf standing on the landing above.

'Marcus, you're early, mate. Come on in.'

Kate watched quietly as Alf speedily descended the stairs and reached out to pat his friend on the back with a smile and friendly welcome, ushering him into the hallway.

'And I see you've met my Kate,' he said, placing a morning kiss on her cheek as she met his eyes with an apologetic glance for her behaviour the previous night. He rubbed her shoulder in quiet acknowledgement before leading the way to the kitchen. 'Let's go through to here and we'll do you some coffee.'

Marcus followed, but not before glancing at Kate with his piercing green eyes, like a bottomless pool of bright-emerald liquid contained by the thickest and most luscious dark eyelashes she'd come across on a man. Something about the way he looked at her, as if he could see into her very soul, unnerved her.

Trying to shake off her unease, she followed behind them, taking in the athletic, toned frame of her guest and the smooth, sun-kissed skin at the base of his neck, peeking out from his shirt collar. She silently hoped Marcus's arrival wouldn't complicate matters further.

It was the last thing she needed, on top of everything else.

Chapter 5

'Physically he sounds like my ideal man.' Megan joked, hardly believing her ears. She carried on walking through the city toward St Mary's Axe, adjusting the volume on her mobile hands-free unit to drown out the nearby cabbie tooting his horn. 'Interesting that he has Spanish heritage. I thought you said he was Alf's friend from school?'

Kate was sitting in the Oak Park staff canteen, mobile glued to her ear, excitedly trying to relay her news about Marcus to Meg in hushed tones. Tasha was eyeing her suspiciously from the far corner, hidden behind a magazine she'd already read the previous day.

'Yes, he's Alf's friend from school. What's that got to do with him being half Spanish?' Kate asked confused. She dismissed the comment. 'So, there's me rushing around this morning trying to get the dog sorted, the washing up done and ready for work – all whilst Alf and him are having a catch-up – when he looks at me with genuine concern and tells me he's got the day spare, so looking after Sam and doing the dishes is the least he can do to help. Honestly, Megan, he seems too good to be true. Even Alf looked surprised.'

Megan was stopped in her tracks as a heavy-set gentlemen in a well-cut charcoal suit barged straight into her, dismantling her hands-free ear piece. Without so much as a backward glance he continued on his way, leaving her seething in the middle of the busy side street. 'So rude!' she exclaimed loudly, catching the attention of three nearby city workers. She fumbled with her earpiece. 'Sorry Kate, an ignorant bastard just bumped into me without so much as an apology.'

Grinning into her mobile and sensing her friend's anger, Kate waited for the rustling sound to die down before she continued speaking. 'Yes, so it might not be so bad having him around the house for a few days after all. I could get used to this.'

Megan raised her eyebrows as she took a sip of the frappuccino she was holding in her other hand. The last person she'd expected to receive a lunchtime call from was a giddy and excitable Kate; especially since it was about a man that wasn't Alf. Marcus had certainly made an impression.

At first she'd been shocked to hear that Kate still hadn't broached the subject of marriage with Alf. She'd seen the look on Kate's face at the party when he'd presented the puppy – she'd felt her friend's disappointment and wanted to run to the stage to hug her. Instead she'd had to make do with giving her a pep talk in the ladies' loo straight after.

Furthermore, she'd heard the office gossip – everyone present at the party had also thought that Alf was about to ask for Kate's hand in marriage. It had incensed her to discover that he had been surprised by this. In addition to the weekend's drama, hearing that Alf had since invited his friend to stay with them had made her despair for Kate.

Yet Kate's energy was infectious. She sounded animated. Megan sincerely hoped that she wasn't setting herself up for a fall. She'd sensed, from Kate's lack of contact since the party, that she'd been mulling over things. It was typical of her to retreat from the world when she was confused. It was her way of dealing with things. She only hoped that having this Marcus around for a few days would be a benefit. She knew how vulnerable Kate could be at times.

'What are you doing tonight? I might have to pop over and inspect Marcus. See if he really is as hot as you're suggesting.' She took another sip of frappuccino. 'Besides, I can worm all of the necessary information out of him so we can make a proper analysis.'

Kate laughed, an odd squeak as her heart pounded in her chest and her mouth suddenly felt dry. 'I can't tonight. It's the monthly staff meeting. I won't be home until late.' She narrowed her eyes, hoping that the lie wasn't too obvious in her slightly strangled voice tone. Tasha was now hovering beside her at the sink and she caught the woman eyeing her curiously.

Megan was about to answer at the same time as spotting a colleague approaching her, pointing rapidly to his wristwatch. 'For goodness sake, I'm going to have to go, Kate. I can't leave the office for five minutes without someone chasing me for something. I'll call you later, okay?'

Without waiting for Kate to reply, she cut the call, all thoughts of Kate and Marcus instantly forgotten.

Pushing back her chair from the dining table, Vivian bade farewell to the others at the table and made her way slowly back to her ground-floor apartment. As she passed the grandfather clock in the main corridor, she was surprised to see she'd spent far longer taking her lunch than she'd allowed for.

Tutting to herself, she tried to hurry her steps, faintly aware of a strong pulling sensation in the upper left region of her chest.

'Are you okay, Viv?' Kate called out, spotting her friend at the far end of the corridor. She noticed Vivian's greying pallor even from a distance. Placing the arch file of paperwork she'd been preparing to deal with under the nearby reception desk, she headed towards her.

Vivian's smile was cut short and she clasped her hand to her chest as another excruciating sensation took hold. 'Hello, love'. Her well-lined face scrunched itself into clear discomfort and she swayed unsteadily on her feet. She struggled to speak. 'Goodness me – I've got heartburn ever so bad today.'

Kate quickly and tactfully drew up a chair from the nearby visitors' area. 'Have a quick sit-down till it passes,' she suggested, carrying the chair closer and gently helping to lower Vivian's large frame into the flimsy plastic.

'Don't mind me. I'll be as right as rain in a moment. Bet it was that bloody fish pie. I've a good mind to put a complaint in to the kitchen again.'

'Oh dear, I bet the kitchen staff will be pleased.' Kate giggled, noticing that Viv's hands were steadying from their shakes. She felt relieved. 'Shall I get you a glass of water?'

Waving her away in irritation, Vivian pulled herself up, her long, pleated navy skirt hitching itself higher on one side of her hip. 'I'm alright now. It was my fault for rushing. I've got visitors coming you see...' She winked at Kate.

'Ah, visitors.' Kate nodded with a knowing smile.

It was often remarked upon by new members of staff that many of Vivian's visitors brought gifts of Guinness and cigarettes. She herself had once wondered why the guests to her room were often a constant and steady stream. However, she'd quickly got to discover why Vivian's nickname was Tea Cup Viv and why the guests were often laden down with the alcoholic beverage of choice. 'How many have you got today, then?' she asked, noticing that the colour was coming back into Vivian's cheeks.

'Two. A mother and a daughter. Let's hope I can work my usual magic.' She chuckled and then suddenly looked seriously at Kate. 'You ought to have one, you know. It might help?'

Kate felt her face flush. She loved Viv dearly, but she still couldn't get her head around the idea of someone being able to read the future. It was an absurd and indigestible theory. And all from a cup containing the dregs of tea leaves?

Wrinkling her nose, Kate tried to think of a suitable response. Although her curiosity was piqued, she felt scared at the prospect.

She trusted Vivian and knew she'd never dupe her into anything, for her heart was pure gold. But what if the predictions that were made did have some vestige of truth behind them? It was hard to consider that possibility, but then why did so many clients return to Vivian time and again?

'Don't look so frightened, love, there's no need to fear anything. You're clearly not ready yet. So forget I suggested anything.'

Kate stared into the distance, considering her words.

'Go on, shoo now. We've both got work to do.' Vivian was already waving goodbye and heading down the corridor before she had a chance to answer.

She looked on as Vivian rounded the corner and disappeared from view. She really was a bold character, much like Kate's Aunt Evie had been. In many ways, perhaps that's why she'd held Viv so dearly in her heart since her first few days at the Care Home eight years ago. She was like the nurturing mother figure she so desperately craved and had lost – twice over.

'Right, where'd I put those files again?' Kate muttered to herself, picking up the chair she'd placed in the middle of the corridor and setting it back in its rightful place. She scanned the corridor until her eyes rested on the reception desk and all at once she remembered.

Hastily walking across to retrieve the files, her eyes flittered over the grandfather clock and her stomach gave an involuntary lurch. Only two hours left of her shift and she'd be going home… and seeing Marcus.

Megan finished typing up the job description she'd spent the afternoon preparing and glanced at her mobile that lay discreetly beside her Rolodex. No calls from Jonnie. On one hand she was relieved, as no news was good news. But on the other, she couldn't help but worry – it had been four days now and the knot of tension in her stomach was beginning to grow with every passing hour. It seemed silly after so many years to still experience the same conflicting emotions as always. She'd come to the conclusion it was a lesson ingrained and experience had taught her that no slip-up was the same as another. Yes, they followed the same pattern – it was, after all, a vicious cycle. Yet the devastation over the years had only seemed to worsen. If that was at all possible.

Her office phone shrilled loudly, disturbing her thought process. She recognized the caller display immediately – TopTen Recruitment. Rolling her eyes, she picked up the handset.

'Good afternoon, Hamilton Insurance Brokers. HR Department.'

'Hi, Megan, it's Kaley over at TopTen.'

'Hi, Kaley,' she tried to sound enthusiastic, even though Kaley was her least- favourite consultant to deal with. 'What have you got for me?'

Picking up her pen and turning the page on her jotter pad, she listened patiently as Kaley's monotone voice rattled off the qualities of various potential candidates. It was a full five minutes later before she ended the call, feeling as if she'd been drained of all life force by the dull conversation. Glancing down at the notes she'd made on her pad, she realised that her mind wasn't in the right mode for candidate selection. She could barely make sense of what she'd written.

Her mobile flashed suddenly and she felt her stomach lurch. Despite being set to silent tone, her brother's name flashed across the screen. Grateful as ever for having her own office, albeit a small one, she slid the slider across the screen, a sickening feeling sweeping through her.

'Jonnie?'

'Sis... Can you come and get m... me?' She noticed the unmistakable slur in his voice.

'Where are you?'

'Sss... Sss... Sid's h-house.'

'You've been drinking' she accused, immediately regretting it. Ten years of the same pattern and yet she'd made the crucial mistake of pointing out the obvious, opening up a door for a tidal wave of denial and abuse.

'Oh, for God… God's sake. I haven't been drinking. I… I haven't touched a drink. Fucking always accu...accusing me of drinking. You nasty bitch.' He spat the last word with such force that she held the phone away from her.

He continued with his rant. 'I just wanted to… to see you. But no, you al-always think th-think the worst of me. Accu… accusing me all the time.'

Feeling sick to her stomach at the rising agitation in his voice and his abusive language, Megan took a deep breath to calm herself. She knew from experience that there was no way she'd be able to help him at this point. It would be a fruitless effort, with him directing his anger at her. It was better to distance herself and be thankful that at least he was still alive. He would undoubtedly begin to sober up within the next day or so.

'I have to go, Jonnie. I'm at work.'

She cut the call with shaking hands. Even though she'd been through similar conversations countless times, the process always affected her emotionally.

'At least he's safe at Sid's,' she muttered to herself, thankful that he hadn't been calling from a police station or hospital, as he had on many an occasion. Megan ignored the once again flashing screen of her mobile, turning the handset face down. She knew that if she ignored the calls for long enough, he'd eventually stop calling.

What saddened her about the situation was that it wasn't directly his fault. Growing up with their alcoholic mother hadn't been the best precedent to begin with. The difference was that their mother, to an extent, had been a 'functioning alcoholic'. Whilst she hadn't provided the same level of care that some of Megan's friends' parents displayed, she had managed to hold down a job and take care of the basic needs of her two children, single-handedly.

Having to learn to be highly responsible from a young age, Megan had automatically taken on most of the caring duties for her younger brother. It was she who ensured he was properly washed and fed. And it was she who eventually took over the role of guardian to Jonnie when, as soon as she turned eighteen, their own mother scarpered off to Scotland with her on-and-off boyfriend.

Jonnie had never really stood a chance. He was just thirteen when their mother had left and, despite Megan's best efforts, the impact had obviously been too great. By the time Jonnie reached twenty, he'd already been in and out of prison for minor offences and began to drink heavily. It was heartbreaking to see her younger brother destroying himself. Especially as he'd been doing so well for the past three months – even securing himself a job at the local builders' merchant.

Megan sighed as her PC monitor dulled and a screensaver took its place. Maybe, just maybe, once Jonnie sobered up, he'd get back on track and finally seek the help she so frequently and desperately tried to convince him that he needed…

She tapped her mouse and brought the PC back to life. Reluctant as she was, she had to get on with her work.

Kate re-dusted the rolling pin with a handful of plain flour and continued to work on the pastry she was rolling out. It had been an unexpected disappointment to arrive home the previous evening and find the house empty – she'd had hopes of getting to know more about her mystery guest, Marcus. It wasn't often she come across men so beautiful and especially one who was going to be staying under her own roof!

Instead, she'd found herself greeting Alf a lot earlier than usual, thanks to an out-of-city local meeting he'd attended. Without waiting for her to ask, he'd explained that Marcus had been commissioned to cover a last-minute story for a national newspaper. Given his circumstances he'd jumped at the chance and headed back up North for the overnight stay. For a moment she'd been disconcerted, until Alf had swiftly followed up that he'd be returning to stay with them the next day.

As a consequence, her best-laid plans for an evening in Marcus's presence instead gave way to a rather sombre affair, especially after Alf had spent most of it recounting the details of his client meeting. Part of her had wanted to tell him that she didn't give a hoot about professional indemnity insurance aimed specifically at engineers and architects, and neither did she care that the chief executive was a 'smarmy git'. However, she'd feigned considerable interest and calmly nodded in all the right places. Only when Alf finally seemed satisfied that he'd exhausted the topic, did Kate dare to bring up the subject that had been niggling at her.

Still raw from the proposal disappointment and without having the distraction of Marcus, she'd felt bold enough to raise the matter of the house being in need of redecoration. On some inner level, the uncomfortable association with the house's neglected appearance reflecting their relationship was eating away at her. And she had wanted to remedy the situation, especially as she still hadn't found the courage to broach the real reason for their issues...

Unfortunately, raising the subject of the house had done nothing but leave her feeling dejected. She'd immediately deduced from Alf's quick glance around the room and nonplussed attitude to her suggestion, that he didn't feel it absolutely necessary. Although she could have easily argued her case – and she was in no doubt that he'd have told her to go ahead if it was what she really wanted – his lack of initial enthusiasm disappointed her. She felt it was an omen of things to come.

A sharp tap on the front door caught her attention, breaking her thoughts. Sam, who had been sitting quietly by Kate's feet, ran cautiously to the safety of his corner box as she dusted off her floured hands on a nearby tea towel. Walking into the hallway, she could vaguely make out the distorted sight of a man leaning against the glass. Her spirits lifted a little. She had high hopes for the evening ahead and was welcoming the much-needed presence of Marcus to distract her from her current relationship situation. The guilty part of her conscience did wonder why Marcus was striking such a chord within her – she'd never felt such felt such a bubble of excitement at the idea of spending time with a man who wasn't Alf. Yet she pushed the self-reproach aside and told herself it was simply a diversion from her own mounting concerns, especially the fundamental issue of her problems with Alf.

Ignoring the thudding in her chest and her quickened breathing, she hastily opened the door.

The sight that greeted her wasn't what she was expecting…

Chapter 6

'Jonnie?' Kate once again impatiently shook the shoulder of the slumping bulk of Megan's brother on her doorstep. 'Jonnie, get up.' She heard the wariness in her own voice and tried to keep calm, despite her escalating sense of dread. Jonnie was refusing to stir and, aside from a gentle snort that assured her he was still breathing, he remained a dead weight half-propped against the doorframe. 'Can you hear me? Please get up,' she urged, knowing it was a fruitless request.

Upon opening the door and looking forward to greeting Marcus, she'd been dumbfounded to see a dishevelled and foul-smelling Jonnie instead. He'd barely managed to stay standing long enough to utter her name, before collapsing into a heap at her feet.

Panic suddenly shot to her core and Kate felt momentarily at a loss as to what to do. Thankfully, Alf wasn't due home for another hour – she couldn't begin to imagine his reaction at finding a drunken, passed-out Jonnie on their doorstep. It didn't bear thinking about. Alf had never attempted to be compassionate or understanding of the situation with Megan's brother, despite Kate's gentle persuasion and subtle hints about the childhood he'd endured. It was no use, often falling on deaf ears. Part of her wondered if Alf's refusal and inability to understand could be attributed to the fact that he'd had a relatively straightforward childhood. How does anyone know about tragedy and loss unless they themselves have experienced it first-hand?

The stories of Jonnie's alcoholic behaviour had only been told as references to Megan's predicament; never had they directly involved Kate herself – until now. She was without doubt that Alf would be livid if he arrived home now.

Trying to calm her anxiety, she thought of her options and decided that the best course of action was to call Megan. Pushing the door to, she ran into the kitchen and hastily grabbed her mobile from the counter, dialling Megan's number and walking quickly back into the hallway. Kate's heart sank as the call immediately went to voicemail. Glancing at the time on her phone display she knew it was highly likely that Megan was on the tube. It would be at least twenty minutes before Kate could reach her.

'What the hell? Mate? Are you okay?' she heard a male voice outside the door. Marcus. Her heart sank a notch further. This was not how she'd envisioned her evening in the slightest. Goodness knows what Marcus would think – not to mention that he'd undoubtedly tell Alf. Kate rushed to the door, dreading a show-down if Jonnie chose that moment to regain his senses. Forgetting pleasantries, she jumped to Jonnie's defence.

'Marcus, it's okay. I know him' she said hurriedly, immediately noticing the shocked expression on his face. She also noticed that he looked exhausted, his olive skin pasty and his normally sparkling green eyes lacklustre.

'What's happened? Are you okay?' he asked in concern, reaching out for her arm.

She waved him away gently and kindly, feeling a strange relief that at least she wouldn't have to deal with the situation alone. 'I'm fine. Nothing untoward has happened.' She gestured to Jonnie and tried to explain quickly, aware of the ticking clock and Alf's imminent arrival home. 'He's my friend's brother and he has a problem with drink. I thought it was you, so I opened the door and he passed out on the doorstep.'

'Shall we get him inside?' Marcus asked, putting down his overnight holdall and pushing the street door open as wide as it would allow. He bent down to hoist up the guy, who looked to be slightly younger than himself.

Kate considered this for a split second, before shaking her head. 'Actually, I think it's better if we get him to his own home.' She wondered if he had a key somewhere. 'You check his pockets for a door key, I'll quickly lock up here – if you don't mind helping me?'

Marcus looked slightly surprised, but quickly nodded his reassurance. 'If that's what you think is best' he said, noticing that she sounded harassed. He quietly wondered what Alf was going to make of the situation.

Kate had already rushed back into the kitchen to turn off the steak she'd been braising for the pie. Between switching off the hob and grabbing her handbag from the dining chair, she locked the back door and tried Megan's mobile once again. Voicemail.

As she reached the door again, she saw that Marcus had put his holdall in the hallway and was attempting to stand up a drunken and ever-so-quietly-slurring Jonnie. A set of keys dangled from his left hand. 'Ready?'

'Oh, that's a relief, he's got his keys on him,' she said, really meaning it. Taking her car fob from the hallway bureau she unlocked her car, thankfully only metres away, and proceeded to help Marcus practically drag Jonnie to the rear of the small Renault. Positioning him on the back seat took some manoeuvring, but they eventually managed it.

'Don't worry, it's not too far a drive. About ten minutes from here and hopefully my friend Megan will be home by the time we get there. She works in the City,' Kate explained, grateful that Marcus had automatically opened the front passenger door and settled himself in the seat. She hadn't taken it for granted that he would accompany her, but she gave silent thanks, wondering how she'd have managed to get Jonnie out of the car alone otherwise.

She got into the driver's side and started the engine.

'Is this a regular thing, then?' Marcus asked, looking sideways at Kate and noticing a small patch of dried flour on her cheek. Her skin was flushed and he considered her slightly shaking hands gripping the steering wheel as a sign of her unease.

'Well, for as long as I can remember he's had a problem with the drink. But he's never turned up at ours before. I can't think why he would either, to be honest.' It was true. Why ever would he knock at her door?

They heard a groan from the back seat and Marcus looked over his shoulder at the fully grown man, head flopping onto his chest and dribbling from the mouth. Instead of disgust, he felt pity.

'Drink destroys people,' he said at the same moment as Kate briefly glanced in his direction. She couldn't be sure but she thought she caught a shadow of sadness pass across his face.

Feeling responsible for the unexpected drama that had welcomed Marcus home – not to mention the change in his mood – and eager to change the subject, aware that Jonnie could awaken at any moment and overhear their conversation, she forced a smile.

'So how was your business trip? Alf told me you went to do an interview up North.'

Marcus nodded his head tiredly. 'Yes, I happen to know the editor and they'd been let down by another journalist at the last moment. So he called me in instead.' He glanced out of the window, thinking about the irony of the trip and how he'd almost been tempted to stay up North.

'Will you be doing the same work here, then?' Kate asked, curious. Alf, never one to elaborate, had only filled her in briefly on Marcus's situation – that he'd split with his fiancée in Leeds and returned to his roots to start afresh. Usually she would have pressed for more details, but knowing that Marcus was coming back to stay with them, she'd thought it wiser to get the story from the horse's mouth.

'Yes, hopefully – well, I have a few things already in the pipeline and then there's my book…' he tailed off, shrugging his shoulders.

'I've almost finished the final draft – I'm hoping something will come of it.'

Kate indicated left, turning into the side road that led directly to Megan's end of terrace that she shared with her brother. 'You've written a book?' She was impressed. 'What's it about?'

Marcus smiled at the sudden enthusiasm in her voice. He liked the way she glanced at him with genuine and pleasant surprise. 'Well, it's fiction but the main character is loosely based on my grandfather. He's had an extraordinary amount of adventure in his years. I thought it'd make for interesting reading.'

He noticed they were slowing to a stop and Kate reached for the hand brake, pulling it up gently. 'That's doubly impressive. Not only have you have written a book, you've based it on your granddad. He must be rather proud.'

Marcus grinned, wondering silently how his grandfather would react when he revealed that he'd chosen him as the main subject of his newest 'project'.

'He doesn't know yet.'

Kate raised her eyebrows in surprise. 'Well, I'm sure he'll be ecstatic – provided you've not included too many of his personal secrets.'

A splutter, followed by a loud sneeze came from the back seat. Jonnie groaned loudly and Kate and Marcus both reacted quickly, their conversation instantly dismissed as she turned off the engine and Marcus undid his seatbelt.

'Let's get him inside as fast as possible. It will be better than if he wakes up – in case he starts being abusive.' Kate began getting out of the car, grabbing her mobile and dialling Megan's number one last time. She could tell from the lack of lights in the half brick and rendered property that Megan wasn't yet home. The call went straight to voicemail.

Marcus was already pulling an incoherent but now semi-awake Jonnie from the back seat.

'Come on, mate, let's get you inside.'

Thankfully, Jonnie seemed to have gained the use of his legs and stumbled out of the car, eyeing Marcus through squinting eyes with an aggressive look on his face.

Kate took control of the situation, sensing that Jonnie would react badly to a stranger giving him orders once he became more aware. She gestured with her eyes from Marcus to the passenger door, nodding her head and hoping he'd understand that it'd be better for him to wait in the car. He did. Except he refused to get into the car, choosing instead to stand beside it, just in case Kate needed assistance.

Kate ushered a staggering Jonnie to the blue street door and opened it, breathing a sigh of relief as he walked straight into the house, without so much as a word or backward glance. Stumbling to the nearest armchair he collapsed into it, his eyes closing again.

Without wasting time, Kate put his set of keys onto the sideboard and hurried out of the house, closing the door behind her with an overwhelming sense of relief. There wasn't any need to stay a moment longer than necessary.

'That was quick.' Marcus commented in surprise as she came up the paved concrete path towards him.

'I know, he passed out on the chair as soon as we got in.' Kate walked straight to the driver's side and got into the car, Marcus following suit. She couldn't help but glance at the overhead digital time display with a cautious expression. 'Oh goodness, it's six-thirty already. Alf will be home soon.'

Marcus heard the distinct tone of anxiety in her voice and looked at her quizzically. 'Are you worried about Alf coming home?'

Regretting her words, Kate started up the engine and shook her head slowly. 'No. It's not that.' She considered how best to put across her worries. 'It's just that Alf's always found fault with my friend Megan, despite us being friends since childhood. If he finds out about Jonnie…' She exhaled slowly, pushing her head back against the headrest. 'Well, it'll just probably cause an argument between me and him and I don't want that. Not tonight.'

'I see.'

Marcus considered what Kate was saying. The last few months of his relationship with Linzie had been especially hard – her wayward friends playing a vital part in the numerous arguments and eventual disintegration. Yet the reasons had been very different to the situation Kate was in.

Despite only knowing Kate for the briefest of time, she'd given him the impression of a kind-hearted person – even her job suggested that. Plus he'd seen the way she'd fussed over Alf – not to mention himself, a practical stranger to her – before going to work the previous day. He vaguely remembered from past conversations with Alf that she had no family, having lost her parents at a young age. Something about this touched him deeply. It seemed she was wise in not wanting to cause unnecessary disharmony with Alf. Although he did wonder what Megan was like, for easy-going Alf to not like her.

'I don't want to put you in an awkward situation and of course if you'd prefer to be honest with Alf that's fine…' Kate began.

'Look, I won't say anything about this to Alf unless you choose to mention it. Okay?'

Kate felt her shoulders relax and her grip on the steering wheel loosened slightly. She smiled and tried not to exhale too heavily. 'Thanks, Marcus. If Alf is home, then of course I'll tell him where we have been.' She hoped this wasn't the case. 'But if not, it's probably best for the moment that he doesn't know…'

Letting her voice trail off, she concentrated on the road ahead. The evening hadn't started at all how she'd hoped and yet despite the circumstances she'd come to experience another side to Marcus that confirmed her initial gut feeling. He seemed to be of that rare variety of men – both aesthetically pleasing and a generous, considerate person to match.

She quietly wondered why his fiancée had let him slip away.

'That was delicious.' Alf commented, pushing his empty plate away from him. He'd been pleasantly surprised to arrive home – albeit a bit later than he'd planned – to find that Kate had prepared his favourite meal. She also seemed to be in high spirits.

Marcus nodded his agreement. 'Really lovely, Kate. If you continue to cook like this, I might not ever want to leave.'

Earlier calamity forgotten and thankful that telling Alf had been averted, Kate grinned from one man to the other.

'I guess we might have to buy a bigger house then, Alf,' she joked, meeting Alf's eyes and waiting for his reaction.

'I thought you wanted to re-decorate this one?' he replied, his tone more serious. He'd toyed with the idea since their discussion yesterday and he was beginning to think she was perhaps right. The rooms did seem rather tired…

Kate shifted in her seat, aware that Marcus was looking at them both with interest. 'Well, yes we can decorate.' She nodded her head slowly. 'Or maybe we could just buy something else instead?' she ventured, feeling braver now that there was another person to witness the discussion.

'You want to move?' Alf asked, surprised. He seemed to consider the idea for a split second then shrugged his shoulders dismissively. 'I don't see there's any point yet; we're happy enough here, aren't we?'

Kate bit down on her bottom lip, stopping herself from instantly retorting something she'd later regret. She tried to not show her frustration. Instead she stood up and began to collect their empty dinner plates. 'If you say so, Alf,' she muttered quietly.

Marcus, sensing that the atmosphere had changed, avoided looking at either party and instead helpfully picked up the used cutlery and glasses, taking them over to the sink.

'What's that supposed to mean?' Alf snapped in annoyance. 'So you're not happy?' He knew something was bothering her, but he couldn't understand why she was being so awkward. And of all the times to do it, why create a tension in front of Marcus?

Surprised at Alf's tone and not caring that Marcus was present,

Kate let the silence linger for a moment before she responded crossly.

'It doesn't matter what I suggest, you always seem to cut me down.' Clattering the plates against the worktop in frustration, she avoided turning around through fear of both men seeing her suddenly teary eyes. She knew she wasn't being entirely fair on Alf, but she couldn't help herself.

Alf stood up, glancing in Marcus's direction and shook his head scornfully. He didn't want to get into a fight when there were clearly deeper things to be discussed. It wasn't like Kate to be like this. 'I'm not going to argue with you, Kate, but I can't seem to win lately either. If you want to decorate I've said that's fine. Do what you want. But I'm not moving on a whim.'

Kate remained silent, staring out of the window into the narrow back garden as Alf opened the fridge for a can of beer and, handing one to Marcus, suggested they retreat into the living room.

'That's if Kate doesn't need help here?' Marcus offered, stealing a sideways glance at her and noticing how she managed a small shake of the head at him.

'I'm okay, thanks. I'm going to tidy here and go up to bed and read.'

'So you're not going to join us?' Alf asked, his tone suggesting that he felt she should.

Before she could answer, Marcus, clearly feeling awkward, cut in and tried to lighten the atmosphere. 'Oh, go on, Kate, unless your book is more interesting than me. Besides, I'm intrigued about your art now that you've mentioned you used to paint.'

Knowing he'd unwittingly chosen a sore subject, Kate forced herself to smile at him and with a reluctant nod of the head she agreed. 'Okay, let me tidy in here and I'll join you both with a glass of wine.'

She didn't notice Alf's approving gaze – instead she felt relieved as they left her washing the dishes in the kitchen and the volume on the television in the adjoining room rose to an unbearable level.

She needed something to distract her mind from the hundreds of burning questions that were once again floating around in her head.

It was time to face the facts. Alf clearly wasn't yet ready for marriage; that much he'd proved the previous weekend. Neither was he interested in babies – for that subject had also been avoided for as long as she could remember. To add to that, he'd barely shown enthusiasm for her suggestion of re-decorating and he'd just more or less outright dismissed the idea of moving. So where did that leave their relationship?

Far from feeling as if they'd reached a comfortable plateau, Kate instead felt that they were both treading quicksand.

It wasn't a welcome experience. She exhaled sadly and began to rinse the dishes – knowing that her own reluctance to speak up was partly to blame.

Chapter 7

'Honestly, though, Kate, thank you so much for bringing him home. Given the state I found him in… well…' Megan paused for a moment, reminded of the image of Jonnie face down on the carpet in a pile of his own vomit. 'I'm just thankful that he chose to come to you. Heaven only knows where he'd have ended up if he hadn't.'

Megan had been dismayed to see the number of missed calls from her friend the previous evening. It had been an unwelcome surprise after an already exhausting experience of getting stuck on the Underground for close to two hours. The lack of ventilation, frustrated fellow passengers and the fact that she'd been forced to stand for most of the journey now seemed like a blessing in disguise. Finding out that Jonnie had made a nuisance of himself by going to Kate's wasn't something she would have had the strength to deal with. Especially after being called into the last-minute management meeting at work and told of the restructuring plan that was to affect the entire staff force at Hamilton's.

'It's just a shame he slipped up. He was doing so well,' Kate said, feeling sympathetic at the weariness in Megan's voice. 'I still can't understand why he came here, though? Did he mention anything to you today?'

Relieved that she wasn't having the conversation face to face,

Megan nodded into her house phone. 'Yes, he did; he said he locked himself out of Sid's and you were the closest place he could think to go to.' It wasn't a lie, but it also wasn't the entire truth.

'Oh, okay, I thought it might have been more than that. I'm just pleased that Alf wasn't home – he wouldn't have been happy.'

Megan agreed. Having Alf involved in the situation would have made things exceedingly complicated. Besides, she wasn't sure that, given her current state, she would have been able to hold back on the news she'd discovered at the meeting, directly affecting him. She tried to put the thought aside.

Just like Kate, she had been baffled as to why her brother had ventured to her friend's house. Rather than pressing him for answers straight away, she'd waited until late morning, when a grey and pallid Jonnie had arisen from his slumber and – then sober – apologised profusely. She'd heard it all before, but with no desire to head down the well-trodden path of lecturing him, she'd instead asked why he'd gone to Kate's. She'd been startled by his response. It seemed that in his incoherent stupor, after locking himself out of Sid's and being 'abandoned' by Megan in her refusal to answer his calls, the only person he could think of who would understand his situation was Kate.

With lowered eyes and stilted words, he'd consciously tried to explain to Megan that he had an overwhelming sense of loneliness. He'd been struggling with feelings of rejection and emotional neglect. Given that he knew Kate had no real family to speak of, he'd hoped to find a kindred spirit in her. After all, she'd made references on numerous occasions in the past to the fact that she, too, had felt empty. He thought she'd understand and maybe have some answers.

It had pained Megan to hear of her brother's troubled feelings, but she was grateful that he'd passed out before he'd had a chance to open up to Kate. She knew her friend well and although she'd have done everything within her power to help Jonnie, Kate would have also been torn apart at revisiting the emotions associated with her parents' and aunt's death. She'd spent so long trying to make peace with everything and the emotions would have undoubtedly opened old wounds. It wasn't a subject Megan wanted Jonnie to raise again – and she'd warned him of this, explaining that Kate had her own issues she was struggling with, without the extra burden of his, too.

Sidetracked by her thoughts, Megan realised she hadn't been paying attention to Kate's chattering. She caught the end of a sentence about visiting Tea Cup Viv for a reading and made what she hoped was the right reassuring response.

'Great. So you're going to have one, too, then?' her friend asked in surprise. Without waiting for Megan's response, she carried on enthusiastically. 'I'll tell Viv. I don't want to do it alone; I'd prefer to have you there. You know – just in case. And it'll be so interesting to see what she gets for you, too.'

Trying to sound enthusiastic, Megan said she'd look forward to it – with no real intention of undertaking anything of the sort. It wasn't that she didn't believe in psychic abilities it just didn't interest her. She had no desire to know anything about the future – she was much more content living day by day.

Kate knew this too, which was why she'd been a little taken aback at Megan's keenness. She'd expected her friend to instantly dismiss the suggestion. She herself had been toying with the idea for most of the morning; gradually she'd come to the conclusion that she needed answers and although she didn't really believe in it, perhaps it would offer some. She was at a loss as to what more she could do. Short of sitting down and having the frank conversation with Alf that was needed, she first wanted some guidance from somewhere – and if Viv could give that in some small way, then why not?

The previous evening, although it seemed to improve as the hours passed and the wine flowed, had left her once again wondering where their relationship was headed. Things, perhaps, wouldn't have been so questionable if Marcus hadn't raised the subject of travelling and holidays. She'd been more than surprised when Alf had piped up with the unlikelihood of them taking a long-distance trip in the foreseeable future. She vaguely recalled the words 'workload', 'financial restraints' and 'priorities' being bandied around by him, but the entire time she'd stayed silent, solemnly wondering why her input on the matter hadn't been requested. Only when Marcus had looked at her for confirmation had she managed to mutely nod her head in agreement, not wanting to cause another quarrel in front of their guest.

Kate couldn't understand what had happened to their plans to spend two weeks road- tripping around California. Alf had seemed so eager to discuss the trip at the start of the year and they'd even looked into excursions. It was now only spring – so when had his change of heart taken place?

So many uncertainties seemed to be dancing around inside her and she knew it wouldn't be beneficial to open up to Alf unless she could make some sense of their meaning first. Besides, the idea of talking to him about things and not hearing the response she wanted to hear, terrified her. She'd lost so many people in her life already. What if there was a possibility that Alf *didn't* want the same things as her for the future? The devastation that rippled through her at the very idea wasn't an emotion that she even wanted to acknowledge. The fear of being alone once again, of someone she desperately loved leaving her, was too overwhelming a thought to consider.

So she needed to be prepared first within herself. Just in case…

She tried to pay attention as Megan's voice boomed excitedly down the phone, telling her about an opening party of an exclusive cocktail venue in the City. As her eyes flitted towards the large staffroom clock, she was dismayed to find that her lunch hour was rapidly drawing to an end.

'I'll let you know if Shilpa can get me an extra free entry for opening night – it's going to be a ticketed event. I think you'll enjoy it.'

Kate groaned. 'Oh, I don't know, Megan, it doesn't really sound like my scene…' she tailed off, wondering why Megan was extending her the invite. Shilpa was usually her partner in crime for these sorts of things.

Megan cut her off before she could protest further. 'Kate, you've been moaning that you want to dress up and go out more lately. This is your chance. You need to let your hair down – de-stress. Come on, it'll be fun.'

It didn't take long for Megan's words to have an effect. Kate knew it was true – since her birthday party, she'd once again gotten lost in a swamp of insecurities and forgotten the glamour and zest for life that she'd briefly rediscovered. She thought of the new cream-chiffon dress, still marked with nail varnish and banished to the back of her wardrobe. Hadn't Alf promised to replace it? In a split second she'd made up her mind.

'Okay, you're right. Count me in. I need a girlie night out.'

Megan whooped in delight and promised to speak to Shilpa.

Saying goodbye, Kate ended the call on her mobile, pleased with her decision and allowing herself to feel excited at the thought of a fun night out. Getting up to put her empty egg-and-cress sandwich carton in the canteen bin, another thought occurred to her…

Maybe, just maybe, she had found an answer to her worries after all. Perhaps that was the key to understanding her future with Alf. Maybe she just needed to make herself happy again – get back to appreciating who she was and enjoying life again. Otherwise, how could Alf even begin to try to fix things?

Alf stirred a generously heaped spoonful of sugar into his mug of coffee. Although the narrow staff kitchen was spacious enough to accommodate two long lunch benches and at least twenty people, he couldn't help but overhear the conversation between Jeanette from credit control and Bea, the personal assistant to the director of the international division.

'So the rumours were true, then?' Jeanette was saying with

dismay, replacing a carton of milk in the shared fridge.

'I think the accounts department will be safe,' Bea replied reassuringly. 'It's mostly the various broking teams and schemes that will be scaled down. Plus a management restructure.'

'I hope you're right, Bea. At my age I'm not likely to be getting another job soon in this current climate.'

Alf glanced at Jeanette as she picked up her mug of tea from the countertop and she lowered her voice as she caught his gaze. Pretending he didn't notice, he picked up his own mug of coffee and made his way back to his desk, a leaden feeling in his stomach. He'd suspected something was amiss, but had naively assumed it was most likely to do with the upcoming salary appraisals being fixed at inflation rate. Despite hoping for an increase, he'd already decided that if he convinced Kate in foregoing any big travel plans, they wouldn't need to worry if the raise didn't happen.

Sitting down at his desk, Alf felt shaken up. He'd worked solidly over the past two years to secure his current role as head of the PI Scheme for Engineering and so many sacrifices had been made as a result, financially and emotionally. His career investment was only just beginning to pay off – he was on his way to peaking. Yet overhearing the conversation had confirmed the hushed gossip that had been making waves all around the department for the last two days. He knew that quiet, straight-laced Bea wasn't the type to involve herself in rumours. Besides, she had direct access to her director, Andy's, inbox. If anyone was going to be aware of developments on a management level, it was Bea.

Setting his mug down next to piles of paper that were swamping his desk, Alf avoided getting caught up in his team's current discussion on Indian food versus Chinese food. His mind was abuzz with new worries. Given that the scheme was a success with him at the helm, and considering the further plans in the pipeline to establish Hamilton's as the leading broker in the engineering industry, he was doubtful that his position was unsafe. Yet there was no guarantee. It was crushing to think that his hard work could possibly amount to nothing. For the first time in a long time, he felt powerless.

Kate was another growing concern. He was sure he wasn't imagining it, but she'd been acting off with him for the past couple of weeks now. It wasn't just her emotional distance that he'd noticed; it was her attitude. One moment she was complaining about decorating, the next talking about selling – he couldn't fathom out the problem. It wouldn't have been so hard to talk things over if Marcus had moved out by now; as it was, he was still with them. Alf was beginning to regret ever suggesting the idea. It was made worse by the fact that he'd quietly raised the issue with Kate, who'd jumped to Marcus's defence and insisted he was welcome to remain a lodger for as long as necessary. Given her already stilted attitude toward him, he thought it best to reluctantly agree.

Although Alf enjoyed his friend's company, the set-up was beginning to wear thin – he hoped it wouldn't be too much longer before Marcus left.

Blowing out a sigh, he wondered why life had suddenly become so complicated. Things had seemed quite rosy not even a month ago. And now, well, he felt as though everything had shifted in unexpected ways – yet he wasn't quite able to pinpoint exactly why.

A new email flagged with a high-priority symbol flashed into his inbox; opening it, he stared at the short note and attachment. A request for the third-quarter pipeline figures. His heart sank. It would take the remainder of the afternoon and well into early evening to get the figures prepared. He'd promised Kate he'd be home on time, hoping to take her to their favourite Italian restaurant and get to the bottom of whatever was bothering her – without Marcus's presence. However, considering the gossip he'd just overheard, a surge of anxiety forced him into necessary action. The idea of leaving on time and rectifying things with Kate would have to be put on hold.

Pushing his relationship concerns aside, Alf opened the attachment and concentrated on the numbers dancing in front of him.

He was prepared to do whatever it took to secure his position. Surely Kate would understand and support that. After all, it was of benefit to them both.

'This is amazing.' Marcus said excitedly, studying a small, soft watercolour canvas of a pastel dragonfly. 'Why isn't it hanging on the wall instead of being tucked away up there in the loft?'

Kate blushed. It had been a long time since she'd seen her own work and now, in the bright light of the living room, she was awed by the beauty of some of the canvases that surrounded her. It was incredible to think that she had been the one to bring them to life. The thought was almost incomprehensible.

'I don't know,' Kate answered honestly, sitting down on the corner recliner and studying a larger canvas of an Indian elephant adorned in traditional festival jhools. 'I guess after my aunt died, my inspiration dried up.' She glanced wistfully at the artwork propped up around her. 'It was as if my art died with her.'

Marcus sat down on the floor, facing her with his full attention. Encouraged by his empathetic silence and seeing the compassion in his bright-green eyes, she carried on instead of withdrawing.

'She was everything to me. I don't remember my parents – I was only two years old when they died in the accident and she took me in, having no kids of her own. She'd often tell me stories about Mum and Dad; she made sure they were a constant feature of my life, despite them not being here...' Kate looked up with a melancholic smile. 'But, really, if I'm honest, she was what I considered my mum. She was the only mum I knew, the only family I had.' Wiping a small tear from the corner of her eye, Kate tried to fight the sadness that was engulfing her. 'I was all she had, too. Her and my mum's parents had died early, too. Ironic, really.' She smiled sadly. 'Maybe there is some truth in life patterns repeating themselves down the generations.'

'I can't imagine how hard it must have been for you' Marcus said quietly, reflecting on his own life. 'I lost my father in my teens and that was difficult enough, despite me and him not having a good relationship. He wasn't the kindest of men. But I've got my sister and my mum, so it's a bit different.'

Taken aback at his admission and frankness, Kate was quick to answer. 'I'm sorry, I didn't know about your dad.'

Averting his eyes and not wanting to talk about it further, Marcus sensed that Kate – like himself – had a lot of unresolved issues.

'Have you thought about trying again with the painting?' he asked gently. 'I mean, now I've seen these canvases, I can understand why you were on the brink of becoming sought after. You have a unique talent.'

Kate shifted uncomfortably. She was reminded of the conversation she'd had with Alf at her party when the sudden desire to go on an artistic retreat had flared up from nowhere. Although he'd swiftly crushed her fervour, part of her agreed with his logic. Wasn't her painting a thing of the past? Didn't she have enough to concentrate on at the moment?

Seeing Kate furrowing her brows in conflict, Marcus pressed on.

'Do you not miss it?' he asked carefully. 'I couldn't imagine not being able to write. It would be as if part of my life force had been cut off.' He looked at Kate intently. 'I'm certain, given the talent and dedication that these creations reflect, you're meant to be an artist. Surely that's what your aunt would have wanted for you. Maybe you owe it to her...'

Touched by his words, Kate wiped another tear from the corner of her eye. She couldn't remember the last time she'd truly felt as alive as she had when she'd spent endless hours painting. It seemed such a lifetime ago. She was suddenly aware that she'd carefully and purposefully buried all associated emotions of her painting with her aunt.

The more she glanced at Marcus and her canvases, the more the idea of uncovering her artistic side again made her heart dance with passion. She felt instantly alive with newfound enthusiasm.

Slowly grinning, she looked at Marcus, who was watching her with a twinkle in his eye. 'I think you're right. I think it's time I picked up a paintbrush again.'

'Good girl.' Walking across to her, he embraced her in a gentle hug, pleased that his probing and efforts had paid off. She was a sweet, kind woman and she deserved to be recognised.

Caught off-guard at the intimate gesture, Kate found herself closing her eyes and breathing in his alluring scent. Wanting the moment to last, she was disappointed as he pulled away and insisted it called for a celebratory glass of wine. She watched him disappear into the kitchen, Sam following behind him hurriedly.

Although she'd been upset when Alf had called and told her that he'd be working late again, it had surprisingly resulted in her having one of the most pleasurable evenings in a long while. She had Marcus to thank for it. She'd never have ventured into the loft for her artwork if it wasn't for his insistence – and it clearly had paid off.

He returned with two glasses of wine and Sam obediently tucked under his arm. Handing her the chilled drink, he held up his own glass to hers. 'A small toast to your artistic venture.'

Laughing, Kate ritually clinked his extended wine glass. Taking a sip of the cool liquid, her smile faded as she heard familiar footsteps on the gravel outside. Alf was home.

Rather than being happy at the prospect, she felt her stomach instinctively tightening. Marcus, unaware of her anxiety, carried on talking and she fixed a smile on her face, hoping he wouldn't notice. Unable to concentrate on his words, she listened intently for Alf's key in the front door.

A strange sense of panic began to wash over her.

What on earth was he going to think of her wanting to take up her art again? Especially after he'd been openly discouraging at the party.

Even more so, how would he react when he walked in to discover that Marcus was the one who had encouraged it?

She took a final gulp of wine as she heard the front door close – knowing she was only moments away from finding out.

'Whoa, what's going on here then?' Alf walked into the living room and felt his irritation rise to new levels. He'd thought of nothing else but his job predicament on the way home and had been hoping to get a chance to share his concerns with Kate. He'd assumed Marcus would be out somewhere. He certainly wasn't expecting to find him cosying up with his girlfriend over a glass of wine. Jealousy prickled inside him.

Setting her glass down on the dining table, Kate tried to look carefree, despite feeling rather guilty all of a sudden. She hadn't even bothered to prepare dinner and one look at Alf's ashen, tired face told her all wasn't well with him… He looked odd, peaky, even.

'I was just showing Marcus my artwork. It was a bit of mission to get it down from the loft…' she tailed off, glancing around at the mess surrounding her. 'I was just about to start tidying up, actually.'

'Great artwork, though, isn't it, mate?' Marcus said, stepping forward with his wine glass in hand, unaware of Alf's silent fury. 'You've got a genius here.' He smiled at Kate before knocking back the remainder of his wine in one gulp. 'Right, I'm off out now. I'm meeting the lads at Eclipse for a few beers.'

Alf, remaining silent, nodded his head slowly, glancing quickly at Kate, who was busying herself with setting the canvases in a neat pile. He loosened his tie, sinking onto the sofa and switched on the television.

'Okay, Marcus. Have fun.' Kate looked up and tried to keep her facial expression neutral as Marcus slipped on his jacket. She could feel Alf's eyes burning into her back, watching her every move. Continuing to tidy, she waited until they both heard the front door close and Marcus walk up the outside pathway before turning back to him.

'What on earth is wrong? You look like you want to murder someone.' She took in his bloodshot eyes and clenched fists. She rarely saw him like this. Standing up straight, she walked across to sit beside him on the sofa, sensing his quiet fury. 'Is this about me getting the artwork from the loft? Or about me drinking wine with Marcus?'

Alf, all of a sudden tired and weary, exhaled slowly and rubbed his burning eyes with the palms of his hands. He didn't have the energy for an argument and Kate's fretful expression was enough to rapidly cool his anger and irritation. He'd always found it hard to stay mad at her.

'It's work' he replied, jaded. 'I'm not sure if my job's safe, Kate.'

She stared at him for a few seconds in quiet alarm, before taking his hand and pulling him toward her in a cuddle. 'Oh babe, I'm sorry… but don't worry. If worse comes to worst, we'll get through it, won't we.'

He didn't answer.

Ignoring the ball of anxiety in the pit of her stomach, she kissed his cheek, wondering how Alf would cope without the job he'd lived and breathed for the past five years.

It was another drama to add to the storm that was brewing.

Chapter 8

'What a wonderful little chap he is,' Alan remarked, his usually stormy grey eyes reflecting a shade of icy blue in the early-morning sunlight. He sounded remarkably content walking in the wooded grounds of the care home with his new aide by his side.

Kate wrapped her light, black coat around her a little more tightly, for despite the bright skies it was a very fresh day. She grinned as Sam obediently sat in front of Alan with an excited wag of his tail, in anticipation of the treat in Alan's hand. 'I still can't believe you managed to get Mr Steinbach to agree to Sam being here on a daily basis.'

Extending the treat to the well-behaved puppy, Alan smiled. 'Ah, my dear, you do not understand my influence.' His eyes twinkled. 'Many of the residents with whom I spoke thought it was an ingenious idea. Walter would have been a fool not to agree.'

'Well, I want you to know how thankful I am, Alan. It's certainly a good thing for Sam, too. I did feel a little guilty leaving him cooped up all day at home.' She lowered her eyes, not wishing to add that the atmosphere in the house hadn't been the most inviting for him either, of late.

'It's my pleasure, dear. I am most honoured to be of use in some way.' He looked forlornly into the distance. 'Heaven only knows how much I need something to occupy my time.' His eyes returned to their stormy shade.

Kate was grateful as Sam, as if sensing the older man's sudden bleakness, gave a small whimper and jumped up against Alan's knees, licking the tweed material of his trousers enthusiastically. Alan laughed, cheeriness returning to him.

'Shall we start to head back?' she asked gently, aware that they'd been walking outside much longer than anticipated. 'I don't want the others thinking that I'm skiving my duties. I'm sure Hilda will be wondering where I've got to.' She shrugged apologetically.

'Of course.' Alan agreed, thinking privately that Kate was always more concerned about other's wellbeing than her own. It would be the downfall of her if she wasn't careful.

They walked together in comfortable silence, both lost in their own thoughts. It was hard to believe that Alan had once been a leading QC and judge. Although distinctly well-educated and articulate, Kate found it difficult to apply the notoriously hard, unyielding reputation that she'd heard associated with him to the kindly Alan that she knew. It was another reminder that people changed in life as time passed.

She wondered if that was what was happening to her, too. She had hardly been able to recognise herself over the past week – her rekindled passion for painting had filled many a spare hour. She knew there were more important matters that she should have been concentrating on, but the heady sense of getting lost in creativity was having an effect on her spirit – she felt stimulated and inspired. It was becoming addictive. Especially more so now that Alf had dropped his latest bombshell.

As if being able to read her thoughts, Alan turned to her with knitted brows. 'I was rather surprised to hear some gossip about you being a remarkable artist?' He looked at her expectantly. 'Is that true, dear?'

Feeling heat rising in her cheeks, Kate blushed. 'Well, I'm uncertain about "remarkable",' she teased. 'But yes, I've recently got back into my painting. When I was younger I used animals as my inspiration, but this time around I'm drawn to flowers.'

'How extraordinary,' Alan remarked as they approached the arched stone porchway of the entrance. 'I'd be very interested in seeing your work one day. I'm sure we all would.'

Entering into the care home's cream and beige foyer, with the smell of the freshly painted corridor still hanging in the air, Alan commanded Sam's attention. 'Right, chappie, you're to come with me now.' He turned to Kate. 'I shan't be needing any further assistance this morning. But before I take Sam on his rounds, I'd like you to consider the idea of showcasing your art here – at Oak Park.'

Stumped for words, Kate could only shrug uncertainly.

'You see, for all the exterior beauty of this fine establishment, the interior décor is rather dull.' Alan pointedly glanced towards the nearest seating area, where only mahogany wood chairs and matching tables occupied the space. 'And for the fees that this place warrants, one should be treated to a little more decorative luxury.'

Kate privately agreed, but was reluctant to voice her opinion. She hesitated. 'I would love to, Alan, but you haven't even seen my artwork…'

Cutting her off with a dismissive wave of his hand, Alan interjected. 'I have it on good understanding that you're more than capable.' He winked at her.

Immediately knowing that Alan was referring to the small canvas she'd brought to show Vivian, she relaxed a little. It was warming to know that Viv had sung her praises, despite it being something she'd shown her in confidence. Still, she didn't quite know how to phrase her next concern without offending.

'The thing is, Alan, I'm pretty sure that Mr Steinbach, not to mention the Board of Oak Park, would not want my art hanging on its walls.' She tried to joke lightly, hoping that she hadn't overstepped her mark.

'Nonsense,' Alan replied quickly, a smirk on his face. 'Leave it with me.'

Looking at him quizzically, Kate decided it best not to challenge the idea further. Instead she unbuttoned her coat, glancing at the grandfather clock behind the reception desk. 'Okay, I had better get going then. If there's any problem with Sam, don't hesitate to call me.'

Alan chuckled, tugging on Sam's lead. 'Don't you worry. We'll be fine. I've had to deal with worse things in my lifetime than a Cavalier King Charles – believe you me!'

Not doubting him for a moment, Kate said a brief goodbye before rushing on with her round.

Approaching home, Kate saw a warm glow emanating from behind the cream roman blinds in the living-room window and wondered whether Alf or Marcus had arrived before her. She was a little later than usual, given that she'd had to locate Alan – whom she'd eventually found in one of the side gardens – and collect Sam. Nevertheless she was pleased that he'd lost track of time due to enjoying the puppy's company so immensely. It made her decision as to whether Sam could eventually become burdensome an easy one. She hadn't seen Alan with such a spring in his step for quite some time.

She parked the car and, reaching for Sam in his small pet carrier, made her way towards the house.

Over the past week Kate had tried to be extra sympathetic towards Alf – the news of Hamilton's restructuring had appeared to hit him hard. She'd tried constantly to reassure him that even if there was an undesirable outcome, it wasn't a devastating situation. She still had her faith in him – he had a proven track record of his ability and drive, he was certain to secure a new job quickly. Plus, it wasn't as though they had financial worries. Their savings fund was exceptionally healthy – it would most certainly tide them over if it came to the worst. But Alf wasn't in agreement. Instead he kept arguing that his career was at stake and that their savings were not intended for situations such as redundancy – the money was for their future together.

This, at least, had warmed Kate to the very core. She'd repeatedly replayed the moment in her head over the last few days, squashing a lot of her doubts. Such simple words had given her a much-needed confirmation of Alf's commitment. Yet she feared it was Alf's ego that was taking the biggest battering. The very thought that he'd worked so hard over the past two years and now found himself at a point where he had little control over the situation demonstrated that he wasn't handling the situation at all well.

'Hello,' she called out, opening the street door and bending down to open Sam's pet carrier.

She noticed her small butterfly canvas, which Marcus had offered to hang, in the hallway. It looked so pretty against the usually bare white wall.

'Hiya,' Megan's voice called out from the kitchen, closely followed by Marcus's.

Surprised, Kate stood up straight – closing the street door behind her and staring in confusion as Megan appeared before her.

'I didn't know you were coming over!' she said, bristling slightly as she noticed Marcus's eyes on Megan's face. Shrugging off her coat, she looked on as Megan bent to fuss Sam.

'I know – sorry, I just assumed you'd be home. You're usually home by now. My battery died on the mobile so I couldn't call.'

Kate was aware that her body language was ever so slightly stiff and unwelcoming as she hung her coat on the banister. She tried to loosen up and forced a smile. 'That's okay. I was held up.' She turned to Marcus. 'I see you two have finally met then!'

The appreciative glance exchanged between him and Megan wasn't lost on her as she walked past them into the kitchen. 'Shall we have a cup of tea?'

'Yes, please,' Megan said, sitting down at the small table. 'Marcus was just telling me about the book he's written. I said he should send it to Samantha – you know – the one who's friends with Jo. Really tall.' She flicked a crumb from the surface of the table. 'Jo told me a while back that Samantha's made a name for herself with her new agency – apparently she represents a few famous writers.'

'Oh yes, I forgot about her.' Kate was relaxing now that she'd got over Megan's impromptu visit. She turned to Marcus. 'Megan's right, she might be worth a shot. I mean, I know you've got your own contacts, but if I get her details from Jo, it might be worth sending her the manuscript.'

Marcus retrieved the carton of milk from the fridge and passed it to Kate. 'Yes, that'd be great. Thanks.'

Pouring milk into the three mugs, Kate glanced at Megan. 'So what's going on with you, then? Everything okay?'

Megan darted her eyes towards Marcus's turned back and shifted uncomfortably. 'All's good, work was busy today, though.' She caught Kate's eyes and made a 'not now' motion with her hand whilst Marcus wasn't looking.

Kate understood perfectly and tactfully changed the subject. 'Are you still coming for the tea-leaf reading the day after tomorrow? I checked with Vivian and she doesn't mind doing it in the evening for you.'

'Oh, about that…' Megan grinned devilishly and Kate knew what was coming.

'You can't come? Or you don't want to come?'

Marcus looked from one woman to the other, keeping quiet.

'It's not that I don't want to come,' Megan began, protesting. 'I will come if you really want me to, but I don't want a reading myself.'

'Oh, go on, please.' Kate urged, knowing that Megan wasn't likely to change her mind. 'She might tell you about a handsome stranger who's going to come into your life and sweep your off your feet!'

Hearing enough, Marcus decided it was time to make a polite exit and allow the women privacy for their girlie discussion. 'I'm going to pop to my sister's – leave you two ladies to chat.'

'Oh, are you sure you don't want to stay and listen to us slag off the majority of the male population instead?' Megan teased.

Marcus laughed, taking a final gulp of his still-hot tea. 'No, I think it might be a safer bet spending time with my four highly strung nieces and nephews.' He set his mug down on the sink. 'Okay, I'd best get going. I'll probably not be back until late. There's a new Indie band showcasing at The Vibe that I'm going to check out.' He picked up his keys from the table. 'Well, it was very nice to finally meet you, Megan.'

The women said their goodbyes – staying in the kitchen and making small chit-chat until the coast was clear. Megan jumped up to watch Marcus's retreating figure from the back window. 'Oh, my God!' she exclaimed, open-mouthed. 'He is so hot, Kate. I nearly had a heart attack when he opened the door to me earlier.'

'Yes, well I did tell you this!' Kate replied, giggling. 'Why do you think I've been encouraging him to stay on longer?'

'I know you did, but I also know what your version of "hot" is. Two words. Luke Drissold. Need I say more?'

Kate rolled her eyes. Luke Drissold had been her first teenage crush and the boy she'd considered the most handsome in their school year. Sadly nobody else had agreed.

'Well, this time I'm just pleased you can finally trust my judgement. The crazy thing is, he's such a lovely guy, too. I always thought that combination didn't exist.'

Sitting back at the table, Megan looked at Kate expectantly. 'So, why is he single?'

'I still don't know. He hasn't really gone into details and I don't feel comfortable to push him,' Kate said honestly. She'd found it rather odd that each time the subject of his life in Leeds had arisen, he diverted the conversation in another direction, but then she wasn't one to pry. People had their reasons for not wanting to talk about certain things.

'Alf's getting antsy about him being here, though. He feels he's outstayed his welcome.' She fiddled with a pen on the table. 'I haven't said anything to Alf, but Marcus told me last night that he might have found a place in North Street. He's viewing it tomorrow. Whether he's mentioned it to Alf or not, I don't know.'

Megan looked at Kate's downcast mouth and felt a twinge of concern. Kate seemed to have grown extremely fond of Marcus, and although she could now understand why, she was relieved to hear that he might soon be moving on. It wasn't a healthy situation, given the current state of her relationship with Alf.

'North Street has some really nice properties. Let's hope it turns out well for him, then,' Megan said kindly.

Kate was quick to reply. 'Well, if not, he'll just have to stay here for a while longer. He's no trouble.'

Biting her lip, Megan decided it was time to change the subject. 'Oh, by the way, Shilpa got you a ticket for the cocktail opening. It's this Saturday night.' Retrieving her oversized handbag from the floor, she rifled through to locate her diary.

'Oh, I forgot about that.' Kate said, suddenly realising she hadn't got around to mentioning it to Alf.

Megan gave her a pointedly suspicious look. 'Don't tell me you've changed your mind!'

'No, no, not at all. I'm up for it.'

'Good.' She opened her diary and ran her slender, manicured nail across the appointments. 'Ah, here we go – we're meeting Shilpa at 8pm at Swoonies.'

'Swoonies? Is that the purple, mirrored place on Ridge Road?' Kate asked, feeling more and more out of her depth. 'The one where all the glamorous people go and you need membership to enter?'

Megan laughed. 'Honestly, Kate, you sound like an old woman. Yes, it's that one. And don't worry – Shilpa has membership. We'll go on to the cocktail place after.'

'I think Marcus mentioned he went there briefly the other week.' Kate said, trying to recall the conversation.

Megan's interest perked up a level. 'Really? I didn't have him down as a party person. I got a feeling he'd be more like Alf.'

Without taking offence, Kate smiled. 'No, actually he's pretty much the opposite. From what I gather, he goes out a lot. Although

I guess living here he's had to curb his ways a bit to fit in with us.'

'Hmm,' was all Megan managed to mumble, reminded suddenly of the time and why she'd decided to drop in on Kate in the first place. She began to feel uncertain and wondered if she'd done the right thing by popping round.

However, on the plus side, meeting Marcus had definitely been an unexpected highlight. She'd felt the chemistry with him the moment he'd introduced himself and they'd sat down. His intense gaze had barely left her own and the electric current between them had been palpable.

That was until Kate had arrived home and ruined the moment.

'So, anyway, tell me, is there a special reason you came over?' Kate asked, brows furrowed. 'Don't get me wrong! You know you're always welcome, but it's unlike you to get here early unless something's wrong!'

Megan looked awkwardly at Kate's concerned face and knew in an instant that, regardless of protocol and ethics, she had done the right thing by coming. 'Well, yes…' she began. 'It's about a proposed change to Alf's role.'

Kate only heard the first few sentences before a swooshing sound of blood rushing to her ears blurred the rest. She felt a lump form in her throat and her heart sink to the floor.

Where would this news leave her and Alf?

Chapter 9

Alf loosened his tie and stared mindlessly into the barely touched pint of Guinness in front of him. He rarely had time to take a lunch break and today was no exception, but Gary had convinced him otherwise.

'I wouldn't have put her a day over forty, but fifty-four, well, that did it for me.' Gary pursed his lips and shook his head regretfully. 'Turned me right off the idea.'

Alf looked wryly at Gary, wondering how a man with so few physical attributes could afford to be so choosy in his conquests. 'Deborah still on the scene?' he asked, referring to the on-and-off long-standing casual relationship that Gary flitted in and out of.

'No, mate, not heard from her in a while. Was getting bored with that anyway.'

Alf raised an eyebrow, certain that Gary could never get bored with the feisty, tattooed blonde. He watched as Gary leaned forward.

'What's going on with you and your missus, then? She got you talking of tying the knot yet? Or should I say noose?' Laughing, he mimicked a rope being tightened around his throat.

The question caught Alf off-guard. All had clearly not been well between him and Kate in recent weeks, but the last person he was going to share that information with was Gary.

'No, Kate's not like that – she's pretty easy going. We're doing alright.' He took a large gulp of Guinness and glanced at his watch. 'Listen, mate, I've got to be heading back – got a meeting at two.'

Gary appeared disgruntled at the news, but he shrugged with feigned disinterest. 'Fair enough. We'll go for a beer next week or something.'

Alf gathered his belongings and took a last gulp of his Guinness. 'Yes, we'll do that,' he agreed, with no intention of following it through. He set down his half-empty glass. 'Right, then, see you next week.'

Walking away quickly, he debated returning to the office or finding a quiet spot somewhere to collect his thoughts. His mind was made up for him as he walked through Devonshire Square and noticed an empty bench. Sitting down, he put his leather document wallet to one side.

Gary's words had hit a nerve. Things weren't right at home. He was relieved that Marcus had finally found a property – albeit North Street – a desirable location where he himself would have loved to be able to live. It irked him that Marcus had been living at theirs and contributing very little towards expenses, and yet almost overnight he'd landed himself a potential book deal, a job on a national newspaper and a stunning apartment. Still, it would be good to have his home back without having to worry about his friend interfering in his life again.

There'd been a definite shift in his friendship with Marcus since the day he'd got home to find him and Kate surrounded by her artwork. Maybe he wouldn't have felt the same way had he not had an unsettling day at work, but it wasn't just his already frustrated nerves that had triggered things. It was Kate's enthusiasm about the entire matter – she might not have been aware of it, but it shone out of her. He'd been furious to see the house scattered with discarded bubble-wrap, dusty easels and of course, her works, ones that she'd long since banished to the loft. Sure, they were good pieces – he knew her capabilities and talent – but he hadn't expected to come home to a bombsite. Plus she and Marcus been so caught up in the art, there hadn't even been a dinner prepared.

Yet it was her sparkle that had hurt him the most. Where had the sudden excitement come from? When they'd first met he'd tried repeatedly to encourage her to continue with her artwork. It had been one of the things that had attracted him to her – the fiery passion and enthusiasm in her eyes when she'd spoken about it. Yet she'd brushed him off every single time.

He'd known back then that it was because she'd been struggling with her aunt's death – feeling totally alone in the world and lost. And he understood that – more than she even realised. Sure, he'd grown up with a family around him, but it hadn't been the ideal childhood. His father had been both controlling and manipulative and his mother had been too concerned with her own needs to shower Alf with the attention he'd desperately needed. Then his father's affair had blown any remaining family life to shreds. So he'd learned to rely upon himself, to be a one-man band. But, of course, Kate – having no parents at all – couldn't truly relate to how a person could feel totally alone, even if they did have a family. And he'd done his best ever since meeting that younger and lost Kate, to look after her in every way that he possibly could…

Yet coming home that night and seeing her eyes shining and flushed cheeks had been a stab to the heart. Especially as there were clearly other issues she'd been struggling with over the past few weeks and not shared with him. She hadn't looked that alive and enthusiastic in weeks…no… months, even. He suddenly realised that that Kate had been gone for a while. The Kate that was more fun and vibrant, that didn't take life so seriously. Somehow both of them had lost their way in the relationship, settled in a routine and dulled down. Had he been just as lacking as she had?

It churned his stomach knowing that Marcus had been the one to influence and help her to feel inspired again. Not him, but Marcus. He'd asked her why the sudden turnaround, hoping for an answer that would contradict the feeling in his gut and make the situation bearable. It hadn't come. Instead she'd mentioned that she'd been thinking of it for a while and had even made a comment at her party, which he'd supposedly been unsupportive about. He vaguely recalled it, but he wasn't having her put all of the blame on him.

Wasting no time in trying to get the situation back under control, he'd pulled Marcus aside and told him in no uncertain terms that it was time to move on. Kate didn't think so, but he sure as hell did. He explained it was for the best as he didn't want to lose the friendship entirely over the matter of him outstaying his welcome and meddling in their relationship. Marcus, although surprised, had seemed to understand this.

Deep down, Alf knew his friend well enough. It wasn't Marcus's style to go after another man's woman – he wasn't that type – he had respect for others' relationships. If he was honest with himself, he was aware it wasn't Marcus's fault – especially after he'd listened to Marcus apologise that he thought he was helping by getting Kate back into something she enjoyed. But hearing that Marcus, too, had picked up on her unsettledness had been the final straw. Her emotional distance and lack of interaction had been going on for weeks and he had to address the issue head on.

He couldn't deny, though, that since she'd started up the painting again, she did seem to be a bit chirpier. And given his current situation at work, she was making a considerable effort to be supportive… Yet there was something still not right.

Breaking into his private thoughts, a middle-aged woman in a slightly too-tight skirt suit plonked herself down unceremoniously on the bench next to him.

Alf looked up sharply, but she avoided his glance, noisily retrieving a foil-wrapped sandwich from her handbag. Irritated by the woman's action, he picked up his document folder and decided he'd head back to work. He reminded himself again that in less than twenty-four hours Marcus would be moved onto pastures new.

It was time he and Kate had a long-overdue chat.

'She should never have told you. Wrong of her, that was,' Viv said, looking to Lillian for confirmation. 'Isn't that right, Lil?'

Lillian nodded grimly without looking up from the complex baby blanket that she was crocheting. 'Agreed. She should have thought twice before opening her mouth.'

Kate considered their opinions and found a part of herself agreeing. She'd been in limbo for the past thirty-six hours, torn with the great burden of the knowledge that had been bestowed on her by Megan.

How could she be expected to keep such a secret from Alf? She couldn't go on allowing him to be filled with stress and anxiety over his predicament when she knew the possible outcome. Yet, she knew the role Megan had played in all of this and the risk she had taken by telling her.

If she told Alf, it was at the peril of sacrificing Megan. She couldn't be sure that he wouldn't implicate her friend in some way and then Megan's job and career would be at risk.

It was an even worse situation given that Marcus had moved out the night before – he'd been her life-line, her distraction and her happy pill, all rolled into one. She felt strangely adrift knowing that he wouldn't be there to greet her when she finished work later on.

'If it comes to it, will you go?' Viv asked quietly. She fiddled anxiously with the bottom button on her lavender cardigan. The thought of losing Kate was enough to start up the uneasy twitches in her chest again.

Lillian stopped her crocheting and looked up, waiting for Kate's response.

It was the question she'd asked herself a million times over since finding out. 'I don't see much choice around the situation.' She sighed sadly. 'So of course I'll go, if Alf wants to take it.' She stopped folding the washing she'd been arranging and sat down on a small stool next to Lillian. 'It's unlikely he's going to decline.

He's worked so hard for this. It'll be a dream come true for him.'

Without skipping a beat, Viv was quick to retort. 'For him, yes. But what about you? Being a couple is about compromise, love. You have a proper think about what suits you, too. You'd be giving up your life here.'

'She's right. Worst thing you can do – give up your own happiness for a fella,' Lil warned, her beady brown eyes looking at Kate reproachfully. 'And I should know that. Why'd you fink I'm in here? I shouldn't have listened to Terence's urges to put the will in his son's name. Fat lot of good that did me.'

Despite the complexity of her own situation, Kate wanted to laugh. Although Lillian was a force to be reckoned with, she was at a loss as to how her late husband's son had managed to force the sale of his father's large estate – thus leaving Lillian effectively homeless and with the only option to reside at Oak Park.

'You've got Viv. You two are a great team. What more could you want?' Kate joked, relieved that the focus was being moved away from her.

'Hmm, well. I suppose it could be worse,' Lil grumbled, voice barely audible.

'What about your tea-leaf reading? Do you want it now instead of tomorrow night?' Viv asked suddenly, a twinkle in her eye.

'Now? But I thought you only liked to do them in your lunch break or evening?'

Viv flapped her hand in front of Kate. 'Don't be silly. For you it's a different set of rules.'

Kate glanced at the clock on Vivian's living-room wall – she was halfway through her morning shift. If she delayed the paperwork that was waiting for completion, then she'd have enough time to spend an extra twenty minutes with Viv. 'Okay, go on then, you've twisted my arm.' She didn't add that her legs had suddenly turned to jelly and her heart had picked up its pace. She realised she was nervous. Really nervous. What if Viv saw something about Alf's new job situation?

'Sit yourself down,' she instructed Kate, pulling out the "special" visitors' table from the nest of tables in the corner. 'Lil, make yourself scarce. Kate and I have got business to do.'

Lillian looked up in surprise. 'You'll tell me all the details after anyway. What's it matter if I'm here or not?'

Shooting her daggers, Vivian tutted and switched on the kettle.

'You're fine to stay, Lil. I wouldn't expect you to leave,' Kate said truthfully. 'Besides, I could do with the support.'

Both Lillian and Kate watched quietly as Vivian poured boiling water into a teapot full of loose English breakfast tea leaves. After a few minutes, she retrieved her special plain, white cup and saucer from its cabinet and poured a small amount of the strong brew into it.

'Drink it when you're ready' she instructed, setting the cup and saucer down on the small table in front of Kate.

Eyeing the steaming cup of tea, Kate waited for it to cool before she drank as much of the bitterly strong brew as possible.

Watching with a satisfied smile, Vivian ordered her to turn the cup three times anti-clockwise and then place the saucer on top, turning both over and allowing the remnants to drain for a full minute. Kate did as she was told, glancing at Lillian with a nervous expression.

'Okay, let's see what the leaves have to say.' Viv replaced the upturned cup back to standing position and stared into the messy interior.

'Interesting. Look at that!' she said, pointing to the bottom of the cup. 'A picture of a house and a number six.' Peering forward into the cup, Kate wondered how on earth Vivian was seeing a house and number in the jumbled mess of brown specks. 'You'll be moving soon. In six months' time.' Vivian said. 'There's a new job opportunity too – you see the balloon?' she pointed to the other side of the cup, where a balloon was supposedly clear to see. Kate nodded, despite not being able to see anything of the sort. 'And a ring – look at the ring.' Intrigued, Kate could vaguely make out a round circle in the spot where Viv was pointing. 'There's an engagement coming to you,' she said matter-of-factly. Kate's heart skipped a beat.

Vivian peered curiously at the cup, holding it at a funny angle. 'Well I never…' she said, her face clouding over.

'What is it?' Lil interrupted, scooting forward in her seat.

'Alf. It says Alf.'

'What?' Both Kate and Lillian asked in unison.

Vivian, failing to hide her concern, looked once again at the cup and the clear 'Alf' spelled out. 'Look here.' She pointed, holding the cup at the correct angle for both Kate and Lillian to view.

'Oh, my good lord! It bloody well does! It says Alf.' Lillian nudged Kate's arm with her elbow. 'Can you see it?'

Kate stared in disbelief at the small, but perfectly formed, three letters. There was no denying they spelled Alf's name. 'That's amazing. What does it mean, though?' she asked, intrigued, noticing that Viv had gone a little quiet.

'Well, dear, it's only ever meant one thing to me, in all my years of experience doing this,' she replied apprehensively.

'Which is?' Lil asked, impatient.

'It's the name of the man Kate's destined for. It's Alf she's going to marry.'

Failing to notice the wary glances exchanged between Lil and Viv, for the first time in over a month Kate felt a great sense of relief.

With Vivian's words she finally had clarity. She felt every nerve ending in her body buzzing with happiness and certainty. Alf was the one. He was the one she was going to marry. Even though she'd always thought it was Alf, there'd been doubts of late, the constant niggles that had started to make her question things. Now she'd just played witness to an undeniable and inexplicable sign of reassurance.

She had her answer and it was the one she'd never expected to hear. Least of all through a tea-leaf reading.

'Why didn't you just keep your trap closed then?' Lillian grumbled, annoyed. It was typical of Viv to act first and think later.

'Well, it wouldn't have been right, would it? The girl is entitled to know.' Vivian took another gulp of her third can of Guinness.

'Well then quit your moaning. Who knows – it might even be wrong.'

'Have you not been listening to anything I've been saying? That's the whole point I'm trying to make. I don't feel that Alf is the one for her – I never have done. But you know how Kate is about him, completely blinded. So, I can't tell her so. I just don't understand why his name would be written in the cup like that.'

She was baffled. It wasn't like her to be contradicted in her readings and yet that's exactly what had happened. And with her lovely Kate – of all people. She'd been hoping it would be the push Kate needed to start making long-overdue changes.

Lillian, despite not fully believing in all things alternative, trusted her friend's judgement. 'I agree. So, let's just let her work that one out herself. She's a grown woman – she'll find out soon enough he's not the right man for her. You mark my words.'

Vivian took another swig of her Guinness. She desperately hoped Lil was right.

Otherwise she had an uneasy feeling that she'd just unwittingly pushed Kate further down the wrong path.

Replacing the phone handset in its holder, Alf stared at his computer screen, his mind racing. He could already feel the perspiration beginning to trickle down his forehead. Clyde had requested to see him immediately. It could only mean one thing – his job wasn't safe. He felt his stomach turn to water.

Getting up from his desk, he consciously wiped the sweat from his brow with the back of his hand and straightened his tie. Trying to ignore the fact that his legs felt like leaden weights, he picked up his ballpoint and note pad and walked towards the chairman's office with as much confidence as he could muster.

Janelle, Clyde's executive assistant, was staring at the spread-sheet on the screen in front of her as Alf approached her desk. She glanced briefly at the printed daily diary that was wedged between her keyboard and hard drive – yet she didn't need to. She was already aware that Clyde had requested Alf – he'd come out of his office two minutes previously to warn her.

'Go on through, he's waiting for you' she said, never growing bored of her role as gate keeper to the most important man in the building. She watched as Alf walked to his fate – unaware of what Clyde had in store for him. As the door closed behind him, she couldn't help but feel slightly sorry for the man.

She, of all people, knew how ruthless Clyde could be.

Chapter 10

Running her hand over the teal-sateen fabric, Kate knew instantly that it was the ideal dress for her night out with Megan and Shilpa. The subtly sexy and stylish design with ruche detailing on the bodice would give her the elegant look she was striving for.

She glanced once again at the more expensive cream-chiffon dress that she already owned hanging on the mannequin in the boutique window. As much as she loved the dress and, with the helpful advice of Hilda had managed to remove most of the nail- polish stain, it didn't feel fitting to be wearing it for a girls' night out. She looked at the hand-marked price tag of the teal dress – very reasonable indeed.

'That's been quite popular, that sateen dress. It fits really well.'

Kate turned and smiled, seeing the glamorous, heavily tanned boutique owner approaching her. 'Yes, I was just thinking it'd be perfect for a girls' night I have this weekend.' She held the dress up against herself.

The owner nodded approvingly, her bright-pink acrylic finger-nails reaching out to touch the capped sleeve. 'The colour really suits your olive skin tone and it's definitely a party dress. Also the fabric is good, it washes well.'

'Okay, I'm sold,' Kate joked, walking across to the counter. She glanced down discreetly at her arms – olive skin tone? The tinted moisturizer she'd continued using – albeit sparsely – since her party, was clearly working its magic. Her arms did have a rather healthy and natural glow.

The owner followed behind her, watching her curiously. 'You've been in here before, haven't you?' she asked, squinting at Kate as if to try to place her. Her eyes suddenly lit up with recognition. 'Ah, I remember you now. You were the one getting engaged. You bought the cream dress, didn't you?'

Blushing, Kate tried not to show her awkwardness as she inwardly cringed, fleetingly recalling the moment almost two months earlier when she'd excitedly shared her news. 'That's right,' she nodded, hoping the woman didn't push the matter further. Thankfully she didn't. Neither did she gaze at Kate's hand for the non-existent ring. Instead, she rang up the purchase on the till and carefully bagged the teal dress. 'There you go, then.'

She passed the bag to Kate, who politely smiled and said thanks, silently cursing herself for ever mentioning the engagement and wanting to get out of the shop as fast as possible.

Moments later, she was walking back to her car, purchase swinging on her arm. Although satisfied that she'd found a wonderful dress, it had only provided a short distraction from more pressing matters.

Spending the entire afternoon thinking about Megan's revelation and her tea-leaf reading, she'd come to the conclusion that she couldn't possibly keep the job news secret from Alf any longer. Two days had been more than enough.

She knew Megan had told her mostly for her benefit and not Alf's. After all – as Megan had pointed out – if Kate was having relationship doubts then this would likely be the make-or-break situation. She'd also urged Kate that it could be a good time to encourage Alf to look into alternative positions, closer to home, before the news broke. Yet the thought didn't appeal to Kate.

Although she'd much prefer to continue living in their home town, she didn't have it within her to deny Alf such a career-enhancing opportunity. It wasn't her nature to be devious or keep such positive news from the person she loved the most. And it certainly wasn't fair on Alf to let him carry on believing his job could be at risk, when the likelihood was the complete opposite.

She was going to have to tell him, and she hoped to God that it wouldn't backfire on Megan. Unlocking the car, she contemplated how best to break the news – deciding she'd tell Alf that Megan accidently allowed the information to slip out and she herself had pursued it further.

The jarring sound of her mobile tone disturbed her careful considerations. Grabbing it from the inside pocket of her handbag, she looked at the blinking screen. It was Alf. Her stomach knotted. She'd built up the courage and planned out what she'd say, all she had to do was tell him there was something that she needed to discuss later. She answered the call. It was now or never.

'Glasgow?' Kate repeated in astonishment. 'But that's Scotland.' She stared at Alf in shock. Nothing was making sense. Megan had warned her that management had ear-marked Alf to be transferred to their Manchester office, yet there'd been no mention of heading up a new division in Scotland. She was at a loss for words.

Alf looked at Kate's crestfallen expression and felt his own excitement waver. The proposition had been the last thing he'd expected when he'd walked into Clyde's office. He'd barely been able to take in what was being said to him. Whilst on the one hand it was flattering to hear that although he'd initially been selected for transfer to the Hamilton Manchester offices, they'd instead favoured him – over their original choice of Henry Cavendish – to head the Scotland start-up, he couldn't help but wonder if there was an ulterior motive behind the chairman's decision. He was in no doubt that Henry was the stronger candidate for the position, given his managerial background. Brushing aside his qualms, he focused once again on the huge opportunity that had presented itself.

'I know it's a shock. It is for me, too' he said, taking Kate's hand in his own. 'But think about it, babe, this is going to open so many doors for us. It's a massive opening.'

Kate didn't know how to respond. The excitement was written all over Alf's face; it had been since the moment he'd arrived home after telling her on the phone that he had something major to share with her. She'd naïvely felt so relieved, assuming that he'd been informed of his transfer to Manchester and that she'd no longer have to endure the uncomfortable presence of the secret hanging over her head.

In one phone call, she'd been let off the hook, never needing to reveal what she already knew. She'd been so excited to arrive home and share Alf's enthusiasm – she'd even felt it could be the breakthrough they needed to lay everything on the table about their future together. How ironic then, she thought bitterly, that there had been a twist in the turn of events. She repeated the word in her head. Glasgow. Scotland. Miles away.

Aware that Alf was waiting for her to say something she kissed him on the lips. 'I'm so proud of you for being chosen. And I know it's a huge opening for you – well, for us, even. But I won't lie, Alf, it's come as a bit of a shock.'

Although she'd begun to warm to the idea of starting a new life in Manchester, she couldn't help but feel anxious about the idea of Scotland. She pulled back from his lips, looking directly into his eyes and felt a tug of familiar connection. 'It's a lot to take in. Scotland's not just up the road – it's as far away as we could possibly get.' She watched as he pondered her words, running his hand anxiously through his hair.

'It is far. But there are trains and even flights. We could be back here within half a day.'

Biting down on her lip, Kate didn't know how to respond. It was true that Scotland wasn't the other side of the world – she was certain that plenty of people commuted on a regular basis in much the same way as they'd have to. But it was much further than she'd expected. The idea filled her with panic – it certainly wouldn't be as easy or economical to hop on a train at short notice to see those she'd be leaving behind.

'Well, look, we don't have to make any decisions right now. Let's sleep on it, give it a day or two and see how we feel?' Alf said, not failing to notice Kate's hesitation. Putting his arms around her waist, he pulled her closer to him. 'But just keep in mind where this could lead us to in a few years, Kate.' He gently stroked the back of her hair and placed a small kiss on the top of her head.

Kate closed her eyes in Alf's embrace, wanting to stay there forever in that familiar, secure and warm place. She wanted to be happy and excited for him – she really did. But she couldn't, because she had an underlying feeling that a tidal wave was heading straight for them – with no way of escaping.

If she was honest with herself, she knew she didn't want to go to Scotland, she certainly didn't want to lose Alf and, furthermore, she didn't want to stay in the same pattern that they'd got stuck in lately. It left little choice.

For the first time in a long time, she felt truly scared for the future.

'Are you sure you don't want me to cook you something before I go?' Megan asked, poking her head through the doorway of the living room. She watched Jonnie laugh at something on television before he turned to her.

'No, stop fussing. I'm fine. I'll put a pizza in the oven later.'

Megan sighed, wishing for a moment that she didn't have such a strong mothering instinct. He'd been doing well since his last slip-up with the drink, but it didn't stop her from worrying about him. It hadn't helped matters to find out his working hours had been cut down at the builder's merchants. She knew that it wasn't ideal for Jonnie to have too much time on his hands – it invariably led to over-thinking and him drowning his sorrows.

'Okay, well I'll finish off getting ready, then.' She hurried back up the cream- carpeted staircase, wondering which of the two dresses she'd chosen would be the most appropriate to wear. She wasn't even sure why she was making such an effort; it wasn't as if she was particularly bothered about Michael. Yes, he was handsome, in a chiselled and preened kind of way, plus there was the added benefit of his intelligent conversation and the fact he preferred the finer spots of London, enjoying both good food and wine. Why then, wasn't she feeling bowled over that the conveyancing lawyer had asked to see her for a third time?

'I'll wear the navy one,' she muttered to herself, grabbing the dress from her wardrobe and flinging it onto the bed. She began to take the bendy rollers from her hair, watching as her already-wavy locks bounced into loose curls.

It hadn't bothered her until now that she'd spent the majority of her adult life relatively single. She'd always been happy in her own little world. She liked her social nights out with friends; she'd enjoyed working her way up the career ladder, affording to buy a decent-sized house for herself and Jonnie. But lately, she'd started to feel differently about everything. There was this strange need to have someone to share her life with, to cuddle when things got too much and to talk with, when no one else was available. She needed someone in her corner, someone to love – for her heart was almost brimming over with love to give and yet there didn't seem to be anybody suitable to give it to.

She'd recently begun to think over the countless relationships that she'd started for a few months here and there – even Simon, who she'd been with for over a year – some of them seeming promising, but she'd broken off with all of them as soon as they had got too close. It wasn't that she'd intended to do it – she'd only ever felt bereft afterwards – but it was something she couldn't help. How could she allow a man close when there was Jonnie in her life? The Jonnie that always fell back on her. The Jonnie that needed her.

Despite the constant drama and heartache that her brother

brought to her doorstep, none of the men in her past had been able to understand her feeling of responsibility and protectiveness towards him – and that was part of the problem. Simon, especially, had proved that, eventually growing tired of her worry over Jonnie.

So how could she form a relationship and think about starting a family of her own, when Jonnie had no one of his own? What man would allow the burden of her brother's alcohol problem eating into his relationship with her?

She'd wondered about Michael, with his compartmentalised ways and his already apparent need to be in control. How would he fare if feelings got deeper and she explained her fears about Jonnie? Sadly, she already knew the answer, despite only having been to dinner twice with him. He would be the same as many others before him. She was confident that he wouldn't be able to understand.

Spraying her curls with fixing hold, she concentrated on adding a final coat of mascara to her already-long lashes. She didn't often wear make-up, but tonight she wanted to 'wow'. She had a feeling it was the last time she'd be seeing Michael and she wanted to make a final lasting impression.

Sighing, she walked over to the bed to put on her dress. She knew that the course of love was never going to be an easy one, but she couldn't help wondering if it was her destiny to remain single.

After all, how many men would be able to relate to her situation?

Kate took a bite of her goat's cheese and pesto Panini and considered Marcus's point. It wouldn't make business sense for him to jump at the first deal offered, especially as he'd since had interest from a competitive publisher; it would be more sensible to wait it out.

'Whatever you decide, I'm so pleased that Samantha has been of benefit to you. It was good thinking on Megan's part to introduce you. I'll be sure to let her know that it's paid off.'

Marcus leaned forward in his seat at the sound of Megan's

name. 'How is she – Megan? I hope that brother of hers isn't giving her more trouble.'

Wiping her fingers with a tissue, Kate chewed carefully before answering. It was a simple enough question, but she'd noticed how Marcus's body language had changed at the mention of her friend's name. 'She's fine. Jonnie's been behaving, as far as I know, which is good, really, considering Megan's started seeing a new guy.'

She watched for Marcus's reaction, noticing a small twitch of his eyebrow on his otherwise unresponsive face. She continued. 'I hope it goes well, she deserves to be happy and she's been single for far too long. It's about time she met someone nice.'

'That's good,' Marcus said, taking a sip of his coffee. 'And you? Have you guys made up your mind yet on the offer?'

Kate sighed, shaking her head. 'No, I can't say we have; and it hasn't helped matters that Hamilton's still haven't confirmed Alf's proposed package.' She screwed up her napkin into a small ball, placing it on the plate in front of her. 'He knows that I'm not making my final decision until we can be sure it's worth uprooting for.'

Marcus considered Kate's answer, a brief scowl passing across his face. 'What will you do about your work?'

'In all honestly, I've no idea,' Kate replied, looking downcast at the crumb-scattered table. 'The thought of starting again isn't something I relish.' She picked at her used napkin. 'It's hit me the past few days just how much I do love my job – Viv, Lil, Alan, even hypo Hilda. I can't imagine starting at another care home, you know?'

Marcus nodded, understanding Kate entirely. 'Sometimes, though, an upheaval can be a good thing. I mean, take me as an example. Six months ago I had a fiancée, a house and a career in Leeds with a bunch of plans for the future that focused on those things. And now, I'm here – in completely different circumstances.' His green eyes met Kate's. 'It's not been easy. I won't lie and say it has. But I'm happy.'

Kate smiled gratefully, aware of Marcus's attempt to help her feel better about the situation. The truth was, though, that she wasn't sure any more about anything. Given that Alf was still awaiting his package offer, combined with his sudden enthusiasm for working longer hours – in the hope he'd convince management they'd made the right decision – it had left little time to discuss her concerns with him.

She looked at Marcus's newly grown dark stubble. It gave him a slightly harder edge, but couldn't take away from his devastating Mediterranean features. She found it hard to believe that he was still single. Although now that he'd settled into his new home and given that his book was in a bidding war, she didn't suppose that he would be for much longer. It was interesting that he hadn't bitten her bait about Megan. Maybe there wasn't that much of an interest there after all… Surprisingly, the discovery filled her with hope.

Kate nodded. 'You're right, I know that. I'm just finding it hard to get my head around everything, though. As much as I love Alf and this is our chance of a fresh start together, I can't help wondering what's in it for me.' She bit the side of her lip tentatively. 'I keep thinking, what if things don't work out – where does that leave me?'

Marcus looked at her quizzically as a deep-crimson blush slowly began to spread across her cheeks. He frowned. 'I'm not sure I'm following,' he said awkwardly. 'Do you mean that you and Alf are having problems?'

Squirming in her seat and wishing she'd never raised the subject, Kate avoided looking at him. She knew he wasn't a girlfriend and the last thing he probably wanted to discuss was her and Alf's relationship issues; but if anyone could give her a man's perspective on Alf's behaviour then Marcus was the ideal person. After all, he knew Alf. He knew Alf well.

Taking a deep breath, Kate decided it was now or never. Although her emotions had felt more balanced and improved concerning her future with Alf since Viv's reading, she couldn't shake off the thought that she needed to consider the Scotland move very cautiously. 'Has Alf ever mentioned to you about marriage or engagement or even kids?' she asked carefully.

Looking startled, Marcus raised his eyebrow as he slowly took a sip of his coffee. He wiped away a thin line of frothed cream from above his lip before he answered, considering his words. 'Not directly, no. But there's been the odd reference to marriage in various conversations we've had.'

Kate squinted, disappointed. She knew that it was unlikely that Alf would have had heartfelt conversations with Marcus, or any male friend, for that matter. But she'd hoped that there might have been something mentioned that could have given her a clue.

'Okay, just forget I said anything.'

Setting down his coffee cup, Marcus wondered whether to say more or to keep his opinion to himself. He knew Alf well enough to know that he could be selfish at times. He'd also observed from living with the couple that there were cracks in the relationship, and ones that needed filling fast. Yet Kate was such a fragile and delicate woman, he didn't want to hurt her with his straightforward observation on the matter. Anyone with foresight could see that the relationship was heading into well-worn and bleak territory. They were too set in routine and their lives were a bit dull, in his opinion.

'Look, if it's marriage you're thinking about – I personally don't think it's unreasonable to raise the subject with Alf. You guys have been together years now and as a man I can say he's probably expecting you to hint at it at some point anyway.' He smiled, lightening the mood. 'It's what women do.'

Grinning, Kate nodded her head in agreement. 'I suppose it is. And anyway, given that the move affects both of us, it would probably be a good time for me to start dropping hints.'

Relieved that the conversation had taken on a lighter tone, Marcus's eyes flittered across to an attractive young woman in her mid-twenties, giggling with a friend. She looked up, as if sensing his eyes on her. 'So, any plans for the weekend?' he asked Kate, suddenly aware of a longing to be spending quality time alongside an attractive woman such as the one now shooting him suggestive glances behind Kate's back. He returned the gaze, drinking in her slim frame and long brunette hair.

'Actually, Megan's convinced me to go to out on Saturday night.' She noticed Marcus's eyes dart towards her with new-found interest. 'We're going to Swoonies and then there's some new cocktail place opening that her friend Shilpa has got us tickets for.'

'Sounds fun – it's about time you got out and let your hair down,' he said pointedly and she felt herself agreeing. During Marcus's time staying with her, he'd made it clear on more than one occasion that he felt her social life was lacking. He was right. Besides, who knew how much longer she'd have to enjoy girls' nights out if she was to be moving to Scotland.

'And you? Any plans?'

'Not at the moment. I might be working, so…' he shrugged, signalling the waiter for the bill. 'I'll see how it goes.' He glanced across at the brunette again, wondering if there was any way he could get her to feature in his weekend plans…

Picking up her handbag off the unoccupied chair next to them, Kate reached for her purse.

'No, I'll get this,' Marcus said as he saw her opening the zip. 'Put your money away.'

Doing as she was told, Kate hesitantly replaced her purse and hooked her bag onto her arm with a smile. She watched Marcus's glinting eyes and wondered how a man with so much charm came to be starting a new life so far removed and far away from his old one. Where had it all gone wrong?

She stiffened when the thought occurred to her that she, too, could soon be doing the same thing. Except in Scotland. Her smile faded just as fast as it had come.

She needed to have the 'marriage and children' talk with Alf. She couldn't avoid it any longer. It was time.

Chapter 11

Alf looked at the offer letter laid out on the solid mahogany and leather-bound desk in front of him, not needing to think twice as Clyde thrust his heavy ballpoint pen towards him.

'It's going to be a pleasure working with you on this new venture. We should expect to see great results within the next three months,' the older man said assuredly, watching as Alf's signature flowed from the ballpoint onto each page of the contract.

Leaning forward to retrieve the signed papers scattered across the desk, Clyde fixed a satisfied smile to his face.

'So that's it, then,' Alf said aloud, partly in disbelief as he once again considered the hefty salary that he'd just secured. 'Four weeks to tie up here and then it's off to Scotland.'

Clyde chuckled, aware that the board's decision to request an immediate answer from Alf didn't exactly comply with protocol. But he'd observed how malleable the newly appointed managing director could be. His hunch hadn't failed him – Alf had barely taken time to ask the basics before he'd agreed. He was most definitely proving to be the right choice for the role.

'Yes, that's it. Megan from HR and Janelle will be in contact to send you across everything needed and a copy of your contract. I suggest you liaise direct with HR with regard to our accommodation budget and suchlike.'

Indicating the end of the meeting and despite Alf being suddenly filled with questions, Clyde stood up and held out his hand. 'Congratulations, Alf. I think it's time you shared the good news with your wife and celebrated.' Walking swiftly across to his brass coat stand, he lifted his Crombie overcoat from the hook, shrugging it on quickly. 'Now, if you'll excuse me – I have a lunch with the CEO of Lloyds to attend.'

Alf followed feebly as the chairman made his way out of the office, the word 'wife' ringing in his ears. His eager excitement had vanished – replaced with a dreaded feeling of anxiety. The one-hour meeting had passed quickly, but had he reacted too hastily? However would he explain his decision to Kate? He knew full well that she'd be livid that he hadn't consulted her first, and rightly so. But how could he have said anything but 'yes'?

Clyde's parting words ran once again through his mind. Wife.

Why did hearing that word fill him with such alarm? He shuddered involuntarily and watched with a pang of nervousness as the mirrored lift doors pinged open in front of him. Everything had suddenly got very complicated.

Megan had only just returned from her lunch break when the new office junior plopped a sealed brown internal envelope on her desk. A post-it note attached was signed by Janelle. She sighed, frustrated at the growing amount of work and pressure that management was placing upon her with the restructure. Putting the envelope on the ever-growing pile of documents she needed to attend to, she one-handedly tapped her password into her keyboard.

A small beep came from deep within her shoulder bag and she rustled inside for her mobile, her spirits rising a little when she saw Michael's name on the screen.

She smiled. 'Well, well, aren't you the keen one,' she muttered happily to herself as she opened and read his message.

'Are you still on for dinner later? Pick you up at 8? x'

Despite having her reservations about him, he'd so far squashed every theory that she'd ever had about men. If she was honest with herself, she was starting to really open up to him and look forward to their dates. She couldn't remember the last time she'd began to feel this way about someone. It made it all the more promising that she'd delicately tried to drop small hints about the situation with her brother and Michael had seemed nothing but reassuring and supportive.

Her phone rang and she saw the chairman's office flash up on the caller ID. Picking up the handset, she noticed two answerphone messages flashing at her.

'Hi, Janelle.'

'Hi, Megan. I sent Casey down with a document for you. It's urgent.'

Megan glanced at the internal envelope she'd dumped precariously on the overflowing pile, and reached for it – thankful that Janelle couldn't see her rolling her eyes.

'It's Alf Stafford's signed employment contract. Clyde's asked that you get everything prepped as priority.'

She heard herself taking a sharp intake of breath. 'Signed contract? But I only prepared the document this morning.'

'Well, Clyde and a few members of the board had a meeting with Alf an hour ago and he signed,' Janelle said flatly. 'Anyway, you were requested to be at the meeting, I left you two voicemails.'

Feeling slightly panicked that the chairman had requested her on the one occasion that she'd allowed herself a full hour's lunch break, she stumbled for something to say. 'Oh, I had to take …'

Janelle cut her off dismissively. 'It's fine, Clyde went ahead anyway. You just need to deal with it as a priority.'

Shocked, Megan mumbled her agreement and replaced the receiver. She'd barely had a chance to think about the document she'd been asked to prepare only that morning. Of course, whilst typing it up she'd been considering the conversation she'd had with Kate only the previous evening – listening as Kate had voiced her concerns about the Scotland move.

Megan still couldn't understand the motives behind the board offering Alf the opportunity to head up the new Glasgow office. Especially since she'd originally been instructed to prepare the offer letter and contract for Henry Cavendish. But nonetheless, it had been a shock when Kate had rang and told her the previous week – only minutes before Clyde's office had confirmed it with her.

Preparing the formal offer that morning, she'd seen that the salary and package that had been laid out for Alf – whilst very generous – wasn't comparable to that which would have been offered to Henry. She knew Kate would be impressed, but then she also knew her friend wasn't over-fussed about the material side of life.

She'd expected that the formal offer would have been tendered to Alf within the next few days and he'd be given a short period of time to make up his mind. She was fully aware that the start date for proceedings in Glasgow was only a month away. It had panicked her to think that in a few weeks her best friend could be packing up her life in London for new horizons. But she'd assumed she'd have time to talk it over with Kate first.

It was astounding to believe that within less than four hours of her preparing the document, Alf had already signed on the dotted line. What on earth had he been thinking, to sign without first consulting Kate? Because surely he hadn't had time to discuss it with her.

Filled with anger and sadness, she picked up her mobile and began to prepare a response to Michael's message. She had a feeling tonight wouldn't be a good time to meet for dinner after all…

Kate would undoubtedly be needing her.

'Do you want a little more milk in your coffee, Hilda?' Kate asked, watching as Hilda sipped the lukewarm liquid and grimaced. Vivian and Lillian glanced at Kate with amused expressions from the other end of the dining table. It was rare that they joined the others for afternoon tea in the main dining area, with Vivian usually preferring her afternoon Guinness in the privacy of her own room. Yet today was the exception. It was Hilda's eighty-fourth birthday and almost all the residents of Oak Park were celebrating. Kate had even bought a special large iced cake for the occasion.

'No, I'll make do with it how it is, thank you very much.' Hilda scowled, taking another grimacing sip – just to prove her point. 'Anyway, you know I'm lactose- intolerant. Too much milk can send me into anaphylactic shock.'

Vivian tutted loudly and shook her head in annoyance. 'Shame I hadn't discovered that a bit sooner. I'd have bought you a cow for your birthday.'

A few of the residents suppressed their smiles at the loud outburst, as Lillian grinned none too discreetly beside Viv. 'Don't let her wind you up. She'll be dead soon anyway – she's supposed to be allergic to caffeine, too, remember.'

Hilda ignored the chuckles that followed, instead focusing on Kate and Alan, both seated to the right side of her. 'It's a lovely cake and my favourite-colour icing too – pink! Back in my heyday, Kate, I used to be called the Pink Lady.' Kate leaned in, trying to concentrate on Hilda's story and drown out the catty remarks coming from Viv's end of the table.

'Ha, pink lady! No doubt because she ate an apple and spent three weeks in A&E complaining of it being stuck in her windpipe.'

Hilda didn't rise to Vivian's bait, instead continuing to relay her tale of the pink hair rinse that everyone had remarked upon as beautiful. Kate marvelled at the way Hilda's face lit up as she took a bite of her cake and relived her past to the other residents. It wasn't often she saw the woman so happy and full of beans.

'If you'd like, Hilda, we can do that for you as a special birthday treat – get your hair rinsed?' She was certain that the care home's resident hairdresser could arrange a pink dye for Hilda on her next visit. She caught fellow care worker, Tasha's, eye and saw the nod of approval.

Hilda brushed her off instantly. 'Oh no, dear. I'd look a fright at my age with pink hair. Best left in the past, things like that. Anyway, you know how sensitive my eczema has become. Not to mention the terrible patches of psoriasis on my head. I couldn't possibly allow my hair to be dyed.'

Catching Vivian's exasperated expression, Kate suppressed a giggle. Hilda was no more susceptible to eczema or psoriasis than she was to caffeine and lactose. In fact, Hilda was probably healthier than most of the other residents combined. Instead, she let the reply pass. 'Yes – you're right. Let's dismiss that idea, then.'

'Is that your phone?' Vivian mouthed at her, pointing to a secluded corner shelf of the dining room, where Kate often stored her phone during working dining times.

Hearing the vague sound of her ring tone, she checked that Tasha was in deep conversation before getting up to discreetly retrieve it. Alf's name was displayed on the screen. She wondered if it was news about his proposal – it was rare of him to ever call during afternoon working hours.

Glancing back towards the dining table, she could see that everything was under control and she stole the moment to slip into the staff room, pressing 'answer' as she did so.

'Hey, babe.' Alf's voice was barely audible above the noisy bustle in the background.

'Hi.' She pressed the mobile closer to her ear, trying not to shudder as loud noises from the other end of the line jarred her thoughts. 'Where are you? What's that noise?'

'I'm walking. It's the traffic. I'm just coming up the underpass near home. I left work early.'

Instantly alert, Kate was quick to reply. 'Is everything okay? Why are you home early?'

'Everything's fine. I've got some good news – actually I was wondering if you could leave work early, too? Meet me at home in twenty minutes?'

Kate's heart skipped a beat. Good news? 'Did you get your

proposed package?' she asked, a sinking feeling in her stomach.

'Yes. I'll explain when I see you.' He sounded ever so slightly edgy. Or perhaps it was the background noise, Kate thought – trying to decipher if it was nerves or dread that was making her feel queasy. She glanced at the clock on the wall; she had just under an hour left of her shift. It wouldn't be a problem to escape a bit early. 'Okay, I'll leave now. See you at home soon.'

She hung up the call and went back into the dining room, thinking about the conversation.

Vivian only needed to glance at Kate's pale face to know that something was wrong. She nudged Lillian and they watched in unison as Kate whispered something quietly into Tasha's ear.

'Good Lord! She doesn't half look shook up. I wonder what's happened,' Lillian said, noticing Kate heading across to them.

'You okay, love?' Vivian asked as Kate got closer and bent down to their level, eyes filled with unease.

'I've got to rush off. Alf just called – he's got news on the job. He's waiting at home to tell me. He sounded weird.'

'That's good news, then, isn't it?' Vivian suggested carefully. 'At least you'll be able to consider things properly now.' From the brief look of despair that passed across Kate's face, she knew that the 'good news' was anything but 'good'.

'Go on now, hurry along.' Lil said, tapping Kate's arm and shooing her off.

Not needing to be told twice, Kate picked up her belongings and squeezed Viv's shoulder. 'I'll let you know all about it tomorrow.' Rushing away quickly, she was nearly out of earshot as Vivian called out her parting words.

'Good luck, love.'

Kate vaguely heard her good wishes and bit down on her lip. For what she was about to do – it was going to be more than luck that she needed.

Alf was pouring himself a glass of tomato juice as he heard Kate's car pull up outside. He waited to hear her footsteps on the gravel and Sam's loud whimpering from his pet carrier before going into the hallway to open the street door for her.

'That was quick,' he said nervously, noticing her slightly jumpy manner and drawn face. When had she lost weight?

It suited her, though; her eyes looked somewhat bigger, doe-like even. She looked more mature, he realised, with a pang of guilt that he hadn't noticed it before.

Bending down, she released Sam from his carrier. 'Well, it sounded important.' She looked up to meet his eyes. 'So I put my foot down.'

'Do you want a cup of tea or a drink?'

'No, I just want to know about the good news? I didn't leave work early for a cup of tea.' She smiled, making light of it. She felt snappy, but was trying to hide it behind casual humour. Her nerves were frayed, for she knew that this conversation was about to open a huge can of worms.

Alf could tell she was nervous. It was the way she always got when she wasn't certain of something. She wasn't the only one – he felt his palm growing clammy with sweat around the small glass of juice he was holding.

Making no move to walk towards the kitchen, Alf realised Kate was looking at him expectantly. She hadn't even taken off her shoes yet. 'They've offered me a fantastic package, Kate. It's over double what I'm earning now, plus a commission and share scheme. On top of that, we get an accommodation budget for the first year, company car and come Christmas time, all going well – the board hinted at a large bonus on the table.'

Kate stood transfixed, not daring to breathe, the words washing over her. Alf, face lit up in excitement, continued babbling on.

'The start date is a month from now and although I know it's really short notice, I just couldn't pass up the opportunity, Kate. Not when Clyde was sitting there waiting for me to decide.'

What did he mean he couldn't pass up the opportunity? Her

heart started to thud in her chest.

'I could hardly say no, could I?' he implored, noticing that she wasn't reacting in the way he'd hoped, prayed, even. 'It was a case of biting the bullet, Kate. I just kept thinking how much we'd benefit if I signed. Hell, we can even afford a Porsche!' He saw her face drop and her eyes narrowing furiously.

'Well, any car you want really. Or holiday?' he added quickly, back-tracking.

Barely able to get the words out, Kate reached for the stairwell banister to support herself. 'Signed? You've signed the contract?'

An uncomfortable silence ensued between them as Alf hung his head, avoiding Kate's searing glare.

'I had no choice, Kate. Clyde asked me to make a decision there and then.' He looked up defensively, just in time to catch the look of absolute horror that was plastered across her face.

'You selfish bastard,' she sneered, feeling a rage so strong that her legs were trembling. 'How could you? You absolute selfish bastard!' She ran her hands through her hair, her fingers shaking with fury.

'For fuck's sake, Kate, there wasn't a phone-a-friend option,' he replied, exasperated. 'I had five minutes to make a decision on our future and I took the option that I thought would benefit us.' His voice cracked with frustration. 'I took the option that I thought you would want me to take.'

Quick as a flash, she pointed her finger angrily into his face. 'Benefit us or benefit you, you mean? And the option I would want you to take?' She looked at him wild- eyed. 'How the fuck do you know what I want without asking me *first*?' She practically spat the last word at him.

Feeling herself sinking back against the staircase, she couldn't believe what she'd heard. It was bad enough that she'd been expecting to come home to news that he'd had an offer he wouldn't want to turn down. But to find out that he'd willingly accepted something that would change both of their lives before so much as consulting her…

The knowledge was too much to bear.

'I'm sorry, Kate. I just honestly thought I was doing the right thing.'

He was hovering over her, looking down with pity in his eyes. Pity for her or pity for himself? She couldn't tell and she suddenly didn't even care. Straightening up slowly, she knew what she had to do. In an instant, everything had become so much clearer.

'You have no idea, Alf, no idea about what I want. Do you really think that Scotland is going to be the answer to all of my prayers?' She looked at him fiercely, her eyes now brimming with tears. 'All I want is for us to be more of a couple, have some sort of future in mind.' She felt her throat tightening with tears. 'Do you never think about the baby we lost?'

Alf, shocked into silence, felt his breath catch momentarily. The question was so sudden and off-topic that it caught him unawares. He stared at Kate, his arms instantly going out to her. She never brought up the miscarriage. Never. He'd assumed that she'd dealt with it and moved on, but one look at the pain written across her face told him he'd been wrong to assume anything.

'Come here.' He pulled her towards him, despite her strong resistance. 'Of course I do. How can I not? Has this Scotland move brought up things about the baby?' He stared at her, clueless. Where was all this coming from? She was looking at him strangely, her face contorted and confused.

Stepping out of Alf's embrace, Kate felt her heart pierce with pain. He didn't get it. He didn't understand. At all. She couldn't breathe. She had to get away. Away from him…. Fast.

Fumbling for her bag, she found it on the stairwell behind her and grabbed it tightly with her right hand, feeling around for her car keys with the other hand. 'I'm sorry, Alf. I'm not sure I can do this any more.' The words sounded strangled, her voice disconnected.

Alf looked at her oddly and moved forward, his expression both crestfallen and flummoxed. 'What do you mean? Why've you got your car keys?' He tried to reach for them, but Kate snatched her hand away and took a step backwards.

'Us. I mean us, Alf.' She stared at him grief-stricken. 'I'm leaving. I have to leave.'

Turning around before he could say another word, she walked towards the front door and opened it – walking out into the cool mid-afternoon air.

She felt sick to her stomach.

Chapter 12

Thankful that Jonnie was on an evening shift at the builder's merchants, Megan took two large wine glasses from her high-gloss cream kitchen cupboard, placing them on the flecked worktop.

'Look, I think the sensible thing to do is to stay here tonight,' she said firmly, taking a chilled bottle of white wine from the fridge. 'I agree there are things you need to discuss, but you're both angry and arguing is not going to solve anything.'

Once again, the chirpy ringtone blasted out from the speakers of Kate's mobile as a picture of Alf filled the screen. 'It's him. This is the sixth time now.' She rubbed one puffy, tear-stained eye and looked at Megan. 'Do you think I should answer it?'

'I think you need to decide that for yourself,' Megan said carefully, aware that she was treading on thin ice by playing agony aunt after such a colossal disagreement. 'Maybe text him later and just let him know you're fine and you're here. Otherwise he's not going to quit calling. He might be worried about where you've got to.'

Kate continued to watch the flashing screen, making no move to answer it. Mercifully, the ringtone soon died away. She knew that Alf was worried about her. She hadn't told Megan the full story – she'd left out the part about the miscarriage. It wasn't something she wanted to face just yet and she knew her friend's sympathy and anger at Alf would only make things worse. 'You know the ironic part of it is that I spent all day plucking up the courage to bring up the marriage conversation tonight. Typical that all of this had to happen today, of all days.'

Megan finished pouring a generous amount of wine and turned to face Kate in surprise. '*You* were going to bring it up?'

'Don't look so shocked,' Kate stated touchily. 'I've been thinking about it since my lunch with Marcus the other day and it makes sense.' She sniffed, her nose stuffy from crying.

Megan sat down on a high-backed stool opposite Kate, pushing a glass in her friend's direction. 'I agree.' She considered her for a moment in stunned silence. 'I'm just shocked, that's all. I didn't think you'd ever be the one to bring it up.'

Kate took a sip of wine, even though her head was pounding and alcohol was the last thing that she wanted. 'It's everything, Megan – Alf, the move, the party, work. At times, I feel like I'm on a road to nowhere and it scares me.' She fingered the stem of her glass. 'I love Alf and I want our future to be together, but I need more than just a hope. I need a commitment.'

'If ever there's a time for needing to know where you stand, then, yes, it's now.' Megan replied thoughtfully, wondering how Alf would have reacted had Kate broached the subject.

'I just cannot get my head around the fact that he agreed to the contract straight off, knowing full well that I had my reservations. I don't know any boss that expects a decision instantly. I mean, surely he could easily have asked for a few hours to consider?'

Megan had already covered this matter countless times since she'd arrived home to find an angry and tearful Kate on her doorstep a few hours previously, but instead of pointing it out, she solemnly nodded.

'And if he can give an answer to Clyde concerning a major life decision – within five minutes of being asked – then why shouldn't he be able to give that to me, too?'

Pondering on Kate's logic, Megan found herself heartily agreeing. She knew full well that Clyde was a persuasive man, especially when he had reason to be. But it didn't let Alf off the hook for dragging his feet on the most important relationship decision that was required of him.

'Because he's a selfish, inconsiderate asshole. That's why,' Kate fumed, ignoring the uncomfortable pulsing ache in her temples and taking another sip of wine.

'So what are you going to do?' Megan asked tentatively, wondering when she'd last seen Kate so riled up. It didn't suit her usually placid demeanour, but in her opinion it was about time that her friend stood her ground.

'I'm going to be honest with him.' She stared at the work surface in front of her, feeling a strong confirmation and conviction in her thoughts. 'Tell him how blown away I am by his decision and lay everything on the table.' Turning to Megan, she shook her head at her own stupidity, with a sudden and apparent realisation of just how easy-going she'd been over the last few months, especially given the circumstances. His reaction to her raising the topic of the miscarriage had been the icing on the cake. 'I'm not going to move to Scotland with him unless he's willing to show me he's as committed to me as he is to Hamilton's. It's as simple as that.'

For the first time in a long time, Megan saw a flash of the Kate she'd once known. The steely, independent and stronger-minded person that had slowly ebbed away over the years as she'd matured in her relationship with Alf.

She had no doubt that Kate would stand by her decision – she had seen the look on her face before – the determined eyes and set jaw spoke volumes. She was finally ready for answers and she couldn't be dissuaded.

'I have to say, I think it's about time you did put your foot down.' She pursed her lips, noticing Kate suddenly looking at her curiously. 'You know I'm always supportive of what you want, but I can't stand by any longer and watch you throw your life away. I've had to do that with Jonnie and it tears me apart. I can't do that with you too.'

Kate looked at her in surprise. 'What do you mean throw my life away?'

'It's Alf, Kate. You're not happy and you haven't been for a long while. It's not healthy to fix your focus on this marriage obsession that you have.'

Taken aback, Kate frowned at her. 'I'm not obsessed! It's normal to want to get married after seven years with the same person, Megan.'

Not rising to the bait, Megan continued, on a roll now that she'd got going. 'Well, maybe so, but, anyway, I haven't seen you have a proper laugh or look carefree in *so* long, Kate. It's like you're living in some sort of bubble with him. And it's the way he talks to you sometimes. He puts you down and you don't even seem to realise it.'

Knowing that she'd struck a chord as Kate dropped her gaze to her lap, she stopped her observations and took a sip of wine. 'I just want to see you happy again. Life's too short to make such big compromises all the time.'

Kate lifted her head, trying not to let Megan's words upset her. She was tired and spent. And deep down, she knew her friend was right. Alf did have a way of cutting her down to size without, perhaps, being aware that he was doing so…

'Well, my mind is already made up. I'm going to stay here tonight and first thing tomorrow morning I'm heading home to talk with him. Things need to get sorted. I can't continue like this.'

Megan couldn't help but feel gratified at her friend's response. Kate was finally taking control.

It was long overdue.

'I've been waiting up for you.' Alf raised his head from the sofa and sat up straight, thankful that she'd finally returned home. He'd heard her car pulling up outside and immediately stirred himself from his stupor. He'd spent most of the night mulling over her reaction to his news and her unexpected questioning about the miscarriage. He still couldn't get his head around the turn of events.

Not saying a word, Kate felt her heart pounding as she walked across to the adjacent armchair and carefully sat down. Alf noted the dark circles under her eyes and her drawn, pale appearance. She looked as exhausted as he felt.

'Do you want a coffee or something?' he ventured, not knowing where to start. Seeing the brief look of annoyance cross Kate's face, he knew he'd said the wrong thing. Yet he wished he'd had the foresight to make himself a coffee. It was barely 7am. He knew it wasn't the appropriate moment to get up and go into the kitchen, so he remained seated, staring bewilderedly.

'I think we're both aware there's a lot of things we need to discuss,' Kate began, eager to get the frank discussion she'd come to have with him underway. She'd promised herself she would be honest and direct – she'd spent the entire evening tossing and turning on Megan's sofa, running over her decision in her mind. She paused, looking up.

Alf seized his chance to speak. 'I don't understand why you brought up the miscarriage, Kate? It's been four years and you've never mentioned it before.'

Taking a deep breath, Kate held his confused gaze. 'It's not that I didn't want to talk about it before, Alf. It's because you never asked. You never brought it up, not once. It's like the whole thing is a taboo you don't want to acknowledge.'

He shifted himself forward to the edge of the sofa, trying to get closer to her; wondering how she could have misjudged him so badly. 'But that's not the case at all. I didn't want to hurt you by bringing it up again. I thought it was best laid to rest. I thought that was the way you wanted it!'

Huffing lightly, Kate shook her head in disbelief. Did he really expect her to want something so important to be brushed under the carpet and forgotten about? 'Of course I wanted to talk about it! Maybe not at the time, but afterwards. Have you never once thought that perhaps I wanted to talk about having another baby or at least some reference to future children?' Her voice sounded whiny and strained, even to herself.

Wearing a puzzled frown Alf scratched his face, disconcerted. 'But we have discussed kids. You *know* I want kids in the future.' He'd referenced children in different conversations many times. He noticed Kate's eyes widen in surprise at his answer.

Exasperated, Kate stood up, too riled to be seated. 'No, Alf. We haven't *once* properly discussed the subject. Have we ever sat down and spoken about *when* we might start trying to have children? Whether it's even possible after my miscarriage?' She looked at him angrily, her voice rising. 'How it'll work with our jobs if we have children? Whether we should consider turning the spare room into a nursery for future children? No. Never. So do not sit there and calmly tell me that we have discussed things.' It infuriated her that he could assume his stupid and general comments about one day having a potentially famous footballing son could be considered a discussion.

Standing up and walking across to her, Alf felt his stomach sink. He had no idea she'd been thinking like this. 'I didn't know you wanted to discuss those types of things?' he began, feeling out of depth all of a sudden.

Ignoring him, Kate stomped across to the television, its screen flickering with an early-morning show and switched it off forcefully. 'I'm sick and tired of not knowing where this relationship is going. I don't even know if you want to get married.'

'Married?' Alf repeated in confusion. 'Of course I want us to get married. You know that!'

'It's not rocket science Alf – it's straightforward. We've been together seven years.' She walked back towards him, holding her fingers up to clarify her point. 'Seven years, Alf.' She watched his eyes narrow in further confusion. 'The last time we had the marriage conversation, which, I should add, is because I brought up the subject,' she jabbed a finger toward herself, 'You said let's wait a couple of years, get the house done, do some travelling, get settled with work.'

Alf suddenly realised where the conversation was going and looked at Kate in surprise.

'Except, two years later and aside from your work changes, we haven't even done any of those things.'

'Oh hang on, let's be fair here. I did suggest travelling this year,' Alf replied, irritated, thinking that it wasn't fair that Kate had kept her concerns to herself and was now offloading onto him – including the blame. He wasn't a mind-reader.

'No Alf, the travelling idea recently went out of the window too – due to financial and work reasons – your decision, remember?' He noticed her eyes had turned a darker shade of blue. She was fuming. 'Not to mention that when I also suggested redecorating last month, you practically vetoed that idea too!'

Quickly thinking back to both conversations, he knew she was right. Despite this, he pressed on. 'But I thought we both agreed that we were waiting, though? Giving it a few years? Why didn't you tell me sooner that you had a problem with it?' He ran his hand through his hair, closing his eyes slowly in the process and wishing he could be somewhere else. His gut was telling him things were about to get extremely complicated and his heart was beating ten to the dozen. He wasn't sure he was ready for this talk any longer.

Kate shook her head in absolute disbelief. 'A few years? No, Alf, we agreed a couple of years. Which, in my vocabulary, equates to two years. Two years from my thirtieth birthday.' Her voice broke, the pent-up frustration she was feeling building up into tears behind her eyes. 'Which is why I guess I had naïvely expected a surprise proposal at my thirty-second birthday party…' She stared down into her hands, wringing them in both frustration and embarrassment and she let the words tail off.

Alf let her statement sink in properly before he dropped his hand from his head to the table. Dumbfounded, he gazed at Kate's face, noting the pain behind her teary eyes. She had thought he was going to propose?

'But whatever gave you that idea? I hadn't even hinted at anything like that, had I?'

He was so confused now. Had he accidently slipped up and said something about marriage that she'd misinterpreted? He'd never meant to hurt her. How had they got to this stage?

Kate felt as if she'd had the wind knocked out of her as she watched Alf's puzzled expression and fought the nausea that was building up inside. 'That's all you have to say for yourself?' She stood up, wiping a lone, cold tear that had fast fallen down her cheek. 'After telling you I thought you might propose, all you can think about is how I came to that conclusion?' Her voice was becoming high-pitched and irate. 'After absolutely humiliating me at my birthday by presenting me with a flipping dog's tag in a box in front of everybody, don't you think I deserve an honest answer?'

Alf rose to his feet, angered by Kate's sudden attack on him. 'I told you the dog tag wasn't my idea. I wish I'd never fucking bothered with the dog now – the trouble it's caused.'

Quick to defend Sam, who was nowhere to be seen amidst the tension, Kate gritted her teeth, seething. 'Don't you dare blame the dog in all of this. This is nothing to do with a dog. This is everything to do with your reluctance to get married and start a family.' She turned her back to him, not wanting him to see the hurt that she was sure was written all over her. 'Because, admit it, Alf. That's the problem, isn't it? You don't want to marry me or have children with me, do you?'

Silence passed between them for what felt like an age, Kate holding her breath whilst she waited for an answer. She felt Alf gently grab her arm and before she knew what was happening, he'd spun her around and was brushing her hair from her teary face.

'Don't be silly! Of course I want to marry you. And I couldn't think of anything better than having another baby together. I love you, Kate. Come here, you daft cow.'

Her heart softened and when she dared to finally take a breath, the emotions were so overwhelming that she didn't resist when

Alf pressed her against him and cradled her, not caring that the tears were wetting his t-shirt. She gently pulled away from him, feeling tired and overwrought.

'Come and sit down.' He steered her back to the sofa and pushed her gently into the seat. 'Babe, I haven't spent all these years with you just to walk out at the last moment – I want you to be my wife. We're practically already husband and wife, for Christ's sakes!' He laughed lightly, grabbing her hand in his and tilting her face towards his. 'And of course I want a baby with you – in fact, I want lots of babies.' He paused and sighed. 'But I don't see the point of rushing into getting married and planning children at this very moment, especially now that the move to Scotland is going to be preoccupying us. Planning a wedding, trying for a baby, as well as settling into a new home and new jobs is going to be a huge strain on us. Surely you can appreciate that!'

Kate felt a whooshing sound in her ears as she sucked in a breath and considered Alf's gentle wording. Her heartbeat, which had slowly settled back into a steady pace, quickened instantly and the anger that had vanished leaving in its place a bone-deep weariness, all at once returned with a vengeance. 'You're unbelievable. Absolutely unbelievable.' She shook her head, and instead of tears and pain, she had a strange desire to laugh. 'You're spineless, Alf Stafford. A cowardly, spineless man. There's never going to be a *right* time is there? That's the problem. Life doesn't give anyone a 'right' moment. And I, more than anyone, know that. Look how many people I've lost.'

'Babe, you've taken it the wrong way. I didn't mean...'

Flinching as Alf instinctively reached out and tried to pull her towards him, she leaned backward. 'If you truly wanted me, Alf, there's no way you'd be putting your work before me. So I'll tell you what I'll do – I'll make things easy for you.' She stood up, resolute in knowing what she had to do, for she was too far hurt by his words to consider any other action. 'I'm done with holding onto hope and illusion, Alf. I shouldn't have to beg you for a future together. I'm sorry, but there's no way I'm going to Scotland with you and certainly no way I'm going to waste another moment of my time with someone who doesn't want to commit to me. Especially the same someone who, coincidentally, has no problem committing to his boss.'

Shell-shocked at the turnaround of events, Alf felt his stomach churning. He'd never seen Kate look this unyielding. He knew her well enough to know how steadfast she could be. There was no way he was going to lose her. Not when everything he was working towards was for her too. He knew what he had to do and it was the thing he had feared the most, for the whole idea of it made him feel confused and vulnerable. She was standing up and picking up her keys – an expression so broken that he just wanted to reach out and hold her.

'Wait.' He reached out and grabbed her arm. 'I know you're angry and I don't agree with your reasoning behind it, because I've already told you I plan to marry you and I definitely want children. Can't you see what Scotland is for us, Kate? It's a chance to get to that stage with enough finances and security behind us. But if engagement is what you want and that's what will make you happy – let's do it now, then. Just don't walk out on me, Kate. I need you. I need you in Scotland with me.'

Kate looked into Alf's familiar, glistening eyes, noticing the prickling of tears in the corners and wiping her own wet cheeks with the back of her right hand. Didn't he see that he'd already had seven years to secure her by his side, to have his babies? They already had all the security and finances they needed for a life together. So why was Scotland going to be the magical answer?

'I'm sorry, Alf, I can't stay.' She choked back a lump in her throat and willed herself to keep strong. 'You've told me everything I needed to hear and I'm sorry, but I can't be with someone who wants me only because they need me.' She glanced towards the fridge, eyes searching for the framed photo of her aunt that stood proudly against the wall, silently asking for her help in making the right decision. 'I deserve more than that. And whilst I didn't expect you to drop down onto one knee and present me with a huge diamond, I also didn't ever expect you to propose to me out of pity or reluctantly, either.'

Alf immediately opened his mouth to protest, but Kate placed a finger against his lips, silencing him. He grabbed her finger and kissed it, his eyes red and watery. 'Don't, Alf. It's too late. It's better this way. My life belongs here and yours now belongs in Scotland.'

He looked like a little boy lost as he stood awkwardly in the middle of the room, arms by his side, hair dishevelled and face etched with dashed hopes. 'So that's it, then? You're just going to walk away?'

'Yes.' Her voice was tiny and barely audible, but the word seemed to echo through the walls of the house and both of their hearts.

Making a momentous choice, she picked up her keys and quietly left the living room, the devastation of her decision heavy in the air. It was only when she reached her car moments later that she fully realised the impact of her words and began to weep wildly.

She'd just walked out on the love of her life.

Chapter 13

Two weeks later

'We'll never get served standing here' Kate moaned, taking into account the three-person-deep queue for the bar. She tugged gently on the neckline of her dress, annoyed that it appeared to be lowering of its own accord. Despite looking a great deal better than she was feeling and her already thinner frame working its magic on a couple of totally unsuitable admirers, she would have preferred to have been curled up on her sofa with Sam, ideally watching back-to-back comedies instead of vying for the barman's attention to get served a drink.

'Stop whinging. Tonight you're supposed to be letting your hair down and enjoying yourself.' Megan scowled, spotting an opening in the queue and seizing the opportunity, dragging a grumpy Kate with her.

'Ouch, mind what you're doing. You nearly pulled me into that guy with the ginger hair.'

Almost immediately catching the attention of the barman, Megan had placed her order within moments. 'You did want another Mojito didn't you? That's what I ordered you.'

'Sure, anything,' Kate replied, disinterested in the specifics of the alcohol and just grateful for anything that would take the edge off the overwhelming sadness that had engulfed her. She was watching as the ginger-haired man standing nearby pulled a laughing woman closer to him and kept his arm firmly around her waist, his head leaning into hers. They made a cute couple – just like she and Alf used to make.

'Here you go.' Megan held out a sugar-rimmed glass, the pungent smell of mint and alcohol in the air as Kate accepted it. 'Let's go back to the others and see if they've managed to get the attention of any fit guys yet.'

Kate looked longingly at the couple now embraced in a laughing kiss and felt herself pining for Alf. She missed him. It had already been two weeks since he'd moved out and gone to stay with his brother, but she missed him so much.

'Okay, let's go,' she said, pushing Megan to lead the way and weaving quickly behind her through the crowd. She needed a distraction – and fast. She couldn't carry on like this – it wasn't healthy. She could feel the familiar lump rising in her throat and knew it wouldn't be long before the onset of hot, fat tears joined it.

Passing the DJ stand, Megan waved to Nathan, who was engrossed in his turntables but looked up as the women passed and smiled, baring his diamond-studded tooth. She carried on walking towards the group of women, who were clustered around a tall table, a group of three dark-haired men standing nearby, with their backs to them. 'Looks like the girls might have company,' she said, turning briefly to Kate. 'Oooh, the one in the biscuit jumper over the white shirt doesn't look too bad from here, does he?'

Kate gazed at the figure, who appeared to be chatting quietly to his friend. The lighting was dim and it was hard to see anyone from a distance, but his stature and build reminded her a little of Marcus. She'd felt guilty ignoring him since the split with Alf, but then she had been ignoring everybody – unable to face the sympathy and questions. Everybody except Megan – and that was only because she had no choice, given that Megan had a spare door key and insisted on using it.

It was also Megan's persistence that had brought them to

Swoonies for the evening, because after two weeks on sick leave and spending nearly all of her waking hours crying into her sofa, she had told Kate that enough was enough. Forcing her into the teal dress – which she'd bought for the cocktail opening that she had ended up not attending – Megan had told her they were going out for the evening. No buts, no excuses and no arguments. It was time to begin moving on from Alf. Starting with a girls' night out.

'Hey, we wondered where you had both got to,' Shilpa said, flicking her black hair behind her shoulder as Megan approached, Kate trailing behind her – her glass of Mojito already almost drained.

'The queue for the bar is ridiculous, as always.' Megan spotted a bowl of olives on the table and popped one into her mouth, making eyes towards the men nearby and raising a questioning eyebrow at Shilpa.

'Hot,' Shilpa mouthed discreetly, noticing Kate's expression changing from intrigue to a wide smile. She frowned at Megan and nodded towards Kate, who was already walking away from them towards the men.

'Kate?' Megan hissed, panicked, spinning around as her friend grabbed the arm of the man in the jumper. Surely Kate wasn't going to do something as stupid as throwing herself on the first attractive guy she laid eyes on?

All at once she recognised the man as he cautiously turned sideways towards the woman that had grabbed him. Megan saw his face light up in recognition – his expression changing from aggravated to exhilarated – and felt her stomach lurch with desire.

'Megan,' Kate called to her, suddenly enthused and jubilant as she hugged him. 'Come over here. It's Marcus.'

Kate turned back to Marcus, seeing the concern as he looked at her sympathetically, his face clouding over.

'I've been calling you' he said, observing her tired eyes and slimmed figure. 'Why didn't you answer? I heard from Alf, of course.' He patted the small of her back. 'I'm sorry to hear it, Kate.

I didn't ever expect that of you guys.'

Seeing Kate's eyes welling up and her bottom lip trembling, Megan quickly stepped forwards into the exchange. 'Hi, Marcus.' She squeezed herself into the gap between Marcus and the window next to him. 'I didn't realise it was you. Nice to see you again.'

Marcus smiled and briefly leaned in for a hug. 'We haven't been here for long.' He pointed to his friends. 'To be honest, I'm not in the mood to be here tonight. We've been here the last few weekends running now. Same old people.'

Kate nodded, agreeing. 'Me too. I'm only here because she dragged me here!' She pointed at Megan and poked out her tongue. 'Apparently I need to start moving on and this is the place to do it.' She rolled her eyes dismissively.

'Well, suit yourself you ungrateful mare, I was only trying to help,' Megan replied light-heartedly. 'Have another drink. It might improve your mood.'

'No bickering, ladies.' Marcus cut in, placing a hand on each of their shoulders. 'But seeing as two out of three of us are bored, how about we get out of here and go elsewhere?'

Kate looked at Megan with a smile, feeling both relief and excitement for the first time all evening. 'I'm up for it – it's still only early. I can't imagine staying here all night. It's too pretentious.'

Megan looked a little reluctant, glancing back at Shilpa and the girls and reminding herself of the text she'd sent to Michael suggesting they meet up after their respective evening apart. 'I'm not sure. I did promise the girls I was in a party mood and they won't be happy if we leave them.' She looked back at Marcus with his sparkling green eyes and expectant expression and felt her resolve weakening. 'But, go on then… you've twisted my arm. Let's make a run for it.'

'Great. The boys won't mind me sneaking off with two beautiful ladies. In fact, they'll be envious,' he joked, turning towards Kate. 'So where do you fancy going then, seeing as it's you that needs the cheering up? Another bar somewhere? Or a bite to eat?

I could murder some food.'

Kate considered her options for a moment, then thought of the one place she'd always wanted to visit and had been limited because Alf hadn't favoured the food. 'What about that huge Japanese restaurant on Frog Street? It's got a bar and dance floor at the back, too.'

Megan nodded enthusiastically. 'Ooh, yes, great suggestion, I could eat a beef Teppanyaki right now, too. Sounds good to me. We can have a boogie later as well.'

'Perfect, I love it in there,' Marcus said, draining his drink and placing the empty glass on a nearby table. 'Ladies, get your stuff, we're getting out of here.' Standing by the exit, he waited patiently for the girls to grab their belongings and say their goodbyes, grateful that he'd finally get to spend the evening with Kate and a chance to, hopefully, lift her spirits. Not to mention have another chance to get to know Megan a little more…

By the time both women were ready to exit the bar, Marcus already had his coat on and was waiting with both arms extended. 'Allow me,' he said, linking his arm through Kate's on one side and Megan's on the other.

Chatting animatedly on the way to the restaurant, laughing and cracking sarcastic jokes with Marcus, neither woman could remember the last time in the past two weeks that they'd felt this happy or lively.

Surprisingly, it wasn't only Kate who was privately hoping it was the start of something new.

'Well, it sounds like you had a lovely time.' Lil said, picking up her half-eaten Eccles cake and breaking a piece off. 'I don't suppose you fink this Marcus has got a bit of a fancy for you – ain't it the second time this week now that he's popped round?

Kate blushed shyly, struggling to find the corner of the clean duvet cover she was changing. 'No, Lil, I think he's just being kind. He's that type of person.' She located the corner and swiftly shook the duck-down duvet into place. 'Anyway, I'm not ready to be getting into something with someone new, just yet.' She straightened the cover once again, before picking up the stacks of pillows from the floor and rearranging them in place.

'I know that. But it doesn't hurt to have a bit of fun. Blimey! I wish I could have an admirer to give me a bit of fun.' Lillian giggled, spluttering crumbs of cake across the carpet. 'The only fun I get at this age is having me blood pressure taken once a fortnight by that handsome Dr Sharman.'

Kate laughed, smoothing the folded eiderdown over the bottom end of the mattress and walked across to join Lillian. 'It's not that I don't want fun, Lil – believe me, I really do.' She sat down on the clothes trunk at the foot of the bed, her expression pensive. 'I guess I'll just feel better about everything when Alf leaves for Scotland next week. Until then, I can't help feeling like things are on hold.'

Lillian reached across and patted Kate's hand. 'I know, darling, it's never easy ending somefink.' She wiped the corner of her mouth where the spittle was collecting, as it always did. 'You'll be better off when he's out the picture for good. And then you can get yourself a nice new young man – maybe even this Marcus.'

She winked at Kate with a cheeky grin.

Zipping his suitcase shut, Alf surveyed the mess around him. 'I don't even need half of this shit,' he muttered to himself, kicking a battered and muddy trainer from underfoot and wondering how he'd accumulated so many clothes over the years.

Ever the helpful girlfriend right until the end, Kate had made sure that his belongings had been placed into storage bags for him to collect, conveniently sorting the things she knew that he regularly used from the old and placing the remains in their loft. He looked at the bags that had neatly stored his goods, now devoid of their contents and dumped around the spare room of his brother's house.

He still couldn't get his head around the events of the past month. He'd barely been able to function at work over the last two weeks – there was a great, gaping hole where Kate had once been. The move had kept him occupied, something to strive forward for and focus on – but it wasn't completely doing the trick. He couldn't stop thinking about Kate. No matter how many evenings he filled with impromptu trips to the pub with his brother, or staying late at work to finalise his job takeover, she was always there – in the forefront of his thoughts.

Pushing a box of documentation that he'd be taking to Scotland nearer to the suitcase he'd just finished packing, he wondered if the agent had received his message about picking up the keys a day earlier.

Finding a property on the budget that Hamilton's had provided him with hadn't been as straightforward as he'd assumed it would. Given that he wasn't familiar with Glasgow and that the new office headquarters were slap-bang in the middle of the city centre, the conveniently located loft conversion apartment he'd originally set his heart on had far exceeded his allowance. The prospect of bachelorhood had lost its appeal as soon as he'd discovered what he could actually afford close to the office.

Still, the penthouse apartment he'd found, complete with open-plan kitchen and wet room had all the trappings of 'luxury' stamped across it, despite being a fair distance away. It was also satisfying to know that it was something Kate would never have gone in for.

In the first few days after she'd walked out, he'd half expected her to ring him and make amends – but when she'd come to the house and told him that they needed to find an alternative living solution, he'd known it was over. She'd seemed so cold towards him. It was like being faced with a version of a woman so familiar and yet a complete stranger.

He'd thought he'd known her inside and out, but the Kate that had stood before him with sad eyes and a determined look had reiterated in no uncertain terms that it was definitely finished between them. It was just a case now of him getting settled in Scotland and then making the necessary arrangements to put their terraced house on the market – after all, it wasn't as if she could afford the mortgage on her salary alone.

'Well, she's chosen her bed. Time for her to lie in it,' he muttered to himself, angered that he was once again thinking about her. It was too painful to try and go over the events of their last conversation in his mind again. Anyway, he'd been doing that too much.

Tony, his brother, appeared on the bedroom landing. 'You all packed and ready to go?' He glanced behind Alf at the ransacked room littered with belongings. 'Bloody hell, Alf, you can't leave the place like that. At least chuck it in boxes. Chrissie will go mental at me otherwise.'

Ignoring his brother's comment, Alf picked up the suitcase and moved it onto the landing. He'd never been close to his half-brother and if he hadn't been desperate for a place to stay then he wouldn't have even considered contacting Tony. His father's affair with Tony's mother had been a contributing cause to his lonely childhood and upbringing. Tony, at eight years younger, had been lavished with the attention that he'd never once himself experienced from their dad. It had been hard to stomach throughout the years.

'You want a hand loading up the car?' Tony offered, picking up the suitcase, seeming as keen to be rid of Alf as Alf was to go.

'Yes, it's only those two and a few boxes. Should be plenty of room to load up.' He glanced at the four boxes of things he'd decided to take with him, wondering if he'd forgotten any necessities. He couldn't remember the last time he'd had to pack without taking Kate's organised and interfering ways for granted. He was sure she'd laugh if she saw his pitiful selection of belongings for his new life in Scotland. Instantly feeling overwhelmed and despondent, he began picking up things from the floor, carelessly and aggressively shoving them back into bags.

Tony was back quickly, selecting two more of the boxes and

nodding with a satisfied smile at the vaguely tidier room. 'Bit better. At least I won't be in the doghouse when you go, now.'

Alf offered a tight smile, unable to find any sense of amusement where Chrissie was concerned. In his opinion his brother's wife was far too controlling. She reminded him a lot of his own mother, with her selfish and demanding ways.

Stacking the last of the bags in a pile in the corner of the room, he dusted his hands on his jeans. 'Right, that's me done I think.' He could hear Tony outside, slamming the car boot closed. Picking up his phone, he tried once again calling the letting agent's number but was met with a voicemail recording. He left another message. 'Hello, Veronica, it's Alf Stafford again. Hoping you've picked up my previous message about getting the keys for 40 Limburg Street first thing tomorrow morning. I'm heading up to Glasgow tonight, so I'll be stopping by the office at 9am tomorrow. Let me know. Cheers.'

Tossing a sports bag over one shoulder, he picked up the remaining two boxes. Tony met him halfway down the staircase and took the heavier top box. 'That's the last of it,' Alf said, following him to the car. 'I'll arrange to get the other boxes collected soon, once I know what's happening with the house.'

'Yeah, no problem. You're staying for a bit of dinner first before you go, though, aren't you?' Tony asked, watching Alf close the rear doors of the car. 'I think Chrissie mentioned she was doing chicken hotpot later.'

Standing awkwardly by the driver's door, Alf took a moment to consider Tony's offer. He knew his brother meant well, even if Chrissie railroaded him into most of the decisions he made, but he and Tony were like two strangers constantly struggling to find a common ground. It had been hard enough living under the same roof for three and a half weeks, let alone trying to form a brotherly bond over the occasional pub beer or dinner. He was relieved to be leaving, looking forward to his penthouse in Glasgow —even if the idea of being totally alone in a new city did unnerve him a little.

'No, Tone, I think its best I shoot off just before rush hour starts. It's a long drive and I'm hoping to get to the hotel by midnight.'

'Righty ho.' Tony walked towards him and leaned in for a stiff hug. 'Take care, mate.' He patted his brother on the back. 'Drop us a line when you're settled in and we might even pop up at some point – me and Chrissie.' He smiled, standing back after the bumbling embrace.

'Yeah, do that,' Alf said, nodding unconvincingly and knowing that the threat was empty and it would undoubtedly be another two years before they met again. 'Tell Chrissie I said bye and thanks for everything.'

'Will do. Safe journey. And don't forget what I said about the birds. Plenty of sorts up there in Glasgow. It'll be no time before you meet someone new.'

Alf laughed weakly and climbed into his car; Tony was already turning away and walking back into the house. Moments later he pulled quickly out of the driveway, clicking on the radio to distract his thoughts. He couldn't quite believe the day had finally rolled around to be leaving his home town, and despite being thrilled at the prospect of the new life that awaited him, he felt noticeably bereft.

Bereft for the woman that should have been sitting in the car alongside him, sharing his excitement and the new start he'd anticipated together.

Reaching out, he turned up the radio even louder in an attempt to dim the melancholy feeling.

'Do you really believe that?' Megan exclaimed, searching Michael's teasing expression and failing to keep a straight face.

'It's a statistical fact.' He removed his tie, slinging it casually over his black-leather dining chair and pressed an illuminated pad on his white living-room wall. The darkness engulfing the room was instantly obliterated by bright spotlights, the television screen flickered into life and electronic shutters closed steadily across the windows. 'Everyone knows that all women hit the age of thirty and suddenly want to marry and have babies.'

Megan shrugged off her suit jacket, still not failing to be amazed at the technology that Michael's city pad boasted. 'But I'm thirty-one and I'm not bothered by those things. So does that make me the exception or the proof that you're statistically incorrect?'

Pulling her close to him, Michael playfully nuzzled her neck, grinning as she squealed at the sharpness of his stubble against her skin. 'What that makes you, my sexy Megan, is the perfect girlfriend.'

She laughed, breaking away from him and kissing him on the nose. 'So is this a good time to tell you that I'm going wedding-dress shopping next week?' She poked out her tongue at his expression of mock horror and slipped off her heels. 'I'm starving. Shall we order something now or did you want to wait?'

'I was being serious, you know.' He walked into the high-tech kitchen, picking up a handful of takeout menus from a pile on the work surface and spreading them on the dining table. 'You really are the perfect girlfriend.'

'Stop, or I'll start blushing,' Megan teased, noting that Michael was no longer jesting and looking at her with intensity.

'I haven't felt this way about a woman before. And even all of this joking around about marriage and babies.' He took her hand in his and placed a small kiss on her forehead. 'It wouldn't be such a bad idea, you know – if it was with somebody like you.'

Speechless, Megan shifted her eyes nervously, unsure how to react – for no man had ever made reference to the idea of a strong commitment with her. It wasn't that she didn't fancy Michael – there wasn't anything not to fancy about him, and she certainly couldn't have wished for anybody more understanding and fun. But she'd assumed they were taking it slowly…

'Wow, that's quite a declaration,' she said carefully, searching his face and sensing his expectancy. 'I don't know what to say.' She looked down at her hands, still embraced in his. 'Except that

I feel more comfortable and happy with you than I have with any other man.' She met his eyes. 'So wherever this leads, I'm open to going there.'

'Well, that's good enough for me,' Michael said, stroking a stray strand of hair from her face and smiling. 'What do you fancy then?'

Unnerved, Megan looked at him. 'What do you mean?'

'Chinese, Indian, fish and chips…' He shook his head at her tense expression and playfully slapped her bottom. 'Remind me to never bring up the subject of marriage again. You're worse than a fella!'

Laughing, Megan gently pushed him away and grabbed the choice of take-out menus from the table, pretending to concentrate on the options.

Grateful for the distraction, she couldn't help but marvel at the obvious fact that Michael had been bitten by the love bug. He had a solid, strong personality – in the couple of months that they'd been dating she'd observed that it wasn't in his nature to speak about emotions. So his comment had most certainly thrown her off balance.

The problem was, she wasn't yet certain of her own feelings towards him. Knowing that part of the issue was her reluctance to expose herself to the possibility of being hurt, she pondered how she could lower her barriers. Michael had made it clear, so far, that her unusual motherly instinct over Jonnie wasn't an issue. From the way he'd acted around her brother, she felt that she might have finally found someone who wasn't put off by his demanding behaviour.

However, she didn't want to think of the alternative reason for her reluctance – the reason she'd been trying to squash over the last few weeks. For it was an idea so absurd that it was laughable – after all, didn't love at first sight only belong in fairy tales?

She pushed the thought away and selected a menu from the array in front of her. 'Shall we go for a Chinese takeaway, then?'

Michael nodded enthusiastically, none the wiser to the conflict taking place in Megan's mind.

'I'm gobsmacked, I really am,' Kate gushed, one hand on her chest, feeling her heart beating rapidly beneath the fabric of her uniform. The other hand was on her neck, which she was certain would by now be crimson – as it always was when she was pleasantly surprised.

'You deserve it, love, and anyway, why shouldn't they give you this opportunity?' Vivian said indignantly. 'Your artwork is a lot better than all of the pieces in this home put together.'

'He's done you a wonderful thing, our Alan.' Lil folded the cover of her wordsearch magazine back into place. 'I know he's got contacts in high places and I happen to know that he's got old Steinbach in his pocket, too.' She winked at Kate. 'But he must have gone all out to convince the board and put a good word in.'

'Oh, he must have,' Vivian said, nodding her head vigorously in agreement. 'I reckon you'll end up making quite a few bob out of this, Kate.' She tapped her nose. 'You mark my words.'

'Well, let's not get carried away just yet,' Kate replied, laughing. 'One step at a time! It's only hanging a few pieces in the entrance and a few in the visitors' area.'

Vivian looked at her sternly. 'You leave it to us – we'll have those pieces sold for you in no time. Won't we, Lil?'

Lillian bobbed her head in encouragement. 'Course we will. I already know that Alma's son is a big-shot businessman. I'll easily have one offloaded onto him the next time he visits. She's always harping on about how much he likes art. Well, good job, too – then he'll be able to appreciate real art when he sees your pieces, won't he?'

'Too right he will,' Viv retorted, reaching for her Guinness can.

'I love you both. I hope you realise that,' Kate said, sitting herself between the two women and placing a protective arm around each. She noticed that although Vivian brushed her off with tutting and Lillian with an eye roll, both women's hands reached for hers, their faces lit up with warmth and affection. 'But you must promise me that you won't go about bullying the other residents and visitors into buying my art. Alan's been kind enough to get permission for it to be hung and shared with the residents and guests, not for it to be sold. Besides, I paint because I enjoy it, not to make a profit out of it. Okay?'

'Oh, do stop fussing, love,' Lil said, rebuking Kate. 'My dear old mum used to say to me, Lillian, never kick a gift horse in the mouth.' She stared at Kate pointedly. 'And I'm going to say the same fing to you.' She looked at Vivian for approval, her lips pursed. 'Anyway, don't you have work to be getting on with?'

Kate stood up, knowing when she was being shoo'ed away. 'Yes, I do. Oh, and I'm leaving a little earlier today anyway.'

'Why's that, love?' Vivian asked, her face tightening slightly.

All too familiar with Vivian's constant chest pains, Kate looked at her with concern, observing how her hand was clasped tightly around the arm of her chair. Her knuckles whitened with the tension of her grip. She knew from experience of late, not to ask her if she was okay, for it would only bring a tirade of expletives and reassurance that she was 'bloody well fine' and 'stop bloody asking'.

Instead, Kate focused on her second highlight of the day – the call she'd taken from Marcus, who'd asked her if she'd like to join him at an art exhibition that was taking place early that evening. As she relayed the news, she saw the raised eyebrows and exchange of suspicious glances between the women.

'That sounds lovely, darling,' Lillian said, patting Kate's shoulder. 'You make sure you have fun with this new chap of yours. He sounds ever so keen.'

'Yes, you go and enjoy yourself, love. Who knows, you might even get a few ideas out of it for your next canvas,' Vivian said cheerfully, her pain seeming to have vanished.

Rather than correct Lillian once again on Marcus not being her 'new chap', Kate instead made sure that both women were well equipped for the remainder of the afternoon and said her goodbyes.

It was only when she was finally ready to leave and had collected her belongings from her staff locker – and Sam from Alan's care – that she allowed herself to consider her developing friendship with Marcus.

If she hadn't known better, she could almost have begun to think that there might be more than just a friendship connection going on. The idea alone was enough to make her feel revitalised.

She picked up her pace – a spring in her step. Things were looking up.

'Do you want to grab some dinner? Maybe a pizza? Or are you heading straight off?' Marcus zipped up his jacket and blew into his cold hands, waiting for Kate to pass him his car keys.

'Yes, sure, good suggestion. Saves me cooking yet another meal-for-one.' Her melancholy smile was fleeting as she brushed away the thick strands of hair blowing into her face. 'Wow, where's this wind appeared from? It's supposed to be June.'

'I know, it's a flipping joke.' Pulling up his sports-jacket collar to brace himself from the chill, Marcus walked briskly across the exhibition car park. 'Let's go in my car. Silly taking two cars for a three-minute journey.'

Almost jogging to keep up, Kate followed until they reached his car. She climbed into the passenger seat, grateful for the warmth that greeted her as she closed the door. 'Great exhibition, but I still can't believe how expensive some of those paintings were.'

Marcus grabbed his seatbelt and clicked it into place. 'Yes, a bit steep, some of those prices. Mind you, if that guy can sell his pieces at that much, then you'll have no problem charging even more.' He laughed lightly at her roll of the eyes and started the car engine. 'You need to start believing in yourself a bit more. You're talented. So own it!'

Brushing off his enthusiasm with a light giggle, Kate continued staring out of the windscreen ahead, trying to keep her lips pursed slightly to hide the broad smile that wanted to spread across her face. Marcus's words had given her a warm rush inside. He really seemed to believe in her.

Lost in her quiet thoughts, his voice broke the silence as they approached the restaurant. 'I'm starving now. I might have to order some wings and garlic bread, too. I might even have a beer or two. As long as you've not got to rush off quickly.'

'That's fine for me, but I thought you were going to meet friends after for that media event?' Kate asked, wondering why he'd changed his mind.

'Supposed to be, but not sure I'm in the mood now.' He brought the car to standstill outside the pizzeria. 'I've had a really nice evening so far with you, so let's just take our time here.' Turning off the engine, he unclicked his seatbelt and patted the top of her leg. 'Come on then, shift yourself, hun. We're here.'

Not able to help herself from reading into his words and body language, she felt a small rush of excitement sparking inside her. He was changing his plans to be with friends because he'd enjoyed his time with her so much? And he'd just called her 'hun'. He'd never used that word before with her. She felt herself blushing slightly.

Walking beside him towards the restaurant she couldn't stop her thoughts from going into overdrive.

Chapter 14

'Penthouse?' Kate repeated, irked. 'Talk about making the most of something.' Frowning, she stopped stirring the Bolognese that she was preparing on the hob. 'And,' she said, as an afterthought, pointing the wooden spoon dripping with red sauce in Megan's direction. 'It also shows that deep down he must have always wanted the bachelor life.'

'That's a little unfair, Kate,' Megan said, breaking up another Parmesan breadstick and popping a piece into her mouth. 'I'm no fan of Alf's, but I agree with his logic.' She crunched loudly as she spoke. 'Surely if you were a single man with a generous housing budget, you'd also choose the most modern, high-spec, airy apartment you could find?'

'I wouldn't, as a matter of fact,' Kate replied tightly, feeling a tiny bit sick at hearing Megan say 'Alf' and 'single' in the same sentence. She tried to blot it out, picking up the red wine and adding a generous amount to the pot. It didn't help. 'So, what's going on with Michael, then?' she asked, desperate to change the subject before her appetite vanished along with her social skills. 'Any more references to you being the type of woman he'd like to marry?'

Megan giggled and picked up a Kalamata olive from the small bowl on the work surface in front of her. 'We had such a good time on Thursday evening at his work drinks – his colleague, Drew, is a nice guy. I thought of you, actually.'

Kate wrinkled her nose. 'No thanks, I'm not up for match-making at the moment.'

Megan rolled her eyes and chewed on the olive thoughtfully. 'And he wanted to do something tonight, but I obviously told him I was coming here. So we're spending tomorrow together. He's suggested a drive out to the countryside – he's quite the romantic when he wants to be.'

'Well, he's clearly smitten, then, if he's wanting to spend so much time with you,' Kate said, opening a packet of dried pasta. 'You've been seeing an awful lot of each other lately.' She took a handful of the spaghetti and placed it in a pan of water. 'I know you, Megan, and you wouldn't be wasting this much time with a man if you weren't interested.' She turned to face her. 'You're falling for him, aren't you?'

The question stumped Megan, who stopped chewing her second olive and in a rare display of embarrassment, started to blush. 'No,' she began, hesitating and uncertain. 'I feel good around him and, yes, I do enjoy being with him. But I wouldn't say I'm in love.' She looked down at her glass of water. 'He's perfect in a lot of ways, but in others, he isn't. He's not at all how I expected the guy I'd fall for to be. That's what I'm struggling with. I just don't know if it feels right...'

Noticing her confused expression, Kate came over to sit with her. 'Hun, more often than not we end up falling for the man who is as far removed from our ideal as possible.' She stared at the kitchen fridge, her eyes drawn to a magnet that Alf had won in a packet of crisps at least five years ago. The memory made her smile. 'I mean, look at me with Alf! Who'd have thought that I would have fallen in love with someone like him!'

Megan smiled and nodded her head in agreement. 'Yes, I have to say it was a bit of a shock to all of us.'

'Exactly,' Kate replied earnestly. 'He was everything I'd always said I didn't want. An office worker, dark-haired, not particularly well travelled…' She stared wistfully at the fridge. 'The list was endless. Yet, I couldn't have fallen any deeper for him – and despite the fact that we obviously weren't meant to be together forever, I still wouldn't change anything about the last seven years.' She looked back at Megan, who was watching her with interest. 'I guess what I'm trying to say is, you can't fight love – love always wins.' She returned to the pasta pot, which was dangerously close to boiling over. 'So go with the flow and enjoy what's developing with Michael, because you might just surprise yourself.'

'I know you're right. And I know I'm maybe reading into everything too much, but I've picked up from a few things that he's said, that he's got this traditional idea about married life.' She collected the used napkins and tea cups from the dining table and walked across to the sink.

Draining the pasta, Kate turned her head sideways at Megan. 'How do you mean?'

'Well, the other week he made a comment that it'd be his dream to one day live in a countryside manor. He also said he's got this future vision of himself wearing a wax jacket and wellies and standing in acres of woodland, clay-pigeon shooting – with his large brood of kids.'

Kate snorted with laughter, almost dropping the colander. 'Okay, whilst that idea would work quite nicely for a large percentage of women, I can see why it would bother you.' She scooped a generous amount of spaghetti and sauce onto each plate. 'I really can't see you in a country manor and I certainly can't see you with a brood of kids. One or two, yes, but more…' She smiled to herself. 'No, I definitely don't see it.'

'I know,' Megan replied, laughing. 'I'd pull my hair out if I was expected to become a country girl in a remote village and stay at home baking stews and bread all day. Not to mention having loads of children running about.'

'Did you tell him this?'

'Well, no, of course not – I mean it wasn't like he was directly asking my opinion. But I did drop the hint that country living isn't something I could see myself doing.'

The women both seated themselves at the small table with their plates. 'Oh, I forgot the wine.' Kate said, standing back up and walking to the fridge. 'What did Michael say to that, then?'

Megan sniffed the heady aroma of the Bolognese wafting up at her, grateful for Kate's skill in producing the dish. 'He asked if I was familiar with the countryside – to which I obviously said not really. And then he stated that it was absurd to judge, if I hadn't experienced it.'

Setting down a chilled bottle of white wine on the table, Kate reached for the two wine glasses. 'I'm out of red, so white it is.' She unscrewed the cap and poured. 'And, yes, he's got a point. However, because I've known you for longer – with all the encouragement in the world, I still don't think you'd ever be able to morph into a country bumpkin.'

Megan picked up her glass. 'And I agree. Which is why, although tomorrow's drive to Essex will be a welcome change, he's certainly not going to sway me longer-term. Anyway, I want to do a little toast.' She waited for Kate to hold up her wine glass before continuing. 'Cheers to you – and this beautiful meal you've prepared – and here's to both of us embarking on new love ventures.'

They lightly clinked glasses and each took a sip.

'Now, tell me,' Megan said, replacing her wine glass and picking up her spoon and fork. 'What's going on with you and Marcus?'

It was a moment before Kate set down her own glass, staring blankly at the meal in front of her. She knew that Megan was fully aware of how involved Marcus had become in his campaign to keep her distracted with fun things to do, but she also knew that Megan wasn't aware of how seemingly close they were becoming. Yet, that was part of the problem plaguing her. She was certain there was a shift happening in their connection and yet neither she nor Marcus had acknowledged it vocally.

'We've met up quite a bit this week. Remember that art exhibition that I told you about on Wednesday? The one he took me to?' Megan nodded her head. 'Well, yesterday he spoke with the owner of the building where it was held – he's a colleague of his – and the guy has agreed with Marcus to rent me the space to exhibit at a really low price.'

'Oh, my goodness, Kate, that's fantastic,' Megan said in surprise. 'Are you going to go ahead with it?' She looked at Kate's reluctant face. 'Kate, this is a huge step to get yourself back into the work that you love. You have to do it.'

'I know.' She played with a piece of pasta on her plate, her appetite vanishing at the prospect of exhibiting. 'And it's good of Marcus to put in a word for me. But honestly Megan, I don't think I can. It's one thing hanging art at the care home, but to put my paintings out there in public after all these years – I'm just not sure.'

'But your art is amazing and unique. I don't know anyone who's seen it and hasn't loved it,' Megan gushed enthusiastically. 'Besides, now that things have changed maybe you need to think more about your future. This could be the start of an extra income.'

Kate stiffened. 'What do you mean – my future?' She stared at Megan in annoyance.

'Look, don't take this the wrong way. I'm only saying it because I care about you.' Yet, seeing the look on Kate's face she realised that she'd already taken offence. 'I just feel it's about time you consider your economic situation properly. This house, for example, you're not able to live here alone on your salary and even renting a small apartment doesn't come cheap these days. Maybe you need to think a bit more carefully about your finances. It's not easy being the single and the only breadwinner, Kate. And I should know – why do you think I worked so hard to get my job?'

Kate sighed, defeated. She knew that Megan was right, but it was a daunting issue that she'd been pushing to the back of her mind, ever since Alf had moved out and they'd agreed to discuss the house at a later date. Her wages weren't bad – there was always double pay on bank holidays and overnight shifts, but they certainly wouldn't be enough to continue single-handedly with the mortgage. Alf had hinted at this, too, and although they had a generous amount in joint savings, part of that was now going towards paying the bills until a decision was made.

Noticing Kate's blanched face, Megan immediately felt guilty. 'I'm sorry, I didn't mean to worry you – forget I said anything. Besides, whatever happens, you know you've always got a spare room at my house.'

Kate took a gulp of wine, hoping the anxiety she was feeling would be eased by the chilled liquid. 'I know you wouldn't see me on the streets and you are correct in everything you've said.' She looked gratefully at Megan – the one person she could always rely on for the truth. 'So, yes, I do need to have a sit down and work out my finances. I guess that can be another job on my list for next week.'

'Good. And you must say yes to Marcus about the exhibit. It's too good an opportunity to pass up.'

'I will.'

Kate smiled and nodded, hoping that her face didn't betray her real feelings – for her life was getting more complicated with each passing moment. She wasn't sure whether that was a good thing or not.

'I've advised Walter you'll be supplying the canvases next week that you feel are most in keeping with the décor here' Alan said, stroking Sam's head gently.

Kate watched as Sam obediently and peacefully lay still across his new daytime master's lap; a seemingly different dog to the highly strung one that she collected every day after her shift. She wondered how Alan had achieved such a miracle.

'Thank you again, Alan.' She reached out and patted his hand affectionately. 'I've already got a few ideas in mind.' She circled her foot above the fluffy head of a dandelion at her feet, the air – heavy with humidity – making her feel slightly sweaty in her uniform.

'Beautiful out here, isn't it?' Alan stated, gazing wistfully into the distance at the large, ancient oak trees that had originally given the home its name. 'If it wasn't for the tranquillity and the setting, I think I'd have given up long ago. This place has somehow kept me going.'

'I'm sure you don't mean that,' Kate replied gently, looking into the familiar forest on the horizon and pondering how much easier life became with old age and the assistance of a carer.

'Oh, I do, dear girl.' He fiddled with his cane, which was perched precariously against the bench on which they were sitting, careful not to disturb Sam. 'You see, when one no longer has a partner to share life with…' He broke off and turned to her with a nostalgic expression. 'Well, life isn't the same.' He gazed back towards the oak trees. 'Nellie always used to say that the love you give and receive is in proportion to the happiness you experience. Wise words, indeed, Kate. A partner's true love really is the most precious gift and Nellie's was mine.'

Feeling the lump in her throat, Kate turned away, quickly shielding her face with her hair, which hung loosely around her shoulders. She'd woken up feeling pensive and lost, the dream she'd had the previous night featuring a younger Alf still lingering in her thoughts. It was already seven weeks since the split, and although her life had begun to change in ways she'd never have expected, she had moments when she missed him and the ease of the life they'd created – even if it hadn't always been happy. It didn't help that they'd had the bare minimum of communication since he'd left. The last time she'd heard from him had been via a text message to inform her he'd paid an overdue council tax demand. She wished things hadn't been left in such an awkward way.

Marcus's message, that she'd secured an exhibit date at the warehouse over the autumn months, hadn't managed to cheer her much, either. Yet Marcus himself was a different matter. Granted, he wasn't Alf, but that was the refreshing aspect in a lot of ways – it was such a contrast being with someone so carefree. Spending time around him made her feel light, positive and fun. He brought out a side of her that she had forgotten existed, a side that she liked, but she was so confused about the situation. It was perplexing trying to understand his feelings in return. Did he or didn't he want her? All of the signs were there, but she wasn't sure if she was reading them correctly. Then there was the question of whether she really wanted him…

'Are you quite all right, dear?' Alan asked, breaking into Kate's thoughts.

She swallowed back the lump, inwardly chastising herself for not being able to control her emotions. 'I'm fine, Alan.' She looked on as the dandelion head beneath her foot caught against her heel, its small, delicate seeds floating upwards in the wind.

Alan caught her gaze and winked. 'You ought to make a wish,' he said, taking her hand in his and gently squeezing it.

Looking at him curiously for a moment, Kate closed her eyes and wished for the one thing she felt she needed most at that moment – clarity on her situation with Marcus.

'All done.' She grinned, feeling surprisingly better.

'You'll be fine, Kate.' Alan said suddenly, his tone more of a whisper, but serious. 'I know the ending of a relationship is never easy, but sometimes it's necessary in order to reveal a person's true intentions.'

The unexpected shift in the conversation caught Kate by surprise. Her eyes pricked with tears as Alan gazed at her with sorrow in his own.

'I had an experience much the same as you, although both circumstances and times were different back then,' Alan explained, his voice cracking slightly. 'I was in love with this person for many years but never knew where our future was heading and if they really felt the same. I took the decision to end things, and after a short while met Nellie – the true love of my life.' He smiled at the memory of his beloved wife.

'What happened to the other person?' Kate asked, intrigued.

'They didn't seem too bothered at the beginning, but as time passed they realised the gravity of their mistake and tried to rekindle things.' He smiled sadly. 'By that time I was too far involved with Nellie and I knew things could never be the same again with myself and the other person.'

Kate thought of Alf and wondered how she'd feel if she learned that he was dating another woman. The thought sickened her to the depths of her stomach.

'Did the other person settle down?'

'Yes, eventually they met someone, but never married. They were happy enough – happier than I know they'd been when with me. It just took them a longer time to realise that.' He lowered his eyes and gently rubbed Sam's ears. 'Therefore, in my experience, dear Kate, if two people are meant to be together they'll find their way back to one another, regardless of circumstances. If not, well – then you'll know you've made the right decision.'

Kate thought quietly about his words before speaking. 'The thing is, Alan, although I miss Alf and I do still love him, I can't honestly say that I wholeheartedly want him back.' Saying the words aloud filled her with a deep sense of peace – she was finally confirming her innermost thoughts with someone. 'Ending things with him hasn't been easy – in fact it's been a battle at times. But I know it was the right thing to do because of certain circumstances and although it's hard at the moment to see a clear future for myself, I feel freer than I have in a long time.'

Alan smiled and nodded his head. 'Well, then, Kate, it seems that you've most definitely made the correct decision.' He tapped his watch. 'And on that note, it's time we headed back inside for afternoon tea.'

Without another word, Kate stood up, watching as Alan fumbled with his cane and gently placed Sam on the grass. For the first time all day, she felt more at ease.

Maybe things weren't as complicated as she was making them out to be.

Chapter 15

'It's Charlie Ward from Henderson's on line two. Do you want to take it?'

Without looking up from the contract in front of him, Alf barked his order. 'Tell him I'm in a meeting at the moment and see if you can arrange a lunch this week with him.'

Hearing Sarah scuttle back to her desk directly outside his office and try, inefficiently, to ascertain dates for the lunch he'd requested, he shook his head in annoyance. It had been a mistake hiring the slim and curvaceous twenty-four-year old. Perhaps he'd been blinded by the flirty nature of her interview and the endless legs that had presented themselves under the barely-there short skirt she'd worn – but he'd assured himself that it was her CV that had been the problem. It was plainly clear, within the five weeks since they'd been operating, that most of the secretarial experience she'd claimed she had was a gross exaggeration. Even Kate would have made a better job of it – and that was saying something, considering her open distaste for anything corporate.

Sarah poked her head around his office doorway. 'Shall I still keep the 27th August free for the meeting in London headquarters?'

'Has Janelle from Clyde's office not confirmed it yet?' Alf asked, irritated.

'Erm.' She looked down at the small ring-bound notebook in her hands. 'I'm not sure. She did call, but I haven't called her back yet.'

Feeling his blood boil, Alf bit down on his tongue to stop himself from swearing at her. 'It's an extremely important meeting.' He spoke in simple terms and as calmly as his anger would allow him. 'Get Janelle on the phone now and get it confirmed. I need to know whether I'm going to London or not. Okay?'

'Fine, I'll see to it.' She sauntered sulkily back to her desk, tottering on heels that were far too high and precarious for carpeted floors. Alf sighed, a long, drawn-out sigh of frustration and disappointment. Getting up, he walked across to his open door and slammed it closed, a little too forcibly – for it shook the grey prefab walls around him.

How had it come to this? Was this the irony of living the dream? He sat back down in his leather, padded swivel chair, the most extravagant purchase he'd made for his office and stared up at the ceiling tiles, his eyes squinting against the halogen tube lighting. It had all been new at the beginning, settling in, making his voice heard amongst his new team, carefully selected by the London head office. Sure, he'd been given a say-so in their hiring – but deep down he'd known his opinion counted for nothing. The hiring process had started long before he'd taken up his position as MD. They weren't a bad team, all twelve displaying strengths in different ways within their roles. Sarah was the only weak link and, considering he'd been solely responsible for choosing his own PA, he couldn't shake off the feeling of it being an omen of things to come. One wrong step…

He still couldn't get his head around his new role. He'd always dreamed that becoming 'boss' would be satisfying and – dare he say it – powerful; but the reality was quite the contrary. He was slowly sinking under the pressure of it all. The constant need to be on top of his team, to be their driving force and to ultimately be held responsible for their performance – it wasn't something he was sure that he was cut out for. Then there was the London meeting that was looming – where he'd be expected to stand before the board and present the first quarter performance figures. And it wasn't as if he had Kate, his rock of support, cheering him on as she always had.

'Oh, Kate.' He tiredly rubbed his face with both hands – seeing her perfect smile in his mind's eye and hoping to rub that away, too. He missed her. He missed waking up to the smell of her vanilla perfume in their bedroom, he missed going home to a lively house, where she'd always welcome him with a cup of tea, even on the days when they'd argued. But mostly he missed being able to hold her and know that she'd always be there by his side.

Except now, she wasn't.

'How did I manage to fuck up so much?' he whispered to himself, letting his arms fall and dangle over the sides of the chair.

A sharp knock at the door disturbed his thoughts and, sitting up sharply, he shuffled the papers in front of him – just in time to look busy as the door swung open.

'Afternoon, Alf,' Clyde said, standing in the doorway in his much-loved Crombie, with a large redwood umbrella tucked under one arm. 'Weather here's worse than London.'

Stumbling for a suitable response due to the shock of the chairman's unexpected visit, Alf stood up hastily from behind his desk and walked around to greet him.

'To what do I owe the pleasure, Clyde?' Alf said, hoping that his grin hadn't turned into a grimace. 'I must say, I wasn't expecting to see you, of all people, last thing on a Friday afternoon.'

Clyde looked at him with a twinkle in his eye and if Alf hadn't known better, he'd have thought the man was humoured by him. As it was, he knew that Clyde's ruthless reputation preceded him. 'I was in the area, thought I'd drop in. See how the office is progressing and how our new MD is delivering.'

Feigning a light laugh, Alf called Sarah into the office – hoping that she'd at least have the etiquette to take the chairman's coat and umbrella and offer him a beverage. Embarrassingly, she failed to take the initiative on all three accounts – resulting in him requesting her to do so. Making a mental note to check her probation period and never again to hire staff based on any aspect of their physical appearance, he glanced nervously at Clyde, who was eyeing Sarah with a lecherous gaze.

'She puts Janelle to shame,' Clyde said approvingly, as soon as she was out of earshot. 'I know what I'd like to do with those legs, given half a chance. You dirty dog – hiring one like that with a wife at home.' He winked and patted Alf on the shoulder with a chuckle.

Feeling his heart sink to new depths at the mention of the word 'wife', Alf smiled unconvincingly.

'So, what do you say to heading off for a drink after you've run the latest figures past me?' Clyde demanded, his presence now ominous. He took a seat on the client sofa by the window.

Panicking at the request, Alf tried to calm his racing pulse. He wasn't prepared in the slightest to begin sharing figures with Clyde – he'd barely got his head around the spreadsheet that he'd asked Sarah to begin preparing. Furthermore, an after-work drink? He couldn't imagine anything worse.

Seeing the flush of crimson spreading across Alf's face, Clyde narrowed his eyes, realising his new MD's predicament. 'Unless, of course, you've already got commitments with the wife and need to phone home for the green card?' he piped up.

Like a rug being pulled from under his feet, Alf realised it could get a whole lot worse.

With that last comment – it already had.

Megan giggled as Michael rested one hand along her bare waist, the other twirling her hair as they laid head to head against the mountain of pillows on his bed.

'You didn't honestly say that to him, did you?' she asked, incredulous. 'You're lucky he didn't hit you!'

Michael laughed. 'Yes I did – and he's a big bloke, but he took it quite well. Although there was a brief moment where I feared for the bridge of my nose.'

'I'm not surprised! You're the only person I know who could call a heavy-weight champion boxer a pansy and get away with it.' She snuggled in closer to him, feeling his slim but toned arms slip around her, totally encasing her. 'Mmm, I like that.'

He kissed the tip of her ear. 'It's all part of the Michael Healy charm.'

She shivered, noticing the change of tone in his now-husky voice. 'Don't start. We need to get out of bed soon. We can't stay here all afternoon.' Not able to resist him, she moved her mouth closer to his.

He laughed, rolling away from her gently and swinging his legs off the bed, standing up naked – not caring that his floor-to-ceiling windows provided a direct view to those in the apartment block opposite.

'Oi, where are you going? You can't do that! That's mean – come back.'

He smiled, taking in every inch of Megan's bare body spread provocatively across his bed. 'I have something for you. I just need to get it.' He bent down searching through the discarded clothes on his floor.

'Everything I want is right there, fixed to you.'

'Well, I have something even better.'

She sighed, pulling a face like a spoilt child. 'Fine, go get whatever it is. It better not be a giant dildo. I don't do plastic.'

Grinning, Michael continued searching through his clothes. 'And there was me thinking you were an up-for-anything girl.' He smiled suddenly. 'Okay, here it is. Something you'll no doubt dislike, but still…'

Megan noticed the sparkle of excitement spreading across his face and peered from the pillow curiously. 'What is it, then?'

'Just you wait and see.'

'At least let me cook you a nice meal one evening, as a thank you,'

Kate enthused, running her hand over the limited edition, signed and dedicated autobiography that Marcus had presented her with.

Rubbing the back of his neck awkwardly, Marcus was quick to answer. 'Like I told you, it wasn't that big a deal. All part of the perks of interviewing celebrity chefs,' he joked, glancing at the cover sleeve of the hardback copy in distaste.

It had been hard to believe that the young chef who had wooed the nation with his idealistic outlook on super-healthy cuisine, was in reality an egotistical chauvinist. Still, the brief from the magazine's commissioning editor had been to portray the celebrity in a positive light – something he'd managed to do, albeit grudgingly. The only upside had been remembering Kate's love of the man and asking for the signed copy. It was a small compensation for a draining afternoon's work.

Kate carefully placed the book into her large bag and picked up her glass of cranberry juice from the sticky bar mat.

'Are you sure you don't fancy a proper drink?' Marcus asked, taking a swig of the bottled fruit cider he'd opted for.

'No, I'm okay thanks.' She shook her head slightly, pausing as she caught sight of her reflection in the mirrored bar décor. The transformation was hard to miss – those were actually high cheekbones staring back at her. It gave her a small flutter of confidence – in some measure the split was, indeed, benefiting her. She'd also noticed more men glancing at her appreciatively of late and her old dresses were starting to fit again. 'I'm saving the alcohol for later. I'm going for a drink with my friend JoJo. We might end up painting the town red.' She noticed Marcus's eyes widen with surprise; her body dared itself to lean in closer.

'Off out to party? You're getting to be quite the girl about the town, now, aren't you?' he joked, pulling away, ruffling his hair as he did so and taking a gulp of his cider.

Filled with disappointment, she straightened herself on the bar stool, hoping that she hadn't made him feel uncomfortable. There's definitely a chemistry, she silently repeated to herself, but it was natural that Marcus would want to hold back – he was Alf's friend. She was certain that he was probably fighting his feelings as much as she was. It wasn't a straightforward situation.

She'd spent the last few days mulling over every detail of their contact since the split, analysing every conversation and action, and coming to the conclusion that there had to be more to it than friendship. Even today's gesture of going out of his way to obtain her a memento from her favourite chef was proof of it. Alf had never done anything like that in all their years together.

Just as she was about to ask Marcus on the developments with his book, her mobile vibrated on the bar top – Megan's name flashed up. She picked up the phone and showed the screen to Marcus. 'Sorry, I need to get this. I told Megan I'd let her know the details for meeting JoJo later.'

He nodded vigorously. 'Of course, go ahead.'

Pressing the answer key, she barely had a chance to say 'hello' before Megan's voice boomed loudly into her ear. 'Kate! Guess what...' Wincing, she tipped the phone away from her ear and grinned at Marcus, who could clearly hear every word.

'Michael's only gone and asked me to marry him!'

Shocked into silence, Kate stared numbly ahead at the neatly stacked rows of spirits on the mirrored shelves, failing to notice the look of surprise on Marcus's face or her friend's voice still chattering from the handset. She was only aware of the sound of her quickened heart beating in her ears. Michael had proposed to Megan? She felt physically sick all of a sudden.

'And he said he knows it's really soon and of course that I'm probably going to say no... but I was...' The line went silent. 'Kate, are you still there?'

'Marry him?' Kate felt the bile rising in her throat and let out a strangled sound.

Marcus gently reached up and removed the mobile from Kate's white-knuckled grip. Her face was completely pale and her eyes stunned, like a rabbit caught in headlights. He saw her bottom lip beginning to tremble and before she had a chance to let out the flurry of tears that he could see building, he lifted the mobile to his mouth.

'Hey Megan, it's Marcus. I'll have to get Kate to call you back.' He glanced worriedly towards the still-silent and unmoving woman next to him.

'Marcus? Hi, what's going on? Is Kate okay?'

Hearing concern in Megan's response, Marcus was quick to reassure her. 'Yes, don't worry, everything's fine. Sorry, got to go. She'll explain later. Bye.' He hung up the call, feeling ever so slightly guilty for the rushed words; but sensing that Kate was about to have a meltdown, drained the last of his cider and gently encouraged her off the bar stool and the short distance towards the car park and his car. He felt her arms trembling as he unlocked his car.

'Five minutes.' The first of the tears began to fall from her eyes. 'She's only known him five minutes!'

Relieved that he was finally getting a reaction out of her, he steered her into the passenger seat. 'Sit there for a bit. I can see you've gone a bit pale.' Kate looked up at him – her expression doleful and sad. There was a childlike quality and vulnerability that made his heart skip a beat. He couldn't bear to watch any woman cry – it brought back too many memories of Linzie. 'I heard what Megan said.'

Rubbing her eyes with the sleeve of her jumper, Kate sobbed uncontrollably, grateful that she had the privacy of the car to shield her from prying eyes. 'I'm sorry,' she muttered at Marcus, through hiccups. 'You must think I'm such an awful friend reacting to Megan's news like this.' She wiped her wet nose with the back of her sleeve. 'It's just knocked me for six.'

'It's okay, I understand.' He fiddled in his jeans pocket, pulling out a crumpled tissue and handing it to her. 'Don't worry, it's clean.'

She took the tissue, not caring that it had fibres of fluff stuck to it and blew her nose loudly. 'Oh, God, what must Megan think?' Taking a deep breath to calm her tears, she used the tissue to wipe what she knew would be streaky mascara from her cheeks. 'What kind of a friend am I, going quiet on her like that and not being excited for her?' Crestfallen, she leaned her head back against the headrest and closed her eyes.

Marcus, who had perched himself on the small brick wall that surrounded the car park, looked past the open passenger door at Kate. 'I'm sure she'll understand. It's the shock, that's all.'

Springing forwards suddenly from the car seat, she fumbled with her bag, which he'd placed in the foot well. 'Where's my phone? I need to call her.' Her face flushed, she began to erratically and frantically search through the contents of the large bag before finally tipping it, in its entirety, into her lap. She couldn't have Megan thinking that she wasn't happy for her.

'Kate, stop.' Without hesitation Marcus bent down and grabbed her arm. 'Enough. You need to calm down first.' He reached into his pocket. 'Your phone is here.' Showing her the white handset, he offered it to her. 'But I don't think it's the right time to be talking about proposals – do you?'

She lowered her head in embarrassment. 'I don't know what happened. I just heard her say that he'd asked her to marry him. I don't know what came over me.' She sobbed once again, noticing tiny pieces of white cotton from the tissue covering her dark jumper.

He rubbed her arm. 'Shh, it's okay. You're bound to be upset and, to be honest, Kate, I was beginning to think you were never going to crack. It's been a long time coming.'

'What do you mean?' She sniffled, screwing the wet tissue into a ball in her palm and looking at him expectantly.

'Well, considering the situation between you and Alf...' He hesitated, unsure if it was wise to open wounds further. 'I thought you were coping remarkably well. Perhaps a little too well at times – I had a suspicion you were bottling it up.' He squeezed her hand. 'It's good to let it out, Kate.'

He was right – she had been holding on to things of late and from nowhere they had erupted to the surface at the sound of Megan's words. Yet Marcus was mistaken; it wasn't just Alf that she was crying for, it wasn't Alf's lack of proposal that she was crying over and it wasn't what she'd lost that she was grieving. It was more than that. Much more than that.

Marcus looked at her softly and she smiled at the intimacy of the moment, searching his face as his kind eyes bore into hers with both sympathy and understanding.

In a moment of absolute clarity and without hesitation, she leaned forwards, tilted her head and kissed him – catching him totally off-guard.

She had been waiting so long to do it and in a blink of an eye her wish had finally been granted.

'What are you doing?' Marcus jumped back from Kate in surprise, gently pushing her away. 'Kate, have you lost your mind?' His eyes widened in shock. 'I'm Alf's friend.'

Kate felt the blood drain from her face, the expression of horror written across Marcus's features making her feel winded with humiliation. She stumbled for something to say, her mind going blank and her only wish being for the ground beneath her to open and swallow her whole. 'I thought that… I…' She couldn't talk. An overwhelming nausea took hold of her.

Stumped for words, Marcus blew out a long sigh, his mouth making an 'O' shape. 'Wow, this is really awkward.'

Kate could feel the pounding of her heart in her chest so aggressively that it took her breath away. Eyes lowered – for she couldn't even bear to glance at Marcus – she switched to auto-pilot and began shoving the possessions littered in her lap hastily back into her bag. She had to go, she had to get away. Her body began to prickle with heat, the realisation of her actions hitting her with full force.

'Hun, listen…' Marcus stepped forwards, his expression softening. He reached out for her arm.

Shaking him off, she picked up her bag and grabbed her mobile,

scrambling from the car as fast as her legs would allow....
What on earth had she just done?

Chapter 16

Kate wasn't sure how long she'd been walking through the park, but the sun had long since faded and aside from the gentle breeze of the early evening wind, she was alone.

Avoiding the well-worn footpath, she'd opted for a more remote route through the edge of the forest. She knew she looked an absolute fright with her puffy eyes and tear-stained face scrubbed free of make-up, but she didn't care. The cool air felt good against her skin and had helped, in a small way, to wash away her frantic thoughts. She paused, hearing a grunting sound up ahead, at the same time stepping on an uneven rock and cursing the thin-soled pumps she was wearing for allowing her to feel every harsh texture.

She frowned, as the moan, belonging to a huskily voiced woman, was halted by a softly spoken man chiding her, his voice carrying an Irish lilt. Hesitating, Kate stopped and considered her options. It was obvious that the couple were potentially enjoying a secluded moment together – not expecting anyone to be passing through this part of the forest. Looking behind her, she saw how dark the route through the trees had become and knowing that the night was fast approaching she couldn't risk backtracking on herself. The only way back onto the public footpath and closer to home would be heading directly towards the sound of voices. The couple were now giggling and whispering in low murmurs.

'Oh, what am I worried about? Who gives a damn?' she chastised herself under her breath. She had more important matters on her mind than the embarrassment of disturbing a couple at it. She pressed on, deliberately treading heavily into the ground, hoping that the crunching of leaves and twigs would be enough to alert them.

As the trees opened into the clearing, she saw the couple ahead, sitting together on the hand-carved wooden bench that few knew about. She let out a sigh of relief at the sight of them fully clothed. Trying to quicken her pace, she kept her distance as much as possible, keeping her head down, suddenly conscious of her blood-shot eyes and blotchy face. Hurrying past them, without looking up, she failed to notice both of them turn to stare at her. She also failed to see the foot-deep burrow that had been covered over with twigs and rockery. In her haste to exit the clearing as quickly as her legs would carry her, she didn't realise that her flimsy pump had lodged at an awkward angle into the rabbit burrow – until it was rather too late. Before she knew what was happening, a sharp pain seared through her ankle and she found herself face down on the rough ground.

'Crikey, are you okay?' a voice called out to her. The crunching sound of leaves was enough to cause her to try and scramble back onto her feet, despite the stinging sensation in her cheek and hands. She made it as far as sitting up by the time the woman and man appeared in front of her.

'Here, let me give you a hand.' A tall man with ginger hair reached out his hand to her and gratefully accepting it, she hoisted herself up, trying to ignore the throbbing in her ankle and the fact that the man was rearranging his unbuttoned shirt in embarrassment. 'You took quite a tumble there.'

Mortified, Kate tried a feeble smile as she glanced from the pretty brunette, who was looking at her with a face full of concern, back to the man, who was reaching down to retrieve her mobile from the dirt. 'Thanks, I'm fine. I guess I wasn't paying enough attention to where I was stepping. Sorry to disturb you.' She reached out and took her mobile from his extended hand and couldn't help thinking that both of them looked vaguely familiar.

'As long as you're okay?' the woman repeated, her arm snaking itself around the man's waist. She watched as the man reciprocated, putting his arm around the woman's shoulder, and she felt all the more awkward for intruding.

'I'm fine. Thanks.' She dusted down her trousers, aware of the heavy dirt stains but pretending it wasn't an issue. 'Anyway.' She gestured ahead self-consciously as the couple watched her, both with a clear expression of pity. 'Best get going. Getting dark.' She started to walk away, trying not to wince with each step. 'Thanks again.'

'Go carefully.' The man called out with a smile, before turning back and kissing the top of the woman's head.

The small and loving gesture made her instinctively think of Alf and she suddenly remembered where she recognised the couple from – Swoonies. The very same loved-up couple who had also made her think of what she'd been missing out on over the last seven years. Swallowing the lump that appeared in her throat, she put it down to a culmination of the day's events.

A full five minutes later she finally felt she'd gained enough distance from the couple to let the first words of pain escape from her lips. 'Ouch' she whimpered, hobbling slowly, yet relieved that the park's green metal exit railings were in sight in the distance. She would have cried, but for the emptiness behind her eyes – for she felt that she'd already drained herself of every tear possible.

Her mobile vibrated in her pocket. Stopping, she pulled it out and glanced at the screen. Megan again. Rejecting the call, she returned the mobile to her pocket, wanting more than ever to be home and in her bed, hidden from the world and left alone with her thoughts. She couldn't make sense of anything.

It was all too confusing.

'Finally,' Megan exclaimed, throwing her arms around the worse-for-wear-looking Kate who stood on her doorstep. 'I was beginning to think I should send out a search party. Do you know how worried I've been?'

Kate pulled her old and comfortable cable-knit cardigan tightly around her, feeling sheepish. 'I'm sorry. I didn't mean to avoid your calls. So much happened today Meg…'

'Well, don't just stand there. Come in – I'll make us a cup of tea.' She let Kate past her and followed her into the kitchen. 'You look bloody awful, by the way.'

Looking down at her blue-and-white floral pyjama bottoms, partially covered by the grey cardigan, Kate shrugged. 'You should have seen me earlier if you think this is bad.' She took a seat in her usual spot at the centre island. 'Firstly, before anything else – I want to apologise.'

Megan filled the kettle. 'What the hell's happened? You've obviously been crying – your face looks a mess and what are you apologising for, you daft cow?'

'Well, for starters I'm apologising for going quiet on you when you told me the potentially biggest news of your life earlier.'

Megan chuckled, replacing the kettle back onto its base. 'Seriously, Kate, you're killing me here. You know I like Michael a lot, but it's hardly as if I've said yes. It was more of a joke than anything.' Picking up the tea towel she patted her hands dry and took a seat opposite Kate at the island. 'Anyway, more of that later. What's gone on with you? Did you drive here in your pyjamas?'

Kate looked at her in confusion. 'So, you're not going to say "yes" to him?' She held her breath, waiting for the answer.

'Well, not at the moment, that's for sure.' Megan narrowed her eyes, sensing her friend's sudden alarm. 'Oh, God! This isn't all about me and Michael, is it?'

Unable to look her directly in the eyes, Kate stared at the counter top and fiddled with a tissue she'd tucked into her sleeve. Megan felt her smile vanish, her happy feelings plummeting to be replaced with guilt, as the realisation sank in. 'Oh, Kate… surely you didn't think? God, I'm so sorry. I didn't think…' She slapped her hand against her forehead at her thoughtlessness. 'I'm so stupid. I just assumed you'd know I found the whole thing highly amusing. It wasn't real.' She bit down on her bottom lip, hoping she'd not made things worse. 'Well, it was real, but what I mean is, it wasn't…'

'I know what you mean, Megan.' Kate smiled sadly. 'You don't have to say sorry, you didn't do anything wrong.' She blew out a long sigh. 'It's me, you see…'

'You're upset because it brought back the situation with you and Alf?'

Taking a deep breath, she took her time to answer. 'Partly. When you told me, I felt blank. Sort of numb and overwhelmed. I was shocked, I guess; not in a bad way – I want you to be happy and nothing would please me more than you getting engaged – but I think it unexpectedly brought up a lot of issues I've been squashing. It caught me off-guard.'

'Why didn't you mention that you've been struggling? You know I'm here for you, hun.' Seeing that Kate was feeling teary, Megan went over and pulled her into a hug. 'You're allowed to fall apart sometimes, you know.'

Kate nodded into her shoulder, feeling reassured. 'I know. I think I've just been trying to hold it together too much and probably focusing my attention on the wrong things.'

Pulling away, Megan noticed Kate was about to say something and then seemed to think better of it, closing her mouth again. She sensed there was something she was holding back on. 'So, what happened today then? Where've you been all this time?' She walked across to the kettle, allowing Kate the space to feel at ease. 'JoJo told me you'd texted and cancelled. But neither of us knew where you'd got to instead.'

'Walking in the park. I needed to clear my head.'

'Oh, I see.' Taking two cups from the rack, Megan dropped a teabag into each one. 'You saw Marcus earlier, too, no?'

Kate avoided looking up, simply nodding her head in confirmation. Megan caught the shift in her body language.

'It's only because I tried calling him when you didn't answer earlier. I thought you might still be with him. I got his number from Lee. He didn't answer, though.'

Kate sighed. 'Well, like I said, I was walking – so I wasn't with him.' Her tone was defensive.

Deciding to change the subject until Kate was ready to raise the issue, Megan changed her tactic. 'How is he, anyway? How's the book going?' She stirred a generous amount of sugar into her tea.

'Can we please not talk about Marcus?' Kate snapped, her voice shaky and cracking.

Megan turned around just in time to see Kate sinking her head into her arms on the counter top. She set the milk she'd just picked up back down and stood in front of her. 'Right, what's going on? Has he said or done something bad?'

Sighing, Kate slowly raised her head, her eyes watery and avoiding Megan's questioning stare. 'I feel so humiliated, Meg.' She felt her bottom lip trembling. 'I don't know what I was thinking.'

'Why – what's happened? What did you do?' Looking at her with a wide-eyed stare, Megan instantly knew the answer even before she had asked – for the embarrassment was written all over her friend's face.

'I kissed him.' Kate scrunched up her face, feeling nauseous at the recollection. 'One moment we were chatting and he was being nice, the next I was leaning in to kiss him.' She finally looked up to meet Megan's eyes. 'He pushed me away, Meg.'

'Bastard.' Annoyed, Megan walked back towards the half-brewed tea, picking up the milk in anger and slopping it into the cups. 'He knows you're vulnerable. I warned him that he was giving you the wrong vibe – I knew this was going to happen. I knew it.' She stirred the tea vigorously, unsettled at her friend's revelation.

'What do you mean you warned him?'

Setting down the two cups on the island, Megan took her seat in front of Kate, dreading the conversation they were about to have. 'Look, don't be mad at me.' She glanced sheepishly at Kate. 'I sensed that you had this secret thing going on for Marcus, but in all honesty I didn't think you'd act on it. Obviously it's a rebound reaction because of Alf – and I get that. But Marcus should have understood that too. Which is why I tried to warn him that night we went for the Chinese.'

Incensed, Kate threw up her hands. 'Oh my goodness, stop right there. I can't believe you said this to him. What were y…?'

'Hang on, I wasn't finished.' Megan cut in sharply. 'Of course I didn't say that to him. I just told him that I think it's good you had him as a friend and steered the conversation to guys being careful of giving off the wrong signals, because as women we are likely to misinterpret things – especially after a breakup.'

'God, this just gets worse and worse.' Kate stared into her cup of tea, waiting for Megan to finish digging herself a hole. 'Why didn't you say this to me, instead of him?'

Megan hesitated, unsure how to explain. 'You just seemed so happy, although I knew it wasn't all as hunky dory, as you believed it was. I didn't want to burst your bubble and, in fairness, I really didn't expect you to be telling me you'd kissed him.' She looked at Kate apologetically. 'I thought it was a slight crush that was giving you the confidence boost you needed. Plus he was helping you with your art and stuff. I just assumed the bubble would burst of its own accord, very soon. Although certainly not in the way it has.'

Kate sighed resignedly and took a small sip of tea, feeling better as the sweet, sugary taste washed away the bitter tears in her throat. 'He was so shocked when I kissed him. You should have seen his face, Meg. If I wasn't so humiliated and wanting to cry, then I'd laugh about it.'

'How did you leave things, then?' Megan asked cautiously, silently deciding that she'd cut Marcus's balls off if he'd in any way made Kate feel even worse.

'I ran off. That's why I went to the park. He tried to follow me, but I told him to leave me alone. I refused to answer his calls as well. He's left me two messages and sent me a text that he was sorry if I'd felt he'd led me on – that wasn't his intention. His messages explained that he loved me as a person, as a friend, but that's all. He just thought he could help me, given that he's recently been through a breakup himself.' She shook her head with a small, sad smile. 'You know, all the usual crap that's supposed to make you feel better about them not wanting you in return.'

Softening, Megan felt her earlier anger vanishing and a new respect for Marcus replacing it. 'Ah, hun, don't feel bad. From his message, it sounds as if he really didn't set out to hurt you.' She tried to choose her words carefully, sensing how delicate Kate was feeling. 'Maybe look at the experience as a positive thing. At least now you know where you stand and it doesn't mean you and him can't still be friends. ' She looked at Kate hopefully. 'I mean, it's not as if he's been awkward about it – he clearly appreciates the friendship.'

'I don't know, Megan,' Kate began, feeling weary and exhausted. 'I know it's mostly my fault – I guess I did read much more into things than I should have, but right now I just feel a fool.'

'That's natural. I've felt a fool many times when it comes to men.' Megan smiled. 'Hey, do you remember the Greek guy?' Grimacing in recollection, she fiddled with her teacup. 'The one that I really liked, who drove the Porsche 911.'

Kate remembered, nodding her head. 'I can't believe he stood you up, especially right outside that restaurant. Did you ever hear from him again?'

'Nope, never.'

'Asshole.'

'Yep, totally. Which is why you shouldn't let something like this make you feel bad or embarrassed. It happens to the best of us. It's part of dating and part of life. If we didn't get rejected, then we wouldn't know real love when it happens.' Megan took a gulp of her cooled tea. 'Besides, Marcus has been understanding and you've got an excuse. You haven't long been single, so it's a given that you're a bit all over the place.'

Feeling a bit better, Kate smiled. 'I guess so.'

'I know so.' Megan replied, grabbing Kate's cup from in front of her and getting up from her stool. 'Right – I'm assuming you haven't eaten, so how about we get a takeaway and a bottle of wine and see what's on TV?

'Yes, that sounds really good.'

Megan threw a magazine from a nearby pile in Kate's direction. 'Okay. I'm just going to ring Michael. Have a look at the TV guide, check if there's a rom-com or something cheery on.' She grabbed her mobile from her bag on the side. 'Back in a sec.'

Kate watched as Megan left the room and, opening the magazine in front of her, she flicked to the correct listings. Every fibre of her being wanted to ask about Michael's proposal, but she knew it wasn't the right moment. She was aware that Megan had deliberately played down the situation – she could see in her friend's expressions when speaking of Michael just how much he'd made an impact on her – she was clearly in love. Even if she was denying it to herself.

Yet she couldn't help but feel satisfied that things weren't going down that serious road, just yet. It had been hard to face up to her true demons during her walk in the park, but she'd had to be honest with herself. It wasn't that she was jealous, scared or even love-sick for Alf, though, yes, she missed him and now and again wondered if she'd made the wrong decision. But the real reason for her fear was abandonment.

She couldn't hide from the fact that every person she'd loved throughout her life had – in one way or another – left her. First her parents, then her aunt, the baby, even Alf…

Megan was the only one she had left. Selfishly, she wasn't prepared just yet for her to be taken from her too.

Chapter 17

'This is the thing with young men these days, cowards the lot of 'em.' Lil said, shaking her head in disgust. 'And to think he could have had a nice woman like you.' She watched in the bathroom mirror as Kate administered a small amount of antiseptic to her upper back. 'Never you mind, darling. There's someone better out there for you. You just wait and see.'

Kate worked the cream into the bruise on Lillian's back that looked a lot worse than she'd been led to believe. 'This should help, Lil, but I'll get you a visit from the doctor arranged, just in case.'

Lillian shooed her away instantly. 'No, no, I don't need to see the doctor – it was just a little fall, that's all. No harm done.' Repositioning her floral blouse, she buttoned it up. 'An' don't think you can fool me. I know you liked him and I'm sorry for encouraging it. If only I'd known he was such a berk.'

Despite her concern for the ugly mark on her ward's back, Kate chuckled and realised how much better she felt being at work. 'I'm still going to arrange a visit from Dr Sharman. And, yes, I did like Marcus, but I can't blame him for not feeling the same in return, can I?'

Harrumphing, Lillian popped out her false teeth and ran them under the tap. Kate passed her a small hand towel and looked on as she re-affixed the dentures.

'That's better. Had a bit of food stuck under the palate.' She checked her appearance once again in the mirror. 'I'll do. I ain't going to win no beauty contest, mind.' She pinched her cheeks in an attempt to bring a little more colour into her complexion. 'And no, I don't agree about Marcus – he's still a berk in my opinion.'

Kate stifled a smile, knowing that it wasn't worth disagreeing with an opinionated Lillian. 'Are you going down for breakfast? Or are you meeting Viv at hers?'

'Meeting Viv, of course. Can't be doing with that old bunch of moaners in the dining room – anyone would think the lot of 'em were on their last legs.' She picked up her purse from her dressing table. 'Listening to them mope over their porridge is enough to put me in an early grave.' Leading the way, Lillian opened her door and walked into the pale-pink and lemon corridor of the East wing on which her room was located.

'Now, tell me again, what's all this about your friend Megan getting proposed to, then?'

Kate's smiled vanished. She still couldn't believe the story herself.

Alf read the email from Janelle for a third time, allowing the meaning of the words that were dancing in front of his eyes to settle in his mind. 'Shit.' Angered, he swiped his hand across his desk in one brisk motion, sending his leather-bound pen holder and all of its contents flying across the room.

Seething, he picked up the phone and dialled Clyde's office, waiting for Janelle to answer.

'Everything okay?' Sarah asked, slipping her head around his office door and staring nervously at the disarray. 'Shall I get you coffee or something?'

Alf shook his head dismissively and she quickly retreated, closing the door behind her. He growled in frustration as Janelle's voicemail service greeted him. Slamming down the handset, he ran his hands through his hair – or what little there seemed to be left of it.

'A sodding coffee for a situation like this,' he muttered to himself in disbelief. 'As fucking useful as a rubber hammer.' Picking up his suit jacket from the back of his chair, he strode across the office and aggressively swung open the door. Startled, Sarah jumped in her seat, minimising the celebrity gossip webpage she was surfing a fraction too late.

'Good to see you're working hard.'

'I was just...'

'Not interested.' Alf snapped, cutting her off. 'I'm leaving the office for the rest of the afternoon. If anyone asks, I'm in a meeting with Branders and you don't know what time I'm back. If Clyde's office calls, ring me on the mobile immediately.'

'Okay.'

Storming towards the lift, he waited impatiently for the doors to open, all the while his mind trying to process the email. Was Clyde having a laugh?

A small bell sounded and the heavy metal doors glided open in front of him. Stepping inside, he considered his options. Given the situation, it wasn't ideal if he spent the afternoon in The Plough drowning his sorrows in pints of beer – he was bound to be spotted there by one of the team passing at lunchtime. He had little choice but to seek refuge in his apartment.

It was almost an hour later when Alf climbed the cream-carpeted staircase to his penthouse. Stocking up on supplies at the local corner shop had been a wise decision – he still hadn't done a full supermarket shop since moving in. Yet living off takeaways and microwave meals from the limited freezer department of Nisa was beginning to take its toll on both his energy levels and his weight. He missed sitting down to eat at a dining table with Kate, instead preferring to stand in the kitchen and eat at the counter – so as not to remind himself of what he'd lost.

The apartment was dull and damp, despite the brightness and dry air of the late- summer weather outside. Setting down the blue plastic carrier bag on the swanky kitchen countertop, he reached inside, pulling himself out a bottle of beer. He'd never been a heavy drinker, but today was an exception, given the culmination of events over the past week.

He tried not to think about Vicky; he was humiliated enough without reminding himself of her knock-back. It wasn't that he'd even liked her much, but the loneliness was starting to get to him. Her glowing smile and doe eyes had reminded him of Kate, even though her sharp personality was nothing like gentle and kind Kate's. It had been tough enough to drunkenly ask her back to his after a late nightcap together; he certainly hadn't been expecting her to say no.

Walking across to the sofa, he sank onto the cool, unforgivingly hard leather – a mocking symbolism of the apartment itself; all for show and totally impractical. Taking a sip of the bottled beer, he considered the wording of the email. He'd been in the role now for nine weeks and had barely been given a chance to prove himself, so how had the board come to the conclusion that he was failing to meet initial targets? Furthermore, he was incensed to discover that there was a consideration of extending his probation period. Could they even do that? The alternative was plainly spelled out, though – 'a discussion of termination and severance package'. He felt bile rising in his throat.

It had always been a quiet concern with him that the first quarter expectations on the new Scotland start-up were beyond realistic, yet he'd truly believed he could single-handedly steer the business to some level of victory. He hadn't bargained for Clyde and the other members of the board vetoing his every decision, though. It wasn't as if the processes and incentives he'd rolled out to his team were even his ideas – they'd been decided by the board. So, therefore, how was it possible that despite his best efforts he was being held responsible for the failings to date?

It was becoming glaringly obvious that he'd been selected for the role as little more than a scapegoat. As much as he didn't want to consider the possibility, it would seem that he'd been drafted into the position to do the groundwork and now the board was clearing the way for a more suitable candidate. It would also explain why he'd seen Henry Cavendish's name in a circulated confidential document the previous week. Surely it was no coincidence that the man Clyde had originally wanted for the role was no longer considering jumping ship for the competition – as rumour had had it.

Sighing dejectedly, he set down his beer bottle on the glass-top coffee table and tried to calm his anger and nerves. It had cost him everything to come to Scotland – his relationship, his house, his friendships – hell, even his family – notwithstanding the fact that he rarely saw Tony anyway.

The only reason he'd even worked so hard in the first place had been to carve out a better lifestyle for himself and Kate. He'd wanted desperately to prove to her that he could be the solid support that she needed. But now, it was likely he was about to lose every reward for the sacrifice he'd made by choosing Scotland over her.

He felt sick to his stomach. How would he ever explain this to her? What would become of their house if worse came to worst and he couldn't get another job?

How could he have been so stupid? Why hadn't he seen the warning signs? The bile rose again and he gave up fighting it down. He sank his head into his hands and for the first time in weeks, he allowed himself to cry.

'Corsica is beautiful. I spent a weekend there last summer with Jerome and Saskia,' Michael said, cutting into his filet mignon, looking satisfied as a trickle of pale-pink liquid spread across his plate. 'Perfectly cooked. That's why I like it here.'

'I'd prefer somewhere a bit more distant, though. I've always liked the idea of Nepal. Or how about Peru?' Megan suggested, waiting patiently for Michael to finish chewing the large mouthful of steak and glancing sideways as the maître d' seated two robust city gentlemen to the left of their table. It was fun discussing potential honeymoon locations. Not that they were 'officially engaged' – but she'd come around to the idea more since her conversation with Kate. Although she still hadn't actually accepted his proposal, she was playfully going along with the idea that if they got engaged then she'd prefer to elope and have a subsequent culture-rich experience on another continent as their honeymoon.

'I'm not keen on South America or Indonesia, for that matter.' Michael replied finally, taking a sip of his Merlot. 'I'd prefer something a little more refined, anyway.'

'I thought this was supposed to be somewhere we'd both like to go?'

'It is.' He portioned more béarnaise sauce onto the side of his plate. 'And I know how much you'll love Corsica, which is why I'm suggesting it.'

Megan rolled her eyes playfully. 'You've only known me for three months – you can't possibly know that I'll prefer Corsica over my lifelong dream of travelling to Nepal?'

'I know more than you think.' Michael retorted with a smirk. 'Especially that you're partial to making men wait longer than necessary for three letter answers.'

The gentle prompt wasn't lost on Megan, who bit down on her lip nervously. She'd come to realise that Kate was correct in seeing that which had taken her a little longer to establish – she was falling in love with Michael. It was hard to believe, for it seemed the feeling had almost crept up on her overnight, but there was no denying that she couldn't imagine her life without him in it now. She knew that logically it was far too premature in the relationship to be getting engaged; even Kate had agreed with that. And yet, now Michael was chiding her – she couldn't really think of any reason not to say yes. After all – the heart's intention and the head's logic were two completely different things and hadn't everybody always suggested she 'follow her heart'? Why wait if something was feeling right? Sure, it was a big decision, but what if it was the correct decision?

She set down her cutlery, her mind suddenly made up. Without hesitation, she knew it was something she had to grab. 'Okay, Michael, let's go for it.'

'Excuse me?' He looked at her bewildered. 'Go for what? Corsica?'

She giggled nervously. 'No, you idiot – I mean let's get engaged. I'm saying "yes" to you.'

'You are?' The sparkling excitement in Michael's eyes was hard to miss. He studied her face quizzically. 'I know you've been humouring me, but are you sure you're serious about this?' His expression hardened, the sparkling eyes darkening.

'I'm sure.' And Megan knew she was because looking at Michael's face had just confirmed everything. Butterflies danced inside her. 'I still think it's soon and I'm not saying we should rush into the wedding just yet, but I can see us growing old together – you with your walking stick and pipe and me with my hairnet and rollers.'

'You do realise this calls for a proper celebration?'

'What, so I can show off my hand-carved wooden engagement ring?' Megan mocked teasingly. Although the African carved ring had been a novelty gesture and part of Michael's 'relaxed' proposal, she'd appreciated the fun and jokey side of it.

'Well, I'll have to get you something a shade more reflective to put on your finger, won't I?'

'Am I going to be spoilt with diamante this time?'

Amused, Michael leaned forward and brushed her fingers with his own. 'I might stretch to a diamond; depends on whether you agree to going to Corsica for the honeymoon.'

Poking out her tongue, Megan picked up her wine glass. 'I'll consider it.' She nudged his foot under the table. 'Come on, let's have a toast then – to ourselves!'

Laughing, Michael picked up his own glass. 'To you, my beautiful Megan and our future life together. Hopefully in the countryside, after our magnificent holiday in Corsica.' He winked and clinked her glass.

Megan couldn't remember being so content – she finally belonged with someone. It was a good feeling.

'I've had two clients this week already comment on that one,' Vivian said, raising her eyes and pointing to the large colourful canvas of an owl above them. 'I've a good mind to get up there myself and stick a price next to it.'

Kate smiled. 'You know I can't put a price next to it, Viv.' She glanced around the entrance hall, a sense of pride swelling in her chest, for her artwork had given the usually drab interior a new lease of life. Even she had to admit that her canvases were eye-catching, and the extraordinary amount of compliments she'd received from both staff and residents was overwhelming. 'Oh, I meant to tell you – Tommy congratulated me this morning. I could hardly believe my ears. Tasha said it's the first time she's ever heard him pass on a good word to anyone.'

'Well, I'll be struck down – that's the first time I've heard of it, too. Miserable old bastard, that one. Although maybe part of it is due to having Tasha as his helper. She's a dragon.'

Kate nodded. 'Yes, but you know how she likes to think she runs this place – and sometimes me, for that matter. I've noticed she's a bit put out by all this attention I'm getting.'

Vivian stopped walking as she approached the dining table and drew out her favourite chair. 'Good, serves her right. Maybe if she was a little nicer to people, then she'd reap the rewards that you do. It's all about what you put out, love. And I don't mean your body, as Lil seems to think.' She grinned cheekily, as Lillian approached with a glass of lemonade.

'What's all this about? I heard my name mentioned.'

'We're talking about Tasha the dragon.' Vivian pointed behind her to the far right corner where the fiery red-headed carer was assisting Tommy to a table. 'And also about you putting yourself about.'

'Well, excuse me for thinking you were my friend!' Lillian tutted loudly. 'My days for all that are over,' she said indignantly, pulling out a chair. 'Besides, it never did me any harm. My second husband, Bobby, bless his soul, said I was the best thing he'd ever had.'

'Is that why he left you, then?' Vivian replied, gesturing Kate to give her the small carrier bag she'd asked her to bring to the dining table.

Passing her the bag, which contained a flask of Guinness. Kate suppressed a grin. She always found it fun watching the two best friends prattle away at each other.

'He didn't leave me. She stole him. Love of my life, he was.'

'Hmm, we know – you've told us a million times before,' Vivian retorted, opening the flask and discreetly pouring a small amount of the Guinness into her empty coffee cup.

'I don't know why you bother with that. All the others know it's Guinness not that espresso stuff you like to pretend it is,' Lillian said, shaking her head. 'Anyway no one drinks coffee with their lunch.'

'Never you mind about me. Worry about yourself.'

'Viv, be nice!' Kate chided, noticing Alan walk into the dining room and making a beeline for them. 'I'm off early today, remember – straight after lunch I've got that meeting with the financial advisor.'

Vivian took a sip of her drink. 'Oh, yes, good luck with that. Let's hope he can find a solution for you to take over the mortgage.' She crossed her fingers and held them up.

'Afternoon, ladies,' Alan said, approaching the table. 'Would you mind if I joined you?'

'Hello, Alan, of course – come and sit down,' Vivian replied, patting the top of the chair next to her.

Kate's mobile beeped from the depths of her pocket, reminding her that she'd forgotten to leave it in her usual hiding place. 'Oh, I forgot my phone was still on me.'

Alan set down his glass of sparkling water on the table and took his seat next to Viv.

Lillian winked. 'Don't worry about that, Kate. Answer it if you have to. We don't mind. Stupid rules they've got here.'

Alan nodded his head. 'Indeed, Lillian, I do agree.'

Retrieving the phone from her trouser pocket, Kate quickly checked the display and opened a message from Megan.

'Are you free later? Need to see you. Got news.'

Intrigued, she rapidly typed out a reply telling Megan she'd be home after her consultation with the advisor and to pop over to hers. She received an instant response.

'Good. See you later. It's important. '

'All okay love?' Viv asked, disturbing her thoughts. What news could be important? It was unlike Megan to text if she had something significant to tell her. But, then, maybe she was busy and couldn't phone?

'Yes, fine. Only Megan – she's coming over later.'

'That's nice. Bit of girls chat will do you the world of good. Viv topped up her coffee cup with the flask.

Lil agreed and Alan continued to study the week's menu card on the table, not wishing to get involved in womanly matters or draw attention to Vivian's peculiar habit with her Guinness.

'Right, I'm just off to get Hilda. I'll be back soon.'

'Just don't be wheeling her in to sit at our table.' Viv said, picking up her napkin to dab at the brown stain she'd made on the white top cloth. 'I don't want to be put off my lunch, thank you very much.'

Alan chuckled, raising his eyebrow at Kate.

'You know I wouldn't do that. I'll make sure I sit her as far away as possible. Okay?' She could just about hear Vivian's sarcastic reply and Lil's subsequent laughter as she hurried off in the direction of the West wing. Thinking once again about Megan's text message, an anxious feeling passed through her – similar to the sensation she'd had the previous day when she'd been unable to shake off the persistent thought that something awful was about to happen.

By the time she'd reached Hilda's room, she was utterly convinced that something wasn't right. Texting wasn't Megan's style and she realised she also hadn't spoken to her properly for a few days. Just the odd email and very brief call. Yet she'd been so busy trying to distract herself from the Marcus situation that she hadn't paid much attention. She'd thrown herself into her painting and given her wardrobe an overhaul with a shopping spree. It had been an enlightening experience to get back in touch with feeling sexy and good about herself again. The clothes she'd bought had reflected that.

Yet thinking about Megan's aloofness over the past days caused concern to build in her – something was definitely amiss.

She really hoped she was wrong.

Chapter 18

Marcus finished typing the feature piece he was working on and glanced at his watch. 'Two-thirty already.' Exhaling heavily, he glanced back at his laptop screen. It had been a gruelling week with work, not to mention the deal he'd signed with the major publisher that was already demanding his attention in unwanted ways.

And then there was the phone call, the call that he couldn't stop thinking about. He knew it had been risky calling Megan, for she could have blamed him in many ways for everything that had happened with Kate. But he hadn't expected her to be so receptive, nice even.

He'd been with a lot of women and liked to think himself quite sensitive to the emotions of the opposite sex, even though he'd failed miserably when it had come to Kate. He'd finally stopped feeling guilty about the mixed messages he'd unwittingly given her. He'd just felt drawn to help whilst Alf hadn't been around, like a protective older brother. In some ways, he'd thought he'd been doing his friend a favour – he knew Alf still cared for Kate. He'd thought that maybe she'd reconsider the breakup once she was seeing clearly again and was happier within herself. However, she'd evidently misinterpreted his actions, thinking that he was interested in her in a romantic way. He hadn't expected Kate, of all people, to be the one to make him question his own judgement.

His mind flitted back to Megan. So much of her reminded him of Linzie, all the good parts – the parts that had made him fall in love. Not the parts that had worn him down and torn his life to shreds. He stopped his mind wandering to his ex and the gossip that had filtered to him since he'd moved back down to the South. He couldn't blame Linzie for wanting to move on; after all, he'd been the one who had walked away. But Linzie getting together with Jackson? On one hand he realised it was inevitable – yet on the other, he couldn't help but wish she'd see sense. It was a dangerous road she was walking down.

Still, he focused once again on the call he'd made to Megan and how much it had given him an insight into her. He knew she wasn't available. Something she'd said had referred to that, but it couldn't hurt to hope. He'd sensed something when speaking with her that told him she, too, was feeling an undeniable chemistry. It pleased him immensely. After all, since the first time he'd laid eyes on Megan he'd always known there was a connection.

'You finished that feature yet, mate? Ed's on my back regarding layout.'

Marcus observed his colleague who'd appeared in his office doorway with slightly more irritation than intended. He didn't like being disturbed midway through thought.

'It'll be with you in half an hour.'

'Thanks.'

He watched him skulk away – thankful that he'd managed to secure himself a position that gave him flexibility to use either home or office as his hub. He didn't envy the colleagues who were forced to spend the best part of their days in the ever-busy office with its constant din of activity.

His mind wandered back to Megan and he found himself thinking about her straightforward chatter. She really was a breath of fresh air. Even the way she'd told him not to fuss over Kate's refusal to acknowledge him, and that she would eventually come round, had been to the point. He didn't mince his words, either, for it had been the reason he'd called – wanting to know if Kate was okay, as she clearly wasn't willing to let him know herself. Yet he couldn't help but wonder if the situation had also presented him with a silver lining – an unexpected chance to connect with Megan again.

He hadn't realised just how much she had got under his skin until he'd spoken with her again.

The only problem was that he didn't know how to take the situation further.

'Sam – dinner time!' Kate stood against the frame of the back door and peered into the garden. Only partially visible through the overgrown bushes, she saw Sam's small head bob upwards at the sound of her voice.

'Come on. Come and eat.'

He didn't need to be told twice, for he was almost immediately at her feet after bounding towards her, jumping up at the silver dish filled with dog meat she was holding in her hand.

She leaned down to place it on the floor. 'You'd better make the most of that, sweetie – because the way things are going we'll be living on bread and water soon.' Picking up the empty foil carton of the premium-quality dog food, she placed it in the bin.

Although she hadn't expected the financial advisor to tell her that things would be unrealistically hunky dory with regard to a secure future, she hadn't been prepared for what he'd actually said. It was grim, all of it. Grimmer than grim. An analysis of her current salary and outgoings, plus various calculations based on present bank loans had brought her sharply to the reality of her situation.

She'd never be able to afford to take on the mortgage single-handed in the foreseeable future. The most realistic option was that they try to sell the property and she rent herself a small apart-ment. Sighing, she took a packet of chicken breasts from the fridge and began to prepare a curry – she didn't have the willpower to consider her predicament without going into meltdown.

By the time she'd added the final blend of fresh herbs to the simmering chicken, Megan was already ringing the doorbell. It did little to calm Kate's anxiety; she was never normally on time, so why tonight? She couldn't help but dread whatever 'news' her friend was bearing. She walked to the street door and opened it.

'Hiya.' Megan breezed into the hallway smiling broadly, clutching a bottle of white wine under her arm and a bunch of flowers in the other hand. 'Got you these. Pretty aren't they?' She thrust the bouquet of mixed freesias towards Kate and slipped off her heels. 'Mmm, I can smell curry – just what I fancy eating.'

Kate eyed the flowers suspiciously and narrowed her eyes. 'They're gorgeous, but why're you bringing me flowers? You never bring me flowers.' She brought the bouquet to her nose and inhaled the sweet fragrance. 'They smell lovely, though.' She lowered the bunch, noticing that Megan was avoiding her eyes. 'Yes, I've cooked a curry.'

'Let's eat, then. Glass of wine and curry. You always make the best curry!' She led the way into the kitchen, dumping her bag on the hallway floor as she did so.

Kate followed, heart pounding. She knew something was up. 'Meg, what's going on?'

Putting the wine down carefully on the counter top, Megan stood still, holding her breath – her expression of utter happiness replaced with a worried glance. 'Is it really that obvious?'

Kate smiled, despite herself. 'Well, yes; firstly you brought me flowers and secondly you're doing that overly positive thing you do when you're about to drop a bombshell.'

'Oh goodness – I can never fool you on anything, can I?' She shrugged sadly with a small grimace and took a deep breath, facing Kate. She knew it was better to do it quickly, or else she'd be on edge. 'It's Alf, Kate.'

'What about him?'

'I think he's resigning.' She watched as her friend's face lost its colour and she held out her hand to steady her.

Shocked, Kate leaned against the countertop, head whirling with questions and her heart dancing in her chest. 'What? How is that possible? Alf would never resign. Are you sure?' She stared at Megan in confusion.

Taking a seat opposite her, Megan unwrapped the silk scarf from her neck, suddenly conscious of how hot it was in the small kitchen. 'I'm not certain. However, I saw an email that I assume wasn't supposed to have included the part at the very bottom. It was a discussion between two of the board members about Alf's capacity in his new job – I don't think they're impressed with him. Anyway, one of them had mentioned that after a phone conversation they'd had with Alf, he would likely consider the resignation offer proposed.' She let her words sink in, noting how quiet Kate had gone. 'I haven't been made aware of any offer – although I'm usually the one who helps draft such things as HR Manager, which is all the more strange. I've got a sense that Clyde is forcing Alf out of the company.'

'But that's terrible. Can they do that?' Kate asked, feeling sickened by what she was hearing.

'Technically, no. But Clyde is ruthless. I've seen it happen before and I'm sure it won't be the last time. If he's backing Alf into a corner by questioning his ability and putting pressure on him, then it's likely Alf will want to walk away, especially if he's tempted with a generous gardening-leave package.'

'Alf's not a quitter, though. He's worked so hard for your company and look at what he gave up for that position, Meg.' She shook her head in defiance. 'I just can't see that he'd resign….'

'Look, I know it's a bit of a shock. Even for me.' She stared at Kate with a serious expression. 'But it's the way these things work out sometimes.'

Choosing her words carefully, Megan walked across to the hob to lower the heat under the bubbling curry. 'The thing is, I wanted to warn you because, if it's true – it's going to mean he loses all the Scotland benefits. Including his accommodation.'

She watched as Kate looked up sharply, the realisation of the words having their effect. 'Which means it's likely he's going to be moving back here, Kate.'

'But he can't.' Her tone was horrified. 'I mean, I know it's his home town, but I can't bear the possibility of having to see him on a regular basis. ' The thought made her feel sick.

Everything suddenly seemed to be caving in on her. It had been one thing experiencing the separation knowing that Alf was happily tucked away in Scotland and telling herself that she didn't miss him – because realistically he'd disappeared conveniently from her life. But if he was back South, living nearby and a constant reminder of what she'd walked away from... Her stomach churned.

Megan sighed. 'Maybe this is a good thing. It's probably what you need to really move on.'

'But I have moved on. You know that.'

Hesitating, Megan bit down on her lip. She wanted to see Kate happy – she deserved it more than anybody she knew. Yet she also knew that Kate was lost. Although in some ways the split had transformed her friend's life on both a social and a creative level, she wasn't convinced that Kate had truly faced up to her new single status. Her fixation and deflection onto Marcus had proved that.

'I know you have and I think you're a much better person for it.' Megan said earnestly. 'I can't believe how far you've come along in such a short space of time.' She picked up the wine bottle and opened it. 'All I'm saying is, maybe if Alf comes back it will give you the real closure you need – you know – forcing the sale of the house and stuff and properly going your separate ways.'

Kate sighed, defeated. She knew Megan was right. With Alf in Scotland it had been easy to convince herself that the split was necessary and the best thing for both of them. It had also allowed her to avoid taking responsibility for the decision she'd made. Every time she began to think of him and miss him, she'd told herself it had to be this way, because she couldn't possibly leave everything behind to be in Scotland with him. However, if he returned home – where did that leave her excuses to herself?

'Anyway, there's no point reading too much into it just yet. Like I said, I can't be certain because it was only mentioned on an email I saw.' She helped herself to two wine glasses from the cupboard. 'If anything gets confirmed I'll tell you, but I wanted to warn you. Even if I did sort of mess it up by bringing flowers. I just didn't want you to be too depressed about it all.'

Despite the turmoil that was taking place inside her, Kate allowed a small smile and got up to turn off the hob. 'I'm pleased you did. I guess it's the kick I needed, anyway.'

Picking up a spoon from the side, she dipped it into the thick curry sauce and began to stir. 'I met a financial advisor earlier and it was depressing, to say the least. Looks like I'm going to have to call Alf anyway and have a discussion and make a decision about the house a bit sooner than we'd planned to.' She watched as Megan poured a generous amount of wine into one of the glasses, eyes widening as she caught the gleam of the diamond on her left hand.

'Megan! What's that on your finger?' She scrambled across to her friend and grabbed her hand, looking at her in astonishment. 'You're engaged! But I thought you were waiting?' She noticed the tone of disapproval in her own voice and immediately disliked herself for it as she looked at Megan's flushed cheeks. 'Why didn't you tell me sooner?'

'Oh, don't look at me like that.' She pouted in a sad way, making Kate feel even worse about her friend than she already did. 'It was a spur-of-the-moment decision. We were in L'Oranger yesterday discussing possible honeymoon locations and I just decided it was silly to pretend when I could have the real thing.'

She held out her hand in front of her, allowing the small, but very reflective, diamond set in a thin band, to catch the light. 'You were right, I am falling in love with him.' She looked at Kate self-consciously. 'So I thought, what the heck – why not grab happiness whilst it's being offered?'

Mollified, Kate reached out and pulled Megan close to her. 'Congratulations, honey. Come here and give me a hug.' She threw her arms around Megan's slender frame, her earlier fears of losing her best friend totally forgotten as she heard her excited giggle.

'I would have told you sooner, but what with the Alf thing – I didn't think it was appropriate – I wanted to mention that first. Plus I knew you'd notice regardless.'

Kate laughed. 'You know me too well!'

'Besides, I've told Michael I don't want a celebration. We're keeping it to ourselves for now. I still want us to get to know each other more first.' She looked bashful as she poured the remainder of wine. 'I'm definitely not into planning the wedding anytime soon. Maybe a couple of years yet.'

Kate raised an eyebrow mockingly. 'Two years! Isn't that a bit long?' She saw Megan fiercely shake her head and began to chuckle at her response. 'Well, whatever makes you happy, makes me happy. Anyway, who am I to advise you? I'm hardly a relationship expert, am I?' Leaning across the counter she reached for the glasses of wine. 'I'd say a toast is in order, then. One for your engagement and another for my new approach to getting my life in order.'

Megan picked up her glass. 'Hear, hear. I'll drink to that!' Gently tapping her glass against Kate's she took a sip of the lukewarm wine. She'd barely swallowed the mouthful of sweet liquid before she was consumed with an overwhelming feeling that perhaps she'd made a hasty decision in saying yes to Michael. The same paralysing feeling that had been seeping numbness into her since she'd awoken that morning and he'd presented her with the ring – which she could only imagine he'd managed to source from somewhere late the previous evening.

'You do think I'm making the right decision marrying him, though?'

Kate looked at her oddly. 'You mean you're not sure?'

'I didn't say that, did I?' She met Kate's eyes and felt her confidence dissolve. 'It's just that I wasn't expecting him to get the ring so fast and everything...'

Kate bit down on her lip and considered Megan's words. She knew how strong-minded and changeable her friend could be and she also knew how determined she could be when she set her heart on something. But the flipside was that she was more vulnerable than most, for those very same reasons. It was natural that she was already beginning to question the situation when she'd never had to compromise in a relationship before – let alone allowed herself to fall in love.

She picked her words carefully. 'I think you're just scared, and I understand that.' She saw Megan lower her eyes and knew she had hit a nerve. 'The reason that Michael's rushing is undoubtedly because he's eager to make you his wife. He obviously cares a great deal about you to push things to this level of commitment so soon. You're a lucky woman, Megan. Don't fight it – go with the flow. If it makes you happy, then what's to question?'

Megan looked down at her engagement ring and knew she'd heard the words she needed to. Smiling, she glanced back up at Kate. 'What would I do without you, huh – oh Wise One?'

Kate laughed and stood up, opening the corner cupboard, where she kept her rice supply. 'Well – firstly you'd be very hungry, given the amount of food you seem to be eating at my house these days.'

'I'm so looking forward to that curry, though. It smells delicious. I should pop round with important news more often,' she joked, taking a sip of her wine and watching as Kate filled a pan with water.

Rolling her eyes, Kate placed the pot on the hob and added the packet rice and a sprinkle of salt. 'I think I've had more than enough news for one day.'

'You're okay, though, about it all?' Megan asked, concern instantly sweeping through her as she saw the dark cloud pass across Kate's face. 'Alf, I mean.'

'I guess I'll have to be, won't I?'

Nodding morosely, Megan agreed. She sensed by Kate's stiff body language that she was struggling with the revelation, but she was bravely putting on a positive front. It was also an obvious shock to her about the engagement, especially knowing how it had affected her the previous week. Yet she knew that inner strength was Kate's main virtue. She always had a way of holding it together when things got tough or challenging.

Instinctively, Megan reached out and squeezed her arm. 'It'll all be okay, you know. You've still got me. Even though I'm not a hot, hunky bloke, at least I'm reliable.'

Kate sniggered, her shoulders visibly relaxing a little. She turned and smiled. 'Yes, I know that.' And she did; even if Megan was now engaged, it clearly hadn't changed things between them in the slightest. Knowing this helped to ease the tension that she was beginning to bottle up.

'Good. Don't forget it, sister.' Standing up, Megan straightened her skirt and re-tied her hair. 'I'm just going to pop to the loo, then I'll be back to give you a hand.' Walking out of the kitchen, she made the decision to tell Kate about Marcus's call another time. There was nothing to be gained from such a conversation.

She'd already had had more than her fair share of revelations for one night.

Chapter 19

Megan glared at the screen, wanting to throttle the person at the other end of the mobile. It wasn't that she minded giving out advice – and of course she'd never say no to him because she knew that helping him was indirectly helping Kate. But his pitiful tone was driving her to despair. Woe is Alf. Get over it!

'Look, like I've said, off the record they haven't handled it in the correct way – that much I agree on. But, Alf, the offer they've made seems very generous in the circumstances.' She paused, checking there was no one in the corridor outside. 'You remember the situation with Lance? Clyde pretty much ruined his career – his name was tarnished and last I heard he was in Guernsey because he was unemployable in London.' She fiddled with a document as someone passed in the corridor, nosily casting a glance towards the glass window of her office. 'I just don't think that taking Hamilton's to a tribunal would be the way forward. As much as you don't like taking my advice, I think this time you should.'

She knew from his exasperated sigh that he agreed with her; there was a pause while he considered saying something and then seemed to think better of it. Megan saw it as the opportunity she'd been waiting for.

'Anyway, if you take the offer, will you be coming back home?'

He didn't skip a beat. 'Yes, most definitely. It's where I belong.

Scotland's nice, but there's nothing here for me.'

He quietened again and Megan sensed the apprehension even through the phone. The thing that he most wanted to know but couldn't bring himself to ask. 'I see.' She waited, knowing it wouldn't be long before he would be unable to resist.

'So how is she?' His voice was barely a whisper.

It was on the tip of her tongue to ask 'Who?' but she refrained. As much as she didn't like him, she wanted him to know that Kate wasn't falling to pieces without him. 'She's fine. Moving on with things. Doing very well, actually.'

'Has she met someone new?' He knew she hadn't; he'd read between the lines from various conversations with Marcus, but he felt compelled to ask. Just in case.

Megan paused, part of her wanting to let him know that Kate had fallen in lust with Marcus, purely to show him how stupid he'd been at letting her slip away and also the satisfaction of knowing it would destroy him. Yet, she knew it would only cause more heartbreak and problems for Kate. Instead she decided to answer with a bitter tone.

'She's single. You bailed out on her, remember?'

'Don't start, Megan, I'm not in the mood.' His voice was tired, strained. 'Besides, I tried to make it right, but she was the one who didn't want it. And I'm perfectly aware of what I've lost – not a day goes by when I don't regret it. She was the best thing in my life.'

'Save it for someone who cares.' She shook her head.

'Nice' he snapped. 'Some things never change, do they, Megan?'

Sighing, she decided it was best to put an end to the call before they spiralled into a familiar and destructive pattern of snipes. 'Listen, I have to go. For what it's worth, I do hope it works out with the offer, though. Take it.'

'I'm going to.' Begrudgingly he muttered his thanks and said a swift goodbye, hanging up before she had a chance to say anything more.

Tutting to herself at his rudeness, she replaced her mobile onto its charging pod, relieved that she finally had confirmation of Alf's intentions. The only problem was going to be breaking it to Kate.

Seeing her friend's reaction when she'd first told her about the email hadn't been reassuring. She was convinced that Kate still had strong feelings for Alf because although she'd tried to appear normal for the rest of the evening, Megan had seen straight through it. Barely touching her curry, Kate had drunk far too much wine and congratulated her on the engagement too many times. It had been uncomfortable to witness.

Her internal phone rang and she grimaced as she noted the name on the caller display. Janelle. No doubt Clyde finally wanted to bring her up to speed on the delicate situation. She sighed, picking up her pen and sliding her notepad closer to her.

'At least you've got tonight to look forward to,' she muttered to herself, picking up the handset. A small flutter of excitement spread through her. She couldn't wait to sample the food at the exclusive restaurant that Michael had secured a table at.

Besides, she needed something to cheer her mood after the conversation with Alf. It had caught her strangely off-guard. Had he genuinely meant it when he said he missed Kate and that she was the best thing in his life? The thought was accompanied by a niggling feeling of guilt. What if Alf was the one for Kate after all?

These thoughts were wiped away as Janelle's voice boomed down the phone at her.

'The ninth of October? That's barely a month away.' Kate looked up from her mobile in astonishment. 'I can't believe he's expecting me to have everything prepared within four weeks. How the hell does he think I'll be ready for the exhibition in, what…?' She counted quickly on her fingers, her horror growing. 'Twenty-four and a half days…'

Vivian tutted, smoothing her hands across the swirled red-and-purple-patterned blanket covering her knees. 'Nonsense. That's more than enough time. All you've got to do is send out a few invites.'

'I haven't even finished painting the collection yet. I thought I had another month and a half!' Kate shook her head fiercely. 'No, Viv, it's just not possible. I'd rather forget the whole thing. He can stick it.' Her tone surly, she threw down her mobile onto the bed, annoyed that Marcus would do this to her. The thought crossed her mind that he might have done it on purpose, but she dismissed it almost instantly. He'd made it clear he didn't think of her in that way, so why would he purposely change the dates of the exhibition he'd arranged on her behalf.

'Don't be such a defeatist. You've been looking forward to this.' Vivian's voice was stern. 'It's your big opportunity and if you pass this up, then I know for sure that you'll not get another.'

'Thanks a lot for your encouragement.' Kate snapped, regretting it as soon as she saw Vivian's lips purse together. She sighed and sat down next to her, on the special chair reserved for clients. 'Sorry.' She rubbed Viv's arm apologetically. 'It's wound me up, that's all. He knows I'm avoiding him and to send me a text like that...' She picked at her fingernails, noticing how slim her fingers had become. 'Well, it's something I've got no choice but to reply to, have I?'

'Oh, you don't half feel sorry for yourself sometimes, Kate Wilson.' Vivian retorted, wryly smiling. 'You're not a child. You're a woman. He's offering you an olive branch and you should take it – forget this silly business about the kiss.' She noticed Kate wince. 'I'm sure he's had many a woman throw herself at him if he's as handsome as you say. He sounds like a good man and right now he's offering you a golden cup – don't cut your nose off to spite your face.'

Picking up a pleated skirt from the arm of the chair, Kate threw it towards the pile of dirty laundry she'd placed on the floor and considered her options. Four weeks was far too soon, but if she sent out the invites and managed to sort her speech, then really there wasn't that much else to do. She hadn't yet finished painting the collection, that was true, but she knew full well that she hadn't been intending to display the entire collection anyway. She'd already prepared the pieces she wanted to showcase; in fact they were already covered and set to one side against the back wall of the living room. So what was holding her back?

Pride. She still felt stupid in front of Marcus, even though he'd tried to make it normal between them again; she hadn't yet replied to any of his messages. She was behaving like a churlish teenager – not the thirty-two-year-old woman that she was.

'Besides, you might be able to fool yourself, but you certainly can't fool me, Kate – you're going to need a distraction if Alf's coming back. It's written all over your face that you're still in love with him.'

She stopped staring at the pile of laundry and bit down on her lip, willing herself not to cry and wishing she'd refrained from telling Viv about Megan's discovery so soon. 'Don't.' She shook her head and sniffled, feeling her throat tighten. 'I can't think about that right now.'

Getting up, Vivian walked across to Kate and put her arms around the girl, wishing that she had a remedy for heartbreak. 'Now now, don't cry.' She brushed a strand of hair away from her cheek. 'You two were together a long time. Those feelings don't go away overnight, darling. It takes a while.' She patted Kate's back and noticed that her eyes were brimming with tears.

'Oh God, Viv. It's such a mess. If only he didn't have to come back...' she tailed off.

'It's a good thing, if you ask me. You two have a lot of unfinished business – including your house to sort. It's time to face up to it, Kate – you can't keep running away from things. It always gets worse before it gets better. Him running off to Scotland and you fixating on Marcus didn't solve anything, did it?'

Kate nodded. She knew Vivian was right, but she'd been trying to convince herself otherwise for the last few days – ever since Megan had told her about Alf's phone call and his intentions of returning. Yesterday had been the tipping point, with Megan's confirmation that Alf's resignation letter had been received. The news had made her feel nauseous.

She knew that it was only a matter of time before he'd call her direct, wanting to discuss their finances and the house… After all, he had to call, didn't he? Or would he just turn up on the doorstep and let himself in? The thought made her shiver. She didn't know if it was with excited delight or pure terror.

'And don't go worrying about Marcus telling him anything. My sixth sense tells me that the whole episode will never get mentioned. You needn't worry in the slightest.'

'I know that,' Kate answered matter-of-factly. And she did, because although Marcus had become a good and trustworthy friend to her, she knew he wouldn't want to upset Alf. 'I'm certain that he won't breathe a word of it. That's something I'm thankful for, at least. Mind you, I got the impression his friendship has waned with Alf in Scotland. He didn't mention speaking to him regularly.' She paused, thinking. 'But then again, perhaps that was just because he didn't want to upset me by raising the subject.'

'Well, on that note, are you going to reply to Marcus, then? Tell him that you'll be happy to take the new date for the exhibition?' Viv challenged, her steely gaze on Kate.

Kate smirked, knowing that Vivian had achieved exactly what she'd set out to. 'You drive a hard bargain. I guess I'll have to reply, won't I? Otherwise I'll never hear the end of it from you.' She picked up her mobile and began to quickly type out a response before she had a chance to lose her nerve.

Smiling, Vivian took her place again in her favourite chair and readjusted her blanket, pleased with herself. She knew that her days were numbered, what with the strange and increasingly frequent pains she was having in her chest. Her intuition told her that all was not well on a health level, but she daren't seek medical advice. She'd never been one for doctors or hospitals, after all – what good did it do to be palmed off with a prescription for various pills? She'd seen the way many others her age had gone to hospital with a sniffle and come out in a coffin. No, she didn't trust the men in white coats.

She would rather spend her final days helping to get Kate on the right track. That much she'd promised herself.

'It's too soon.' Without looking up from the sports section of the tabloid he was reading, Jonnie reached for another handful of salted nuts, unaware of the frustration he was causing his sister.

'But you said you liked him!' Megan repeated, unsure if Jonnie had heard the first time. 'So have you changed your mind or something?' She paused, waiting for him to look up. He didn't.

'Regardless, still too soon.' He spoke with his mouth full, small pieces of nuts and spittle spraying the page in front of him. Wiping them away with a brush of his hand, he finally turned to his sister. 'Meg, you don't even know the bloke and neither do I. Yes, he seems nice and I do like him, but what if he turns out to be some psycho control freak? Why the rush?'

With a sigh, Megan sat down at the dining table, pushing aside the newspaper and the bag of peanuts. 'We've gone over this already. It's not like I'm marrying him tomorrow – we're going to wait a while. You know that. I can't help feeling like I'm tip-toeing around you at the moment. You're obviously not happy about it, so what's the real reason, Jonnie?' She grabbed his wrist, stopping him as he reached out for the nuts and forcing him to make eye contact. 'Why are you being strange about it all? I thought you'd be happy for me?'

He sighed, gently shaking his wrist free of her grip and meeting her eyes. 'I just don't want you to get hurt, sis. I don't know why, but I've got a bad feeling about the whole thing.' He rubbed his face with his hand, disliking himself for causing the hurt that was evident in his sister's expression. 'I hope I'm wrong because I want to see you happy, but I don't know. I think you've not given it enough time.'

'Is it jealousy? Is that it?' Megan asked angrily, eyes blazing now. Why did Jonnie always have to throw a spanner in the works with everything? Couldn't he just accept that she'd found someone who she wanted to be with?

Jonnie looked at her in surprise. 'Jealousy? Of course not. What have I got to be jealous about?' He stood up and snatched his newspaper and nuts from the table. 'No man will ever come between us, sis, I'll make sure of that.' He patted her head, ignoring her irritated swipe of his hand. 'But please! Just take a bit of notice for once. Be sure not to rush into things. I've just got this feeling Michael's not the right one for you.'

Megan watched him walk away and out into the garden, Jonnie's way of signalling that the conversation was over – at least from his point of view. She felt weary and surprisingly bleak. Michael hadn't shown her anything but affection and adoration. He was kind, caring and generous in every way. She couldn't understand how Jonnie could even begin to think that Michael wasn't right for her. She'd met enough men throughout her twenties and early thirties to know the good from the bad.

It was jealousy, pure and simple. He couldn't accept her being taken away from him – he'd as much as admitted that he'd felt abandoned on many an occasion when drunk and she hadn't pandered to him. It was a mixture of jealousy and fear. As much as she wanted to reassure him that he was wrong and her flourishing relationship with Michael would prove it, she decided it best to let time do that instead.

She heard a faint beep amidst the voices of the cookery programme blasting from the television at the other end of the room. Her mobile. Undoubtedly Michael. Glancing at the clock she realised it was almost eleven; she'd told him she'd be over at his by quarter to in time for brunch.

'Great, now I'm going to be late,' she muttered to herself, fetching her bag from the armchair and retrieving her mobile from its side pocket. Hastily flipping open the leather case, she looked at the screen.

Her stomach fluttered involuntarily and she felt her cheeks flushing, her heart skipping a beat at his name.

Clicking open the message she read it, her bleak mood forgotten as a smile began to slowly spread across her face. Marcus wanted to meet her.

Chapter 20

'Out you go.' Shooing Sam out of the back door and into the late-summer air, Kate inhaled the sweet mix of blooming honeysuckle and jasmine that was creeping up the length of the side gate and fence. Trying not to glance at the overgrown jungle that her garden had turned into, she quickly closed the door, leaving the dog to explore.

Making herself a cup of milky coffee, she sat at the kitchen table and sipped it slowly, thinking over the previous evening.

She should really have expected him to call; after all, texting Marcus had given the opening he'd been waiting for. But answering the phone to him hadn't been easy and neither had it been particularly pleasant at the beginning. She'd felt defensive, vulnerable even, and yet, within a few minutes it had seemed as if the whole kissing episode had never even taken place. Their friendship had picked up where it had left off; he'd even had her laughing at a disastrous evening in a new nightclub he'd visited. They'd spoken for twenty minutes in the end. And only after they'd exhausted all of their news did Marcus raise the subject of Alf and his return to the South.

He said he'd suspected for quite some time that Alf hadn't been happy in Scotland. 'Compromised' as he'd put it. But he hadn't wanted to raise it with Kate before now because he'd not wanted to complicate matters. She'd learned that not only had Alf not taken to the job role as easily as he'd assumed he would, but that he'd also not taken to the bachelor lifestyle. It had felt strangely pleasing and exhilarating to hear it. She wondered if it had given Alf food for thought. As far as Marcus was aware, Alf was still hung up on her, although he hadn't used quite those words – more of an insinuation that this was the case.

The statement had marked a huge shift in her. It was as if she'd finally found the light after months of darkness and confusion. Alf wanted her. And she still wanted Alf. Vivian had been right, there was far too much unfinished business between them. She'd been kidding herself to think otherwise, but then again, she knew that was because she'd tried to hide from her real emotions and feelings. Marcus had aided her in doing that – unwittingly of course – but he'd been the perfect distraction and medicinal dose. He'd shown her an alternative possibility that she'd thought was what she'd wanted and been missing out on.

The past week's reflection as well as their phone conversation had marked the turning of a corner in that respect, too. Although she still considered Marcus a lovely, light and fun person, it was obvious to her now that she'd never fit with somebody like him. She'd blindly overlooked his love of going out, partying, of wanting constant excitement and fun in his life. She'd thought that was what she'd been missing out on with Alf, but the realisation was that she didn't want those things after all. She was no longer the young Kate that she'd thought she'd lost out to. Yes, the occasional night out was enjoyable and she'd been making more of an effort to make plans, but ultimately she was happiest spending time indoors.

Then there was the home environment that she'd so desperately wanted to change. She'd been thinking over Marcus's aspirations to decorate his snazzy apartment on North Street with the latest mod cons, his insistence that things be minimalistic and streamlined. But she didn't care about those things either; all she wanted was a homely home, one where cushions got scattered and the air was filled with a family vibe. One that she could share with a partner and know they could welcome their children into.

She realised suddenly that she'd finally found the balance. The balance between her young carefree self and the thirty-something with low self-esteem that she'd morphed into.

The whole experience had been a wake-up call; one that had shown her what was important to her. The results were surprising and yet also hugely relieving. She realised it was her confidence and inner happiness that she'd lost touch with. She'd pinned all of her hopes of happiness on a future with Alf; all of her thoughts concentrated on babies and marriage. She'd thought that these were the only things that could make her life right again and give her the inner contentment that she was lacking. But marriage and children would come at the right time, when she wasn't trying to control everything.

The past months had taught her that she didn't need a man or anything else to begin to feel good about herself; that she was perfectly capable of functioning on her own and feeling happy from within by being true to herself. Even the small things like changing her image and losing weight had boosted her confidence in unimaginable ways.

The fear of abandonment that she'd had for so long had begun to lose its power over her. She'd finally accepted that the miscarriage was something that had happened for a reason and she felt more peaceful with that knowledge. She knew now that she had the inner strength to cope with anything; she was finally back in tune with herself.

She partly had Marcus to thank for the changes. He was the one who had made her aware of the things she appreciated the most, including her art work. She now understood that his place in her life as a friend was the correct one and it was exactly how she wanted it. Nothing more, nothing less.

All she needed to do now was work out her next steps with Alf.

She was ready to acknowledge that she wasn't quite ready to let what they had slip away entirely. He still held a place in her heart.

Alf surveyed the pitiful collection of boxes that signified the end of his new life in Scotland. If truth be told, he was relieved about the chain of events that had resulted in his demise at Hamilton's – something that he'd have never thought he'd feel.

He hadn't had to wait long for his resignation to become effective – in fact it was pretty much as he'd suspected. Henry Cavendish was conveniently in Scotland within an hour of his submitted formal resignation and introducing himself as the temporary MD. It didn't bother Alf as much as he'd thought it would; perhaps part of it was the substantial amount of money he was walking away from the arrangement with – the payoff that would enable him to, hopefully, rectify things with Kate and do some of the things she'd wanted to do together.

Alf's heartbeat picked up its pace as he thought about her and how best to contact her. She'd know all about it by now – of that much he was sure. Motormouth Megan would have made certain of that. Part of him had hoped that she'd call, although he knew it was a fruitless hope – after all, she'd made it clear that she didn't want him or their life together – so why would she be concerned with calling him? But he knew Kate, he knew how kind and compassionate she was. He was in no doubt that she'd be worried for him. He knew that when he did make contact, she would at least hear him out. It was his one chance at righting so many wrongs.

Picking up his keys from the kitchen worktop, he glanced one final time around the penthouse that had been his home for the past months. He felt nothing but elated happiness to be saying goodbye. Closing the door without a second thought, he picked up the boxes that were closest to hand and headed for the car.

One thing was for sure, Scotland had put everything into perspective for him. Life wasn't about work or power or penthouses – it was about love, support and togetherness. He could have kicked himself for not appreciating what he originally had a lot sooner. Still, better to find out late than never.

He had one last shot with Kate and he was going to make it worth her while.

Megan spotted him even from a distance. He was sitting at the dark wooden bench nearest to the pub entrance, nursing a beer with a pensive expression. His almost black wavy hair gleamed in the sun, and she felt her palms getting sweaty. There was something about him that did this to her every time.

Without warning, and as if sensing that she was near, he suddenly looked up and gazed in her direction, his face breaking into a grin, flashing perfectly straight white teeth as he noticed her approaching. She couldn't help but smile back; her jaw was acting of its own accord, as was her heart – racing wildly in her chest. She picked up her pace, Michael's disappointment that she'd changed their plans forgotten as she drank in Marcus's appearance.

'Hi, you look great.' He stood up kissing her on each cheek, noticing the slight curve of her waist and her slim wrists as he did so. She tossed her loosely curled hair self-consciously; a waft of vanilla hair product floated towards him, making him feel weakened. 'Thanks for agreeing to meet me. I hope I didn't drag you away from anything.'

She sat down opposite him, trying to avoid staring at the hint of tanned chest visible through his unbuttoned granddad top. 'It's no problem. I wasn't busy so…' she tailed off, feeling a combination of unease and guilt. Why had she lied to Michael? Surely there would have been no harm in telling him the truth about her meeting Marcus. When all was said and done, it wasn't as if she had anything to hide. Or did she?

He continued to stare at her, an awkward silence ensuing. The chemistry between them was palpable. She wanted nothing more than to reach out and pull him towards her, run her hand beneath his shirt and over his toned chest. She looked away, shame-faced at feeling such desire for him. 'So, you wanted to discuss Kate and Alf?' Forcing her eyes to meet his, she reminded herself of why she was there.

He had a hint of a wry smile on his lips, as if able to read her thoughts. His eyes twinkled in amusement and she felt her resolve weakening again. 'Yes, I spoke to Alf earlier this morning. He's heading back today.' He glanced at his watch, Megan following his gaze and resting her eyes on his masculine but slender hands. 'Well, actually, he'll already be on the road right about now.'

She was pulled back to the moment, her surprise obvious. 'Oh, I didn't expect him to leave so soon.' Her brow furrowed. 'He resigned on Friday, but the company gave him the option to stay on in the accommodation for a fortnight. I just assumed he'd stay and make the most of it.'

Marcus nodded, shrugging his shoulders. 'Yeah, I know, he mentioned it to me and I couldn't understand his haste to get back either. But he was insistent. He said he has things to sort out with Kate and the sooner the better.'

This was news to Megan. Her eyes widened in surprise. 'So he means it, then? About missing her.' She watched as Marcus took a sip of his beer. 'He did mention something the last time I spoke to him, but I have to say I wasn't very forgiving and cut him off.' She picked at a beer mat in front of her, thinking of Kate.

'Oh, yes, he means it. He's determined to get her back, from the things he was saying to me.' He looked at her, waiting for her response.

'Wow. I guess I wasn't expecting that. He's usually crap at recognising a good thing, let alone making amends.' She smiled at Marcus apologetically, suddenly remembering he was Alf's friend. 'Sorry. I'm sure you're aware there's no love lost between me and Alf, but I'll hand it to him. I'm impressed.'

Laughing, Marcus reached up and ran his hand through his hair. He liked her feistiness; in fact, he realised there were many things he liked about her. Really liked.

The harassed-looking waiter finally approached their table, interrupting them for Megan's order. 'I'll have a white wine, please,' she requested, feeling Marcus's eyes on her as she ordered. 'So, where were we?' she asked as the waiter retreated. 'Oh, yes, Alf… hang on a minute – where's he staying then if he's back tonight – surely not?' She was alarmed suddenly by the thought that he might be intending to head directly to Kate.

Sensing her panic, Marcus was quick to reassure her. 'No, no, don't worry, he's not going to theirs. He's staying with me.' Megan noticed that he didn't look entirely thrilled at the prospect. He turned his palms upwards as if in explanation. 'Least I can do after him and Kate put me up for a month.'

'Yes, I guess so,' she agreed, not envying him.

'So what do you think then?' he asked at the same time as the waiter approached them with her glass of wine. Nodding her thanks, she gratefully picked up the chilled glass.

'About Alf?' She took a sip of her wine, conscious of his eyes on her lips.

'Yes, about his chances with Kate. It's the reason I thought it was a good idea to meet, us being the pair closest to each of them.' He fiddled with his near-empty pint glass. 'I thought, you know, we can perhaps give them a helping hand in sorting it all out.'

'Play cupid, you mean?' she asked playfully, her flirty smile not lost on him.

'Something like that.'

She was serious again, remembering with a start that she was engaged. To Michael. Her lovely, kind and spontaneous Michael. 'I'm not sure.' She screwed up her nose, considering the idea. 'The thing is, although Kate's not completely over Alf, I still think it's better that she's moving on from him. If we start meddling, then it might send her backwards. It's going to be enough of a shock for her that he's returning so soon.'

Marcus shook his head. 'Megan, you know as well as I do that Kate will only go back with Alf if she decides that it's the right thing to do. She was the one who called it quits in the first place, remember? But you've got to agree on the pair of them meeting up and discussing things.'

'Yes, of course.' She looked at him in confusion. 'You said Alf is on his way back to do that, though? Why do we need to get involved?' She was wary. It wasn't their place to play matchmakers.

Marcus sighed, knowing he'd have to tell her the full story. 'Because Alf is intending to go about it completely the wrong way. He hinted that he's thinking of buying an engagement ring and proposing unexpectedly in a few days' time. He's convinced it's the only way Kate will forgive him.'

'Seriously, does he never learn?' Megan replied, incredulous. She knew that Kate would have loved this gesture a few months ago, but what with everything that had happened... she was sure that the pair of them needed to at least sit down and discuss things first. It would be foolish to arrive on the doorstep with a ring in hand and expect all to be forgiven in an instant.

'Exactly. He's a man on a mission. Which is why I'm suggesting that we arrange some kind of impromptu meeting between them – one that neither will expect. It'll give them a chance to see each other on neutral ground. A chance to talk honestly without any preconceived speeches.'

She sighed, knowing that he was making sense. If Alf was expecting to walk back into Kate's life with the intention of marrying her, then Kate at least deserved the chance to be prepared and open to the idea. As her friend, she would be helping to make that happen.

'Okay fine. Let's arrange something.'

Marcus smiled. 'See – I knew you'd be on board.' He winked at her and drained the last of his pint. 'I was thinking maybe tomorrow? A Sunday lunch here? You suggest it to Kate, I do the same to Alf and bingo – the both of them arrive and we bail out.'

'This had better not backfire. What if they argue?' Megan bit down on her bottom lip. 'Or worse, what if Kate hates the idea, blames me and never talks to me again?'

'No. You worry too much. That'll never happen, silly.' He reached across and grabbed her left wrist, his fingers locking gently around it causing a jolt of electricity to shoot through Megan's body. She shivered involuntarily and as if experiencing the same thing, he quickly took his hand away, embarrassed.

Why had he reached out to her? Why didn't Michael's touch have the same profound effect on her? She looked at him with questioning eyes.

'You're engaged now?' he asked, his eyes lowering to her hand and the wrist he'd just grabbed. She looked down, noticing for the first time since she'd sat down, her new diamond ring sparkling back at her.

So that was why he'd grabbed her wrist. She felt her heart sink and forced a smile. 'Yes.' She searched for the words, but none came.

'Wow. Congratulations. Fast work. I don't recall you being engaged when we went to the Thai restaurant that night with Kate?' He looked into her eyes, searching for something. 'Who's the lucky guy?'

He knew already, of course he did – he'd been there when she'd made the phone call to Kate. But she didn't know that he knew. He noticed a flicker of disappointment spreading across her face and it pleased him. She felt it too. He could sense it by her body language. There was something there between them. Something so much more than the chemistry he'd had with other women.

She regained her composure and tried to act happy. 'Yes, it was quite a surprise when Michael asked me. But you know…' she glanced down and stroked the diamond, tailing off.

No, I don't know, he wanted to say. So why are you marrying him? Why aren't you single and available so that I can pursue you? Instead he nodded. 'Yes, I do know. I was engaged to my ex.'

Megan's interest was sparked; it was the first time he'd mentioned his ex to her. Kate had once disclosed that Marcus had never spoken about what had really driven the breakdown of his relationship and his eventual decision to move back South. She narrowed her eyes, her intrigue overwhelming. She wanted to know all about him, every last detail. 'What happened?' The words were out of her mouth before she could stop herself.

The cloud that passed across his face was one of painful memories. It was all she could do to stop herself from reaching out and taking his hand in hers. She waited, noting his eyes dropping to the empty glass in front of him.

Silence pulsated between them for what felt like an age, before he finally spoke. 'Linzie was an addict. Cocaine.' He looked up and met her eyes. 'Well, she still is an addict as far as I'm aware. Seven years.' He sighed sadly. 'Seven years of trying to get her clean. In the end I couldn't do it any more.' His voice cracked and he turned away, embarrassed, coughing to clear his throat.

Instinctively Megan reached out and took his hand and squeezed it, feeling as if her own heart were being squeezed in a vice. Jonnie. It was just like Jonnie. 'I understand,' she said simply.

When he finally looked back at her, he squeezed her hand in return. 'I know you do, Megan. I know you do. I've met Jonnie.'

She gasped, not quite believing that she'd finally found someone who could relate to her.

He cleared his throat again and gently removed his hand from her grasp, drawing back and away from her, breaking the intimate moment.

'So where were we? What time for lunch tomorrow, then?'

The conversation was over, but she couldn't help wondering if she'd finally met her perfect match.

Chapter 21

'Why this place? Is the food any good?' Kate asked, scrunching up her nose at the traditional-looking pub they were heading towards. Its peeling black paint and wilted hanging baskets did little to give it credit. Yet from the throng of people standing outside, she knew it must be a popular choice. 'I hope we can get a table. I don't want to have to stand around for ages waiting. Not when I could have just cooked us something at mine.'

Megan wasn't listening; instead she was desperately scanning the crowd for Marcus, wishing she'd never agreed to this ridiculous plan in the first place – not only had it taken her all morning to convince Kate to accompany her, but she was anxious about the possible outcomes. All of them were currently looking increasingly likely to be bleak – especially given that Kate appeared to be in a grumpy and less than pleasing mood. She caught sight of Marcus's head, swiftly followed by Alf's torso, obscured behind a large potted plant. Relieved, she quickly stepped in front of Kate, blocking the view in the boys' direction. 'Yes, yes don't worry – a table's reserved. I did it when I was here yesterday.'

'Yesterday?' Kate frowned. 'You were here yesterday and you wanted to come again today?' Baffled, she shook her head and fanned out the pretty, recently purchased pastel summer dress she'd chosen to wear. The dress had been Megan's idea – a suggestion that she make a bit of an effort given her new single status. Stupidly, despite feeling bloated, premenstrual and stickily hot, she'd agreed. 'I wish I'd worn something looser,' she complained, feeling uncomfortable.

Waving a hand dismissively, Megan marched ahead. 'Stop moaning. We're here now.' Pushing past the customers milling outside, enjoying their drinks in the sunshine, she headed for the entrance, keen to get the introduction over with. 'This way.'

Heading left, towards where she'd previously spotted Marcus and Alf and planning how best to handle the approach, it was a few moments before she realised that Kate had stopped following her. She was surprised to feel a firm hand on her right shoulder. She jumped in response and span around. It was Marcus.

Her mouth formed an 'Oh' in surprise, her eyes flitting towards Alf – who was standing next to him, very still, with a shocked expression – then to the deathly pale Kate who stood a couple of yards away, bewildered.

'Alf?'

'Kate?'

Alf sucked in a deep breath. She looked like a vision, an absolute vision – he couldn't quite believe that she was standing there in front of him. He rushed to speak, a wave of ecstasy and fear coursing through him all at once. 'What are you doing here?' What was she doing there? He looked towards a shifty Marcus, and then at Megan, her eyes lowered guiltily, confusion muddling his thoughts. What on earth was going on?

'You're back?' Kate spoke at exactly the same moment, surprising herself at the buoyancy in her tone. It was absurd, how was it possible that Alf was here? Why wasn't he in Scotland? Her heart was banging against her chest as she looked into his familiar eyes, noting the tiredness and dark circles, but wanting, all the more, to rush forwards and cuddle him. A million questions danced through her mind, all of them overwhelming her with the urgency for answers.

Squeezing Megan's shoulder, Marcus stepped forwards. 'Guys?' He looked apologetic as he interrupted, drawing their attention reluctantly towards himself. 'Sorry to lure you both here under false pretences, but we thought it would do you good to chat.' He caught Megan's eyes and tried to reassure her with his gaze, noticing that Alf and Kate were eyeing each other with nervous expressions 'So if you're up for chatting, we've got you a table reserved under my name.'

He waited for someone to say something, wondering if it had been a good idea after all. Aside from the loud buzz of activity around them, the four of them stood in uncomfortable silence, Megan looking more and more edgy by the second.

Finally, Alf turned to him with an exhilarated expression. 'You planned this?' He rubbed his face with his hand, going quiet. After a moment's hesitation, he slowly patted Marcus's back, a smile breaking out across his face. 'Well, I guess I should say thanks, mate.'

'Kate, are you okay with it?' Megan asked, flustered, conscious of her part in the matter and reluctant to leave her friend, who was wide-eyed with shock and staring transfixedly at Alf.

Kate slowly shook her head, incredulous, before allowing an exuberant smile. 'I can't believe you two arranged this.' She glanced from Megan to Marcus, her brain trying to assimilate all that was taking place. Her eyes eventually met Alf's again, a burst of emotion rising up from the depths of her stomach.

Unable to resist Kate's captivating presence and timid glance, he seized the moment to pull her gently into his arms, embracing her smaller frame. 'Come here, you, I've missed you so much, babe.' She wrapped herself instinctively around him, closing her eyes and relaxing her head onto his shoulder. He smelled familiar and safe. She heard a whooshing sound in her ears, the unheralded situation making her feel lightheaded. Nevertheless, she knew she didn't want to let go of him, so she kissed him – a small, tender kiss – before pulling away. 'I've missed you too, Alf.'

Marcus leaned in closer to Megan. 'I think that's our cue to get the hell out of here before they change their minds.' He rested his hand lightly against the small of her back, giving her a gentle push forwards.

At the tender exchange taking place between the couple, Megan felt relief flood through her. Pacified, she smiled up at Marcus's suggestion and nodded her head in agreement. 'Definitely time to go.'

'Yes, I'm back down to a size ten,' Kate replied confidently as Alf's gaze swept appreciatively over her. 'And I got the highlights in my hair last month. I wasn't sure at first, but I love them now.' They were seated in a quieter corner and although their food had been served twenty minutes earlier, it remained barely touched, neither of them having the appetite to tuck in.

'So, you're sure about wanting to give things another try, then?' Alf asked carefully, waiting apprehensively for Kate's confirmation. Seeing her sitting in front of him, looking more radiant and far more peaceful than he'd see her in a long time, was making his heart contract with overwhelming desire.

'Of course I am.' She reached across the table, grabbing his hand and squeezing it in her own. She held his stare. 'Like I said to you before, I feel there's been a silver lining in us having this time apart and both of us being able to reassess things. I'm so much happier in myself at the moment, Alf, and I know that was part of the problem before. Me not being happy.'

'It was me as well, though, Kate. I see that now. I was too wrapped up in work, thinking that if I could achieve a good level, then it would benefit our relationship in the long run. But look where that attitude has got me.' He sighed, gazing sentimentally into his pint of bitter and absentmindedly tickling the palm of her hand with his fingers.

'Well, we've both been at fault, but let's not focus on the past. If we're going to make amends then it's got to be with a fresh perspective, agreed?' She tilted her head sideways, smiling adoringly at his tender expression.

'Yeah, I agree.' He reached across, delicately stroking a lock of hair away from her face. 'As long as you promise to open up to me about things, too. No more holding back about how you feel. If you ever want to discuss stuff, I'm right here, okay?'

Knowing from the way he spoke that he was referring to the miscarriage, she nodded her head slowly. 'I know. I won't hold my thoughts in any more. It's a new start for us.'

And it was. For if she'd learnt anything from being apart and having time to reflect, it was that experiences of the past were no longer to be given power over the present. She'd made her peace with her loss and it was now time to move on.

Megan felt the vibration of her mobile in her shoulder bag, but chose to ignore it, instead licking her thumb as another drop of vanilla ice cream landed on her hand. 'This is melting too fast. I haven't even eaten the flake yet.'

Marcus glanced at her barely touched ninety-nine and then back to his own, already empty of ice cream to the rim of the cone. 'No, you're just a slow eater, Megan. You'll be wearing it soon if you don't hurry up.'

'Or maybe you're just a pig!' she joked as he crunched down on his wafer cone, half of it disappearing into his mouth.

He smiled, wiping the crumbs from his lips with the back of his hand. 'Maybe.' Narrowing his eyes, he slowed his steps and cocked his head. 'Can you hear that noise? Like a buzzing sound?'

Feigning straining to hear, she discreetly slipped her hand inside her bag and pressed the silence button on the mobile. The vibration stopped. She knew it was Michael wondering where'd she'd got to – she was already at least an hour late, but she'd have to think of a suitable excuse later. She hadn't been expecting Marcus to ask if she wanted to take a stroll by the river – her plan had been to head straight home after the pub incident, but the suggestion had made her heart leap. 'No, I can't seem to hear anything...' She shrugged her shoulders and moved closer to him as a group of people almost collided with them on the narrow riverbank edge. 'So how'd you think they're getting on?'

Marcus finished chewing the last of his cornet and wiped his hands on his jeans. 'Well, I'd say if that kiss is anything to go by, and the fact we haven't had a phone call from either one of them yet – then they're doing okay.'

'I hope so. Kate's going to go mad at me otherwise.'

'Na, she won't.' He shook his head. 'She's going to thank you. You wait and see.' He pointed at a nearby canal boat painted in bright yellow and red – its deck adorned with various exotic and colourful potted plants. 'Look at that, that's a beauty. I've always wanted to live on one of those.'

Megan looked at him curiously, a strange feeling in her chest. 'Have you really?' She couldn't hide the surprise in her voice. 'When I was younger that was my dream too – to live on a narrowboat and go where the wind blew me.'

'Really?' He looked at her oddly, checking that she wasn't humouring him. She wasn't. 'Wow! You're the first woman I've met that's shared that same idea.' He grinned at her.

She smiled back, feeling her stomach fluttering in a way that it had never fluttered before. The sensation scared her – it was overpowering. Michael's face flashed into her mind and brought her back to earth with a bump. 'I don't know about now, though. I'm a bit older and obviously there's my shoe collection...' she joked, feeling guilty for encouraging things and wanting to put a stop to the idea before it got out of control. 'Plus Michael isn't really the type to go in for something like that.' She let the words hang between them, resurrecting a barrier and reminding them both of their places.

Sensing her change in mood and reminding himself that she was off-limits – an engaged woman, for Christ's sake – Marcus glanced at his mobile. 'Time's flown. Can you believe it's almost three o'clock? I'll need to head off soon – I told my sister I'd pop around and see the kids.'

Disappointment swept through her as she silently cursed herself for bringing up Michael. She tried to remain upbeat, keeping her tone even. 'Goodness, I didn't realise it was that time already. I need to get going soon, too.'

'Let's start heading back, then,' Marcus replied reluctantly, not wanting the moment to come to an end. 'I think we must have caught some rays on our arms – look at that.' He lifted the cuff of his t-shirt, showing a distinct tan line between his exposed arm and covered shoulder.

Extending her right arm in front of her Megan observed the golden glisten of her skin. 'Yes, we have actually. We should have put some sunscreen on.' Not paying attention to the ice cream she was eating, she didn't notice that the bottom of the cornet had cracked, a large dollop of ice cream falling from its base and onto her chest as she bit into it. 'Oooh, damn, that's cold!'

Laughing, Marcus instinctively leaned forwards and wiped away the melted ice cream from her bare skin, not considering the intimacy of the gesture until he looked up – his face only inches from Megan's.

Locking eyes, it was as if time had stood still. Neither of them daring to breath, Megan tilted her head ever so slightly – hoping it was incentive enough for Marcus to kiss her.

He pulled away quickly, the spell broken, flustered and avoiding looking at her. 'Right, I really must get going. My sister will be wondering where I am.'

Megan agreed with a nod of her head, feeling flummoxed by the countless emotions that were threatening to drown her. Never had she so strongly wanted a man to kiss her. Feeling awkward she quickly discarded her ice cream in a nearby bin, glad of the excuse to move away from him.

Marcus picked up speed, busying himself with riffling through his pockets and making a show of checking his mobile. He stopped suddenly as they came to a narrow walkway. 'I'll slip off here, if that's okay. It's a quicker route to my sister's.' It wasn't. But he needed to get away from her. Her presence was too powerful, too alluring. He didn't trust himself not to do something he'd regret.

'Yeah, of course – no worries.'

He kissed her quickly on the cheek, before she had a chance to react. The smell of her skin made him want to throw his arms around her and never let go. Instead he backed away rapidly. 'I'll catch up with you soon, then, once we know how the guys got on today.'

Standing there with mixed emotions, Megan found it difficult to focus on what he was saying. She was watching his lips move and the way his mouth curled upwards at the corners. He had her insides in a twist.

'Bye, then. Talk soon.'

She forced herself to stay rooted to the spot and not go after him. 'Bye, Marcus – I'll text you when I hear from Kate.'

He smiled, knowing that he'd hear from Kate directly as well – but happy that Megan was finding an excuse to stay in contact. 'Yeah, do that.'

She watched him walk away with a heavy heart, knowing that she shouldn't be pining for a man she barely knew.

As if on cue, her mobile began to vibrate again. It was a harsh reminder of her fiancé. The one who was calling to find out where she was. Riddled with guilt, she gingerly retrieved the phone from her bag and pressed the answer key.

It should have felt like the most natural thing in the world, having Alf sitting back at the kitchen table for breakfast. Instead it felt a little odd – almost as if he didn't belong any more. Kate busied herself with making them a cup of tea and looked on in amusement as Sam continued to wag his tail furiously, unable to contain his excitement.

'I can't believe how well I slept last night. I've missed our bed.' Alf smiled, watching Kate with interest. It had been a magical night together, one that he'd recreated countless times in his head since the split and yet, in reality, it had been so much more explosive. They'd certainly made up for the time apart.

'It was nice having you there again. It's not felt right without you.' Kate brought their tea to the table, a packet of biscuits under her arm. The past twenty-four hours had been a whirlwind of changes and totally unexpected, but she couldn't remember feeling so happy. It was refreshing having Alf back in their home, even if it did feel weird.

'I've been thinking about a lot of the stuff you were saying yesterday.' Alf picked up his mug and took a gulp of the strong tea, wondering how receptive Kate would be to the idea he was about to propose. 'What do you reckon about selling up? Starting afresh, you know – somewhere a bit bigger, with a bit more space.' He paused, noticing her eyes widen. 'I mean, it doesn't have to be a different area. We both like it here.' He set down his mug. 'I just thought it could be a good thing. A fresh start?'

Kate was bewildered. Who was this man sitting in front of her? He most certainly seemed different to the Alf she'd spent the best part of seven years with. She wasn't complaining; it was a welcome change. She couldn't quite get her head around his complete about-face, though. First his declaration in the pub that he'd messed up by allowing her to walk away – and now this?

'Do you really mean that?' she asked tentatively, wondering whether he was saying it purely because he knew it was what she'd love to hear.

'I do. And I'm not saying it because it's what you wanted.'

Kate suppressed a smile. He knew her too well.

'I'm saying it because I really think it could be good for us. I was pondering on it on the drive back from Scotland. I was hoping that if you did have me back, it would be something we could consider. You were right, this place was never going to be our forever home anyway.'

She shifted uncomfortably, not wanting to state the obvious

but needing to – given that he was serious. 'What about you not having a job now, though? How're we going to get a mortgage – especially for something bigger?'

'Let's not worry about that yet. We've got the payoff money to add a bit to the deposit and I'll have a job soon enough.' He reached for a biscuit. 'Which reminds me – did you know Megan's offered to keep an ear out for any positions coming up?'

Kate looked at Alf in surprise. 'Has she?' Since when did Megan do favours for Alf?

'Yes, she's got those contacts at that recruitment company that deal with Hamilton's and the competitors; she said she's always getting wind of when a job's coming available elsewhere and she'd let me know.' He dunked the oat biscuit in his tea, eating it in one go. 'Got to say, I'm pretty impressed at the change in her since she's met this new fella Michael. He's sorted her right out. She's no longer a nasty witch.' He laughed as Kate playfully slapped him on the arm.

'Don't be mean. That's nice of her to do that for you. And yes, she has changed a lot recently – she's a lot calmer.' She considered the changes in Megan and took a sip of her tea, allowing Sam, who was whining for her attention, to jump up onto her lap. 'So, about the house. Do you think we should get it on the market soon, then?'

Alf nodded. 'Sooner the better. It might take a while to sell, babe – these things can take time. We might as well prepare ourselves for a wait before we receive an offer.' He chewed his lip. 'That's a good thing, though – it'll give me time to get a new job sorted, anyway.'

'That's true. I suppose it wouldn't hurt to tidy the place up a bit, either. A lick of paint to make it more appealing to the buyers, perhaps?' She felt suddenly excited, her senses flared up for the new adventure that awaited them.

'We can go to the estate agent later this afternoon if you want? After you get home from work? Get the ball rolling and maybe have a nosy at what's out there for us if we do sell.' He felt himself getting fired up at the idea – just as he had the previous night when he'd lain awake next to a sleeping Kate and thought about how best to plan their future together. It was the first step of the many changes he'd been considering. It felt right. His severance with Hamilton's had taught him that it was pointless to try to always be in control. It was easier to surrender to the flow of life and treat it as an adventure.

'Yes, that'll be great. I can't wait now. How exciting,' Kate replied enthusiastically, picking up her teacup. 'Speaking of work, though, I've just seen the time. I'd better get a move on or I'm going to be late.' She stood up, Sam jumping to the floor.

'Wait.' Alf grabbed her hand, pulling her towards him and wondering how he'd managed to spend so long taking her for granted. She was perfect, everything he wanted in a woman. 'I love you, babe.' He stood up and wrapped his arms around her waist as she gazed at him. 'I hope you know that. This time around, it's going to be different. So different.'

Searching into his eyes, Kate knew he meant it. She could feel the validity in her heart and everything he'd said to her yesterday had proved it, as had his gentle lovemaking and reassuring cuddles.

'I know it is. This time around it's going to be for good.'

And it was. Otherwise she would never have let him back into her home, her life and her heart. Alf Stafford was her destiny. She was sure of it; more so than ever before.

Chapter 22

'I wasn't expecting to see you, Grumps, that's all.' Marcus replied, bringing his grandfather a large tumbler of whisky and taking a seat on the recliner opposite him.

Roberto raised an eyebrow, sensing the nervousness in his grandson's actions. 'Well, I'm staying with your sister for a while; it's only natural I was going to want to see you.'

'Of course. And I'm pleased you're here.' It wasn't a lie. What with the move back South and the way things had turned out, it had been on Marcus's mind to make the trip to Leeds to see his grandfather, but he just hadn't found the time. 'Sorry I haven't made it up to see you.'

'It's okay, son, I know you've been busy. Your sister's been filling me in on everything.'

Marcus couldn't be sure, but he thought he saw a twinkle in his grandfather's eyes. He clutched his own whisky glass a little tighter, knowing he needed to say something about his manuscript soon.

Leaning forwards and sloshing the ice around his glass thought-fully, Roberto enjoyed the moment of keeping his grandson in suspense. The boy clearly had done well for himself; he was pleased to see Marcus looking more relaxed, his face free of the worry that had been troubling him for so long. It was a far cry from the last time he'd seen him – what with that Linzie dragging him down.

Good riddance to bad rubbish was his thought on the matter. The boy had finally seen sense.

'So, this book deal, then.' He watched in amusement as Marcus's head shot up, his cheeks colouring.

'Grumps, listen…'

Holding up his hand to his grandson, Roberto pressed on. 'Your sister tells me I might be something of a star once the manuscript's published – being that my life story is the main basis of it.' He looked at Marcus pointedly. 'So would you care to share exactly which of my many secrets you're intending to divulge to the literary world?'

Marcus grimaced, embarrassed to be caught out. 'I was going to tell you sooner…' He stared down at the new beige carpet of his North Street property. 'The thing is, I knew you might not be okay with me using parts of your life – the affairs and so forth, I mean – so that's why I've also added in a lot of fictional twists. No one, except maybe those closest, will even know that it's inspired by you.'

He looked back at his grandfather who had a mischievous grin on his face. 'Son, you worry far too much.' He shook his head with a chuckle. 'I'm truly made up that you've found a positive way to use my misgivings.'

'Really? You're not pissed off about it, then?'

'Well, only the fact that you've gone and mixed it up with fiction. I wouldn't have minded my photo and dedication on the cover.' He grinned, took a gulp of his whisky and relaxed back into the sofa. 'I'm proud of you, Marcus.' He looked around the room. 'You really have started over and it's the best decision you could have made.'

Marcus felt relieved. His grandfather meant the world to him and the last thing he'd wanted to do was upset him. He allowed himself to smile and thought about how far his life had come in such a short space of time.

'Who's the lucky woman, then, son?' Roberto asked, leaning

forwards again and narrowing his eyes. It was obvious from the look on his grandson's face that there was a special someone; he was too old and wise not to notice.

'Megan.' Without skipping a beat, Marcus answered instantly – shocking himself in the process. He pursed his lips and gripped the whisky glass with both hands. He had to stop thinking about her, it wasn't right to… she was an engaged woman after all.

'Problematic is she?' Roberto asked, aware of the change in his grandson's mood and hoping to God that he wasn't involved with another type like Linzie. He knew Marcus was always drawn to the ones who needed help; the ones that he could try to be a saviour to. It was his downfall when it came to women.

'No, she's lovely, actually. Works in London, very beautiful. A really direct and honest person. The thing is, she's already engaged to someone. She only met him a few months ago and the cheeky bastard has gone and got a ring on her finger already.'

Roberto listened with interest, never taking his eyes off Marcus. He stayed silent for a few minutes after before deciding it was time to finally talk about the only woman who had ever won and then broken his heart. Broken it by not being able to forgive him for the affair he'd stupidly had.

'Son, let me tell you a story. It's about my first marriage to a woman called Lillian, right here in London.' He smiled fondly at the memory, wondering what had happened to his beloved Lil.

Marcus set down his glass in surprise, wondering why he'd never heard this story before. Besides, how could his first marriage have been to a woman called Lillian? Hadn't his first marriage been to a woman called Mercedes in Spain?

His grandfather was already lost in the process of storytelling, a melancholic expression on his face. 'It all began with an introduction. She was the only one who ever called me Bobbi, you see…'

Pressing the doorbell, Kate stood back and waited.

She heard Megan's mumbled voice from inside the hallway,

followed by a rattling sound.

'Just a sec.' Moments later, the door opened and Megan stumbled from behind it – awkwardly tugging a long green t-shirt over her head. 'Sorry – was getting changed. Had to get my suit off – I've felt uncomfortable in that bloomin' pencil skirt all day. '

Kate stepped into the porch and kicked her pumps off. 'I know how you feel, I've been on my feet all day. They've been killing me in these pumps.'

'How was work?'

Following Megan through to the kitchen, Kate hung her handbag over the banister. 'Not bad. I'm a bit worried about Hilda, though. She's got this awful-sounding cough – I think it might be serious this time.'

'Is that the hypochondriac one – the one I met at the fête that year and she told me she was on the donor waiting list?'

'Yes, that's the one. The doctor saw her earlier; he took me aside and said it could be the onset of pneumonia.'

'Goodness, that's an awful shame. She seemed very sweet, even if she was a bit of a loon.' Megan picked up the kettle and set about making tea. 'Do you want tea, or something stronger?'

'Tea's fine, thanks. I told Alf I'd be back by eight o'clock – he's booked a table for us at Pedro's.' She couldn't help but smile happily as she said this. It had been a nice surprise to receive his call at lunchtime and be told that he wanted to treat her to a special meal.

'So I take it that you guys are very much back on, then?' Megan asked carefully. 'Are you still getting along fine at home?'

'It's early days yet – I mean it's only been just over a week, hasn't it, since he moved back in – but so far things have been going well.' She scratched her arm, noticing the oil paint that she'd been using the previous night staining the undersides of her nails. 'The agent said the photos of the house will be ready for us to check over tomorrow, too.'

'The estate agent? Already? But I thought you were going to decorate a bit first?' Megan replied, stunned that things seemed to be moving along so fast.

'The decorating has been done!' Kate said proudly, noting the look of surprise on her friend's face. 'It's only because he's not working. It's given him something to do all week. The agent took the photos yesterday; he reckons we shouldn't have too many problems with selling fast because of the location.'

Picking up two china cups from the draining board, Megan put a teabag into each. 'That's great, hun. Are you going to start looking for something soon, then, just in case it does sell quickly?'

'No,' Kate replied, shaking her head. 'I've said to Alf that anything we do now has to be considered and thought out properly. No more rushing ahead for the moment. I'd just prefer to take things slowly for the time being. After all, he rushed ahead with the whole Scotland thing and look where that got us!'

Megan nodded. 'I think that's wise.' She thought about her own predicament. 'If I'm honest, I'm wondering if things have bounded ahead too quickly with Michael and me.'

'How do you mean? I thought all was great between you two.' Concerned, Kate came over to her friend. 'Has Jonnie been stirring things up again?'

Turning to face her, Megan failed miserably to hide her unhappiness, feeling tearful as Kate touched her arm. 'No, it's not Jonnie. He's not mentioned anything else.' She picked at the sleeve of her t-shirt, feeling sheepish. 'It's just that I'm not sure if Michael is the right one for me. The more I'm getting to know him, the more I'm beginning to doubt.' She turned back to the tea and stirred in the milk.

Kate frowned. 'Why the sudden change of heart, though?' she asked, wondering what had prompted such feelings. 'Do you think perhaps the honeymoon phase is wearing off and you're just a bit scared of the idea of commitment?' she probed gently.

Sighing, Megan picked up their teacups and carried them to the island counter. Grateful for the chance to have her back to Kate, she used the opportunity to get what was really troubling her off her chest. 'No, it's neither of those things.' She set down the cups. 'I've met someone else, Kate.'

Before she had a chance to turn around, Kate was already in front of her, wide-eyed with shock. 'You've what?' She stood agog, staring at Megan. 'Since when? Why didn't you tell me? Who is he?'

Despite her guilt at the admission finally being spoken aloud, Megan smiled. 'Who are you – PC Plod?' She took a seat, sinking her head into her hands – Kate waiting patiently for her to begin explaining. 'It wasn't expected. I've known him a while, but there's something there – something much deeper than I've got with Michael. I know he feels it, too. And we've got a lot in common.'

'Where did you meet? At work? Is it anyone I know?' Kate asked, intrigued.

Megan bit down on her lip, feeling torn. Ever since she'd thought about telling Kate of her feelings for Marcus she'd debated whether it was the right thing to do. She wanted nothing more than to be honest, but was that really fair on any of them? What if Marcus didn't feel the same way – was it wise to reveal his name before she even knew where he stood?

No, it wasn't. So as much as it pained her to lie, she'd decided that until she had a definite confirmation of Marcus's feelings it would be a lot easier and kinder to Kate if she wasn't aware that she was referring to Marcus. She also didn't want to put Kate's reconnection with Alf into jeopardy. Surely if Kate knew, she was certain to be flummoxed and maybe even angry; it was only natural that she wouldn't immediately be able to understand the strong connection that Megan felt, especially after Kate had thought she'd had that same connection with Marcus herself. And then, what if Alf questioned things and discovered the truth about Kate's previous fixation?

Besides, it had only been a month since the kissing incident, and given that the bridge between the pair had only just been rebuilt, she didn't want to cause more friction.

'Look, it's someone at work. That's all you need to know until

I'm clearer on the matter.' She lowered her eyes at Kate's sympathetic expression, feeling even more of a traitor than she did already. 'You're my best friend and I value your advice more than anyone's – if I'm having doubts about Michael and experiencing a stronger connection to somebody else; even though nothing has happened, doesn't that mean I shouldn't be engaged to Michael?'

Kate reached across and grabbed Megan's hand supportively, noticing how uncharacteristically guilt-ridden and embarrassed she appeared to be. 'Hun, whoever it is, if the feelings for him are really that strong and it's more than lust and sexual chemistry.' She nodded gently. 'Then, yes, I suggest you need to have a good think about whether being engaged to Michael is the right thing. It's too soon to be having doubts only a few months into a new relationship. Especially one that you're intending to stay in 'till death do you part." She smiled wryly, watching as Megan slumped in her seat in disappointment.

'I know you're right,' Megan muttered, although she'd half-hoped that Kate would have given her another answer, one that told her to be happy with what she had already. One that didn't make things even more complicated. What if Marcus didn't feel the same, though? What if she was mistaken?

'Have you told this other guy how you feel?' Kate asked, her curiosity getting the better of her and wondering who at Hamilton's it could possibly be. Surely not Tray from Compliance? Hadn't Megan once said she thought he was quite nice? No. Surely not?

'No, I haven't.' Megan stared into her tea, wondering how Marcus would react if she did tell him. 'Do you think I should do that before I make a decision on Michael?'

Kate considered this for a moment before answering. She'd never seen Megan as happy with a partner as she'd been since meeting Michael – maybe this other guy was a distraction, something she was focusing on out of fear that things could be too good to be true? But, then again, perhaps she was truly falling for another person. Didn't they say that once the heart was open to love it could feel a lot deeper? What if Michael was her warm-up for the real thing? She thought of something her aunt used to say and found herself repeating it.

'No, if you don't know what to do, then it's best to do nothing at all.' She smiled as Megan looked at her quizzically. 'It means wait until you've had the chat with the other guy, to find out where he stands – before you make a decision on you and Michael.'

Exhaling loudly, Megan dismally agreed. 'Okay, advice taken. I'll have the chat first, then take it from there. In the meantime, though, I'll just try and focus on being happy with Michael.' She picked up her cup and absentmindedly took a sip of tea. She knew how impossible it was going to be to try and put Marcus from her thoughts – after all, she'd barely been able to think about anything else for the past week.

'On another note, I've got some good news' Kate chirped, a bright smile on her face.

Forgetting her sullen mood, Megan looked at Kate curiously. 'Go on, then – what news?'

'I've had offers on three separate paintings that were hung at the care home!' She clapped her hands in elation. 'I can't believe it, Meg. I mean, I didn't think they would actually sell to anyone – let alone visitors.'

'Goodness, hun, that is amazing.' Standing up, Megan quickly moved across to congratulate her. 'I knew this painting thing was going to pay off. I told you you're too good to be wasting yourself.' Putting her arms around Kate, she swayed her playfully from side to side. 'Don't forget your best friend when you're rich and famous,' she joked.

Chortling, Kate pulled away, radiant. 'I won't – it's only thanks to you and Marcus that I even gave it another shot.' She sat back down. 'Alan told me about the offers this morning – they're good ones, too. He said it's up to me whether I want to accept them – but if I do, then the board apparently wants replacement paintings.'

'Fantastic! You've got to accept, Kate – this is your new beginning with your art.' Megan walked to the fridge, remembering that she had a box of unopened Belgian truffles that would suit the mood perfectly. 'So, are you all set for your exhibition?' Opening the fridge door she reached for the gold-and-blue box of chocolates. 'Oh, and I meant to ask, do you want me to pick up Vivian and Lillian on my way there – it will save you rushing about and have time to get ready properly?'

Kate took a deep breath, the mention of her impending exhibition making her heart dive into the depths of her stomach. It had come around so quickly and although she was prepared, she couldn't help but wonder if she was mad to go ahead with it. Yet the news of the offers received at the care home had been the encouraging push she'd needed – it was a confirmation of sorts that her paintings were good enough. Besides, she'd come too far to back out now, even if the thought of Saturday did terrify her.

'That would be a great help, thanks. I'll let Viv and Lil know. That'll give me more time for any last-minute things.'

'Good, that's sorted, then.' She thrust the box of truffles towards Kate, opening the lid in the process. 'Here, have one of these. Michael bought them for me.'

Picking a chocolate from the box, Kate noticed how Megan's face clouded at the mention of Michael's name and realised how heavily the connection with the new guy was weighing on her friend's relationship and mind.

She decided to change the subject and lift the mood again – there was nothing to be gained by raking over things they'd already decided. She suddenly remembered something she'd wanted to tell Megan. 'Oh, listen to this.'

Megan looked up intrigued, popping another soft and chocolaty ball into her mouth and thinking how much calmer and content Kate looked in herself. It was madness that their roles had pretty much reversed within the space of a couple of weeks. Hadn't she been the happy and peaceful one just a fortnight ago? She focused again on what Kate was saying. '… and then Marcus told Alf that...' The chocolate ball lodged itself in her throat at Kate's mention of his name.

Perhaps things were going to be a lot trickier than she'd expected.

Chapter 23

'What about that one?' Kate pointed towards a luminous-green leather recliner at the opposite end of the furniture showroom. 'Or not quite bright enough? She giggled and bent down to pick up a colour chart for the fabric-covered sofa they were standing in front of.

'That's bloody awful.' Alf laughed. 'I'd have a headache after five minutes of having that in the house. Do people really buy chairs in that colour?' Alf shook his head in disbelief.

'Apparently so.' She nodded discreetly towards the young couple who had stopped to consider the garish option. 'I think leather is a good choice, though. This fabric one is lovely, but with Sam jumping all over it, it'll be ruined in two minutes.'

'Cor, that's pretty cool.' Alf said, his attention caught by a children's bedroom unit he'd spotted nearby. He eyed the fire-engine structure in awe. 'I'd have loved one of those as a kid.'

'Oh, look over there, there's a princess castle for a girl's room, too.' Kate signalled to the left, looking at the pretty pastel-coloured bed tower. 'I don't think we'd fit in either, though. Especially you,' she joked, digging him lightly in the ribs with her elbow.

'You might have half a chance, I certainly wouldn't. But we're definitely getting one for our future son one day.'

'Yes, definitely.' Kate smiled, her heart beating ten to the dozen.

It was such a simple sentence and yet it spoke volumes. Alf leaned in, resting his hand on the small of her back.

'Oooh, look at that up there. That's unusual. Never seen a painting like that before.' He stared up at the huge piece of artwork mounted on the upper level – a colourful mix of oils depicting a vintage car. 'That'd look fantastic in our lounge.'

Kate followed his gaze, turning up her nose as she studied the creation. 'Hmm, no I don't think so! There's no way I'm having that in any new home we move to.'

'Oh, don't be a spoil sport,' he replied, mounting the stairs to take a closer look. 'Let's just have a see how much it costs. I could get it for the office or spare room?'

Following behind him with a shake of her head, she watched as he stepped in closer to the price code on the wall. 'Eleven hundred quid!' He turned to her, whistling loudly. 'They're having a laugh, aren't they?'

Kate chuckled. 'Well, if you really like it that much, I can paint it for you!' She leaned in closer to the painting, studying the brushwork. It would be extremely simple to replicate.

With a shrug of his shoulders, Alf waved a hand dismissively in front of her. 'No, you don't want to be wasting your time painting. It's pointless.' He was already turning away and walking towards a mirrored dining table.

Kate felt herself bristling. Wasting time painting? Pointless? What did he mean by that? Trying to rationalise her thoughts, she glanced at Alf with a questioning expression, relieved that his back was towards her.

'When we finish here do you fancy popping to the pub for a bit?' he turned to her, unaware that he'd said anything wrong, and stepped forward to plant a small kiss on her forehead. 'You look gorgeous today, by the way.' He smiled at her as if she was the prettiest thing he'd ever seen.

Mentally chastising herself for doubting him and being quick to jump on his words, she softened and nodded her head, linking her arm through his. 'Sure, that'll be lovely.'

'Well, it had me shocked, I tell you.' Vivian tutted in disdain, dipping her spoon into the thick leek-and-potato soup. 'They call this soup? It's like eating an onion-batter mix. It's disgraceful.' Grimacing, she ate a single spoonful before surrendering her cutlery to the bowl. 'No, I shan't be eating any more of that.'

'Fancy making us soup in this hot weather, anyway,' Lil grumbled, equally unappeased by the lunchtime offering. 'I have to agree about Kate, though – she has looked happier this past week. Even if it does seem as if she's gone backwards instead of forwards.'

'My intuition says it won't last, but she'll realise that soon enough.' Vivian said, unscrewing her flask and pouring Guinness into the empty coffee cup. 'I've got a feeling this exhibition on Saturday will show her a thing or two.'

'Ooh, speaking of which, I'm ever so excited about it. I can't remember the last time we had a night out away from this place. And it's really nice of Kate's Megan to collect us.'

Vivian raised an eyebrow at Lil's enthusiasm. 'Hmm, don't you go thinking it's going to be too wild a night. It's Kate's night, not a chance for you to get dosed up on free wine. We're only there to support her – not for you to make a mockery of yourself.'

'Ha!' Lillian exclaimed. 'Hark at you, dishing out the orders. Keep your knickers on, I'll behave – oh, and don't you go forgetting your flask or else we'll all be in for it.'

Seeing Kate enter the dining room with Alan, the two ladies stopped sniping at one another and settled into a comfortable silence.

'All okay?' Kate asked, walking across to the table. 'Why aren't you eating the soup, Viv?'

'It's bloody diabolical, that's why. I'm going to have to have another word with that chef – he's useless.'

'Do you want me to see if I can get you something else from the kitchen?'

Glancing pointedly at her coffee cup filled with Guinness, Vivian winked. 'I think I'm okay, love, got me medicine there. That keeps me going – it's full of iron, it is.'

Kate grinned and pulled out a chair, sitting down to join them. 'If you say so. Anyway, I just spoke with Alf, he says the agent has already got a couple lined up for a viewing of the house this weekend.'

'Cor blimey, that's good news for the pair of you, ain't it?' Lillian replied, carefully buttering a soft, white roll. 'You two had better start looking for somewhere new, then. You never know, they might have it, this couple.'

Kate shook her head uncertainly. 'No, it's only the first viewing, so I don't think there's any rush just yet. Anyway I want to get the exhibition out of the way first – that's my main priority.'

'And what's Alf think about all this with your art work?' Vivian piped up, intrigued that in the two weeks since Alf had re-entered Kate's life, his thoughts on her new-found success had barely been given a mention.

Kate felt her face growing hot and wondered why the question had made her feel suddenly uncomfortable. 'Yes, he's been very supportive; he's helping me to set up tomorrow night, too.' She averted her gaze from Viv's steely stare, feeling caught off-guard.

It wasn't strictly true. Although Alf had been supportive of helping her to make the last-minute arrangements regarding free beverages and nibbles, she was acutely aware that he hadn't been overly complimentary of her paintings. She'd told herself this was normal – after all, he wasn't 'into' art – so therefore how could she expect him to want to ask the reasoning and concept behind her creations? It was natural he wasn't going to be over-enthusiastic, wasn't it?

'Oh, that's good, darling. As long as he's encouraging – that's what you need. I'm so pleased it's all working out well for the pair of you.' Lillian dunking a piece of her roll into the soup and taking a bite. 'Oh, it's not half as bad with the bread dipped in,

Viv. Give it a try.'

'Any news yet on the hypochondriac, love?' Vivian asked, wisely changing the subject. 'She still at hell's door?'

'Viv, you can't be talking about Hilda like that,' Kate replied quietly, discreetly making a 'shhh-ing' sound at her. 'Dr Sharman came and checked her over this morning and he said she looks to be over the worst of it, which is good news.' She pointedly glanced at Viv as she said this.

'Depends how you look at it. I suppose it's good news for him downstairs – it's not for us unlucky ones still lumbered with her, though.'

Lillian chortled, spluttering a piece of bread into her glass of water. She picked up her napkin and wiped her mouth. 'Either way, it keeps us entertained for a bit longer, eh, Viv? Otherwise who else have you got to moan about?'

Folding her arms across her chest, Vivian ignored the question and stared at the giant clock on the wall. She couldn't help but feel that something strange was about to happen. It was the feeling she'd always got when unexpected change was in the making. This time, though, it was different. It was much stronger.

'Okay, ladies. I'd best get going; I need to crack on with paperwork – I only wanted to share the house news.' Kate stood up, noticing that Viv had gone very quiet and pale. 'You okay, Viv?'

Looking up at the mention of her name, Vivian stared into Kate's midnight-blue eyes and felt an overwhelming sense of protectiveness. Kate was such a sensitive and kind soul; she deserved a man in her life to truly appreciate that. 'I'm fine, love, don't you worry about me. You go and see to your paperwork.'

'Okay, good. See you later.'

Vivian watched as Kate walked away, all at once realising the meaning behind her strange feeling. There wasn't much time. Pushing out her chair, she slowly stood up, clutching her flask to her. 'Lil, I've got something I need to attend to. I'm going back to my room. I'll catch up with you after lunch.'

The feeling was getting stronger; there was no time to waste. It had to be done soon. She had an urgent letter to write.

'Horse-drawn carriage?' Megan scrunched up her nose. 'I'd rather arrive on the back of a goat.' She laughed, watching as Michael tiredly rubbed his face with his hand, his expression grim.

Sighing, Megan rose from his lap, changing position to sitting upright, tucking her legs underneath her and folding her arms across her chest.

'What's wrong, grumpy?' She poked his bare chest with her index finger, chasing the trail of hair down to his groin with her other hand.

'Don't.' He moved away from her slightly, his tone severe.

Picking up the television remote from the side table next to her, Megan pointed it at the large screen, clicking it off. The room sank into silence as she turned to face Michael. 'Right, what's going on? You've been off with me all evening and now you're being plain rude.'

'I could ask you the same thing, Megan.' He stared her down, unflinching. He knew there was something wrong – he could tell from the way she behaved every time he raised the subject of their engagement and from the lack of contact they'd had in the past week due to her mysterious 'unavailability', but mostly it was obvious from the way she refused to be serious on any matter of importance concerning their relationship.

Her heart pounding in her chest, Megan knew that this was the perfect moment to be honest – the moment to tell Michael that she'd been having doubts and felt she needed more time to consider things. 'I don't feel I've been any different. It's you who's the one with the problem,' she retorted defensively.

'You're sure about that, are you?' he challenged, noticing a blush spreading across her cheeks. 'There's nothing that's bothering you about us?' He stared at her intensely, daring her to open up to him. She lowered her eyes, picking at her toenails.

'I don't understand what you're getting at, Michael. If there was something bothering me, I would tell you.' She stared up at him again, mustering as much conviction as she could, willing herself not to crack and allow everything to come tumbling out. His eyes were kindly, but there was an air of defeat about him, as if he knew already that he'd lost the battle. She couldn't tell him yet. She wasn't ready. She'd been going over everything in her mind for the past two days and it was all so confusing.

His shoulders relaxing, he softened his tone. 'Okay, as long as you're sure.' He pulled her towards him, resting her body against his chest and putting his arms around her. 'I just want you to be happy.' He stroked her face with his finger and she felt herself shiver at his touch.

'I am happy.' It wasn't a lie, because on one level, she was happy – very happy. She'd never felt quite this optimistic about the possibilities for the future. Yet it wasn't entirely Michael giving her that happiness – it was also Marcus; Marcus and the possibility that he felt the same way as she did. Tomorrow she would know, finally. Tomorrow she would have her answer. She tried to concentrate on Michael again, the secure, stable and solid Michael who was now gently stroking her hair. She really did appreciate him; it felt so natural and comfortable here with him – but something was missing….

'I spoke to my mother earlier, she's looking forward to our visit at the end of the month.'

Trying not to stiffen, Megan forced her breathing to stay calm. She'd forgotten entirely about spending the weekend in the Yorkshire Dales with Michael and his parents. It seemed completely inappropriate now that she was in quandary with her feelings toward Michael. She couldn't possibly spend the weekend with his parents, knowing that her heart might lie with another man. It was all the more reason why tomorrow couldn't come soon enough. She had to know Marcus's reaction. 'Great. I'll have to check again with Jonnie, he's probably forgotten.'

'Jonnie? You want Jonnie to come with us?'

Megan sat up slowly, noticing the consternation in Michael's tone. 'Not particularly, but you were the one who invited him, remember? You told him that he was welcome – given that he wanted to learn to clay-pigeon shoot and your father can teach him.'

Groaning, Michael closed his eyes tightly. 'Ohh, so I did. I forgot I'd mentioned it to him.' He chewed on his lip thoughtfully, a mischievous smile appearing. 'What if we pack him off to rehab or something instead? Solve two problems at once.'

Appalled, Megan flinched, backing away from him. 'How can you talk about my brother like that? His addiction isn't a joke, you know.'

The smile rapidly disappeared from Michael's face and he reached out for her, grabbing her hand. 'Oh, come on, gorgeous, I was only kidding around. Of course he's welcome to come.'

Slapping his hand away, her earlier feeling of uncertainty was replaced with intense dislike as she looked into his eyes. 'Is that how you see him, then? The "inconvenience" that can be shoved into rehab in order to suit your requirements?' She knew she was being unfair, but she didn't care – she thought he'd been different to all the others – that he'd empathised with Jonnie's addiction. But he wasn't any different; his comment had just proved that. He was exactly like the others.

Michael grew wary looking at Megan's thunderous expression, confused as to how she could react so harshly over a flippant comment. He hardly recognised her of late; not only was she being distant but she was overly temperamental - this wasn't the fun, easy going Megan that he'd asked to marry him.

'You're over-reacting and it's ridiculous. You know, I appreciate that Jonnie has an addiction – but he also has issues he needs to deal with.' He gently touched her shoulder, feeling hurt when she moved away from him. 'It's time you faced up to it, Megan – Jonnie needs to get himself sorted. Maybe rehab would be good for him. We can help him with it.' Encouraged by Megan's silence, he continued, on a roll now and wanting to get the issue that had – subconsciously – most been worrying him, off his chest. 'Any celebration that we arrange to do with our engagement, Jonnie's going to be tempted to drink – you know that.' He watched her for a reaction and was pleased when she looked away, feeling that he was finally getting through to her. 'We need to get him sorted out before then. We don't want to risk him falling off the wagon again, especially if it's our special evening or party. He could ruin it for us.'

Megan felt physically sick. She hadn't expected Michael to fully understand Jonnie's addiction, neither had she particularly wanted him to – all she'd hoped for was that he understood her part in the matter. Yet, his suggestion had confirmed things. He did view Jonnie as a liability – as a potential threat to his perfectly thought-out engagement party plans. So his answer was to pack Jonnie off to a week's or month's retreat and hope to 'cure' him – in order to save them the embarrassment of the drama Jonnie could bring to the evening. She turned away from Michael, seeing a side of him that she didn't particularly like.

'Let's not talk about Jonnie any more. I'm not sending him anywhere.' She stood up, slipping on her shoes, which were beside the sofa.

He looked at her in alarm. 'Er, where are you going?'

Ignoring him, she reached for her jumper tossed across the back of the dining chair. 'You just don't get it, do you? You can't force an alcoholic to stop drinking. They have to be ready to. It has to be their choice – their decision.' She took in Michael's perplexed expression and the way he was running his hands, agitatedly, through his hair and continued. 'It's not for us to "fix" Jonnie.'

Michael stood up angrily, grabbing Megan's arm. 'To hell with Jonnie, I don't care about him. I was trying to be helpful.' Forcing her to stand still and listen to him, he grabbed her other arm. 'I don't know what your problem is, Megan. I'm trying here – really trying – and all you're doing is pushing me away. You've been like this all week. What the hell's going on?'

She stopped struggling against him, feeling deflated and lost. It wasn't fair of her to take her confusion out on Michael, but it was becoming glaringly obvious that they didn't share the same ideals as she'd initially thought. Megan knew that although he thought the suggestion of rehab was helpful, he'd ultimately distanced himself even further from her. It wasn't his entire fault, though. She too had been playing with fire.

'I'm sorry.' And she was, truly sorry. 'I'm tired, emotional and everything's getting on top of me this week.' She looked up into his eyes and took a deep breath, knowing she had to be fair to him; he was a good person – he didn't deserve to be kept in the dark. 'I'm not sure things are working, Michael. Between us, I mean.'

He dropped his hands from her arms. 'I knew it. I knew there was something wrong.'

She reached out for him, wanting to reassure him, seeing the crestfallen look on his face and feeling immediately guilty. 'I'm so confused about everything. I need time to think, time to see if this is really what I want. I can't help but feel that maybe we've rushed into this engagement too quickly. I'm not sure if it's right for us.'

'So, let's call it off.' His tone was heavy, unyielding and icily cold. He moved away from her, picking up the empty pizza box from the coffee table. 'I can't be with someone that isn't sure. I'm certain – one hundred per cent certain – that you're right for me. But if you can't say the same, then, I'm sorry, but that's not good enough.' He crushed the pizza box with one hand, the veins in his neck pulsing outwards in rage.

'Michael, wait.' She reached out to stop him from walking towards the kitchen. Ignoring her, he strode ahead. 'I didn't mean I don't have feelings or love you. I do. I'm just saying I'm uncertain whether we should have spent more time as a couple – getting to know one another – before we rushed into engagement.'

Turning to her with a look of absolute fury, Michael banged

down the empty pizza box onto the work surface. 'Go home, Megan. You've said enough and right now, I'm too hurt and angry to speak any more on the matter. Go have your think, but in the meantime I'm calling things off. I deserve more than someone who isn't sure if I'm what they really want.' His voice cracking, he turned his back to her, feeling as if she'd opened his chest, pulled out his heart and ripped it into two pieces.

'I'm so sorry, Michael.'

There was nothing more to be said. Picking up her bag, she made her way out of his apartment; never in her life had she felt more awful and disapproving of herself for causing someone so much heartbreak. By the time she'd reached the ground floor, she couldn't distinguish if the tears that were falling from her eyes were from sadness, guilt, pain or pure relief. Her own heart was aching, but she didn't know why.

She was more confused than ever before.

Chapter 24

Alf finished loading the weeds and twigs into the specially purchased garden-refuse sacks, wiping his forehead with the back of his hand. He'd never been the gardening type, but given the amount of spare time he had on his hands and knowing that the overgrown mess was bound to be off-putting to potential buyers, he'd set himself the task of tackling it. It was just a shame he hadn't factored in the unexpected heatwave the forecasters had failed to predict. The sweat was pouring off him.

'Kate will be pleased, won't she, mate,' he said to Sam, who was eyeing him from his splayed position on the grass with a cocked head.

He stood back admiring his handiwork. Granted, it still wouldn't win them the Chelsea flower show, but the garden once again looked recognisable and neat. 'Time for a beer, I think.'

Heading into the house, he kicked off his dirty boots and opened the fridge, getting himself a cool can of lager. Pulling his mobile out of his pocket, he took a seat at the kitchen table and re-read the job vacancy email that had been forwarded by Megan. It was a great position, one that he knew he had the skills for; not a managerial role, but one where he would run his own scheme once again and be responsible for its growth. The company was an up-and-coming broker's that was already gaining itself a name within the industry. Fired up, he decided to get working on his CV – he didn't want a role like this passing him by without giving it a shot. He could already see the potential.

Taking a long swig of his beer, he reluctantly stood up and felt the ache of the morning's efforts in his limbs as he moved. He switched on his laptop at the dining table and it immediately sprang to life, greeting him with his last-viewed internet search; photos of engagement rings. Closing the page, he smiled, pleased with himself that the search for the perfect ring was already as good as done. He'd seen it the previous afternoon in the local jeweller's, of all places, antique, with a ruby and diamond centre. He'd known instantly that it was the ring for Kate – unique and one of a kind, without being flashy or vulgar. Managing to secure it with a small deposit, he'd hardly been able to believe his luck when he noticed the matching earring set. Without hesitation, he secured those too, deciding that he wanted to go to every length to ensure Kate had what she deserved.

'Sam, get away from those.' He reached out his leg towards the dog, who was sniffing precariously close to Kate's stacked canvases, and pushed him with his foot. 'No!' Instinctively Sam scuttled away, but not before his tail had flicked against one of the smaller paintings, causing it to topple over. 'For heaven's sake…'

Alf stood up, walking over to where the dainty canvas lay and carefully picked it up, surprised to see the intricate detail and creativity that had clearly gone into its making. He couldn't be sure if it was supposed to be a flower or abstract, but its beauty was captivating. 'Not bad at all,' he muttered to himself, replacing it against the others.

He sat back down at the table in front of his laptop, surreptitiously eyeing the forty or so canvases that were taking up most of the space along the back wall of the room. There was something about their presence that was slightly off-putting. He couldn't be certain, but he wondered if it was because they represented a part of Kate that he no longer knew – a new Kate, one who had defined herself without his presence. The thought wasn't a welcome one. In fact, he found himself feeling oddly envious – he'd never had a hobby that he loved and poured his heart into. Not to mention that she'd made a quite a few quid out of it so far with the offers she'd accepted from the care home. There was a pride within him that Kate was capable of such creations, but there was also a feeling of insecurity that came with it. It left him with an unsettled feeling – one that he didn't know how to address.

Sam padded back into the room, catching Alf's attention with a deliberate raise of one paw in the hope of a reward. 'Enough of that, mate – I've got no treats for you.' Shaking his head at the dog's persistence, he turned back towards his laptop – his mind once again focused on the engagement ring he was planning to collect at the weekend and the best way to go about the proposal.

For a few days now, he'd been toying with the idea of asking her after the exhibition, when he knew she'd be on a high – one that he'd be able to top even further by popping the question. However, he'd decided against it; a part of him disliked the idea of their special moment being based upon something entirely linked to Kate. Besides, it wasn't as if her artwork was always going to be a focus point in their life; it was natural they'd soon start planning for a family and Kate's time would be taken up in other ways. He wanted to be sensitive to that.

No, the proposal needed to be special this time – a memory to look back on that was for both of them, for it marked a new era in their relationship. A completely new beginning – after all, since he'd returned from Scotland it was hard to remember a time when they had been so happy and enthused about one another. Life was giving them a second chance; he wasn't going to let her slip away this time. This time he wanted to make everything perfect.

Opening his CV document, he put aside all thoughts of the engagement and concentrated on the task ahead. First and foremost, although he had a more relaxed attitude to his career, it was still important that he secured a role good enough to provide for their near future. After all, he was the man of the house and it was his duty to bring home the bacon, not vice versa. On that thought, he couldn't help warily eyeing the paintings across from him one last time, silently hoping that their potential success wouldn't come back to haunt him.

Dialling Michael's number for the ninth time in succession, Megan waited for him to answer. Her patience had long since waned, the irritation building inside her by the second. 'Answer the fucking phone,' she muttered, once again pressing his intercom buzzer before walking back onto the street and glancing up at his living-room window.

She knew he was home because the lights were on inside the apartment. She also knew he'd undoubtedly listened to her countless voice messages by now and got the message that she wanted to speak to him about the engagement. She'd hinted that she was calling it off but she had wanted to explain her reasons properly – to do the correct thing and tell him in person. He deserved that at the very least. Yet by avoiding her fully, he wasn't even allowing her that option.

Pressing the buzzer one last time, she called his name through the intercom, begging him to give her a last chance to come and explain. She was greeted with no answer.

Left with no choice, she picked up her already damp umbrella from the porch entrance and opened it up, shielding herself from the fresh spattering of rain that was gently beginning to fall and began to walk away…

'Are you sure you're okay about this?' Marcus asked cautiously. 'Alf or Kate might pick up that we're acting strange around one another?'

'I'm sure, Marcus.' Megan brushed her hair away from her mouth and smiled. 'Besides, Kate knows we're going in one car because of limited parking and it's her special night – she'll probably be too wrapped up to notice us anyway.' He gave her hand a gentle squeeze and opened the passenger door of the car for her.

It was crazy that within the space of not even a week, things had taken a complete shift around her. The confusion that she'd felt was gone. She still hadn't heard from Michael – it was undoubtedly his pride causing him to be silent towards her. However, the matter of her breaking off the engagement was resolved. She'd had no other option but to post the sparkling diamond that he had bought her into the slim mailbox of his apartment-block lobby, accompanied with a heartfelt letter. Deep down, she knew that she wouldn't be receiving a response. In some ways, it made the entire situation a lot easier to deal with and experiencing his complete detachment gave her confirmation she'd made the correct decision. She couldn't be with a man who disappeared at the first hurdle.

She certainly hadn't expected things to develop with Marcus as quickly as they had. Meeting him the day after her argument with Michael had been gut-wrenching – mainly due to the uncertainty of whether she'd made a grave mistake in misreading his feelings and causing unnecessary tension in her relationship with Michael. But it had, in fact, been a life-changing conversation. She was surprised at how easily she'd found herself opening up to him and hinting at the underlying chemistry she sensed between them. It was ironic that she'd assumed she'd have to be the one doing the questioning to know where they stood with one another.

It hadn't been anything like that. Marcus had automatically taken matters into his own hands; he hadn't hesitated for a moment in steering the conversation towards his own feelings and being honest and reassuring. His evident relief and surprise that her relationship with Michael had taken a turn for the worse was enough to confirm every notion that she'd had. Moreover, he'd been direct enough to tell her that he'd been unable to stop thinking about her ever since the first time they'd met at Kate's house; it had been driving him wild with jealousy that she belonged to another man, because he'd never felt this way about someone before. She was left with no doubt that it was something special between them.

Allowing herself to acknowledge that she'd felt exactly the same about him had been both exhilarating and comforting. Deep inside, she knew this was it – exactly what she was supposed to feel about the man she'd hopefully spend her future with. In fact, she realised that on a subconscious level, she'd known for a long time that she'd felt this way, which is why she'd always had a small doubt about her relationship with Michael. But that didn't matter now – if anything, the experience with Michael had allowed her to be receptive enough to recognise the special connection she'd struck up with Marcus.

She could hardly contain the breathtaking mix of emotions that the past few days of getting to know one another had left her with. It had barely been seventy-two hours since they'd laid their feelings on the table, and yet Megan couldn't imagine considering a relationship with Michael again – everything she'd felt for him had ebbed away since spending time with Marcus. The emotions that she'd had for Michael were well and truly eclipsed by those she was feeling for Marcus. In spite of this, she'd agreed with him that, for the time being at least, to everyone else they were to still appear as 'friends', taking it very slowly in a new direction. After all, how often was it that people fell for one another after only a few days? There were bound to be a few surprised reactions.

Starting up the car, Marcus turned to Megan. 'Before we get Kate's friends from the care home, I need to swing past my sister's and pick up my granddad, if that's okay.'

'Of course. So he did want to come in the end?' She grinned, aware of Marcus's frustration at his grandfather's insistence that he was past his days of gallivanting.

Marcus nodded. 'Yep, I knew he would. He called me earlier and said that if he had to spend another moment with my sister fussing over him, he'd go insane.' He pulled the car away from Megan's house, noticing Jonnie at the end of the road with a large holdall slung over his back. 'Hey, there's your brother.' He pointed ahead.

'Finally,' Megan whispered, straining her eyes to see how sober Jonnie looked. She was relieved to see that he was walking straight and looked clean. It was an indicator this his AWOL status for the past few days hadn't led to a big bender. Whatever had happened with his drinking, at least he was managing to get it under some level of control.

'Do you want me to stop, so you can chat to him?' Marcus asked, fully aware of Megan's predicament and knowing that she was most likely assessing him for signs of his sobriety.

She shook her head confidently. 'No, it's okay – he looks fine. Let's leave him to his business.'

If the argument with Michael had given her any lasting thoughts, it was that he was right in one thing – Jonnie did need to get himself sorted. It was no longer for her to worry so much on his behalf. He had his own life to lead – as did she. It was time she moved forward and put her own self and happiness first.

The car drove past Jonnie at the very moment that he looked up in their direction, noticing his sister. Breaking into a happy grin, he waved before turning back to the road ahead. Megan waved back, feeling consoled and justified in her decision. The last few days had been the first time that Jonnie had gone drinking without the usual calls and demands on her and seeing him wave in such a carefree way was an unusual gesture. Perhaps things were finally changing for both of them. It was most certainly long overdue.

By the time Marcus arrived at his sister's, his granddad was already waiting outside the red iron gate of the semi-detached house.

'No need to get out. He'll get in the back, he won't mind,' Marcus said, lifting the handbrake and opening his driver's door.

He walked across to his granddad. 'Grumps, you okay?' He patted his back. 'You're alright to get in the back? I've got Megan in the car and we've got to pick up some of her friends on the way.'

Roberto walked directly to the back door of the car, shooing his grandson away. 'Yes, yes, stop fussing. I've had enough of that with your sister. I'm fine in the back.' Opening the car door, he lowered himself in, immediately reaching across to Megan. 'Nice to meet you, my dear, I've heard a lot about you. I've never seen Marcus quite so taken with a woman before. And what a beauty you are, I should add!' He winked at her, tellingly.

'Thanks, Roberto. I hope it was all good things Marcus told you.' Intrigued, Megan glanced sideways at Marcus, who was settling back into the driver's seat, and noticed a faint colour in his cheeks. He glanced at her with an embarrassed smile before turning to put his belt on.

'Right, let's get going, then. Where exactly is this Oak Park place, Megan – Kate did tell me once, but I can't remember?'

Forgetting all about Marcus's granddad's words, Megan instantly began pouring out directions, giving them a rundown of the beauty of the Care Home as she did so.

From the back seat, Roberto could only watch as the pair in front of him giggled and smiled their way towards their destination. He wasn't an intuitive man by any means, but he knew all about women and was certain that this one was something special for his grandson. It was a million miles away from how Marcus had acted around Linzie, or any woman, before. From the way the pair of them looked at one another to the way their body language already mirrored each other, it was obvious that they were destined to be together. It was a rare and special thing, true love, but he was in no doubt that these two had found it. Just as he had – some fifty-odd years previously.

Kate stared at herself in the full-length mirror, the cream-chiffon dress hanging a little more loosely on her slimmer frame than it had the last time she'd worn it months before; nevertheless, it still looked elegant and chic – the stain that had once made it un-wearable was now long gone. It made her feel every inch the confident and glamorous woman that she now felt within. She teased her chignon a touch more tightly into place, securing it with more hair pins and stood back to assess the overall result – she was startled to realise how far she'd come in herself in such a short space of time.

It was strange to be wearing the dress that had been specifically purchased for a different purpose – a purpose that hadn't been fulfilled and had consequently brought about so many changes in her life. It was even more absurd that, not so long ago, she'd associated the dress with a time of heartache and missed opportunity. And yet now, standing barefoot and feeling so much more settled in herself and her life, she didn't feel anything but the buzz of excitement and anticipation for the evening ahead – her evening.

She could hardly believe it was finally here; granted, she might be a little over-dressed for the occasion, but she didn't care. Her theme for the exhibition was 'The Hidden Beauty' and fittingly, the cream dress had marked a fork in the road where life had brought out parts of herself that had been hidden – parts that had since had a chance to flourish and open new doors for her.

She glanced at the clock on her bedside table. 'Better get my shoes on,' she muttered to herself, wondering how Alf was getting on at the venue with her instructions of where to affix each canvas in the layout. She couldn't help but feel a little disappointed at his lack of enthusiasm for the evening; she knew part of it was due to his deflation at not being considered for the job he'd applied for, yet she felt he was also holding something back from her.

In many ways, the weeks since they'd been back together had been idyllic – she couldn't remember them both feeling so happy and at ease. But there was also a feeling that there was something she wasn't seeing; every time it arose, she told herself it was probably because things were at an emotional peak. It was natural to be anxious when life reached a point of seeming too good to be true – it wasn't going to last, she knew that much. So she'd decided it was pointless to burst her own bubble when she should be making the most of it. It was her time; Alf was by her side and all was relatively smooth around her. Sure, they hadn't spoken too much about the longer-term future – apart from the house sale – but that no longer weighed so heavily on her mind. If the last few months had taught her anything, it was that life was best lived in the moment, day by day. Besides, given that she had love, health and blissful happiness at that very moment – what was there not to be thankful for?

Reaching for her mid-heel shoes, ones that complimented the dress, she slipped them on and picked up her mobile, feeling a pang of guilt as she noticed a text from Megan. She'd been so wrapped up in the last few days, ensuring all was prepared for the exhibit – as well as working and trying to reassure Alf about his job plans – that she hadn't had time to properly discuss Megan's dilemma further. Her stomach somersaulted at the thought of seeing her friend at the exhibition, along with so many others who would be joining her in support of her evening – she really was a lucky woman.

Marcus had already told her that the turnout for the exhibit was expected to surpass expectation, as informed by the venue manager; she knew part of this was thanks to Marcus pulling a few strings with media coverage. Either way, she didn't dare to expect much – if only one of her paintings sold, then she would be ecstatic. Her main hope was that others would find as much pleasure in viewing them as she'd had in creating them.

Without reading Megan's message, Kate put the phone into her bag and went downstairs, her heart banging nervously in her chest with each step. Despite not placing too much emphasis on the potential success that the exhibition could bring her, she couldn't help but silently wonder if the evening was a marker for a new beginning. Subconsciously, she crossed her fingers.

Chapter 25

The grandeur and presence of Oak Park was hard to miss on the winding country lane that led to it.

'Now this is what I call a retirement home,' Roberto piped up from the back seat, impressed by the stately building that outshone any version he'd mentally envisioned upon hearing where they were going. 'Bet it costs a fortune to reside here.'

Megan turned to him, nodding. 'Yes, my friend Kate knows a lot of the backgrounds of the residents and none of them are particularly hard up.' She pointed to the far right entrance, tapping Marcus's knee gently. 'Go that way, Marcus. Kate said Viv and Lil will meet us by the East entrance.' She turned around to face Roberto again. 'The pair you're going to meet are lovely, a bundle of fun – especially when together. They're both very close to Kate. That's why they're coming along tonight.'

Marcus glanced at the dashboard clock, aware that they were running a bit later than planned. 'I think we might end up being a bit late getting to the venue. It's already seven now.'

Megan was scanning the car park as they were approaching, trying to catch a glimpse of where Vivian and Lillian might be – very few people were milling about and most of them were staff workers, evident from their familiar fuchsia-coloured uniform. She was certain Kate had mentioned the East entrance, but maybe she'd meant West – after all wasn't that the main entrance?

A sharp, strangled intake of breath from the back seat caused both of them to turn around in surprise, Marcus stamping sharply on the brake. 'What the hell? Grumps?'

Roberto spluttered as his breath caught in his throat, causing a coughing fit. He couldn't believe his eyes; surely they were playing tricks on him? It couldn't be – could it?

Megan watched as Marcus repeated the question to his grandfather, whose face was ashen – as if he'd seen a ghost. Her attention was caught by a red flap of fabric in her peripheral vision and, turning her head to the left, she saw the pair of women they were there to collect – both dressed up to the nines.

Roberto finally stopped coughing, caught his breath and cleared his throat.

Confused as to what was going on, and aware that the women seemed to be checking their watches in the distance, Megan used the moment's silence to point towards Vivian and Lillian. 'Marcus, I can see them. Look – they're just over there.' She wound down her window and shouted across to the women, one of whom looked up and waved in recognition.

Roberto chose the very same moment to speak. 'My God, I can't believe it – after all these years – it's her.' His hands shook slightly as he regained his composure, before turning once more towards the window and eyeing the woman in the green coat in the distance, now making her way slowly in their direction with her friend.

Marcus looked in bewilderment from his grandfather to Megan, who shrugged her shoulders in return, equally puzzled. 'Who, Granddad? Who've you seen?' He pulled the car forwards slowly, in the direction of the pair, who were making sluggish progress towards it.

'Lillian. It's my Lillian. Her in the green coat.'

Megan turned around in surprise. 'You know Lillian?' Well, that was a turn-up for the books. Kate was always saying Lil was a lonely woman with no remaining family to speak of except her friend Viv. She genuinely hoped Roberto wasn't mistaken.

Marcus slowed the car to a halt, just a few metres from the women. He could clearly see their features now, especially the one wearing the thin, flapping mint-green coat that came to her knees, a slim and elegant woman with dark, large eyes and a warm smile. 'Lillian – your first wife Lillian?' he asked in astonishment, still transfixed by the small woman, who was now patiently re-adjusting her hair fascinator. He turned to his grandfather, whose eyes were twinkling in a way that he'd never seen before.

'My God, she's still a beauty.'

'Wife?' Megan repeated in astonishment, aware that both ladies were only feet away from the car and looking in at her curiously. She opened her passenger door quickly, unsure how to react as Vivian stepped forwards and swooped down on her.

'Hello, love – we thought you must have got lost.' She embraced Megan, who noticed Lillian behind her, fussing with her handbag and paying no attention to the exchange.

'Sorry, we're late. We had to collect Marcus's grandfather Roberto on the way.' At the mention of his name, Megan saw Lil's head snap up at the same moment as hearing the back door of the car open. She heard a stifled gasp and saw Vivian's head swivel back around at her friend in surprise.

All eyes turned to the left side of the car, where Roberto was scrambling to climb out adeptly. The sudden sprightliness with which he found himself on the pavement and propelled towards the woman of his focus was startling. The words weren't thought through and they tumbled out in quick succession. 'Good Lord, Lillian, it is really you? Can I dare to hope it's you, after all these years?'

It took a five full seconds of silence before Lil found her voice. She could hardly believe that the man standing before her with the green eyes and square chin was the same one who she had carried in her heart for over fifty years. He'd aged considerably;

weathered skin and heavily lined features replaced the smooth, tanned wrinkle-free face that she remembered. Life hadn't been particularly kind to him in the years that they'd been parted, but nonetheless, it was most definitely him. Her stomach somersaulted in a way that she'd forgotten was possible.

'Bobbi?' Her voice was small and barely audible. She felt Vivian's hand rest gently on her shoulder and her heart beating wildly against the restraint of her chest.

'Yes it's me, my love.'

She didn't know whether to laugh or cry. It was really him. The man she'd always loved with every part of her soul. And the very same man who had cheated on her with another woman.

The venue was big, bigger than she'd remembered – it was hard to imagine how it was ever going to be filled with enough people. 'Did I do okay?' Alf asked, coming up behind her with a glass of champagne and resting his hand on her back. He kissed her on the cheek. 'By the way, you really do look beautiful, babe.' He held out a flute of the sparkling pink liquid.

Kate flushed with excitement and pride, accepting the glass. 'Thanks. I can't believe how well you've done. It looks fantastic.' She gazed around once again at the many canvases mounted in white frames against the exposed red-brick walls, the strategic warehouse track lighting above them creating the perfect ambience. Alf had clearly taken note of her instructions; prices were mounted correctly, as were the descriptions of the works that she'd felt it was imperative to include. 'Better than I could have ever imagined it would.' It was hard to believe these were the very same paintings that she'd painstakingly created in her makeshift workspace of the upstairs spare bedroom. It was like viewing them for the first time. They looked magnificent with their lively, colourful tones against the warm backdrop of the exhibition room, even if she did think so herself. She took in the table lined with bottles of chilled wine and champagne, the various canapés arranged neatly alongside them. The soft music that she'd chosen to compliment her theme was already beginning to play in the background.

'There are quite a lot people in the reception area and it's not even seven o'clock yet. Due to the turn-out, Daniel's keen to be opening the doors in the next few minutes or so.' Alf pressed his hand against the small of her back as he said this, noticing Kate instinctively chew down on her bottom lip – something she only ever did out of anxiety. 'It'll be a wonderful evening, babe. Just enjoy it.'

'I know, it's just hard to imagine that I'm actually here.' Her eyes sparkled and she suddenly thought of her aunt, who had always been so encouraging of her talent – what would she make of it if she were here now to see her? She choked back an unexpected lump in her throat and concentrated on the startling sense of purpose that accompanied it. She knew that fate was giving her another chance to carve herself a name in the art world – an opportunity that she'd already shelved in the past. This was her moment; she had to put every part of her soul into making the evening a success – one that would make her aunt proud.

Noticing the twinkle in Kate's eyes, Alf looked around the room and had to admit that he was rather impressed with the way things had turned out. It had been hard for him to imagine how the gallery, with the bare brick walls and slightly musty smell, would transform itself into an environment so welcoming and polished; yet he'd somehow made it happen and the excitement on Kate's face was enough to know that he'd done her proud. As if on cue, the black-metal entrance doors swung open followed by Daniel and the first trickle of waiting visitors. Alf stepped aside, nodding at the exhibition manager's discreet thumbs-up sign.

Kate took a deep breath and fixed a smile into place, even though her insides were already jittering with nerves and she was finding it difficult to keep her hands steady. She tried to concentrate on the initial reactions of the first guests, feeling relieved when she saw smiles and approving nods. She knew she would have to mingle – there would be plenty of people wanting background knowledge on each piece and besides, she was quite looking forward to meeting others who shared her passion – even if it did mean taking a step outside of her usual reserved comfort zone. Taking a generous gulp of champagne to calm herself, she turned to Alf and fixed him with a determined expression. 'Right, I suppose I'd better get networking. Let me know when the others arrive. I can't wait to see them now.'

'Oh, okay. Sure.' A little taken aback at her boldness, Alf nodded slowly, watching intently as Kate quickly sipped a little more of her champagne. With a brave smile and squeeze of his arm, she turned away from him, tentatively making her way towards the gathering group of people admiring the first showpiece of her collection. He wasn't sure what he'd expected, but he hadn't bargained on her taking to the business side of the evening quite so quickly. He guessed he'd also hoped to be more personally involved in some way.

Alf watched from across the room as Kate – seemingly unaware of his confusion at her flightiness – said something in Daniel's ear, making him feel all the more dismayed. He wasn't an arty type and so far no one that he recognised had put in an appearance, despite the steady stream of guests making their way through the doors. He was effectively alone. Pulling back the cuff of his jacket, he checked his watch, wondering when the others would arrive; the last thing he wanted was to be standing around like a spare part.

Grimly walking towards the drinks table, he refilled his glass of wine and picked up a canapé. From the corner of his eye he could see Kate throwing back her head in self-assured amusement The gesture was innocent enough, but Alf couldn't help the stirrings of resentment that were quick to pop up inside him.

It was going to be a very long evening indeed.

'Ooh, and what about the time you took me to see Buddy Holly at the London Palladium.' Lillian nudged Roberto; the initial mix of emotions she'd had at the totally unexpected re-encounter had now settled into a comfortable mix of excitement and happiness. The anger that she'd silently held against him for cheating on her melting away as she'd chatted with him, recapturing their past.

'Best night of my life,' he answered, without skipping a beat and breaking into song "…Well that'll be the day…"

'Pack it in, you two, we're here now. You've got all night to reminisce – you don't need to do it right in my earhole.' From her squashed corner position Vivian shook her head in good-natured humour. She'd had a feeling all day that something special was in store for Lil – but what a revelation it had been. She couldn't believe the turn of events and, apparently, neither could Lillian or Roberto. For the last twenty minutes, nobody else in the car had been able to get a word in edgeways.

'Don't mind her – she's just a moany old bat sometimes,' Lillian chirped up in playful response.

Marcus laughed from the front seat. 'Well, you lot have certainly made for an interesting journey – but thank goodness we've arrived before Grumps had a chance to launch into another song.' Spotting the only remaining parking space outside the red- brick exhibition centre, he deftly managed to squeeze the large car into the narrow gap. Turning off the engine, he glanced at Megan. 'You're a bit quiet – you okay?'

'Yes, fine – just been listening to the others.' She smiled warmly at him and looked at her watch, unfastening her seat belt. A flurry of activity from the back seat commenced as Roberto opened his side door. Megan lowered her voice to almost a whisper. 'Kate's going to be shocked when Lil introduces her to your granddad. Talk about unexpected – how're you feeling?'

Marcus shrugged, glancing over his shoulder and was thankful that all three back- seat passengers were engrossed in helping each other exit the car. 'It's a shock, but she seems lovely – a bit like you.' He grinned cheekily and opened his car door. 'Right, come on. Let's go and see how Kate's doing.'

It took five full minutes before everyone was out of the car and a further five minutes to find the correct entrance to the warehouse building. 'About time,' Roberto mumbled, taking Lillian's hand as Marcus led the way through the intricate, arty wrought-iron doors.

'Are you okay, love?' Vivian asked, hanging back from the others and reaching for Megan's arm in support. 'You look a bit nervous.'

It had been a while since she'd last seen Megan in person and, although she knew a lot about her life through Kate's stories, she strongly sensed there was something bothering the girl. She'd been aware of it in the car, noticing how the excited energy that had been there when she'd first greeted her had started to lull. In its place there was anxiety.

Megan turned to her, a soft smile on her lips and nodded. 'I'm fine, Viv. It just hit home a bit – hearing Roberto and Lillian's story. Made me realise how important it is to never let go of someone you love, despite any setbacks.' Downcast, her gaze fell to the grey-flecked carpeted floor beneath them.

Vivian stopped walking suddenly and looked at her, her intuition going into overdrive. She'd known there was something about the girl that she was missing and couldn't put her finger on, but now the message was coming as clear as day to her mind. 'Megan, you've made the correct choice. He is the one for you – the one that destiny has chosen for you to be with. But you mustn't worry about what others will think. True love happens fast – the heart knows when it's met its match.' She saw an image of Marcus, followed by Kate and then realised Megan's predicament. She smiled, knowing that Megan was worrying where there was no concern for worry. 'Don't worry about what Kate will say. Whatever her reaction, with time all will be well. She will see with her own eyes the special connection that you and Marcus share. She will be happy for you and it will help her in her own path.' She squeezed Megan's hand. 'Don't hold back, love, go for it. None of this "just friends" business. Life is too short.'

Up ahead, Marcus and the others had turned to look at the

hushed exchange taking place between Megan and Viv.

'Are they okay?' Roberto asked, his tone concerned.

Lillian, sensing that Viv was passing a word or two of her wise advice, patted his arm. 'Don't you worry, I'm sure they're fine.' She looked at Marcus – startlingly the image of his grandfather fifty years previously – noticing that his eyes hadn't left Megan. 'So, any special woman in your life then, lad?'

Before he had a chance to answer, she heard Vivian and Megan break into laughter behind them and saw Marcus's face visibly relax at the sight. Suppressing a smile, she narrowed her eyes and glanced quizzically at Bobbi, who had always had a knack of knowing what she was thinking. He nodded his confirmation with a small smile, his eyes never leaving hers.

Marcus, who hadn't noticed the discreet exchange between the older couple, finally dragged his gaze away from Megan, who was now approaching them. 'Yes, there is actually.' He glanced back at her, his face illuminated with glee. 'Someone very special indeed.'

Megan, catching the tail end of his sentence, looked at Viv, who discreetly gave her a tap on the leg. It was now or never. What was the point of holding back? Vivian was right; love didn't wait for anybody. So why force it to?

'Me, too. He's very special indeed.' With a grin on her face she walked across to Marcus and put her arms around him, ignoring his surprised expression. 'Aren't you, Marcus?'

To the delight of the others, Marcus drew her towards him and, without hesitation, kissed her on the lips. 'Are we making it official, then?'

'We certainly are,' Megan replied, the butterflies in her stomach growing stronger.

'You don't half make a lovely couple,' Lillian said, touched at the gentle and sweet display of affection. She now knew why this man would have never been the right one for Kate. Everything about him fitted perfectly with Megan – it was like they'd been made to be together. Who'd have thought? Especially since the last she'd heard, Megan was already engaged…

Vivian nodded in agreement. 'Oh, they do. They make a lovely pair.'

'I don't want to ruin the moment, but I really think we ought to go inside now. We're rather late already,' Roberto said, noticing that music was coming from somewhere just a little up ahead of them.

'Sorry, granddad – you're right.'

'Yes, he is right.' Vivian frowned anxiously, her mind suddenly drawn to wondering how Kate was faring. 'I do hope Kate's getting on okay.'

'Course she is. Our Kate's a little star.' Lillian piped up, reassuring Viv.

Taking hold of Megan's hand, Marcus led them towards the room at the far end of the corridor – each of them silently hoping that the sight that greeted them would be a positive one.

When they finally reached the open doors, Megan let out a happy sigh of relief as Vivian clutched her hands to her chest in excitement.

It was better than any of them could have expected.

Chapter 26

'My favourite one.' Vivian remarked, staring up at the large canvas in admiration. She leaned in to Kate's ear, covering her mouth with the back of her hand so that the group of people around them couldn't overhear. 'You ought to have charged far more than that, though. No wonder it was snapped up so quickly.' She tutted in mock disapproval at the 'sold' sticker that Daniel had placed underneath the painting.

Kate laughed. 'I can't believe how many have sold already,' she whispered back in an elated tone. Her attention was drawn to Lillian and Bobbi, who she could just about make out through a gap in the crowd of visitors, giggling together in the far corner near the canapés. 'Oh, look at those two lovebirds. I still can't get over how uncanny it is that long-lost Bobbi happens to be Marcus's granddad.' She shook her head at the extraordinary turn of events. 'Marcus must be pretty shocked, too.'

'I know, darling. Join the club; I don't think any of us saw that one coming.' Vivian followed Kate's gaze to where Lil was now sitting on a chair, with Roberto towering above her, in deep conversation. 'I'm so happy for her – I can't begin to tell you what a weight off my mind it is. He'll be able to step into my shoes now.'

Kate glanced at her and was about to say something when Alf appeared by her side and grabbed her arm, a wide smile on his face. 'Sorry to interrupt you, Viv.' He nodded apologetically.

'Babe, have you seen that fella over there? The one in the yellow trousers.' He jerked his thumb to the right of them. 'Me and Marcus have just been chatting with him. Turns out he's Nigel Lambert. Would never believe it to look at him, would you.'

Frowning, Kate looked at Vivian, who appeared just as lost as she was. Alf shook his head in disbelief. 'Surely you've heard of him? He's one of the owners of Grobert Corporation.' He waited for a reaction, but seeing both ladies shrug with as much confusion as before, he waved his hand dismissively. 'Well, anyway, he's one of the big financial players and apparently there's a new project in the pipeline that he's keen to get me involved in.' He smoothed down his shirt with a smirk, pleased with himself.

'Oh, that's fantastic,' Kate replied encouragingly. She noticed Vivian looking at her curiously. 'Did you give him your details?'

Alf was already looking past her, straining his head in Marcus's direction, noticing him once again chatting with Nigel. Marcus was making eye signals for Alf to join them. 'Oh, he's beckoning for me again. Hang on, I'll go and see what he wants.' Nodding his head at his friend in confirmation, Alf hurriedly turned away from them. 'Sorry, I'll be back in a minute.'

Vivian pursed her lips, watching him go. Despite already having been there for over an hour, not once had she heard Alf make a single reference to the success of the evening. Her irritation growing, it made her feel rather unsettled that he'd once again drawn the conversation around to himself and Kate appeared far too blinded to notice.

Nonetheless, she was so proud of her Kate. She'd literally felt blown away upon entering the unexpectedly large exhibition room and seeing the hordes of visitors admiring paintings adorning the walls. The evening seemed to have gone from strength to strength. Kate was in constant demand for one thing or another and none of them had managed to get more than five minutes alone with her.

'Are you okay?' Kate asked, her face a picture of concern as

Vivian stood there lost in thought.

'I'm feeling wonderful, dear – happy to be here and happy to see you enjoying yourself so much. I'm just thinking how much of a success you're going to be. Tonight's enough proof of that.' She reached out and rubbed Kate's back. 'It's going to be the beginning of good things for you, Kate.'

Kate beamed; Viv's compliments meaning more to her than anyone's. She reached across and hugged her. 'Thanks, Viv. I have to say I can't believe how well it's going.' She felt an arm going around her shoulder and turned her head to the left. 'Oh, there you are! I've been wondering where you disappeared to.'

Megan laughed as she came up to Kate's side and lowered her arm, catching Viv's warm smile. 'I know, it's crazy busy, though. Every time I've walked over to chat with you, someone's stolen you first to talk about paintings!' She reached out and readjusted Kate's diamante neckline that had caught upon itself. 'You look gorgeous in that dress, by the way – so pleased you've finally worn it.'

'Thanks. I'm glad I made the effort now, especially given that there's so many influential people here.' Kate watched as Megan nodded her head excitedly. 'I know – Marcus was just telling me that he saw the arts editor of the *Telegraph* earlier.'

'Goodness me, that's wonderful news,' Vivian said, nodding her head approvingly.

'I know – it is, isn't it, Viv,' Megan agreed, rubbing her hands together. 'Let's hope he's impressed. Be lovely to see Kate get a nice review in the paper, wouldn't it?'

Intrigued by Megan's flushed cheeks and sparkling eyes, Kate studied her friend more closely, noticing the radiance and how her actions were unusually larger than life. 'Listen, sorry we've not had a proper chance to catch up yet.'

Megan waved her away. 'Don't be silly, it's your night – you've got to network, hun. Make the most of it.' She looked to Viv for approval. 'Anyway, I've been with Marcus and the others.'

Kate took a sip of wine. 'Good, Marcus will look after you.

He's good company – mind you, I haven't had a proper chance to catch up with him yet, either.' She noticed Megan's eyes dart towards Vivian and wondered if she'd missed something. 'By the way, have you sorted things with Michael or...?'

She watched as Megan, flushed to a deep crimson, her eyes bulging slightly. 'Erm, well.' Her glance shifted towards Vivian again, who lowered her eyes, causing Kate to do a double-take. 'The thing is...'

'What's going on? You're both acting strange. Have I missed something?' Kate asked, suddenly anxious as she caught Megan's eyes flitting towards Vivian for a third time.

'Go on, darling, you might as well tell her. She obviously hasn't noticed yet,' the older woman encouraged, ignoring Kate's perplexed stare.

Megan swallowed, clearing her throat and feeling unusually self-conscious. 'The thing is, Kate, things have kind of developed with Marcus...' She tailed off, uncomfortable as Kate's eyes widened in surprise. 'I didn't know how to tell you. But he was the one I was torn about...'

The words were spoken so quickly that Kate took a few seconds to digest the information. 'You and Marcus? Together? What about Michael? What about the guy from work?' Her mind was instantly awash with questions. She stared at Megan waiting for an explanation; the stirrings of frustration were flaring up somewhere deep inside as she slowly began to piece things together.

Megan had the good grace to look away, sensing the excitement around Kate dissipating as her warm smile was replaced with a cold stare.

'There is no guy from work, is there? It's been Marcus all along, hasn't it?' she whispered dispiritedly. Megan's silence confirmed her suspicions.

'Oh Kate, I'm so sorry I wasn't honest with you. I didn't know how you'd feel about it all.' She glanced towards Vivian pleadingly, who gently nodded for her to continue. 'It all happened so fast – ever since the day we set you and Alf up at the pub. And then you guys got back together and Marcus and I started to hang out, but I wasn't even sure if he felt anything in return. I was so worried about telling you, in case you were annoyed and it messed things up with you and Alf.' Megan lifted her hand to her neck, all at once feeling guilty and stupid for holding back the truth. 'I understand if you're angry with me.'

Feeling crushed, Kate sighed quietly and looked at Vivian for support. The older woman affectionately patted her shoulder. 'You can't control matters of the heart, Kate. You know that well enough by now,' she remarked, sensitively glancing at Megan.

Noticing Megan's despairing expression, Kate instinctively reached out and caught hold of her wrist. 'I'm not angry, Megan, I'm just disappointed. Why didn't you tell me this from the beginning? I'm your best friend and that's what friends are for.' She paused for a moment, glancing in Marcus's direction. 'Despite what you may think, Marcus never meant to me what Alf means to me; he was just a rebound in a crazy moment.' She smiled at her friend. 'All I want is to see you happy; Marcus is a lovely guy and I couldn't think of a better person for you. If you two want to give things a try, then I'm right behind you. But what about Michael? The engagement?' Seeing Megan's watery eyes and ever so slightly trembling bottom lip, Kate hugged her. 'Don't cry, you silly moo! You never cry.'

Overcome, Megan smiled remorsefully and embraced her friend tightly. 'Sorry, I've been a bundle of nerves since we arrived. I think it's finally got the better of me. Especially now that you've said all that.' She stepped back, laughing at the absurdity of the situation and wiping a tear from the corner of her eye. 'I've called it off with Michael and what a drama that's turned out to be. Yet, I'm so happy with Marcus, Kate. But I didn't want to keep it from you any longer. Viv here was the one who convinced me to be honest with you.' She gestured to Viv, who held up her hands with a shrug.

'Well, my darlings, as they say, true friendship is to understand

and to be understood.' Vivian shook the small flask in her hand. 'And, on that note, I'm absolutely parched. So I'm going to leave the pair of you to it, have a top-up and see how Lil's getting on with her toy boy.'

Giggling, both women watched as Vivian turned and slowly weaved her way through the thinning crowd. Before either of them had a chance to pick up the thread of their conversation, Daniel appeared by their side with a clipboard under his arm. 'Kate, can I have a word?' He glanced apologetically at Megan. 'It's about tonight's sales.'

Megan jokingly made a bored face at Kate. 'Right, that's my cue to leave. I'll be over with the others.' Turning away from Daniel, she took a few steps before changing her mind and turning back again. 'And Kate...' she scrunched up her nose sentimentally, a habit Kate knew well. 'Thanks for understanding. You're the best.'

Kate smiled as Megan walked off.

'So, tell me about these sales figures then?'

'Ooh, what a lovely evening that was. I haven't had that much fun in a long time,' Lillian said, feeling tipsy as Roberto clumsily helped her into the back seat of the car. He lowered his tall frame into the cramped space next to her as Marcus looked on.

'You okay there, Granddad?' It hadn't gone unnoticed by him that his grandfather had made full use of the free wine and appeared slightly the worse for wear.

Roberto nodded wryly. 'Don't worry about me, son. I'm over the moon tonight.' He laughed and squashed up against Lil, kissing her on the cheek as Vivian shook her head reproachfully.

'You're like a pair of teenagers, you two. You ought to get a room. And before you get any ideas, Bobbi, I'll have you know that Oak Park doesn't allow overnight guests – isn't that right, Lil?'

Roberto turned to Viv, his hand waving wildly in her direction. 'My Lil's no floozy – I wouldn't dream of coming back to yours. I'm a gentleman – aren't I, Lil?'

'Oooh, I dunno about that, Bobbi,' Lillian answered, grinning. 'I've certainly been a floozy in my time.'

Clicking her seatbelt into place with a chuckle, Viv shifted herself further along, before leaning forwards and grabbing Megan's front-seat headrest. 'Here, listen to this, Kate just told me on the way out that she sold thirty-seven of her paintings and has been commissioned to do two other pieces. How wonderful!'

Marcus pulled his driver's door closed and slipped the key in the ignition. 'Yeah, Daniel just pulled me aside and said that Kate's been so well received that he'll be contacting her for another exhibition.'

'Oh, that's fantastic news – she's going to be on cloud nine. I've honestly not seen her looking as happy as she did tonight for a long time,' Megan replied, reaching across and placing her hand on Marcus's knee.

Roberto made a loud, incoherent comment followed by a belch, causing the others in the back seat to break into laughter. Aware they weren't paying attention, Megan reached a bit higher towards Marcus's thigh.

'Oi you, we've got company,' he whispered coyly. 'Wait until we've dropped this lot off.'

'Put your foot down a bit, then. I'm not sure how long I can wait.' She traced a figure of eight along his thigh with a cheeky grin.

He slapped her hand away playfully. 'Are you happy knowing that Kate's okay about us, then?' he asked suddenly. 'Alf guessed straight away, you know.'

She stopped what she was doing, turning down the corners of her mouth in surprised contemplation. 'Did he? I would never have guessed. He kept it well hidden if he had his suspicions. He was a bit quiet tonight, though, anyway, wasn't he? Oh but, yes, I'm so relieved about Kate.' She sighed happily. 'Her being okay about us means so much to me. I really thought that she was going to be upset, but she was fine. Did she say anything to you?'

Marcus shook his head. 'Only that she thinks we make a great couple. That was about it, really. But then again, Alf interrupted us, so she didn't really have a chance to say any more.'

Viv leaned forwards, unexpectedly grabbing Megan, who hadn't been aware of her listening in to the conversation. 'Did you get that impression too, then – that Alf wasn't happy tonight? I didn't see him crack a smile once, unless it was about himself.'

Marcus raised his eyebrows discreetly at Megan, keeping wisely quiet. He glanced in his rear-view mirror, noticing his granddad peacefully resting his head against Lil's, who suddenly hiccupped. Vivian turned to say something and noticed her friend soundly asleep.

'Well, I didn't get the sense of him being overly enthusiastic about the whole thing, if I'm honest, Viv. I think Kate was a bit too overwhelmed by it all to notice, though,' Megan ventured. Aware that she was speaking out of turn, she was nevertheless pleased to have the chance to voice her concerns. 'But, then again, you know what Alf's like.'

'Hmm, that's just it; sadly, we all do.' Vivian slumped back into her seat, mystified as to why Kate – kind, generous and creative Kate – would settle for a relationship that clearly wasn't right for her and a man who didn't seem to appreciate her true worth. She'd rushed back into things with him far too fast and too soon. Still, at least the evening had been a roaring success. That alone was enough to give her the peace of mind she needed – to know that Kate was going to be okay. She had no doubt her artwork was the start of new things for her.

As Vivian caught sight of Megan's hand snaking back towards Marcus's knee, she suppressed a grin. 'I think you'd better take note of your lady here and put your foot down a bit, Marcus.'

He laughed, not needing to be told twice.

'Morning, sleepy.' Kate watched as Alf stretched and kicked the lower part of the duvet away from his feet. 'I thought you were never going to wake up.' Her voice was chirpy and full of promise, still buzzing from the previous night's events.

'Don't do that, mate.' Alf gently pushed Sam's inquisitive and wet nose away from his face, turning to Kate who – considering the still-early hour – looked radiant and alert. She was tying her hair back into a loose ponytail and it pleased him to see just how naturally attractive she was. 'Morning.' He propped himself up on his elbow, not wanting to forsake the warmth and comfort of the bed too hastily. 'Wow, I slept like a log last night.'

'Don't I know it?' she joked, replacing her hairbrush on the dresser. 'The phone's rung three times already this morning and you didn't even stir.'

Yawning, he ruffled Sam's fur playfully, noticing Kate's disapproving gaze. 'Were any of the calls for me?' He thought of Nigel Lambert, his pulse suddenly picking up speed.

'Sam shouldn't be on the bed – get him down. And no, they were for me.' She finished securing her hair and turned to him with an excited smile. 'Guess what – Daniel wants me to do another exhibition!' She waited for him to reply, her smile slowly wilting as she saw the dismay written all over his face.

'Oh, that's good, huh.' He threw back the covers, feeling a sudden need to get up and get out of the house. Kate's oppressively positive vibe was irritating him. 'Why are you dressed so early anyway?'

Turning her back to him, Kate found it hard to keep her voice steady. It hadn't gone unnoticed that the previous evening there had been a distinct lack of support on his part. If she didn't know better, she'd have thought he'd been avoiding her – only paying her attention when he had something exciting to share about a contact he'd made. After returning home, despite being high on a mix of euphoria and champagne, she recalled Alf's sullenness. It had been easy at the time to attribute it to his drunken state and excuse his behaviour for being in an environment that wasn't his 'thing' – but now she wasn't so sure.

'I thought I'd pop round to see Viv and Lil. That's if they're not hung-over – they both had quite a bit to drink last night.'

Alf looked up, surprised. 'But it's a Sunday! You'll be seeing them at work tomorrow, won't you?'

She turned back to him, careful not to show her disappointment at his surly expression. 'Well, I want to tell them the good news about Daniel.' She couldn't be sure, but the slight flex of his jaw was enough to suggest his disapproval. Walking towards the wardrobe, perplexed at his behaviour, she retrieved her comfortable pumps. Why was he suddenly acting so off with her? 'Plus I want to find out the full story about Bobbi – what a surprise that was – and I can't do that if I'm supposed to be working, can I?'

Alf scratched his back with one hand and stood up, naked. 'Okay – if you're visiting them, then I think I'll give Marcus a call, go for a game of snooker. Maybe when you're back we'll go for a pub lunch?' He glanced at her, his expression hopeful.

'Yes, that'll be nice. Let's do that.' She watched as he nodded and walked out into the hallway, towards the bathroom.

'Alright, that's a plan then' he called out. 'Have fun. I'll see you later – I'm going in the shower.'

She softened as he blew her a kiss before pushing the bathroom door to behind him. Walking down the stairs, she grabbed her keys from her coat pocket on the banister. Maybe she was over-reacting? Why on earth would Alf be unsupportive of her? They'd been getting along so well in the last couple of weeks; it was hard to imagine that he'd want to deny her a chance of being successful at something she loved.

She wondered if his lack of work was getting to him – could it be that? After all, he was used to being busy; surely it wasn't easy having that taken away from him, if only on a temporary basis. She made a mental note to delicately raise the subject at lunch and, feeling appeased, headed towards the front door.

"Like a mill-ion dollar bill, oh, oh, oh, oh, oh…"

Approaching the Oak Park main entrance and seeing the flashing blue-neon lights of the ambulance, Kate's exuberance immediately vanished. She ceased singing, reaching for the radio volume and muting it.

There was a flurry of activity outside the care home as Sunday staff rushed between visitors and residents, some looking harassed and others standing around in groups, their body language sombre.

Kate's stomach somersaulted as she sped toward the nearest available space – reserved only for emergencies.

She knew it was Hilda – the pneumonia had been getting worse, not better. She felt winded, bile rising in her throat. Why hadn't she taken her more seriously? Hadn't the doctor warned her that she could relapse easily? Kate hadn't been the only one to remark on her yellow appearance on Friday. What if they hadn't acted quickly enough?

'Oh, please God! Don't let it be serious. Please let her be okay,' she whispered aloud. Her heart was thumping in her chest as she imagined tiny, frail Hilda being carried out on the makeshift frame. She squashed the rising anxiety that was threatening to choke her.

Fumbling with her gear stick, Kate watched as paramedics in green uniforms rushed past Alan; standing on the steps of the building, his dishevelled appearance was in visible contrast to his usual suave self. She felt her chest constricting, her body trembling as she forced her physical self to co-operate with her thoughts. She was trained for this, trained for health relapses of residents and used to emergency situations. But she couldn't shake off the immense feeling of doom that was surrounding her. Something was wrong. Very wrong.

With shaking hands, Kate hurriedly switched off the engine and opened the car door, rushing towards Alan. He looked up in dazed surprise as he saw her approach, his face paling. She noticed the redness of his eyes, followed by the trembling of his bottom lip. He looked at her in confusion.

'Kate? You're here. But it's Sunday?' Finding it hard to control his speech, she saw that he was quivering. 'Someone told you already?'

'Alan, what's going on?' she asked, her voice coming out strangled.

It all happened so fast, she didn't know which came first – Alan pulling her towards him in a tight embrace, or the paramedics pushing her aside and out of the way of the trolley they were wheeling frantically towards the ambulance.

In a rushed blur of green uniforms, she could only see the top edge of the black body bag covered with a white sheet. By reflex, her hand went up to her mouth in shock – her brain registering despair. No, surely not! Hilda – dead?

Her heartbeat thudding in her ears, she felt Alan's strong arms cradle her tightly as from somewhere nearby Lillian's shrilling, loud voice was echoing in painful, wailing, sobs. 'No, no, no, no. She can't be. Not my Viv, please not my Viv.'

Clarity hitting her like a brick. Kate looked up sharply at Alan, her thoughts streaming from her mind as she tried to fight the dizziness that seemed to be engulfing her. He nodded his head as her legs gave way beneath her. 'I'm so sorry, Kate, it's Vivian. They think it was a heart attack.'

She heard the words as if she was under water, her throat tightening and preventing her from breathing. She tried gasping for air, but it wouldn't work. Her body was rigid, frozen, Alan's arms the only thing keeping her upright.

'Not Hilda? Viv?' Her voice was tiny, barely there and punctured with heavy grief.

She was unaware whether it was Lillian's despairing wailing from a distance or her own animalistic, anguished screams that were the last thing she heard.

Shortly after everything went black.

Chapter 27

'Is that all you're going to eat?' Megan asked, looking down at the barely touched chicken baguette that sat in front of Kate.

Kate shrugged, disinterested. 'I've got no appetite.' She pushed the plate away from her slowly, reaching instead for the sickly sweet tea she had come to rely on of late.

Megan observed the dark, puffy circles under Kate's eyes and her drawn, pale and lacklustre appearance, trying not to sigh. 'Oh, by the way, Marcus heard that *Art and Culture* mag are running a piece on you this month.' She nudged her friend, trying to provoke a reaction, but gave up when she was met with a thin smile accompanied by a vacant stare. Tired of pussy-footing around the subject, she decided it was time to take control – even if Kate didn't agree.

'Hun – it's been nearly two and a half weeks now.' She looked at Kate imploringly. 'You can't carry on like this, it's ridiculous.' She watched as Kate rested her elbow on the tabletop, her chin sinking into her raised hand and her eyes purposefully averted. 'I'm not saying you can't grieve. I know how much Vivian meant to you. But she wouldn't have wanted to see you like this – maundering about so woeful and gloomy.'

She noticed the glassy sheen appearing in Kate's eyes and felt momentarily guilty, but knew that it was imperative to continue – her friend's state of mind was far from healthy. 'Vivian was so excited for you on the way home from the exhibition that night, Kate. Don't let her down by giving up on something that she encouraged you with. That would be an insult to her memory. She would want you to be taking control of your life again – she was a strong character and you are, too. It's time to start living life again, Kate, not hiding away in this house.'

Kate shifted uncomfortably on her stool, Megan's words pummelling into her consciousness, making her feel uneasy. She'd tried to drag herself out of the great black hole that she'd found herself sucked into – she really had. She knew as well as anyone that if Viv were still around she'd be cross at the way she was behaving. Even Lillian had tried talking her around, failing miserably. Alf wasn't much help; he did his best to understand, but she couldn't explain her feelings. They were too warped and confusing – even for her. She knew the letter had been intended to help her – Vivian's parting wisdom and advice – but instead it had thrown a shadow of doubt upon everything.

She'd begun to question her place in life, what it was that she really wanted. If Viv's passing had taught her anything, it was that she had to seize the opportunities of life, follow her heart's desire and not take a single moment for granted. Yet, ironically – as she listened to Megan's stern words – she realised that that's exactly what she had been doing. Taking life for granted, wallowing in self-pity and loathing and hoping that her grief, doubts and illusions would resolve themselves.

'She knew, you know,' Kate said, surprising Megan, who had taken the lulled silence to mean that her urgings were falling on deaf ears. 'The letter she wrote. It was dated a week before her passing – she knew her time was near.'

Megan considered this, glancing wistfully into the garden and thinking what a remarkable and inspiring woman Vivian had been. It had been a frequent thought in the past two weeks – for had Vivian not intervened in her relationship with Marcus, then who knows whether she'd still be playing the 'friends' card now.

The news of the letter didn't shock her. She'd already come to learn, in a short space of time, the influence and impact Vivian had on others. The funeral alone, with its crowd of distraught mourners – way beyond a number that could comfortably fit in the church – had been evidence of that. So many lives had been touched by her.

'Do you think she was scared about it?' Kate asked suddenly, picking at a piece of chicken from her baguette. 'I wouldn't like to think so.'

'No, Kate,' Megan said confidently, with a certainty inside that she couldn't explain. She reached across and squeezed her friend's hand. 'Vivian always looked life in the eye and I've no doubt that she did the same with death. The letter should prove that to you. She wasn't scared – she was prepared.'

Kate smiled, a real smile that reached her eyes. 'You're so right, Megan, that's it. That's what I wasn't seeing – she was prepared. Just like I need to be.' Looking down at her pyjama bottoms and reaching up to feel her greasy hair, she was overcome with the realisation that she'd allowed herself to sink too far. 'And, yes, it's time for me to snap out of this grey mood.' She jumped off the stool, reaching for the discarded lunch plates and cups on the surface, feeling a strong desire to get her life cleaned up and put back in order. Her voice was strong and clear; the grogginess that she'd been unable to shake off was beginning to dispel, leaving a sharp, stark clarity in its place.

She glanced back at Megan, who was watching, dumbstruck, this almost immediate change in her friend.

Kate shrugged apologetically, sensing the need to explain. 'The letter had me thrown for a while, but I think I'm finally beginning to understand why. I wasn't ready to face up to it before and I wasn't ready to accept that she was gone. But it's okay because I know what I have to do now and I also know that although she's not here, I have support in other ways.'

'Exactly, hun, we're all here for you. We always have been.'

Walking over to where Kate stood, Megan silently wondered what the letter said. Whatever it was, it seemed to have made a profound impact on Kate.

She noticed her friend's sombre but determined expression and tried to lift the mood. 'So does this mean you're going to go and have a shower, then, and finally wash that greasy hair of yours?'

'You nasty cow!' Kate replied laughing, before picking up the soapy dishcloth lying in the sink and whacking it against Megan's arm. She ducked, playfully screaming as Megan picked up a tea towel and swiped her in return.

The moment provided Kate with a startling awareness that she'd been so very off-kilter for the last couple of weeks. Where had her laughter and positivity disappeared to? She'd been living inside a shell of herself, numbed down and functioning on a basic level. She mentally affirmed to herself that the moment had come to buck up; to take control again. There would be no more falling back and brooding on Vivian or the letter and the stirrings of changes it was prompting her to make. It was time to take action – starting with being happier again.

The other changes, the bigger ones that she was fearful of – well, those would come at the right moment, just as the letter had suggested.

Megan watched Kate with curiosity as she stood staring into the dishwater, lost in thought. Seconds later, looking up with a satisfied grin, Kate caught her friend's bewildered stare.

'So, about the shower – do you think I should make the effort to put on fresh pyjamas too?'

Keeping her expression serious and suppressing a smile, Megan shook her head. 'No, I wouldn't bother. You're rocking the grubby look pretty damn well. Besides, Alf said he's never seen you looking so sexy.'

Kate laughed. It felt good to giggle again.

'I've popped the receipt in there for you,' the shop assistant said, handing Alf the small, red paper bag. 'Thanks again and good luck.'

Crumpling the remainder of his wad of banknotes, Alf shoved them hastily into his jeans pocket. 'Thanks.' He didn't know why, but he was surprised by the lightness of the bag, which was quite absurd since it only contained two small boxes – one being the vintage engagement ring and the other the matching earring set.

He hadn't planned it this way; in fact it was far removed from the overblown idea he'd been formulating before… well, before 'the incident'. He couldn't use that phrase around Kate, of course, since she'd virtually been a walking zombie since Vivian had died. It seemed anything he said of late was offensive in one way or another; she was constantly snapping at him – when she bothered to engage in conversation at all. But talk about timing… Vivian couldn't have chosen a worse moment. Not that she'd chosen it, but still…

He was relieved that Megan had finally managed to get through to Kate – for two weeks he'd tried his best to be there, supporting, comforting, even being playful. Yet it hadn't worked. He'd had to watch as she grew more and more distant, building a wall around herself that made it increasingly difficult for him to reach her. But that had all changed in the past forty-eight hours. His Kate was back. Not entirely mended, for he knew her scars ran deep – he, more than anyone, knew the demons that Vivian's death had brought with it. The reminder of other losses and the abandonment that she'd once tried to describe to him. He'd only been able to hold her and listen – not fully understanding her pain, but nonetheless trying to share it. However, he was just grateful that the veil of grief had seemed to lift a little; Kate was behaving much more like her usual self. He couldn't suppress his delight.

He'd woken up that morning knowing it was the day – the one that he'd already had to delay by nearly two weeks and he didn't want to waste a moment longer. In another respect, Vivian's death had hammered it home that life was short; he didn't have time to waste. Kate needed this engagement, something to give her hope and a new focus – a new beginning to look forward to. A new life together to plan.

With the spring back in her step, Alf was confident that she would fully understand his reasoning behind choosing tonight. He couldn't wait to see her face; he knew how much she wanted this – and he wanted it too. Viv's death may have put a hold on his proposal, but it had also made him appreciate the strength of his bond with Kate, of the unity that had weathered so many storms. It no longer mattered what life threw at them, he knew he'd be there to protect Kate – one way or another helping her and guiding her. Her port of call in stormy waters – the one who knew her better than anyone. She needed him now, more than ever.

Smiling to himself, he tucked the small bag into the inner pocket of his sports jacket and headed back towards the parking lot. Despite the dry summer air, the forecasters had predicted rain in the evening, but Alf desperately hoped it would hold off. If not, it could threaten to ruin everything – and he certainly wasn't about to let that happen... not again.

Reaching the car, he suddenly remembered that he'd forgotten to buy the ice bucket that he'd hoped to present the bottle of champagne in. He hesitated for a moment, wondering if it really mattered. After all, he'd already put the first and most important part of his plan into place – making sure that Kate was out of the house for the afternoon. All he needed to do now was head home and prepare the garden.

He rubbed his hands together, feeling energised by envisioning Kate's reaction when she saw the array of splendour that he had planned for her. If she was expecting another night in together watching the television, then she was in for a very big surprise indeed. One that she would remember for years to come – he was sure of it.

Hardly able to contain his excitement, he unlocked the driver's door – unable to think about anything but the life-changing evening that lay ahead.

Kate Wilson was about to agree to become Mrs Alf Stafford.

'So he wasn't as in love with me as he originally thought he was, was he?' Megan relayed, raising her eyebrows with a wry smile.

Kate leaned back against the sofa, blowing out a reflective sigh at the news. 'Well, clearly not. I mean, it's one thing you falling for Marcus, but what are the odds of Michael getting involved again so quickly, too?' She twirled a strand of loose hair around her finger. 'All rather odd, if you ask me.'

Megan nodded in agreement. 'It's done me a favour, though. I don't feel half as bad about the situation now. I was dreading having to say to Michael that I'd met someone else.'

Kate grinned. 'You don't have to now. He's probably too caught up with Rachel to care.'

'Well, from where I was standing it certainly seemed that way,' Megan replied, recalling the moment she'd spotted Michael and Rachel kissing passionately in a bar two days previous. 'It was strange seeing them together, though, especially since I remember him telling me that he'd never even contemplate the idea of dating his secretary – so it just goes to show.' Pouting her lips, she applied a thin layer of clear gloss. 'And it's made me realise how we can think someone is right for us and be so *very* wrong. I can't believe we were engaged.'

Considering this, Kate stopped flicking the pages of magazine on her lap, glancing up at Megan, who was applying the last of her barely-there make-up. 'You honestly don't feel anything for Michael at all now? Those feelings have gone?'

Megan replaced the lid on her lip-liner and set it down on the table beside her, looking at Kate earnestly. 'In all honesty, the moment Marcus opened up to me, it was as if any feelings for Michael just floated out of the window. I know that sounds harsh, but it's true. What I have with Marcus is something totally different to what I had with Michael.'

Kate tilted her head, intrigued. 'How so? What's different about it?'

'It's hard to explain, but it's a sort of peacefulness inside – an inner knowing, if you like. There's absolutely no doubt in my mind that Marcus is the one I'm meant to be with. It's so comfortable and *right*, I guess…' She stopped talking for a moment, noticing Kate looking at her intently. She carried on, trying to find the words to express what she could hardly get her head around herself. 'I suppose comparing it to what I had with Michael, it's not so much based on chemistry or lust, it's just more… hmm… what's the word?… natural. That's what it is, natural.'

'So you think Marcus is the one?' Kate questioned, raising an eyebrow, a small smirk on her face at Megan's enthusiasm.

Without missing a beat, Megan nodded fiercely. 'I've absolutely no doubt.' She smiled at Kate. 'It's true what they say, isn't it? When you find the right one – you just *know*.'

Something in those words made Kate feel suddenly uncomfortable and picking up the magazine from her lap, she flipped it onto the floor, changing the subject. "Where are you guys off to tonight, then?'

'Liberalisi,' Megan replied, carefully smudging the light line of eye-shadow across the top of her right eyelid. 'It's a new wine bar in Smithfield. Marcus knows someone who knows the owner. It's guest list only – there's meant to be a lot of press coverage, too.'

Kate sat up straighter, contemplating the excitement in Megan's tone. 'You know what?' she began, thinking about how awestruck Marcus appeared to be since the pair had become an item. 'You guys suit one another so much – you're very alike in a lot of ways. I think I saw it before, if I'm honest – but I was a bit jealous.' She cringed shyly and felt herself blushing at the admission, noticing Megan's intrigue as she glanced up from her make-up mirror.

'Jealous? How do you mean?'

'Well, you know – you and Marcus, the connection. I noticed it that day I came home from work and you two had already intro-duced yourselves to one another. I was a bit miffed. I wanted him for myself.' She giggled, shrinking in embarrassment as Megan's expression changed to incredulity. 'I know, I know.' she held her hands up in mock surrender. 'It was very childish of me.'

Megan threw a pencil sharpener at her, smiling as it hit Kate squarely on the forehead. 'All I can say is that it's a good job we've been friends forever. And a good job that you were quite clearly on the rebound and not meant for Marcus. Otherwise who knows how it might have ended?'

Kate felt the sofa beginning to vibrate and a loud chiming interrupted the conversation.

'Goodness, that's a loud ringtone.' Megan said, wincing and chucking her make-up carelessly back into her purple floral toiletries bag. 'Alf?'

Reaching for the phone balanced precariously on the edge of the sofa's arm, Kate nodded. 'Hey, babe, I'm still at Megan's.'

Megan glanced at the clock, noticing that Marcus would be arriving soon to collect her. She watched as Kate fiddled with the hem of her top, looking disinterested in whatever Alf was saying.

'Yeah, okay, then. I'm leaving in a minute anyway.' Kate glanced at Megan, rolling her eyes at the handset. 'Right, okay, yep, won't be long. See you soon. Bye.'

'Everything alright?' Megan asked, suddenly catching sight of the AA information leaflet that she'd meant to give to Jonnie tucked under the fruit bowl. 'Oh, there it is.'

Kate stood up, stretching her arms above her head. 'Everything's fine. Alf was just wondering what time I'll be back. He wants to order a takeaway so I'd better go home.' She walked across to where her friend was standing. 'What's that, then?'

'Marcus picked it up for me. It's a local AA group. He thought it could be good for Jonnie.' It was on the tip of her tongue to say how relieved she was to have Marcus's understanding and own personal experience of the matter when she remembered that neither Kate nor Alf knew the full extent of his history with Linzie, she knew he'd only told them an edited version. She stopped herself in the nick of time. As much as Marcus was close to the couple, he'd told Megan he didn't want to rake over the past by sharing every detail with others. And she understood that completely.

'Well – it's worth a try. Why not?' Kate said sympathetically.

Megan nodded. 'It is.' She also knew that Jonnie still had a long way to go, but any attempt at trying to push him in the right direction and help him was worthwhile. She saw Kate reach for her padded jacket. 'Anyway – I know you need to head off. Thanks for coming over. I'm pleased you're feeling a bit better about everything.' She reached out and rubbed Kate's arm. 'And listen, all that stuff you were saying earlier about the changes…' Tailing off, she looked at Kate with a serious expression. 'If that's how you're truly feeling, then you should follow it through. Vivian's letter was right. Don't be scared. It'll be okay, hun.'

Kate leant in and hugged Megan. 'Thanks. I know it will.' And she did. 'Enjoy your night with Marcus, and make sure you get some of that press coverage!'

'As long as it's not for the wrong reasons,' Megan joked, walking behind Kate to the front door. 'Bye, then. Catch up tomorrow, no doubt?'

Kate stepped into the cool, early-evening air, the beginnings of a drizzle of rain lightly falling around her. 'Yes, I'll give you a call – if you don't answer I'll know you've got a hangover. And then I might pop around with a nice warm tuna milkshake.'

Megan laughed, waving as Kate hurried the short distance to her car. 'Oh, and… Kate?' she called out, a thought striking her. 'You did the right thing by saying yes to Daniel and the exhibit.' She made a thumbs-up sign, smiling.

Kate unlocked the car with her fob, shielding her eyes from the droplets of rain that were now turning heavier. 'Thanks, I think so, too.' Grinning, she waved a final goodbye and opened the driver-side door.

Little did she know it, but the changes had already begun.

'It would have been better if we wasn't sitting here in the pissing-down rain,' Alf said, trying to be light-hearted but feeling altogether disillusioned. This was not at all how he'd envisioned the evening. Four hours of DIY, stapling vines to the gazebo frame, littering the garden with tea-light candles – not to mention the MDF small dining table he'd erected specifically for the purpose. And it had all been in vain. Thirty minutes before he'd anticipated serving his home-made prawn cocktail starter, the heavens had opened and shit on his parade.

Kate took in Alf's deflated expression and glanced up at the makeshift covered gazebo. The heavy-duty polythene plastic was crackling noisily above them as rain pelted down onto its surface. She desperately wanted to make light of it, but refrained from doing so. Alf had clearly gone to a great effort for her – despite not factoring in the forecasted rain – hence the plastic tenting. Sensing he wasn't in the mood for jokes, she silently bit down on her lip, reluctant to make his misfortune appear all the more dire.

Besides, her own feelings weren't exactly jubilant – her earlier intention of having a frank talk had all but disappeared. It most definitely wasn't the right time or the right place.

Rummaging through the chiller box beside him, Alf placed a heart-shaped chocolate mousse on a small plate in front of her. 'Here you go, dessert time.'

'Wow, this looks lovely,' she enthused, careful to sound encouraging. She watched as he reached for the champagne bottle to top up her glass. 'Well, all the food tonight has been lovely, actually.' That part wasn't strictly true; cooking had never been Alf's greatest strength – the steak had been extremely tough, but sensing his anxiety and disappointment she'd forced herself to eat it appreciatively. She was just thankful that the mousse was shop-bought – she'd seen the packaging stuffed in the bin bag on her way to the loo a few moments earlier.

'So you had no idea at all that I was planning a surprise?' Alf asked, dipping his spoon into the mousse. Under the table, his spare hand instinctively reached to his jeans pocket, feeling for the small box that he'd hidden there only moments earlier. Fumbling, he quickly and discreetly removed it, placing it in the crease of his lap. 'Belt's too tight' he said, noticing Kate's curious glance across the table. He felt himself growing hot, his heart beginning to race at the thought of what he was about to do. 'So, no inkling then?' he repeated, distracting her. 'Even when I called you at Megan's and told you to come home?'

'None at all,' Kate answered honestly. 'But what a lovely surprise it's been. I can't believe you went to all this trouble just to cheer me up.' Having never been one for romantic gestures, she was staggered at the effort Alf had put in. She reached out and grabbed his hand. 'I really appreciate it. Even if it did rain without you expecting it to.'

She was torn. Although it had been a welcome surprise to come home to something so thoughtful and unique – on a melancholic note, it made her decision regarding the changes she was about to undertake all the more difficult. She gazed at Alf, her stomach twisting in growing concern.

His eyes met with hers and she was shocked at the anxiety she saw behind his smile. She felt herself sinking lower into her seat, aware that he was suddenly looking as nervous as she'd been feeling since arriving home. She watched as he fumbled again with his belt, a small trickle of sweat building around his hairline.

Her heart plummeted to the depths of her stomach.

Why hadn't she noticed it sooner? It was obvious now – crystal clear. An immense feeling of wretchedness started to wash over her as the realisation sank in. How had she missed it? All of the signs were there. They had been there for the past hour – the dinner, the gazebo, the champagne...

Clearing his throat, Alf took a deep breath and with one finger flipped the lid on the box held tightly within his discreet grasp. Not wanting to prolong the build-up of jittering anxiety that was wracking his nervous system, he finally brought his hand up from under the table.

Kate felt her insides whirling frantically in pandemonium. She breathed in sharply as she fixed her eyes on the ring that glistened before her; a perfect combination of sparkling diamond and deep, luxurious ruby. Her beating heart seemed to suspend itself in time as she watched Alf lean forwards and ask the question that she had so longed to hear.

'Kate.' He cleared his throat again, in one swift move removing the ring from the box and holding it out to her. 'Will you do me the honour of marrying me?'

Alf watched as Kate's eyes widened in surprise, her features frozen in a state of shock. His hands were trembling slightly as he extended the ring a little further towards her, waiting patiently for her to overcome the initial surprise and delightedly accept his offering.

Despite her shocked silence and racing heart, Kate felt her lips moving and desperately wanted to stop the words that were tumbling from her mouth from being spoken. But she knew it wasn't possible. They were words spoken from the heart. Words that had true meaning. A meaning that she knew was going to tear Alf's own heart apart.

'I'm so sorry, Alf. I can't.' The sentence was spoken so softly that she saw Alf squint in confusion. Clearing her throat, she willed her voice to gain strength. 'The answer is no.' Her tone was surprisingly calm despite the tension and sickness that were making her insides dance. She saw the flicker of excitement and hope extinguish in Alf's eyes – as clearly as a bright light going out in a dark room, his expression crushed.

She had never wanted to hurt him – had never intended it to end in this way. The irony was bittersweet. He'd finally given her the one thing she'd always desired on the very same evening that she'd intended to have a frank talk with him. The same evening that she'd planned to open up to him about the decision she'd made about their relationship – to be honest about her true feelings.

Hearing his sharp intake of breath, she looked on tormented as Alf got up from the table in clear angst, dropping the ring amongst the clutter of discarded plates. She wanted to comfort him, but she knew she couldn't, shouldn't. Reaching out to him would only make things worse for both of them.

He turned to her then, his eyes glassy, his voice shaking with anger and dejection – his tone carrying his pain. 'You don't even need to explain. It's written all over your face. It has been for the past week. I just didn't want to believe it.' She watched as his shoulders slumped in defeat, as he reached up to rub his eyes – the hopelessness pouring from him.

He shook his head at her one last time, a persecuted expression on his face and walked away.

Kate watched tearfully as he disappeared into the house and moments later heard his car engine starting up outside.

An inexplicable sadness engulfed her; every fibre of her being was shrouded in sorrow and guilt. For allowing it to get this far. For allowing her to give him false hope. But for all of the sorrow and guilt, an even stronger feeling was accompanying it – that of profound freedom. It was the freedom of knowing that she could finally go into the future without being held back by old ties. The future that held every possibility of newness. She felt a flutter of hope and instantly knew that she had made the correct choice for her heart.

It was the letter that had decided it. Vivian's letter that had made her see things clearly and opened her eyes to the situation she'd enveloped herself in. She'd been considering everything for a couple of weeks now. Considering how the love that she'd felt for Alf had been anchoring her to a situation that she'd long outgrown; that both of them had long outgrown but refused to acknowledge.

It had taken her a while to understand, but she finally realised the key element that she'd been missing for so long. She loved Alf, but she wasn't in love with him. She was simply in love with the idea of being loved. It wasn't fair on either of them to continue holding on to a relationship based on illusion. A relationship that she'd leapt back into solely because Alf was better the devil she knew. She owed it to herself to desire more than that. She deserved true love and true happiness, as did he. She'd once thought that she was incapable of being totally alone but Viv's death, just like her temporary split with Alf, had shown her that even when circumstances changed in her life – she would still manage to find her footing again.

The dreams that she'd once had for herself and Alf were no longer the dreams that she had for her future. Since giving it another try together, she realised she'd changed in a lot of ways. She didn't need his approval as she once had. She'd finally accepted her own strengths, that she could carve a new career for herself and that no matter how many people left her life, she'd always have the strength to continue and move forwards.

Sitting down and visualising a marriage and family with Alf didn't give her the same peace and excitement in her heart as it once had. Megan's words earlier that day had especially hit home – for they were the ones she'd been questioning of late; when you know it's the right man, you *know*. But that was part of the problem; she hadn't been feeling that way in the past week. She was finding herself hoping for someone different; for something new and exciting; for far more than Alf could give her.

Although Alf had changed in many respects since his Scotland stint, it still hadn't been enough to cement the bond between them again. She knew the silent doubts she'd been having were founded. She'd changed too much in the past months to continue treading the dirty waters that she'd been tiredly fighting against for so long. She had stepped into a new positive cycle of her life – one where Alf no longer belonged by her side as a partner. And one where she would own her power and take control of her life, to go after what she really wanted.

Wiping a tear from her eye, Kate pulled from her pocket the letter she'd religiously been carrying around for the past three weeks; her eyes falling on the part she needed to read for reassurance. The words that had prompted everything.

'Never be fearful of the unknown, Kate. Settling for familiar and safe isn't always the soul's answer to true happiness. True happiness can sometimes only be found by taking a leap of faith – even if that means letting go of something familiar that you love.'

It was only fair that she had let Alf go.
The time had come for her to go in search of true happiness.

Epilogue

Four months later

Kate unwrapped her grey lambswool scarf, dropping it into her lap. Despite the early-February chill, the sun was putting in an unexpected, but welcome, late-morning appearance. It made her second and final day in Brighton all the more appealing, given that she wanted to fit in as much as she possibly could around her already busy schedule.

Sinking back against the hard, wooden-slated bench, she considered the couple of hours she had to spare and wondered whether to head towards the beach for lunch or browse the nearby lanes for gifts. Daniel wasn't expecting her to give him a decision until later and, besides, she'd already made up her mind after spending most of the previous evening thinking about the proposition.

Her mobile beeped with a message from Megan, 'Aloha from Honolulu' accompanied by a photo of her tanned and happy friend wearing a bright-blue bikini and drinking from a coconut shell, relaxed in Marcus's sandy embrace. Kate was instantly transported back to the couple's very small and informal register-office marriage only ten days previously. It was hard to comprehend the pace at which the relationship had developed. Hard to believe that Megan – the very same Megan who had shrugged at the idea of marriage and commitment for so many years – was now a married woman. The irony of the situation wasn't lost on her, for she had been the one to spend seven years in a secure relationship, wanting nothing more than marriage. Yet Megan, so clueless to love, had not only found true love quickly – but wasted no time in taking the ultimate step of commitment.

The register-office ceremony had been awkward in many ways; awkward because she'd had to face Alf – to act civil and friendly, even though she knew that he despised the sight of her. It was clear that he still blamed her and held her responsible for ruining their future together. It was saddening that he still couldn't understand her reasoning, that he was still adamant that they were a perfect match – still living in a state of delusion. She knew that he missed her, but she also knew that it wasn't for the right reasons. She'd come to understand his need for control – even though he wasn't aware of himself doing it and she was thankful that they had as little contact as possible.

Closing the image of Megan and Marcus, Kate tossed her mobile into her bag, gazing absentmindedly at the Royal Pavilion building in front of her. Such little time had passed since that fateful day with Alf and yet it felt like an eternity. Her life had changed in so many ways, ways that she'd never have imagined possible. The completion of the house sale had been the biggest blessing to date – had finally enabled her to free herself of all ties to Alf, ties to the life they'd shared together. It had sold faster than any of them had expected. To Kate, this was further confirmation that she'd made the right decision – it was meant to be. Especially given the opportunity that she had floating before her now; the chance to own a small but perfectly located shop in Brighton, where she could sell her artwork and her newly inspired craft paintings, made of material offcuts.

Given the national media coverage that had come her way since the second exhibition two months earlier, plus the astonishing demand for bespoke pieces, it made perfect sense to have a base from which to work and sell from.

Daniel had been the one to suggest it. He'd almost taken on a managerial role and, whilst it sometimes made her bristle to be pushed into avenues she wasn't comfortable with, she was beginning to see how much his influence was benefiting her. She'd never imagined that she would be so blessed with the openings that were presenting themselves to her.

Besides, Daniel knew Brighton well – he'd once lived there and Kate had fallen in love with it since her frequent visits over the past month. The little old lady who was retiring from the current memorabilia store – which would become her very own art studio if she chose to go ahead with the business offer – was also moving back to London. This meant that the flat above the store was vacant, too. It was a big decision; one that she had weighed up carefully. After all, how would she feel about leaving behind those who were closest to her, and especially breaking away from Oak Park and its many memories after so many years?

She noticed a small white dog bounding towards her across the grass and smiled. The dog could have easily been a carbon copy of Sam. She watched as its owner called its name and it came to a sudden halt. Thinking of little Sam almost brought a tear to her eye. Ever since the split and her temporarily moving into Megan's to save Alf the angst of leaving home for a second time, it had been a concern to her that Sam was clearly distressed by the upheaval. When Alan had kindly offered to take Sam on a more permanent basis, at first she had firmly refused. After all, Sam's place was with her and the care home rules didn't allow pets anyway.

It was Lillian who had told her… Apparently she'd known for a long time, as had Vivian. Yet they'd vowed to keep the knowledge a secret, knowing the havoc that a revelation so shocking could cause to the care home and its residents. It all made sense now – the many things that Alan said or did; the influence he seemed to have over Steinbach. She should have guessed it herself.

She thought back to the afternoon when Alan told her that he'd been in love with someone else before his wife – the person that he couldn't be with – the person he'd turned down to marry his wife. It hadn't come as a shock to her to learn that Alan was bi-sexual, although she couldn't imagine how difficult it would have been back in those days to live with such a secret. However, it was hard to believe the person that Alan had been in love with all that time was Walter Steinbach. The same bitter and nasty Walter that she'd feared throughout her working years.

It had only been recently that she'd allowed herself to consider Walter's lonely existence – wondering if his bitterness could be attributed to having to conceal his own homosexuality for so long… to often be near the man he had always loved and not be able to display his affection. It had made her soften towards him a little. Even more so when she'd been called into his office along-side Alan and told that the Oak Park policy had been changed to accommodate a residential pet. It had been Alan's elation at the decision that had made her change her mind about Sam. She knew that Sam belonged to her, but the dog had always seemed happiest around Alan – he brought out a side of Sam that she never could.

Alf hadn't taken much persuading, despite her fears that he would object just to spite her. Besides, with his new job working for Nigel Lambert – an opportunity he'd worked hard to achieve and wasn't going to sacrifice – he was too pre-occupied to participate in Sam's fulltime care anyway.

Sam had taken to the arrangement of being with Alan like a duck to water. Kate wondered if the ease of the transition was partly because she still saw him on a daily basis through work. Whilst it had broken her heart the first two weeks to let him go, his obvious contentment whenever she saw him was enough to reassure her that she'd made the right choice. Sam was where he belonged – with Alan.

Glancing at her watch, Kate realised with a jolt that it was already nearly midday. She retrieved her mobile and dialled Lillian's number, but there was no answer. Leaving a message on the answerphone, she ended the call. It had become a regular thing, their 'midday catch-up' as they both liked to call it. Except the past week, Lillian had become more social with Roberto and never actually seemed to be around when Kate called. Not that she minded, of course; it was heartwarming to know that Lil had settled in Leeds so easily. Kate had already been up to visit her numerous times; the detached and leafy bungalow in which she now lived was filled to the brim with her many belongings. They always spent Kate's visits alone, talking about Vivian and bringing all the old memories back to life. For both of them it was a special time together – a reminder of their past and a way of reinforcing hope and strength for their future. There was no denying that Kate missed Lil at Oak Park. She'd found it especially hard at the beginning – so soon after Viv's passing, when Lil had gently told her of Roberto's offer to go back to live in Leeds with him. Yet she knew that Lillian had lost everything in losing Viv; her only friend, her only family – perhaps even more so than Kate.

She hadn't wanted anything more than to see Lillian happy in a new home with a new person by her side – filling the great gap that Vivian's legacy had left behind. And Roberto had given her that. The twinkle in her eye was finally back again.

'Excuse me, do you mind if I join you?'

Kate squinted as she looked up at the tall man whose messy ginger hair failed to shield the rays of sunlight from behind his head.

'Sure, go ahead.' She grabbed her bag, shifting it closer to her whilst studying the willowy man with the awkwardly big nose, shrugging off his coat to reveal an orange jumper – one that clashed sharply with his hair. Something about him reminded her of someone. She looked at him quizzically.

He smiled; a warm, inviting, kind smile that flashed perfectly straight teeth. 'You probably won't remember me, but I think we've met.' He sank his tall frame into the seat, noticing Kate's taken aback expression.

'I thought I recognised you,' she began, studying his face once more and taking in the unusual dark-hazel eyes that betrayed his red-orange hair.

'Lanesborough Park?' he said softly, a hint of an Irish accent in his sing-song tone.

Kate flushed, realising all at once who he was and the circumstances under which they'd last seen one another. 'Oh, yes...' she cringed slightly, embarrassed. 'The evening I tripped over in front of you and your girlfriend.' She tried to make light of it, feeling her cheeks burning bright. 'Goodness, what a small world, though? Seeing you here, of all places.' She refrained from mentioning she'd also seen him once in Swoonies. It didn't seem right – almost too coincidental.

'I know. I had to do a double-take when I first spotted you.' He looked at her with a cheeky grin. 'Especially as you look quite different.' He watched as she laughed, knowing full well what he was hinting at. 'I wasn't sure if it was you – all the more because it's Brighton not London.'

Kate nodded her head, thinking about how the night of Marcus's rejection and hearing about Michael's proposal to Megan hadn't been her finest hour. 'Well I'm surprised you remembered me in the first place.' She brushed back a strand of hair from her mouth, feeling suddenly self-conscious, his gentle-giant presence intimidating her. 'So what brings you here? Are you on holiday with your girlfriend?' she asked, a part of her feeling intrigued to know more about him, this stranger with the soothing voice.

He shook his head, a brief shadow passing across his face. 'No, nothing like that, I'm afraid. My fiancée and I split up – nearly five months ago now. So it's just me.' She noticed how he looked down at his feet, reflective. 'I grew up in Brighton, even though I'm originally from Ireland. So it seemed the right time to head back here. I'm staying with my mum for a bit. It's a good place to be.' He looked at her then, his expression a wistful, peaceful one.

'I'm sorry to hear that.' And she was, because hearing his words and watching his reaction brought her own feelings of loneliness back to her. The ones that she'd successfully managed to keep at bay since her split with Alf. It was only in the last few days that they'd began to sprout up… The small fears that maybe she wouldn't have her happy ending with love after all. She forced a smile.

'I'm in a bit of the same position, actually. I recently split, too.' She was grateful when he nodded sympathetically and didn't pry further. 'Anyway you're lucky to have such an eclectic and creative place to take stock. I think I'm falling in love with Brighton myself.'

'You're only here for a visit, then?' he asked, his deep-hazel gaze flitting around her face as he waited for her to answer.

'Yeah.' She hesitated, picking at her scarf. She noticed he was looking at her, waiting for her to say something more. She took a deep breath, knowing that once she said the words aloud, they would make things somehow all the more real. 'As a matter of fact, I'm here to discuss a business proposition – to take over a small shop and possibly the flat above it.'

He grinned then, a wide flourishing smile that made her heart skip a beat, for some insane reason that she couldn't understand. 'Wow, that's great news. So does that mean you might be moving here, then?' His eyes held her gaze and she could see the sparkle of expectancy within them.

'I suppose it might do.' She couldn't help but laugh as his smile got even wider at her words. 'And why are you grinning at me like that?' she asked, watching as he ran a hands through his floppy, messy hair.

'Well, you're a familiar face and I'm in need of new friends.' He laughed then, a hearty laugh that she didn't expect from someone so softly spoken. 'Besides, I need new guinea pigs for the taster evening I'm about to do.'

She raised an eyebrow. 'Taster evening? What's that, then?' She narrowed her eyes suspiciously.

'Don't look so apprehensive. I'm a trained chef.' He was pleased at her pleasantly surprised expression. 'Well, I was a trained chef before I moved to London and started a successful career in advertising.' He picked a piece of fluff from the leg of his jeans. 'Since I moved back here, I decided to get back into the work I love.' He stretched his arm along the back of the bench, not noticing as Kate flushed – a strange feeling was taking a hold in her stomach. 'So I'm opening a Deli-Bar, somewhere to grab lunch or buy my unique and experimental combinations.' He waited for her to reply, almost holding his breath – wanting her approval.

Kate was startled. Not only had she expected him to be a corporate type of person, but from the sound of it, their current life situation was strikingly similar. 'I think that's amazing. It sounds wonderful. Good luck with it.' She meant it. It was inspiring to hear of a fellow creative person following their inner urging. ' You're very brave to be returning to the work you love and leaving your advertising behind.'

He shrugged, considering her words carefully. 'Well, the way I see it – you've got to follow your heart. It's easy to stay doing the thing that's familiar and safe.' He turned to her again, not noticing her paling expression. 'But sometimes to find real happiness you've got to take a risk.' He grinned at her again, then, another thought occurring to him. 'A bit like love – don't you think?'

Before Kate could answer – for she was rooted to the spot at his comment, eerily similar to Viv's letter that was etched into her memory – a shrilling sound came from the mobile that was perched on the bench beside him. He glanced towards the screen and she noted his expression of surprise. He stood up clumsily.

'So sorry, you'll have to excuse me. I really need to take this – I've been waiting all week for this business call.' He hurriedly pulled a card from his pocket. 'I don't know how long I'll be – so here's my card.' He slipped the card into her hand – the exchange causing both of them to experience a jolt of chemistry as electric as lightning. He straightened himself, not quite understanding what he'd experienced, but quickly drinking in Kate's loveliness – a feeling of absurd regret that he was having to leave her so soon. 'Please give me a call, I'd very much like to see you again – even if it's for that taster.' He smiled at her then, before nodding apologetically and answering his phone.

'Hello?' She watched in longing as he turned to walk away from her, getting as far as a few metres before he turned back, covering the mobile mouthpiece with his hand.

'By the way, I didn't catch your name?' His tone was hopeful, full of promise and Kate felt herself blush. It was a new experience, one that she couldn't describe. But a good one – one that she wanted to last forever.

'Kate. It's Kate,' she called out, standing up, still holding his card tightly in her hand where he'd left it. 'And yours?' she asked, noticing how he smiled as he repeated her name back to her.

He was already waving now, bringing the mobile back up to his ear and turning away from her, seeming not to have heard her question. She watched as he walked away, a strange sense of harmony coursing through her; feeling like she'd discovered something that she didn't know was lost.

Glancing down at his business card, she smiled at the bold and interchanging colour – so very much like him, a myriad surprises. Her gaze slowly settled on his name and with a jolt she felt herself sinking back towards the seat she'd just stood up from.

Surely not? It was almost impossible. Incomprehensible.

'Alf,' she said aloud to herself, reading the small squiggly print in rainbow colour. Alf O'Reilly.

And suddenly everything that Vivian had ever told her made complete and perfect sense. She smiled, reaching for her mobile.

She couldn't wait to tell Lil.

Acknowledgements

A special thank you to those closest whose love and support made this third book possible. You know who you are and I love you all dearly. Especially you, Amelia. You brighten my world.

My huge thanks to fellow author Sylvia FitzSimons for the endless encouragement and help. You're an absolute star.

And to you, the reader – thank you for taking the time to delve into my fictional world. I truly hope you enjoyed reading this novel as much as I enjoyed writing it.